THE EIGHT OF EARTH

RICHIE SHAFFER

DEDICATION

To anyone ready to reinvent themselves.

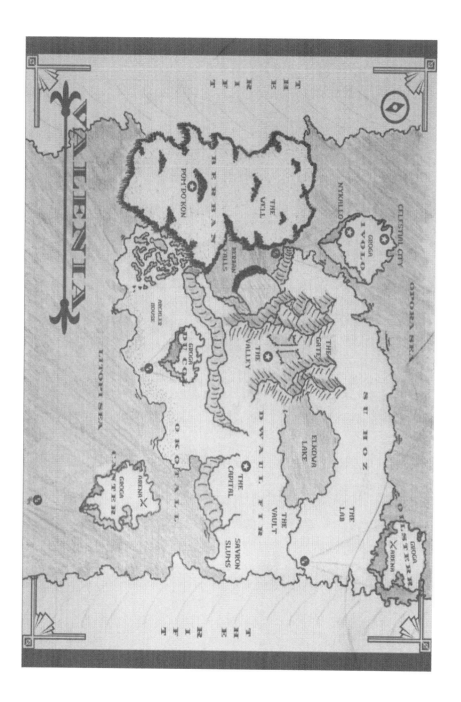

PROLOGUE

ARCHIE ABERNATHY

Journal

The Antarctic sand bleeds in between my fingers and vanishes into the howling winds of the desert. Heat radiates off the dunes along the horizon, swirling gusts kicking up in all directions. I stare. A heaviness burrowing inside me as the scorched landscape I gaze upon taunts me. Eerie waves of tension scratching at my skin, just as the sand does. This morning, Terry asked me how many people I thought were still alive... at this point, it can't be many.

I wouldn't have believed this was once all ice if I hadn't been shown pictures. Thirst is a silent, unstoppable death... Drought is no different.

A horn groans from the mouth of an obsolete speaker along the perimeter wall of the mountain of steel we call the Redemption. The speaker looks out of place, set against the impossible feat of technology behind it. The Redemption towers miles into the sky, the most sophisticated transportation vessel ever constructed. I sit in the shadow of its launch pad atop two insulated blankets, a tombstone of scrap metal reading my wife's name, is half-buried in the sand. I haven't mustered up the courage to say goodbye to her

1

yet... but I'm getting there.

"It's time..." I say. The words fight their way out. This is what my angel has been reduced to; a piece of discarded hull metal. "I wish you could come with me." I remove my glove, and my skin blisters the moment it touches the metal. Tears welt in my eyes, but I had to touch her once more before I left.

The edge of the shadow is just a foot from my blankets now. My time is up.

I stand and fold the blankets under my arm and crouch down to her. My whispers seep off scorched, cracked lips whose only reprieve are the tears that stream into the corners of my mouth. I bury a creased page from my journal into the sand below her name, then turn and leave and fight every instinct in my heart that begs me to stay here with her and let the desert swallow me whole. But if humanity is to live on... I have to fly this ship.

Journal
To my son Leo... Or whoever is reading this.
Year 1: Day 1

Construction of the Redemption is complete. A flying city made of metal and hope. I've thought a lot about how to describe the feeling of stepping foot in the command center today. Sobering is a word that came to mind. Terrifying was another. I should've wiped the simulation logs after our last training session. It was the first thing that popped up when I logged into the system... Years of sim results scrolling down the screen. Most of them red. Not the most encouraging start. But I tried my best to shake that sense of dread as the crew reported today because as Terry would constantly say: "A Captain sets the tone." So that's what the crew saw; firm posture, square shoulders, confident eyes, steady voice. They saw poise...

In five days, what's left of humanity leaves Earth forever. We leave on a flying city we could never test launch. To relocate to one of six planets, we can only guess are habitable. With a crew of 330 that we can only hope is up for the task. And carrying a herd of human embryos suspended in artificial wombs we aren't positive will activate properly when we arrive.

If anyone tells you they'd be poised in that situation... they're a damn liar.

Year 1: Day 2

The Redemption is constant motion. A colony of ants streaming through the tunnels and hallways. Boots clicking against the metal grates of the floor. The steady murmur of efficient communication. We're far more organized than I anticipated. And if anyone is terrified like I am... they don't show it.

Crew members, all with pimpled faces and wrinkleless skin, give me half salutes as they hurry by to whatever task they've been assigned to. Some even smile. Maybe, I've been a bit cynical about this whole mission?

Then, I catch a glimpse of the Personnel Appeals Display, and all those negative thoughts flood back into my mind when I think of the thousands we'll leave behind to wither away and die. I can't even begin to imagine how miserable a death that will be.

I scan through the display screen's bullet points listed in two columns under the title, Essential Personnel Qualifications, and quiver when I read disqualifications like: *AGE > 35* and *pre-existing genetic conditions.*

An older man wheeling a yellow biohazard cart backpedals by me, his eyes follow mine as he continues down the hall. He doesn't seem angry, but a constant gnawing in the back of my mind convinces me he is. A black band is wrapped around the sleeve of his right arm, designating him: *nonessential personnel.* Another passes by with a blowtorch, and another hauls a spool of wiring.

The man leans his crate down, and a botanist in sleek white garb scans the bin and points into the cargo hold. The man disappears into the unit, and I realize that's the last time I'll ever see that man. I didn't know him, but it still rings through me. Thousands scurry through these halls with black armbands. All deemed nonessential. Yet, they help with no resistance. It's the single greatest show of bravery I've ever witnessed. In four days, we'll launch off the planet, and those we leave behind will be left to deal with the barren, scalding rock that is Earth.

Journal
Year 1: Day 2

I gave a speech today... it was just a few minutes, but my

God, did it feel longer. I can still picture all their eyes staring at me. They believe. They truly do. It's beautiful, honestly. And I've come to realize they have no reason NOT to. Before I ended the assembly, each division presented a different component of the Redemption, non-essentials included. And I have to admit, it's hard to hear the comprehensive capabilities of this ship and the crew that runs it, and not have confidence that this will work. But when I finally stood up and looked out over that mass of people clinging to every word... well shit, I nearly puked. These people are counting on me... I suppose humanity itself is depending on me...

I hate to say it, but I think I realize it was never the mission I doubted...

Year 1: Day 3

The automated doors hiss open and slide into the walls as I step through them. For once, I'm met with a delightfully pleasant scent instead of the sterile metal of the ship's bowels. A lavender breeze dances across the room. It reminds me of my wife's shampoo. I always loved that smell.

"Captain, what a pleasant surprise."

Joanna Reins is tending to one of the hundreds of cryopods that line the habitation unit. A pad in her hands is linked to a cord that attaches to the back of the egg-shaped pod.

"Just wanted to come check on my little man," I say, trying to find what to do with my hands. She notices and laughs to herself.

"Don't worry, Captain, there's nothing in here you can break. Relax."

I smile and gesture to the pod. I feel like I'm awkward, but maybe I'm not.

"Can I... touch them?"

"Go ahead. Would you like to see Leo's?" She asks. My ears perk at his name.

"Yea, if you don't mind..."

"Of course not." She puts the pad down and gestures for me to follow. We walk through the equivalent of a human hydroponics lab. Pods are lined in rows, with hoses attached to the ceiling. The lights are far dimmer in the habitation unit then they are in the other hubs of the ship.

"Alright, just need your face for the terminal here, and we can access the protocols and see which one is little

Abernathy," She says. Her cheeks pinch up in a cute way when she smiles. It's an easy, comforting smile that makes it obvious why she has this job. She has this nurturing presence to her and the intelligence to match.

I lean my face down to the podium, and the terminal scans my features. A digitized female voice comes over the speakers.

"...*Facial Recognition Success. Clearance approved. Captain Archie B. Abernathy.*"

"What's the 'B' stand for?" She asks with a grin as she glances through the cryopod manifest. I cross my arms.

"We could be on this ship for thirty years... can't give away all my secrets yet." I smirk. She laughs and shakes her head.

"Found him."

A pod on the left side of the habitation unit hisses and elevates about a foot and a half.

There he is.

I never knew that staring at a piece of tinted glass could be so overwhelming, but just knowing my son is in there is more than I can handle.

I run my palm over the glass of the pod and just picture how proud Christine would be if she could see this. Our son... he's a microscopic speck, but he's our son nonetheless. "So, he just sits here frozen until it's time to hatch?" I ask. She chuckles as if she's about to attempt to explain quantum mechanics to an infant.

"Well, sort of. It's complicated, but the WOMB keeps the embryo in a suspended state until the birth sequence is initiated. Then, he'll begin to grow, just like he would in his mother."

I can tell she's doing her best to make this process digestible for me, but it still seems unfathomable.

"It's remarkable," I say.

"If they work... then, yes, it is." Her face tightens, and it's the first time I've seen her show any sign of worry. We share a quiet moment of hope. "Expedited development, cell generation, resource management..." Her voice trails off as she stares down at her life's work, and I can tell the same doubts that flooded my mind yesterday plague hers as well.

"They'll work," I say. Her cheeks pinch up once more. I don't know her well, but I put my arm around her, and together we stare at the future of the human race. "They'll work."

Journal
Year 1: Day 3

Today I met you! (Leo, that is...) Met Hub A's entire habitation unit, too, technically. What a moment! I had to make my rounds, inspecting Hubs B through K, but nothing quite compared to being in the same room as you. I want to know so badly if you have your mother's eyes or her infectious laugh. Here's to hoping you don't have my hairline! Twenty-two and nearly bald... less than ideal, but I promise there are some desirable genes mixed in there somewhere! But I must admit, seeing you today sparked something inside me. A flare of hope. Of optimism. Of purpose...
I will find you a home, Leo... I promise.

Year 1: Day 6

I can feel the grooves of the metal thruster along my palm. The blood pushes from my nails as I squeeze its handle. There's no need to hold it this tightly, but spasms of stress detonate in every corner of my mind.

"All systems clear," Terry says behind me. "Launch on your command, Captain."

Dozens of the command center's eyes crawl over me like swarming insects. They wait. The future, our destiny, waits in the small steel lever I hold. Humanity waits.

Bile stings my throat as I force it back down to the furnace that's become my stomach. All I can picture is my wife's face. Her smile. That laugh. The way I would tuck her hair behind her ear. The way she would run her nails along my back. I think of her. I think of how horribly I miss her and how lonely this will be without her.

Silence hangs in the air.

Up through the nose. Out through the mouth. I focus.

The time for action is now. Ready or not, I must lead.

I promised my son a home, and I intend to find one.

"To the redemption of man!"

I punch the throttle.

Journal
Year 1: Day 6

The first night in space was bizarre. So quiet. I had grown so accustomed to the constant howling winds of the desert. But here, there was nothing. No noise. No rattling of loose doors against the winds. No whipping of sand against the thin metal walls. No cries from desperately thirsty neighbors. Nothing. Just silence. That is going to take some time to get used to. I also quickly realized just how bored I'll be. After launch, I routed our course to a planet elegantly named C-0821. Once routed, I check in every few hours to maintain route safety and projected course variation. But after that, my responsibilities end. I'm not sure I had thought about what fifty years on a vessel that practically flies itself would look like. I can't help but feel underwhelmed by my role in the saving of the world. But I'll man my post and keep us moving straight.

Year 5: Day 1849

The crest of planet C-0821 peeks out from massive bay doors that hiss open as a recon vessel makes its landing inside the hanger.

Few speak as they crowd around the observation glass, and those who do only whisper. The hanger doors' teeth feed into one another, and the bay pressurizes and releases the airlocks to the rest of the hub.

I push through the unlocked doors into the hanger as the four-man crew climbs down from the vessel.

"And...?" I say.

Journal
Year 5: Day 1849

C-0821 was a null candidate. The scientists say something about tidal locking for a red dwarf star, not exactly sure the details. I know enough to get by, but I'm not a Planetary Biologist. The more I think about it, maybe I need to understand it better. Not like I've got much else to do to kill time!

Morale took a small hit, but I'm hoping they didn't anticipate it being that easy. I understand the anticipation of five years of waiting just to be let down, but unfortunately, our next trip will be longer.

Year 16: Day 6128

"Relax."

I flinch at Joanna's hand on my shoulder. She gives me a tender smile and kisses me on the cheek, but I'm too tense to reciprocate.

"I'm fine..." I say.

"Your beard says otherwise." She reaches up and stops my hand from stroking it. "You've been standing here, pulling at it for over an hour."

"Look at them," I say, nodding to the observation glass.

Dread fills the eyes of those waiting here.

You can almost see the next decade between planets reflecting off the shimmering pools of desperation that build along their eyelids. Joanna tries to weave her fingers into mine, but I'm already pushing through the airlock doors.

Journal
Year 16: Day 6128

Our third failed planet. Morale is lower than ever. Life is truly beginning to blur into nothingness. The pain of Earth is only a fragment of a memory at this point. I think most of us don't care if humanity survives anymore; we just want off this damn ship. I try as hard as I can to keep up some semblance of optimism, but what can I say to them after another failure?... "We'll try again in a decade?" Not that inspiring...

God, I hope this fourth planet is the one. I don't know how much longer I can keep it together for them. If it wasn't for Joanna, I'd have already lost it.

Year 30: Day 11,078

The coordinates of our fifth planet sit blinking across the dash of the command console. I can't push them. My mind simply won't let me. This one was supposed to be it. Number Four. The astronomers said it over and over, *"GZ-923 has a ninety-four percent compatibility rating."* Six percent...

Terry and I sit in silence in our pilot chairs. Our flight crew is with us in the command center, but everyone else has been ordered to get some rest.

"Fifteen years 'til five..." I say to Terry.

"We'll be what... sixty-seven?" He says.

"Sixty-eight..."

Terry sighs.

A disheveled voice of the maintenance department comes on over the comm system.

"Attention crew..."

"Ugh, what's Dave want now?" I groan.

"...maintenance has detected a ventilation malfunction in the barracks sector. Until the malfunction can be confirmed, all crew members must report to hanger bay A to await verification."

I roll my eyes to Terry.

"When it rains, it pours, huh?"

Terry can't help but chuckle an exhausted, defeated laugh.

"I'm staying here, I don't know about you," He says. I slouch down into my chair and prop my feet up on the dash. The flight crew all glance to me for direction.

"At ease, fellas... we can follow procedure tomorrow. Tonight, let's forget." Smiles that haven't shown themselves in some time stretch across the crew's faces as I tear open the vacuum seal of a whiskey bottle. "We only have two bottles left... so enjoy it." My throat burns as I take a pull and wipe the wetness from my beard. The crew passes the bottle around.

Time has passed, but I couldn't guess how much.

I turn the bottle up, but nothing comes out. When did everything get so blurry? I use the command stations to steady myself as I stagger to the flight deck overlook and stare out into the empty blackness of space. Is there anything out there for us? Honestly? Or will the last years of humanity be spent inside a flying metal crypt? I have no idea anymore.

As I press my forehead to the glass, a siren wails from my dashboard. I snap around. Even in my state, I recognize it. I hurry to the dashboard, stumbling as I go, and bring up camera footage of the hanger bay. A brawl has ensued.

Terry has seen it as well, and we dart from the room, down the corridor, toward the hanger bay.

"What's happening?" I yell.

"I don't know." He answers.

Turning through the endless halls, we reach the observation deck, and I try to push into the hanger bay, but the airlock doors are sealed. Through the glass, the gears of the exterior bay door begin to churn.

I press the internal comm and immediately hear the shouting.

"... I'm saving us!" David screams. "... it's madness!"

Dozens of men overpower him and yank him from the control panel on the wall.

"It's no use!" He screams as the crew smothers him.

I kick at the airlock door, screaming. This can't be happening...

I push past Terry and slam on the observation glass over and over.

The gears of the exterior doors spin even quicker now. The siren pounds against my ears. But it isn't until I see *her* that my heart plummets.

Joanna walks calmly by the mob and meets me at the glass, pressing her palm to it. Her cheeks pinch up in that why that has always warmed my soul, and tears flood her eyes.

"Jo!"

The bay doors pry open, and the last thing I see before she is yanked into the void of space is the frozen tear crystallized on her cheek...

Journal
Year 30: Day 11078

They're dead. Gone. Everyone. Drifting through space like a human asteroid field...

The flight crew... we're it. Ten of us. That's it. That's all that's left. David, he... Jo... I can't. I'm sorry, Leo, I just can't write anymore today.

Year 45: Day 16683

The empty halls whisper at me. I walk without purpose through them. Past empty tables in the cafeteria and through dust-coated shelves in the armory. Beyond the habitation unit where I sit every night and fight the urge to bring my son into this world, knowing he'd suffer the same hopeless fate I do. I simply wander.

It was so lonely at first. But I've grown to enjoy the

isolation.

It's given me more time to think of *them*. Of the loves of my life that have been ripped from my world. Of the brilliance of a child, I'll never watch grow. Of all the friends and loved ones whose only chance at life was this miserable doomed existence. I think of them all.

The whispers echo once more, and it seems I can't ignore them any longer.

"Terry," I say over the wall comm. "...Terry?"

No response.

I pry off the panel face and am met with yet another frayed wire.

"Great..." I sigh and begrudgingly march back to the command center.

Terry spends nearly every waking moment in his station, obsessing over projections. I used to admire his dedication, now it's become a bit exhausting.

"The wall comm on grid c5 is busted," I say. Terry doesn't look up; he just mumbles at me.

"Add it to the work orders." I'm not sure why I bother, but I scroll through the hundreds of itemized listings until I find the new entry slot and insert the work order.

"Heard some groaning down c5 as well. Be nice if we had someone who could do an exterior check for us, ya know?..."

Terry stops and finally glances up.

"Arch... just give it a rest, brother. We're not activating the wombs."

A moment hangs in the air where I can tell he hopes I won't contest it. But I can't help myself.

I go to plead my case, but he stops me before I can get a word out. He's heard this plea countless times.

"I won't hear it again, Archie. I refuse." He struggles as he pushes himself out of his station. "You don't think I want to meet my daughter too? I'd give anything."

"Obviously, you wouldn't!"

Terry clenches his jaw and shoves me out of the way as he activates a wall screen behind me.

"Look!" He points to the ship's diagnostic results that flash across the screen. "Oxygen quality is down thirty-eight percent. Our rations are tight as they are, without anyone in Botany. Three of the water recyclers are inoperable. We can barely keep the Redemption running as it is. You want to try to take care of a couple dozen infants as well?" He stews. "And what about medical? The whole staff is gone? What about the

11

fact that we're nearly seventy and we'll be lucky if we make it another ten years? Then, what? They'll be kids, Archie. They'll starve to death or suffocate, or who knows what?" Terry clutches his chest and has to sit down.

I hurry as quickly as I can to him and help him into his seat. Tears water each of our eyes as we both know he's right. He puts his arm to my shoulder and points to his work.

"I know it's hard, Arch. But their only hope is if we find a planet."

Journal
Year 45: Day 16683

It seems as if we'll never meet, my son. I want to, though. Terribly. If it wasn't for Terry, you'd be here. And I could hold you and tell you of my life in person, instead of you having to suffer through page after page of scratched out words and squeezed in sentences. But that would be a mistake... I know that. I'd see you born, just to leave you abandoned on a hunk of metal floating to nowhere. That is not a life you want to live... trust me. Our clock says it's been almost forty-six Earth years since we left that dying rock. Who knows how long it's actually been? It was so over my head that I never bothered listening to the theorists about speed and time and how that'd affect everything. All I do know is, not a moment has gone by that I haven't thought of you. Leo, I promised you a home, and I intend to keep that promise.

Year 56: Day 20800

Terry's hand feels like tissue paper. It's so thin. The steady beep of the pulse reader taunts me. At any moment, I could be met with that dreaded flat tone that'll signal I'm officially the last human in existence, and my dear friend of seventy years, is gone.

"It's the one, Arch... I know it." Terry's words creep from his dry, wrinkled lips. "It's the one..."

I rest my forehead on his arm and think of a lifetime of friendship that lies on this medical bed.

"I know it is," I say. "You did it."

"We did it." The faintest semblance of a smile curls around his breathing tube. I laugh and wipe a tear from my eye.

"Hey, I'll take credit. Who else is here to refute it?" We share a strained smirk, and he gives me a look that tells me its time.

"I love you, brother... Thank you."

And without another moment, my dearest friend drifts away from this world, and I am, completely and utterly alone.

Journal
Year 56: Day 20800

I am the last human alive. What a terrifying thought. Terry passed away today, and I fear I will be soon behind him. So, my son, this will be my last entry. I feel the heat of life slipping away from me even as I write this. But for the first time in nearly thirty years, I have hope. Because of my dear friend Terry and his relentless research. He did it. Found us the type of planet that we've searched almost a century for. I've programmed its coordinates into the dashboard and commanded the Redemption to land, no matter what. The journey will take six years, and I know I will not be alive to witness it. I've never been a real spiritual man, but tonight, I do pray. I pray life exists on that planet. Intelligent life... one that can figure out how to activate your wombs, learn how to raise and care for you. Life that can provide you safety and structure. Life that can give you purpose. Who knows what waits for you there? I can't begin to guess. But just know, if you're reading this, you are a miracle. Humanity is a miracle. DO NOT WASTE IT! Species do not slip through grasps of extinction to be given a second chance, so cherish it.

The legacy of mankind rests on you and the others born with you. I wish like hell I could be there to guide you through it, but as I sit here staring down at the pod you rest inside, I know you will be capable of greatness.

So, to Leo, or anyone else who gets to read this, good luck. And bring us back!

From the last human alive to the first...
Captain of the A.C.R Redemption,
Archie B. Abernathy

PART I

SPARK

1

LEO
ABERNATHY

Metal Eggs

I was not born like a human. I did not tear from my mother at the end of a rope. Squealing. Hysterical. Natural. No. I was hatched from a metal egg. On a planet unthinkably far from Earth. Alone. Quiet. And helpless.

No mother. No father. No siblings. No humans. Alone. Yet... not exactly alone.

Creatures were there. Staring into the egg at a being not from their world that, for all they knew, began materializing out of thin air.

How terrifying that must have been for them?

Their horror would only multiple in the minutes to come.

For another would hatch...

And another.

And another.

And another.

Hundreds, possibly thousands of these metal eggs lined the halls of the alien craft they stood in. Surely, an infestation was under way.

Is it of any surprise the actions they took to solve it? Certainly not. Panic is nature's reaction to the unknown. I would've considered destroying the other eggs as well. So, how can one resent a decision made that they themselves would've also made? You can't. But it doesn't change the simple truth that my species was robbed of its resurrection that day. That is why I hunch over this table in the dimness of our lab and squint at microscopic strands of life.

Sure, they allowed the eight of us already hatched to live. But whether their motivations stemmed from a sense of moral obligation, sheer curiosity or sinister intent, it doesn't matter. As one life does not deem humanity reborn. Nor do eight. I signal my technician to increase the magnification of the lens I stare through because the dream of my father was not for a lone generation of humanity to experience life, only to disappear once again into the ethers of existence. No... His dream was that of a second chance for mankind. A lasting civilization where we could start over and redeem ourselves from the transgressions of our past.

That simply cannot be done with eight people. So, if humanity is to be anything more to this world than a fossilized moment in time, the cloudy solution in this petri dish is that answer.

The sole window of the laboratory is a tiny square on the door that lets in light from the hallway. The only other light in the room shines up from under the petri dish and illuminates the strands of my DNA that lay inside it.

Sweat beads along the ridge of my brow. Patawa wipes it away so it doesn't drop in the solution and ruin the formula. I can feel her constantly glancing at Bryl, who stands guard at the door. As if my nerves weren't shrieking already, every set of footsteps I hear in the hallway makes my stomach drop. But I trust my crew. It doesn't matter if they aren't human, they're still family. Besides, I wouldn't dare look away.

My open eye burns as I squint through the microscope. I don't remember the last time I blinked. Focus. Even the tiniest of errors and my formula is ruined. I run my thumb along the stitching of my father's journal that sits in my lap and concentrate... Too much has been sacrificed for the formula to be ruined.

I swallow and try to control my breathing but it quivers. I haven't uttered a word in so long, the order I give my technician comes out in a hoarse whisper.

"Spri, increase levels on two and seven by half a percent."

Through the lens, a tiny orange protein fluid disperses into the solution and snakes in between every crevice of the oval shaped receptors of my DNA. I just need one receptor to bind to the fluid. Just one. One bind and I can save the human race from its second extinction in 100 years. One bind and everything my father sacrificed will have been worth it. One bind and this planet will know more than eight humans. One bind and I can change the world...

"Boss they're coming," Bryl says.

I don't look up.

Patawa shoots from her seat and begins hiding our work.

"Leo, we have to move!" She urges.

I need to see this...

The fluid swirls and mists like a feathery cloud, curving around each receptor, but none binding. *Come on... Come on...*

The legs of a table screech against the ground as Spri tries to drag it back to where it belongs, but he's too frail to move it. I glance up and bark at him.

"Spri! The sequence, how far along is it?"

Bryl interjects before he can answer.

"Boss, enough! There's no time." I glare at him as he hustles to the other side of the room and lifts the enormous table over Spri's head, putting it down in front of an industrial size freezer. Patawa pulls open the freezer door, and a frosted swirl gusts out as she lets a frozen *Oltish* corpse slam down onto the table. An antenna-like appendage snaps off the man's skull as it impacts the table and disappears somewhere deep into the lab.

I turn my attention back to the formula. There's time... there has to be.

Thoughts flood my mind as mayhem swallows the lab and I watch this orange fluid dance around the DNA receptors. I think of the Redemption and how miraculous it is that the ship even made it here. The hysteria that must have ensued the day it broke up in the atmosphere and scattered its debris across the planet. The fear, the curiosity, the obsession. I think of the 100 years in between that crash landing and the moment Valenian scientists figured out how to activate our wombs. I think of Earth. Of humanity. And of the sheer impossibility of our existence... I think of it all.

The fluid settles for a moment. Fully engulfing a receptor.

I jump from my seat. *Bind you son of a bitch! Bind.*

The orange lining gets thicker and thicker around the oval, the fluid beginning to draw toward the receptor like a microscopic magnet.

"LEO!" Bryl shouts.

My throat begins to tighten. The noise around me blurring into a muted symphony. And for a moment, there is nothing in this world clearer than these unimaginably small particles flirting with one another. The missing piece to breeding synthetic humans at the precipice of creation. And upon its creation, the answer to my species' impending demise.

But as I stare down the lens with tear-filled hope, the microscope is snatched out from under me and all I'm left staring at is the scuffed reflection of myself in the metal table.

"NO!" I shout, the roots of my hair screaming as I pull at them. "What are you doing?!" Bryl yanks me toward him, nearly dislocating my arm he's so strong. He snorts, the slit of his nose flaring in anger.

"Are you trying to get us killed?" Bryl yells. It was there... it was right there. All the thoughts of before fade away and are replaced with an image of Gwinn's face. One twisted into a smug expression. One that laughs at me for failing once again. A polluted smile that stretches across her face, glad the womb accelerant didn't bind and our species will forever stay plummeting toward extinction.

I bury my head in my hands and have to sit back down. Months of work gone. The resources, the money, the risks... meaningless once again.

Pain burrows behind my eyes. A searing headache.

It isn't until I feel Patawa touch my shoulder that I realize just how selfish I've been.

I glance up and am met with three desperate faces. Ones that urge me to hurry before we're detained for performing illegal experiments with High Council property. I bite down as hard as I can, eyes clenched, and bury the devastation. For I've already lost Riley, Gwinn and my formula... I refuse to lose my crew as well.

My apologetic nod doesn't feel like enough, but it'll have to do for now.

Against the far wall of the lab, remnants of one of the metal eggs we were hatched from lay scattered in pieces across a digitized screen. Holograms rotate slowly above each component. We're doing everything we can, but we haven't been able to reverse engineer this miraculous device. Gwinn constantly tells me it's a sign. That the universe is trying to purge itself of the plague that is humanity... I shake her cynicism from my mind and hurry to push the screen into a secret compartment in the wall. Now is not the time to falter in my convictions. Not when we're this close. But as I shove

18

the microscope into the compartment as well and watch the failed formula solution drip down the side, I worry if I'm wasting my time and risking all of our lives for nothing... That's Gwinn for you... Give her ten minutes in a room with the devil and he'd walk out doubting fire.

I move to help them clean.

I knew these Oltish bastards were ugly, but I didn't realize how heavy they were. Bryl and I strain as we waddle the table to the examination scanner. It's an odd feeling to look at a corpse that's so unmistakably alien. Whatever sympathy you want to experience for it, just doesn't seem to register when you can't relate to its features. I can *see* Patawa's concern in the compression of her brow. Bryl clenches his jaw as he strains, much like I do; Spri's eyes dart back and forth in concentration... They aren't exactly the same but these are at least expressions I can translate. But this thing... my brain never knows how to process the races that look nothing like humanity.

The table finally screeches to halt and we huddle around the body, assuming our fake positions.

The laboratory doors pound open as we do and debris blows in from the hall.

This debris is unfortunately High Councilor Russa, not literal trash. Although, if you ask me, there's not much difference.

"High Councilor," I say without looking up. I push the nerves from my body through a silent exhale and I exchange a relived glance with Bryl. That was close... "To what do we owe the pleasure." I act as if I'm pausing my diligent work on the corpse to address the *Ancient* leader. The crew is much more formal in their greetings, letting out a sort of purr my human tongue simply can't replicate.

"Leo, how we doing kid?" Russa towers over the table as he approaches, the obnoxious grin that perpetually splits his beak-like face, tilting there once again. "The brain trust here looks hard at work. Hopefully you brought a ball or something to entertain the big guy." He winks at Bryl, the lens over his eye folding in from three different directions. Just one of the many human habits Valenians have integrated into daily life.

Bryl snorts once again, but thankfully shows restraint.

I have the utmost confidence in Bryl, but Russa is not just one of the most powerful men on the planet, he's also enormous.

Standing nearly eight-foot-tall, his body consists of

thousands of fibrous cords that unwind from a long, tightly concentrated stem of a neck and bundle themselves in heaps like limbs made of intertwining tree roots. The cords tangle and untangle themselves at will from permanent knots along his body, acting much like my own joints. So, as he moves and gestures, his number of "limbs" constantly shifts.

As much as I'd love to watch my massive enforcer tear Russa apart, bit by bit, some men are just untouchable. I answer the obnoxious prick so Bryl doesn't with a fist.

"Progress has been slow, High Councilor. It would help if we could study a body that hasn't been mutilated before getting to us."

Russa grins at my subtle criticism.

He paces around the examination scanner, the ends of his cords working like fingers on the thawing body. Patawa glances to me as he inspects the man's missing antenna and I shake my head at her, begging her not to say anything, but her words are already coming out.

"It's just... studying live cultures of the Rotting would be much more efficient. That's all..." Her voice drifts off as Russa turns his attention to her. A cord slithers up her cheek and Russa lowers himself to her level.

"Seems we're all just full of opinions today, hmm?" He stares at her, his presence alone enough to shatter her. "If you're implying, we jeopardize the sanitization of this lab by bringing in unsterilized bodies... you aren't as bright as I thought," He says. She winces, doing a poor job of masking her discomfort. It pains me to see her squirm but there's nothing I can do. What I've learned over the years is Russa is nothing more than a bored pet looking for something to chew on. Entertain his bullshit for long enough and he'll eventually grow bored of you too and move on. The only people who can hold the attention of this asshole are Gwinn and the Regal himself, Trakstull.

"Of course not." Patawa replies. "That would be foolish..." She shoots me another distressed glance. But I don't take my eyes off Russa.

"Yes. Yes, it would." Russa lets go of her and pushes the head of the corpse to the edge so can he sit down on the table. His casual demeanor is always so frustrating. "So, tell me of this *slow progress*, Abernathy."

He's such a hard man to read.

He grins and smirks and mimics my posture and carries himself with such arrogance and assurance that I'm convinced he knows exactly what we've been up to. But we've gone to great lengths to ensure that he doesn't. So, the more logical answer is he's just an insecure toad who hates the fact that he isn't as powerful as Trakstull and isn't as loved as Emoss.

"Well, when I said slow progress, I really meant no progress," I say. I shoo him off the table so I can show him the corpse and he reluctantly obeys. "See these caverns here along his torso?" I point to chiseled out fissures along the man's side that look like cracks in a dried out river bed. "Unless we observe the disease at a structural level before it melts through the skin and leaves us with this... there's not much we can do."

Russa inspects the wounds along the corpse, leaning in to examine them closer. He murmurs as he studies the body without looking up.

"Far less capable men have accomplished more with less."

I shake my head, huffing.

"Then get them to do it. Because I'm telling you, there's nothing else we can do, short of studying Tanya in Su Hoz," I say, my frustration spilling into my tone. "And the Grogan islands would fall out of the damn sky before you let that happen."

Russa shifts uncomfortably.

"Careful, kid..." He warns.

My stomach chews on itself. Anger burning a hole inside me.

"What kind of leader lets his people die while the only survivor of the very disease that's killing them, is locked away at the edge of the world?"

Russa's grin descends slowly into a scowl. He steps so close to me I have to crane my neck back to look into his eyes. The stench of his fibrous core somehow wafts out from under his flowing shawl. A mildew and decaying scent that makes my eyes water.

"You humans... always paying for your words with your blood. You'd be wise to take a note from your *Reyllion* friend behind you and temper that emotion," He says as he tilts his head to look at Spri. "You willing to die because of an outburst from a human?"

Spri stares at the ground of the closet off to the right. Who knows how long he's been fixated on whatever he's staring at? Spri answers in a flat tone. Emotionless and indifferent.

"Death is a certainty. Am I supposed to fear it? The sun

21

disappears every night. Am I supposed to fear the moon as well? The cause of my death is of no concern to me. Nor is the timing of it. The quality of my life will not be determined by the duration of my life, yet the company I keep *during* that life." Spri shuffles casually past Russa and disappears into the darkness of the lab, returning with the broken antenna of the Oltish corpse. "Leo is an unobjectionable companion. I speculate worse deaths exist." He reaches up to hand the antenna to Russa and pushes out the door of the lab.

My frustration is overthrown by a huge smile that spreads across my face and I try not to laugh.

Russa grins once again, yet this time it's painted with a sinister brush. The type of smile that only those who control your life can express. A smile that slithers into my mind and gnaws on my soul. My face quickly sours.

"Have I ever told you of the day we voted to destroy the other human eggs?" His voice darkens. Lowering so much I have no choice but to lean in. "I voted no... Did you know that? Emoss, Yara and yours truly. That's it... We were the only ones who tried to save you all. The rest didn't hesitate." A cord of his snakes around my arm. "Emoss is dead and Yara has been missing for years, so who do you think wears the brunt of the blame for this mysterious, foreign disease?" His cords twist up my shoulder and pull me close. My fingers begin to throb as their circulation is cut off. I try to push him away but it's no use. "You ungrateful little shit. Maybe it's time we revisit that policy," He says. "Can you picture the headline: *Defender of the people, Russa the Righteous, saves the planet from disease ridden pests.*" He yanks me so close I can feel the heat of his breath. His beak-like jaw barely opening as his words slither out. "Question my integrity again and I very well may try." Bryl shoves his way in between us and snorts. The veins of his massive neck pulsing. Russa stumbles back, but steadies himself, quick to show he's unfazed.

He rolls the antenna in between his fingers, staring at the dislodged appendage. He nods.

"I like the big one." He points the antenna at Bryl. "He's lucky the world has changed or else his insides would be splattered all over that wall behind you, but I do like him."

Bryl peels from his shirt, each of his four arms swollen with twitching muscles nearly bigger than my head.

"Try me," Bryl says as his chest heaves up and down. Aggression seeping from his pours with every pounding breath. I reach out to pull him back. As much as I appreciate Bryl's loyalty, I can't have him getting killed because I ran my mouth.

Russa dusts himself off and hides his shaken demeanor behind a smirk as he always does. Bryl calms himself. "Yea, that's what I thought."

Russa waits a moment before turning and heading to the door, speaking over his shoulder.

"Ya know, it doesn't have to be this way Leo. The others love me," He says. I chuckle to myself. Please... Gwinn loves him as some twisted father figure, that's about it. And Gwinn clearly isn't in her right mind lately. A twinge of sorrow stabs at my side at the thought of her. I have to shake her from my mind once again.

"How about you just take care of her and I'll handle our business," I say. Russa stops as he notices something peculiar along the ground. He bends down and runs his fingers through a small orange puddle. My eyes widen. Patawa darts to action, wiping the remaining spilled formula up.

"Defrosting fluid," She says with a nervous smile. "Frozen bodies and all." Russa glances to her and back to me. He grabs the rag from Patawa and wipes the fluid from his fingers.

"First thing tomorrow you four ship out. New mission to the east. Details will be sent your station," Russa says as he tosses the rag at Patawa. "Redemption salvage located. Could be useful."

I suck at my teeth and try to stay respectful.

"Understood, High Councilor," I say.

Russa pushes through the door when something he said hits me.

"High Councilor." I call out. Russa pauses and retreats back a step. "East? It's not..."

A final grin peels across his face.

"It is..." He says with a wink and disappears into the hallway. The color washes from my face. Bryl notices, glancing to Patawa.

"Where we going boss?" He asks.

My mind drifts to a distant memory and the word barely falls from my lips.

"...Paradise."

2

VICTOR BELLS

Sweat and Glory

Metal and fire and guns and rage and violence. This is my life. And I love it. I don't know where the anger comes from, but it's there. Thick as mud, entrenched in my soul. I love the pain and the fury. The pure energy that follows me like a shadow from hell. Chaos. Demonic frenzy. A man possessed. There is no one more terrifying when I step into the Arena. No one as ruthless. I ooze venom. Pure hate and disdain. To see my eyes in the Arena is to know agony. I've never been defeated, and I never will. I was born to battle.

Calm before the storm.

We stand as a constellation, specks of glowing light huddled together, swallowed by unfathomable darkness. Except our lights are flashing gauges and sensors that flicker as holograms against the visors of our Warlord suits, and our darkness, the bowels of a tunnel that feeds into the Arena. The reflection of a visor against the wall illuminates the metal armor plates of one of my competitors. I watch as he checks the joints of his suit.

Those joints will not save him from my wrath.

Nothing will.

The darkness funnels my vision to the mouth of the tunnel, where I watch the occasional flash of an oscillating spotlight illuminate the madness that awaits us at the end.

A battlefield.

Droves of blood-lusting fans.

Glory.

The Arena.

My body trembles uncontrollably. Silent impatience bulging against the veins of my neck. I can taste blood. Eager. I close my eyes and think of the first time my father, Dansro, took me to a Battle of Warlords fight. I was just a child. Young and violent and obsessed with the glory of battle. Mesmerized by the Arena. Gawking at the Warlord suits covered in dazzling paint, shimmering against the bright lights. Spellbound by the towering statues carved from myrite and galestone and all the rare minerals of Valenia. Duzarod the Wild. Pyra the Immortal. Dansro the Noble.

Legends. Their names to live on for eternity.

I knew, at that moment, my destiny was inside these indestructible glass walls. Warhammer in each hand. An exoskeleton of relentless metal. A storm of rage and violence and pleasure brewing inside. A human face to be chiseled among these alien Gods. Never to be forgotten.

I open my eyes.

That will be my destiny... if Hades allows it.

The compression hinge of my suit's elbow hisses as I lift my forearm to inspect it. I run my fingers along four symbols disguised within the flames and the chaotic patterns that streak across the metal's warpaint.

A peacock for my brother, Fargo. A lotus for my dear friend, Miku. A quill for my father, Dansro. And a crescent moon for my idol, Pyra.

As the tunnel's tension builds, I sway side to side, letting the thoughts of them placate my mind.

Fargo, my brother in every way but blood, is no doubt sitting somewhere in the audience tonight surrounded by a flock of fame-addicted leeches. Insincere barnacles who love to be seen in the company of two exotic creatures... humans. He'll bask in the attention they give him and spin tales of my triumphs to impress the shallow horde. On the other hand, Miku will politely laugh and try her best to stomach the unbearable company.

Dansro will probably have a new prodigy by his side. Talking him through my moves. My decisions. My tactics. Building the next great Warlord.

And Pyra... well... Pyra is gone.

I snap to attention when a bassline begins to pound

throughout the Arena.

It's nearly time.

I close my eyes once more and quickly plot through my eleven opponents one final time.

Two Wraiths; stay in the open, avoid the corners, and keep your eyes alert for their cloak. Weak armor at the core, make your strikes count. Strong, deliberate, and accurate.

Three Phoenix; not threats. Keep your eyes up; flight is their only advantage. Avoid their carpet bombings, and they are easy picking. Don't chase, or you could walk yourself right into a real threat. Eliminations are great, but we play for the win.

One Berserker; a rookie. He's young and inexperienced, talented, but undisciplined and reckless. Try to avoid him until later in the match. He will discharge his shield too soon and leave himself wide open. Patience, then unleash.

Two Specters; both formidable. Avoid their stuns and gadgets, and maintain aggression; they can't take you one on one.

Two Behemoths; use armor-piercing rounds against their heavy armor. Hammers on their legs only, anywhere else will be useless. Take cover if they get positioned with their stationary Gatling. Counter if you feel they're low on ammo. High priority, these two are good.

and last,

One Banshee; ......

"Daddy's tricks won't save you this time, *Victor*." I'm shoved mildly to the side.

He interrupted my thinking; I hate being interrupted.

"You'd be careful the tone you take with me, Silva, I'd hate for you to get hurt again." My eyes remain closed, trying to finish my pre-match ritual.

One Banshee; fast. Very fast, Silva will...

"Hurt? Please, I was back in my suit within a week. You, on the other hand, were gone, what... a month? Two?" Silva says. "Everyone else may have bought the extended Champion's Tour excuse, but I know you're full of shit," Silva says, trying his best to get under my skin. "Just like your grimy brother Fargo and your little girlfriend Miku and all you worthless little human *Surgs.*"

He steps in front me, an irritating grin on his face that I'd love to stuff down his throat. His beady eyes try to act as if he's not intimidated by me, but I see right through him. He runs his fingers sarcastically across my chest plate. "We both know why you weren't fighting." He slowly circles me once more, trying to meet my eyes even though he stands much shorter. He knocks his metallic knuckles against my right leg as he puts two of his other arms around my shoulder. "How is the old wheel, Vic?"

My eyes snap open. This runt has officially ruined my concentration. He needs to be reminded who the alpha is around here. "Leg doesn't hurt a bit. I get you'll never understand what the Champion's Tour is like, but try not to act like such a sniveling bitch about it." I finally meet his eyes and pull him in even closer, our visors pressed against one another. "Plus, *your* little girlfriend Maloree was so incredibly generous she volunteered to host me when I was in *Ivolo*. She just begged me to stay." Silva tries not to react, but I can see the pain behind his eyes. "Poor girl also needed a month off when I was done with her." A devilish smile cracks across my face, and Silva pushes away in disgust. "I keep telling you Silva, but you don't listen. There's nothing women love more than a big gun." I wink, draping my rifle between my legs. "Now get the fuck out of here before *Hades* sees you. He seems angry today." I shoot him one more victorious warning glance, before closing my eyes again. Silva leans in and knocks on the glass of my visor, speaking once more before he leaves. His tone reeks. There is nothing more pathetic than insecurity.

"Tell that psycho, if he's in there, I'm not scared of him. He's no God!" He can conjure such little conviction in his voice I almost feel sorry for him. But Hades doesn't. Hades never does. Hades whips his arm around and grabs Silva by the neck, slamming him into the wall and pinning him there. He pushes Silva to the floor. I can feel his eyes manic with rage, as he snaps his teeth at him. His brow and lips quiver, breath now nothing but endless heaves. Silva squirms to his feet and retreats down the tunnel.

The time has come. *Hades* is awake.

The tunnel to the Arena is dark, and the fervent crowd that awaits us at the end is dying to explode into pandemonium. Muffled rumblings of chants and cheers spill down the tunnel where the twelve of us linger until we've been announced. The tunnel reeks of tension as warriors try to settle their nerves. Steel feet on stone ground scrape and clap as we approach the exit of the tunnel. I stand silently in the back, focused, and poised. *Hades* is restless, though, his upper lip still twitching, snapping his teeth and rocking from side to side.

The lights from the Arena go dim, and a loud booming voice amplified by massive speakers calls out to the crowd.

"People of *Canter*, are you ready?!" The crowd roars in excitement. The voice continues to woo the crowd, calling out in emphatic chunks. "Today's Battle... A free for all... Twelve of the best Warlords from across the world... Only one can leave here victorious..." The crowd begins to stomp its feet in unison, creating a thunderous rhythm. They accompany their stomping with a chant in preparation of their heroes storming the Arena "B.O.W.! B.O.W.! B.O.W.! B.O.W!....."

As the rhythm grows faster and louder, the voice releases his beasts with a passionate growl.

"BATTLE! OF! WARLORDS!" The speakers nearly break with the intensity of the volume, and as a bone-rattling cannon sounds off, we spew from the tunnel like ash from a volcano. The crowd erupts into full madness as we weave our way through the open Arena. Lights of all colors flood the stadium, fireworks crackling above our heads as fog and colorful smoke plume from vents in the ceiling. The sight is mesmerizing. The roars of excitement from 200,000 strong congest my thoughts and make it hard to focus. There is no better feeling in this world. Nothing can replicate the high. For less experienced fighters, though, the rush can be disorienting. There is no preparing for the first time you step foot inside these glass walls. I can see it on the rookie Berserker's face now as he scans the Arena. A storm of emotions. Awe, bewilderment, excitement, fear, fulfillment, insecurity, intimidation, joy. The pendulum swings in his mind from end to end so fast can't he process it all. The one thing I don't see on his face is focus.

That's why *Hades* is so good. The insanity fuels him. He grows stronger every second, soaking in the craze like a sponge. He is unhinged. Deranged. Unpredictable. So, so angry. Violent to his core. When he's in control, there's nearly no stopping him.

As the announcer goes through an introduction of each fighter, I look out over the Arena. 100-meter x 100-meter grid. A playground for warriors. Boxes, ramps, slopes, buildings, hallways. A true Arena for battle. Each area is designed for the strengths and weaknesses of each fighter. Know the land, know your enemy, know their plan.

There are wide-open areas and areas of tight quarters. Balconies perched high above, and troughs that run below. An encounter with an enemy could play out in infinitely different ways, depending on where you find him. And all of it encased inside a massive indestructible glass box. So, I must be prepared for it all.

I hear a buzz as the announcer finally gets to me.

"And finally, the man who needs no introduction. Undefeated at a flawless sixty and zero, he's returning to the Arena for the first time since winning his third straight B.O.W. Championship. He's the new record holder for Eliminations in a year at a staggering eighty-four. The son of Dansro... The Alien Assassin... the Hammer of Earth... the Pride of Groga *Ivolo*... Your champion. The one. The only. *HADES!*"

I raise my fist in the air.

The crowd tips from excitement to full-on anarchy when they hear his name. Their love for him is beyond reason. If only they knew the demon he truly was. But instead, they chant his name with pride. "Hades! Hades! Hades..." The announcer gives the final commencement and the grids under each of our feet open, and we drop into the small tram baskets under the floor.

A web of tram tracks under the grid carries each Warlord's basket to a random tile on the map. There's a brief moment for dramatic effect. I hate this pause. It always seems like an eternity. Sitting in darkness, waiting. The adrenaline cools, and you become all too aware of everything around you. The stench of your sweat punches you in the gut. The harsh angles of the suit dig into your thigh. That tiny sliver of fear begins to whisper into your ear. But with one word, it all evaporates.

"BATTLE!"

The grid floor opens on his cue, and the baskets catapult us into the air and onto the battlefield.

The fight has begun.

The moment I'm thrust into the air, I feel him take over. I've done all I can to hold him back, but *Hades* has clawed his way in. The monster is in control of me now, and any semblance of Victor has been burnt away by a flare of hellfire.

The fury roars through me. Anger so intense, my skin feels it may rip from my bones. Every pour in my body slams shut, trapping the heat within me. I can even feel the vessels of my eyes bulge. Bloodshot like a man possessed, red crackling across them like lightning in the night sky. My heart rate soars, and muscles contract until they nearly rupture. I have one more moment of clarity before I land on the deck of the Arena, and my body lets out a gut-wrenching screech.

I try to move my arm, but nothing happens, and my feet begin to stride forward without command.

A Specter tries to flee from my left. My body purses without my control.

It charges full boar ahead, a Hammer in each hand. The Specter is terrified. He knows he's unprepared for this fight. He fires his stun pulse in my direction. A ring of static-charged energy rifles toward me. My body slides underneath and pops to its feet without breaking stride. It counters immediately. Rearing back and heaving a Hammer. The instant it's let go, the heavy bolt pistol on my thigh is in my free hand. The pistol recoils. A round shatters the Specter's knee hinge. He buckles. The thrown Hammer connects, knocking the warrior to his rear. My body is on him before the Specter can stand. A massive two-handed swing of my other Hammer sends the Specter skidding on his back with a crushed chest plate. The dazed Specter shoots a grappling hook that connects with my foot, and he yanks the rope, flipping my body onto its back. But the Specter is too panicked to capitalize. My rifle is already out and screaming ammunition.

The Specter lays in agony, crushed ribs making his lungs wheeze with every gasp.

The crowd begins to chant.

"HADES... HADES... HADES..."

My head turns toward the crowd, and my fist rises in the air. The fans roar as their hero acknowledges them.

Hades pushes my feet forward, pacing toward the downed Warlord, and I know there is nothing left I can do to control my body. I am a prisoner inside my own mind. My body is Hades' now.

Hades props the fighter up on his knees and shoves the Specter's head under Hades' groin. Hades shoves a fist into the sky once more, wrapping his other arm around the waist of his victim. His manic eyes stare out into the crowd, and he beats on his chest as he lets out a victorious wail.

Hades grunts and lifts the Specter onto his shoulders. The enemy sitting backward, legs straddling Hades' helmet. He holds him there, waiting for his flock to give the Specter his final words. The crowd goes wild in approval and in unison cheer, "TO HELL YOU GO!" just as Hades slams the Specter to the ground with all his force.

A siren sounds as the Specter is eliminated, and Hades belts out a ferocious roar, his foot atop the battered Warlord. The grid tile opens, and the eliminated fighter falls through the tile, taken away in a basket.

In the blink of an eye, Hades has his first victim.

Part of me can feel the rage that courses through Hades. Part of me can't. I watch my arms and legs move with surgical precision, but also feel as if my hands are tied behind my back. I sometimes worry that I actually enjoy how devastating Hades can be. That maybe we're not that different after all. That potentially the violence and fury and insanity that operate on the surface for Hades are nothing more than carnal desires buried deep within me, that I refuse to acknowledge. I can't be this monster, can I? I fight for glory and pride and the high of success. Hades fights because he loves pain. Loves gore and adrenaline. All he wants is to hurt people.

When I look at Hades, it's as if I'm inspecting my reflection in a pond, and someone drops a rock in it. The ripples distort the image, leaving a morphed and abstract face, one I don't recognize. Yet, the longer I look, the more I see myself. The more the waters calm and it becomes clear that nothing really changed, it's been me all along. The beast and I are one. But I must fight at all times to resist his barbaric urges. Because if Hades were to ever completely shut me out, there's no telling the damage he could do. But he's too strong to be completely shut out either. So, I let him loose in the Arena. Give him unrestricted control, so I can save my energy in case I ever need to stop him. He's an insatiable fiend, but he'll run his course. Hades picks up his weapons, and we start off again, deeper into the Arena.

From high above the battlefield, we look like ants scurrying through a colony. Ceaseless motion. Weaving through tunnels and arches, climbing over mounds, and dragging bodies with us. The battle rages on as the numbers start to thin. One by one, sirens scream out the tone of defeat. With it, washing away their hope of unknown heights.

When once there was twelve, only four remain.

Littered with shells and debris, the previously chaotic battlefield has now frozen into a chilling hunting ground.

Weakened prey hiding in the weeds, clinging on to what

little time they have left. Bloodthirsty predators stalking the grounds, emboldened by their conquests. It's now a game of patience or pride.

To some, to hide is to lose the respect of your fans. To lose their respect is to lose everything. So, some will engage even when they will surely fail. Even if they are hurt and outgunned. Because to fight with courage in the face of sure defeat is what their fans have grown to expect. Valiance until the bitter end.

But others don't share the same righteous mindset. To hide is to survive. And for every spot higher up the leaderboard they place, the larger their purse. Their motivations aren't spurned by loyal fans or the glory of battle. They enter this Arena solely for the pursuit of fortune. Riches nearly unattainable elsewhere in this world. Opportunistic vultures who try to exploit others' aggression and principles for their monetary gain. They sacrifice their health and their pride for excess. But I'm in no position to judge. I've never lost. Racked up eliminations. The wealth I've accumulated has allowed me luxuries many only dream of. So, I understand the mesmerizing pull decadence has. The endless desire for more. It's a sickness I willingly bare. Hades is still pure, though. Albeit for the wrong reasons, he doesn't care about the money or the fame, just the violence.

A hush has fallen over the crowd as the four Warlords cautiously navigate the field. Hades knows there's someone nearby. He can feel him. A broken shoulder plate lay on the ground. A trail of empty shells. Someone nearby is hurt. Hades creeps his way around a corner.

Enemy.

Half a clip to the chest and the wounded Wraith is eliminated. No theatrics, no bravado, just purpose. The prize is in sight.

Hades steps over the Wraith and continues down the hall. Rifle ready. He clears each room and each corner with speed and sharpness. Two are left.

A confused murmuring rumbles throughout the audience. It's distracting. Moments later, a flock of boo's follow. What is happening?

Hades climbs to the top of the south building and looks out over the battlefield. Directly in the middle stand Silva and the rookie Berserker. But they're not fighting. They're waiting. Waiting for me.

What has Silva roped this poor kid into? That rat.

Anger makes my veins feel as if they course with lead. My record will not be tarnished by this cheat.

A wicked smile spreads across Hades' face and his narrow eyes stare daggers through his two opponents. Atop the building, he raises his fist once again and beats upon his chest. "TO HELL YOU GO!!" Bedlam erupts as the crowd has entirely swayed to Hades' side. Their champion is fearless. The uproar is so loud I can't hear his feet hit the ground as he jumps from the balcony. The moment his feet touch metal, the bullets rain upon him.

Hades' shield that pulses around him eats most of the first barrage. He finds cover and moves for his assault.

He rolls to his left and lobs a scatter core into the air. Just as the core reaches above the Warlords, he pulls his bolt pistol and fires a shell into it. An explosion bursts into the sky, sending shards of metal misery down upon his foes. Sharp, jagged edges chew through suits like teeth on meat. Seconds later, the scatter rounds explode again into even smaller pieces. The scatter core breaks their formation, as the two retreat in pain. Hades' shield recharges.

Hades sprints to the higher ground and fires clip after clip. He lobs another scatter core. This time Silva bails from his cover as he sees it float his way. Silva moves left, but where is the Berserker? Hades catches a glimpse of him to his right, moving just beyond the edge of his visor. The rookie has flanked him.

He tries to turn and fire a shot, but it's too late. The rookie unloads a massive payload of ammunition into Hades, knocking him to the ground. He manages to fall behind a box and stows his pistol. He can feel the Berserker is pressing him. The rookie pushes closer, inexperience convincing him this is his moment. At the same time, Silva closes in swiftly from the left. Time feels as it screeches to a crawl. Hades' mind runs through the options as the two bear down on him. The rookie is too impatient. I knew he would be. Hades does too. Hades waits until the very last moment then darts at Silva.

A massive swing from Silva's Greatsword sheers its way toward Hades. He jumps and flips, passing just over the hurling blade and lands on the opposite side of Silva. As Hades lands, the rookie unleashes his devastating shield pulse, which now is aimed directly at Silva. The burst lands with full force and launches Silva into the air. Hades fires his last two heavy bolts into the weaselly rat as he crashes to the ground. Then spins and clamps down on his rifle trigger as the Berserker attacks.

Staggering and nearly gone, the rookie is left on one knee as Hades' rifle clicks empty. Smoke pours from the red-hot barrel. Hades pulls out his Hammer and charges to finish the job. He pulls back to swing, but just before his Hammer lands, the rookie falls to the ground... An arrow lodged in his back.

Silva crumples to the ground in exhaustion, his bow splashed across his chest. Vulture! Hades walks over and looks down upon Silva. Silva laughs as blood outlines his teeth. I hate this man. Hades melts away as my heart rate lowers, and I feel myself regain control of my mind. I drop a Hammer to the ground and raise my fist to the sky.

"TO HELL YOU GO."

3

FARGO SHEPHERD

Snakebitten

A party is a place of transformation. I walk through the arching doors of my home, passing by hundreds I do not know, and become someone else. It is impossible to just be. Because that doesn't exist. Yourself, even when alone, is nothing more than the combined values and behaviors your society allows. A spectrum. Extremes on either end, yet they're still tolerable in that society. The only ones that are truly themselves are the people so far removed from that spectrum, they can't even see it. Hermits, recluses, psychopaths. People so distant from the boundaries of the world around them, they cannot be influenced by them. If you're on the spectrum, you're nothing more than your version of what your society can create. Real individuality is the rarest form of existence. But what good is individuality if you have no one to impress with it? I'll keep my act and the spoils that come along with it.

A band of Heplin... entertainers... call my name as I pass. It's an unnatural name for their tongues but an arousing accent for my ears.

"The night is still so young, my beauties. What would the

party do without me?" I smile at them as I continue by and grab some helpless Oltish buck instead. "It's your lucky day, my hideous friend. Enjoy." I sling the man into the waiting arms of the Heplins and shout back to them as they disappear into the crowd. "Humans, such a generous breed, are we not?" I spin back around and smile at the energy that builds around me.

Droves of power-hungry hyaenas flock to my parties. Each desperate for attention. Compensation for their shallow lives is all too present in everything they do. Extravagant dress. Bulky jewelry. Dates on their arm have lust written across their eyes, and they call out to anyone willing to answer. I've been known to fall for their siren song a time or two. I'm a lover, I feel no shame in it. I know they're motives, but that doesn't make them any less fun. I feel obligated to maximize my advantageous position. It'd be a shame to shield myself from a world so eager to expose itself to me. Miku is the saint in this house, not Victor or me.

Our house is perched at the end of a long winding driveway, a galestone gate wrapping the property. Akin to Earth suburbia. Sleek and modern. Crisp. A design only the elite of the elite can afford. Our resident Warlord champion qualifies.

And oh, how these pretentious Grogan dolts love ancient Earth architecture. *So romantic.* I'm not judging; I do love the privacy. Better than living full time in the Valley with Geeva and Cyto, that's for sure. It's just humorous to watch a civilization mimic one that ended in a pile of dust.

Chauffeur's line the drive, emptying their VIP clientele onto glassy stone. Servers wander about holding trays of drinks and drugs. There is no subtlety to this celebration.

The house is purposely dim. I prefer it this way. Soft light shining from the moon is brighter than the dull yellow hue that spits from the house's lights. The darkness gives my minions privacy within the festive madness. Combined with steam that rises off the ground, it creates a fog that hangs over our scandalous behavior. Victor and Miku lounge in a booth in an especially dark corner of the house.

This celebration is for him, yet he sits in the back, hidden from his worshipers. And we can't have that!

"Oh my. Aren't you the mighty Hades?!" I slide myself into the booth, wrap my arm around Victor, and shoot him a smile.

"I'm sorry, I think you have me confused with someone

36

else. I did see him walking around, though. Tall, ruggedly handsome, dazzling eyes, massive biceps?" Victor says.

"Yes, yes. That's him. If you see him, tell him there's a party I've thrown for him, and he's missing it."

"I'll be sure to let him know."

"And who is this, and what has she done with the Princess of Groga?" I gesture towards Miku and tap my nails against the glass she holds.

"Don't call me that.." she looks back unamused. "I needed a drink when I realized hundreds of *Fargos* were going to be rummaging through my house once again."

I raise my glass to cheers.

"To one hundred Fargos. Every woman's dream!"

Miku shakes her head, and even boulders-for-brains, Victor cracks a smile.

"I'm not toasting to that." Miku chuckles. Always so noble this one.

"Fine." I reach my glass up once again. "To the twins, gone five years to the day. May their certain mauling have been quick and painless. God rest their souls." I drink.

Miku apparently doesn't appreciate my flattery or my humor.

"They're not dead, stop," She says.

Victor turns to see if she's serious. Somehow, she is.

She can be optimistic all damn day, doesn't change the fact that they fled Archler House after Emoss died and haven't been seen since.

"The way I see it, if you go running off into Berban, you're asking for one of two things. One, you end up a steamy pile of Tyko shit. Or two, some giant Gaz warrior is wearing your teeth around his neck like a psychotic arts and crafts project. Either way, you're dead."

I take a long pull of my drink and watch a striking Brushu woman walk by. God, I love parties. Miku has her arms crossed, clearly hurt, when I turn my attention back to her.

"They're smart, and they have each other," She says, a tear welting in her eye. Shit... Victor notices and kicks my shin so hard under the table I somehow feel it in my balls.

"Fargo's an idiot, don't listen to him," Victor says as he wraps her in a hug.

"I won't contest that," I say with a grin.

Miku still looks upset, and it's ruining my buzz. I apologize. "Hey, I'm sorry. I'm sure the twins have found a way to stay alive out there." I raise my glass. "To the eight... not the six." I smile, and she rolls her eyes but smiles as well.

"To the eight."

We clink our drinks together and enjoy watching the creatures that slither through the party.

My bodyguard, Geeva, drags a heavily intoxicated Heplin by his hair to escort him from the party. We share a strained glance as she passes by. I think Victor notices but doesn't say anything. Miku watches on in disgust.

"Honestly Fargo, who are these people?" She asks.

"The who's who of Valenia, of course. Everyone and anyone. The usual crowd." It's a vague answer, but honestly, I can't give more specifics.

The truth is, I don't know.

I started hosting these parties after Victor's win a year back, and they somehow grew into the spectacles they are today. They grew in size and scale and flare, and with it, so did my reputation. I became the foremost expert on social status. Every part of who I became was what everyone wanted to be. To be trendy was to be Fargo Shepherd. I had climbed out of the shadow of Victor to become the pinnacle of celebrity. These people may come to drool over Victor, but they come wearing my clothes, speaking with my words, and trying to live my life.

"We need to talk about these parties, Shep. They really are getting out of hand. I bet half these people have never even seen Victor fight." Miku finishes her drink and slides it onto the table, leaning back into the cushion.

"Out of hand? Nonsense. Controlled chaos, my love. Controlled chaos." I reach over and kiss Miku on top of the head. She shakes her head and rolls her eyes, but I see the edges of a smile break in the corners of her mouth. "Why does it matter if they've seen our beloved champion fight or not? All these people want is to be seen anyway."

We sit for a while enjoying drinks and telling stories. When Miku speaks, Victor listens. Intently, completely. He'll never admit it, but he loves her. I know he does. All the man knows is aggression, yet he balks when he tries to express how he feels to her.

Such an oaf.

A blunt object.

I'm more refined. My skills are less forceful, more indirect. She talks of current events and the world and deep, meaningful purpose, and I begin to lose interest. I'll let the star-crossed lovers ponder the meaning of life; I'm more concerned with who I'll share a bed with tonight. I grab two glasses from a server who struts by and make my way toward her.

Across the room, just at the edge of visibility, a frame I'd like to meet leans against a wall. Her details blurred from the thick air. The occasional glow of a smokewrap ember burns near her mouth and is followed by twisting streams of smoke. Tall and curved, with strong, broad shoulders and powerful legs, there's no mistaking her for anything other than *Brushu*. No other species' women have such stature.

Her characteristics begin to emerge as I draw closer in. She's stunning. Flawless straight amber hair. Large seductive eyes that are scattered with amber and gold, mesmerizing. Her dress plunges deep and teases with the very edges of her most vulnerable areas. Her skin is smooth like a pebble buffed by a flowing creek. She's a Goddess of fiery beauty.

"Thank you," her voice purrs, and she takes the glass I offer. She flicks her smokewrap off to the side and seals her lips around the crest of the glass, taking a slow pull. Her eyes never leave mine.

"Fargo." I reach my hand out as I sip my own drink.

"Zina." She gently places her hand in mind.

"Where are you from, Zina?"

She looks at me, sarcastically. Unimpressed.

"Where am I from? Small talk from Fargo Shepherd. I must admit I expected something more... mysterious? Unique..." She raises an eyebrow as she surveys me from over her glass.

"Mmm, I'm sorry to disappoint. You're right though, the billionaire playboy who is one of the last surviving members of an extinct alien race card is overused right now. There's just too many of us. I really need to differentiate myself somehow..." I mock.

She laughs, and I can't help but be hypnotized by this woman. She's different. The typical party girl I meet here is dim-witted and simply motivated. A river of drinks and drugs operate their body. They are lustful, aggressive, purely physical creatures who act more like dogs in heat than intelligent beings. They do not care for unique or mysterious. They just want a story to tell their friends. And I absolutely love to be their story. It's what I've done for years. But Zina carries herself with poise. She has an expectation to her. A posture that demands I labor for her attention. It's a refreshing sensation.

"The capital..," She says.

"Excuse me?"

"You asked where I was from... I answered. The capital, Dwaul Fir."

I wait to answer for a moment.

"... that might be where you live now, but that's not where you're from. You don't have the city on you." I scan her up and down. She's too patient, too collected. The capital is constant motion. Frantic and sloppy. She's anything but.

"There's the mysterious I was looking for." She rolls onto her shoulder, still leaning against the wall to face me. "What do you see when you look at me then, if you don't see the city?" She inquires.

I take another moment to soak her all in.

"Poise. Pace. I see someone raised in a slower world than the city. One that could afford deliberate behavior. My first guess was a farm in Su Hoz. But it couldn't be. Your skin is perfect." I trace my fingers along the bulk of her shoulder. "You'd have blemishes, scars from the labor. My next guess was a suburban part of a Grogan island. Maybe *Oilsterr?* But that couldn't be right either. Your confidence is palpable. You didn't grow up in a cookie-cutter home with a dull, lifeless parent who just existed. You're a Brushu. You grew up in a powerful home. Important. My guess is you're the product of old wealth. Probably raised by a Savron servant, so you learned toughness and respect at a young age. A single child, yet you never got the attention from your family you deserved, so you sought out the city. You could make your own family there. Use your name to get ahead, yet forge your own path from it."

A sly smile curls from her lips.

"Well, well, bravo. Maybe there's hope for you after all." She gives me a look that tells me I've won her over. "If you knew all this, why still ask where I was from?"

I grin.

"Unique and mysterious reasons."

Zina's eyes narrow, devouring me. She finishes her drink, her other three hands spilling down my body like rain streaking down a fogged window. Two of them pool together at my groin, and the third wraps around my waist, pulling me in so close I can feel the muscles of her throat contract as she swallows. I slowly begin to vanish. Falling deeper into the trance of this seductress.

I must have her.

The chill of her breath on my ear consumes me as she

40

whispers.

"*Do you have secrets?*"

My head nods. Her pheromones making a mockery of my mind.

"*Show me.*"

Our eyes meet. I weave my fingers into hers and begin to lead her to my room.

"FARGO!" Victor's booming voice jolts me from my trance. I barely see him before his massive paw is clenched around the collar of my shirt. "What the hell are they doing here?"

The noise and commotion of the party all rush back into focus. The worst sensation of all, clarity.

I do my best to hide it from Victor, but I almost vomit when I see the herd of bodies coming my way.

In the distance, through the fog, all-black gloss tunics shimmer in the low light. Pointed hats cast sharp shadows over their faces. They consume the staircase. Widebodies push flush against the wall like water in a hose as they flow toward us. *Vipers.*

Shit... so much for meeting in the Valley.

I check back at the table for my gun, but it's not there. It hits me that I never brought it out... I pat through the pockets of my jacket for anything else, but they're all empty. My stomach moans.

"Geeva?!" I yell out. Where the hell is she?

The exhausted butt of Zina's smokewrap smolders at my feet. I realize she's gone, but I have far bigger issues at hand. And right now, I just need anything to settle my nerves.

"Let go of me." I snap free from Victor's death grip. "I don't know why they're here." I lie and pick the burnt stub off the ground and try to steady my hand as I suck at what little is left of it.

I exhale silently, eyes glued to the floor.

I can feel Miku and Victor staring at me, but I can't let them see my fear.

The *Vipers* are here... I have to deal with it.

Seven gangsters stand firmly behind their leader, one shorter, older man. Each one is a hybrid crossbreed of species more terrifying than the next. Their hats point down, covering half their faces. Cloudy eyes staring out from under the brims.

Their leader, Deterro, is holding a thin metal case covered in High Council glyphs. He tosses it to me. Acting as if he isn't implicating me in a black-market transaction in front of all these people.

I chuck the case to the table like it's radioactive. I can't be seen taking shit from him. Has he lost his mind? Especially something with "High Council property" plastered all over it. I scan the room, praying I catch a glimpse of Geeva's emerald eyes watching over the situation. I don't.

Some bodyguard she is...

Deterro smirks, watching me squirm. His gaze is wretched. Staring at me as if he's envisioning which way he'd prefer to butcher me. He says all he needs to say at this moment with those sharp eyes. I understand. But these are not men you can allow to sense your fear.

"I'm sorry, gentlemen, but this is a private party. I'm going to have to ask you to leave." I take another step forward and gesture toward the door. A knot builds in my throat so tight I start to get lightheaded.

The *Vipers* hold their ground for a moment, letting me know they're leaving because their business here is done, not because I asked them to. Honestly, I don't give two shits why they leave; I just need them gone. The herd of men turns to leave and vanish as quickly as they appeared.

"Are you kidding me, Fargo?" Victor wastes no time. His anger and disbelief are written all across his face. He lunges toward the case on the table, but I snatch it away before he can grab it. "Fargo! You promised me." I hate when he looks at me like this. Condescending prick.

"I promised you I knew what I was doing. And I still do, so you can wipe that patronizing look off your face." I tuck the case under my arm and push past Victor.

"Patronizing?! Are you serious?! *Vipers* were in our fucking house Fargo. *VIPERS!* You clearly have no idea what you're doing?" Victor and Miku follow me down the hall.

"Yea, and now they're gone. So why don't you back off? I've got it handled." I roll into my room and unlock a small safe in the wall. I shove the case in.

On a shelf in the safe rests a block lined with rows of tiny green vials. I pull one from the block and press a button on the side. The top opens and out shoots a thin green cloud of vapor. I inhale deeply, lungs swelling, and instantly feel the drug spill through me.

The world slows, and my eyelids glue themselves shut. Weightless and silent, the world around me drowns out. I can feel Victor yelling at me, but the sounds are muted. Miku comes close and puts her hand on my shoulder.

"Fargo... we're worried about you." She's a hazy silhouette

of herself, but I can still see the compassion in her eyes. The pain on her face makes my heartache. But the Venom pulsing through my system numbs my soul. I try to speak, but my tongue forgets how to move. I brush her cheek with my thumb and pull her into a hug.

"*Get the hell out of my room...*" I whisper. Miku pulls away, upset, and before I can even blink, Victor's huge fist thunders against my jaw.

I wake precisely where I had crumbled to the floor hours before. My jaw screaming in pain, my entire body pounds. You don't come down from Venom, you crash. The high is incomparable, but so is the low.

My senses are overly heightened. Noise is my enemy, each scent overwhelms my brain, and opening my eyes is torture. The party has all but died out. The only people left are those too drunk or high to function, and the servants tasked with cleaning this disgusting heap.

I step gingerly through the scattered mess of my house. Time crawls along as my hangover continues to win the battle for my soul.

The sun breaks over the horizon, and with it brings a full view of the aftermath. I can't look.

I walk out to the edge of my balcony and peer out over the world below. I wish I could feel some form of remorse, but I can't. I don't feel regret or embarrassment or shame. Just indifference. I make my choices, and I live with them. I drink and take drugs and enjoy the company of women and carefully construct the Fargo I want the world to see. Perception is always reality. But one thought does play over and over in my mind. Zina. She seemed different. For a brief moment with her, I thought I sensed a side of myself emerge that had been long abandoned. But it was just a moment, and the moment faded. My thoughts rumble on like a rusted transport rig until a voice breaks my train of thought.

"Sir Shepherd? There's something you need to see." A servant nervously stands at the entrance to the balcony. His tone worries me.

I trudge back down the hall; my body still angry with me. We stop at my room, and the servant points inside.

"Oh no! No, no, no, no..." I hurry over to the wall safe. The door rests wide open, and everything inside is gone. My heart nearly stops. Panic avalanching through me.

"Sir be careful!" The servant runs over to catch me and helps me into a chair. "We found the safe like this last night, sir." The servant keeps his head down. He doesn't want to see my reaction.

"Last night?! Then why the hell didn't anyone wake me up?" I bark back.

"We tried, sir. Many times. You were firmly unconscious. I believe Mr. Bells struck you quite hard."

I stare daggers through the man.

"You get me a list of every single person who was in this house. Do you understand? Stop cleaning, stop everything, and find out who was here. Right fucking now." The servant darts off, and dread fills me to my core. Dread is replaced with terror when I remember the metal case from the *Vipers* was in there. I run back to the wall safe, desperate for a miracle.

There is none.

But I did miss something the first time I looked in. A card lays leaning against the back of the safe.

I reach in and pull it out. It's a small white card with a dark red crescent moon in the middle. On the back reads a hand-written note:

You were wrong, darling. Born and raised in the alleys of the city.

In another life, maybe you could have been more than a mark.

I'm sorry.
Goodbye Fargo
Z

Zina. My head spins. Even as I read confirmation of her betrayal, I am still intrigued by her. Images of her spark colored eyes flash before mine. And the sounds of her seductive voice still echo in my ears. Reality strikes when I realize she has taken me for everything, and I've been played the fool. But she doesn't realize the true damage she's caused. She's killed me. She's killed herself. The drugs are replaceable. I can make more money. But what the *Vipers* gave me was a loan; they expect it back. And when they don't get it...

They'll eventually kill me, but it will be slow and painful

and gruesome. Then, they will hunt it down, find Zina, and kill her too.

The thought makes bile climb to the top of my throat.

4

TANYA CROWN

The Sick and The Saint

The lights always hurt my eyes when I wake up. Bright and harsh, the constant hum of power coursing through them. The room, stark white. My sterile prison cell. The melody of machines monitoring my vitals is the only noise that slices through the maddening silence. Antiseptic's chemical stench burns my nostrils. I know every inch of this ceiling. I hear the intercom click, and Qwillow's soft Heplin voice projects over the dull speakers. "Hi, sweetie." I roll my head to the side, tubes and wires pulling with me and glare through the glass at her. Her apologetic smile and sympathetic eyes aren't enough. They're... She's...... I know she's sorry, but I still hate her.

She tells me she loves me every day. But if she truly meant it, she wouldn't do this to me. Wouldn't put me through such torment. How can you love someone and treat them like this? Her words are hollow to me. Actions speak louder. Maybe if I were her daughter by blood, she would see the pain she causes. Maybe she wouldn't be able to see me in states like these. Maybe she still would. Maybe I truly am too valuable to not be the subject of permanent exploitation.

What an utterly worthless word *maybe* is.

I hate these thoughts.

One life for the sacrifice of the many. What's the point?

Why is my life less important than the lives I'm supposed to be saving? Just because there's more of them? I'm no martyr. What if two of us had my genes? What if all eight did? Would we never had been allowed a life of value? What's the number of sacrifices to lives-saved ratio to justify their actions? Some bullshit formula for morality. That's not how it works.

I peer through the loose neckline of my med gown at the wide scars that streak down my side.

My life's story is written in these scars. I'm told I contracted the Rotting as a child and survived. The only being on the planet to do so. I have no recollection of it, but apparently, it was a miracle. I suppose I'd consider myself lucky if it hadn't resulted in a lifetime as a lab rat.

I lay here. Machines cycling my blood, bone marrow, spinal fluid, mucus, and every other genetic material I possess to find a cure. *Please*. The cure is to let the weak rot away and begin again stronger with the remaining crop. Forgive me if I'm not the cheeriest individual, but the footlong tube up my nose makes it a little difficult.

"Just a few more minutes and we're done, ok?" The intercom clicks once again, and my angry tirade of thoughts slip back neatly into their deep corner of my mind. Until next time.

An alarm rings out mildly as the machines begin their shut down sequence. A soft hissing disengages the airlock doors, and Qwillow hurries in to untangle me. Pressing buttons, turning knobs, unclipping wires, she detaches me one piece at a time. She doesn't meet my eyes while she's doing it, but I can tell she feels my stare through the back of her head. If looks could kill.

She finally glances at me as we prepare for the worst part. Her voice doing its best to soothe me. "Ready?"

"Let's just get this over with," I say, tilting my head back. Qwillow gently wraps her impossibly frail hand in mine as she takes hold of the tube in my nose. I close my eyes and try to relax.

"Here we go," She says. Qwillow begins removing the tube.

Inch by inch, it slides from my nose, scraping against my sinuses. My back arches, throat closing up as the pain rifles through my body. It feels like she's pulling out my soul. "Try to relax," Qwillow says. My nasal canals constrict even more as her comment infuriates me. *I'm trying to fucking relax.*

The moment I'm free from my medical torture device, I bolt to my feet.

"Whoa, easy." Qwillow flinches toward me as she grabs onto my arm. Our eyes meet, and we stand there. A timid smile tries to push its way out, but she knows the scowl on my face needs time to cool. She lets go and backs away as I push the wetness from my eyes, and she attends once again to her precious machines.

"We're so close, you know?" Qwillow speaks out the side of her mouth; she never knows how to act the minutes after. I don't blame her. I honestly don't know how *I* want her to act. This is who she is. I'm proud of her. I'm proud to have been raised by her. I truly am. She is an inspiration to me every day. That doesn't mean I don't hate her. Doesn't mean I don't love her too. Love and hate, they're far closer than people are comfortable to admit. You can only love or hate something that strikes at your core. And you care about something you love just as much as you care about something you hate. They share the space. It's murky.

"I'm going to my room." I walk out of the observatory. It doesn't make sense, but the first thing I want to do after laying down for twelve hours with machines attached to me, is lie down. But this time, in the warmth of my bed, with covers tucked tight around me.

Su Hoz is a miserable place to live, but it is breathtaking. From my room, I can see in all directions. Gorgeous isolation. Curvy plains roll and bend for miles. Wildlife dot the distant horizon, and the sun is just cresting, bringing with it its soft morning glow. I may be a cynical bitch, but some things are too pure to hate. Gazing out at the wilderness, Qwillow walks by and delivers me a tray with two small cups and a note. One cup, an internal cleansing fluid, and the other a giant pill. The note reads:

Spoke with the High Council about the pill. They said they're working on a suppository version for you. I know you're into that kind of stuff.

I nearly spit my fluid out when I read the note, and a smile splinters my permanent scowl.

"You're gross!" I peek my head down the hallway, and Qwillow is pretending to read her dataplate while she waited for my reaction. She was already giggling to herself before I yelled down to her. "But you're right, I am into that kind of stuff!" I smirk at her as I saunter back to bed.

"STOP! You're *gross!* Why do you have to ruin everything?" Qwillow's face pales, the Heplin equivalent of blushing, and covers her ears as she tries to erase what she heard. I laugh to myself and roll back over in bed.

Out the window, a faint figure is speeding its way toward the lab. Ripping through the grass, leaving a sleek trail behind it.

Miku!

I hop out of bed, run down the stairs, around the corner, and to the entrance of the lab. Still wearing my med gown, I bounce out onto the grass and wave! The wind whistles, and I have to fight my gown from flying over my head.

A swanky RotoBike powers its way to me and slides to a stop. Miku pops her visor up and smiles.

"What's up, girl?!" She hops off the bike, and we slam a hug into each other.

"I've missed you! I'm so glad your here." It's felt like forever since I've seen her. I know it hasn't been, but it feels like it has. I have no one else. My only social interaction since we moved to Su Hoz has been Qwillow and the crew of bureaucratic puppets that come to collect the test results.

Oh, and I guess Gwinn.

When I was younger, I spent more time with the rest. Honestly, we all did. The older we got, the more the novelty of our existence began to wear off. And as it did, society let us live closer to normal lives. As normal a life the first extraterrestrials a world has encountered can have, I suppose.

But with a normal life comes normal issues. People grow apart. Their lives diverge in different directions.

Except for her random visit the other day, I haven't seen Gwinn since Emoss died. Barely anyone has. I have no idea where the twins, Riley and Remmy, are? Leo is always locking horns with the High Council, so they don't give him clearance to visit. And the guys in Groga are just... guys. I know they still care, but affection isn't at the top of their priority list. It's just Miku Hayashi. My most loyal, best friend.

I don't want to let go of her, but eventually, I do peel myself out of the hug.

I always dread when it's time for another test, but Miku almost always comes to visit me after, so in a way, I look forward to them. Love. Hate. Always connected.

"I see you've been *really* productive today. Still in your pj's, huh?" She pulls her helmet off and hooks it around a handlebar, raising an eyebrow at my gown.

"Test was twelve hours this time. They're getting worse. I just got out..." I roll my eyes and motion for her to come in. "Let's go."

After Miku pulls a small bag from a hatch in the back of her bike, we walk back into the lab.

"Did you bring me goodies?" I playfully try to grab the bag and look inside.

"Well, we'll see. Gotta ask Q first how cooperative you were today." She glances at me, already knowing the answer. "Today's top prize for good behavior is... candy!" Her hand overflows with blocks of sugary treats.

"Oh my gosh! Where did you get these?!" I ask as I try to snatch them from her hand. She pulls away with a smile and wags her finger.

"This cute little vendor in Okotall. It was right on the beach. I'd just finished up a shoreline clean-up event I hosted with some locals and saw this little booth selling replica Earth treats.

How cool, right?"

My eyes roll as if by instinct.

"Shoreline clean-up? Really? Your generosity can be nauseating sometimes, you know that?" I grin, and she plucks a piece of candy in her mouth and points back toward the door.

"Oh… I'm sorry, I can leave. Should I go?"

"No!" I snag her arm and pull her close to me, and we laugh. "You're not going anywhere, missy." I rest my head on her shoulder. "I'm just saying, you don't have to spend every waking moment doing some feat of extraordinary altruism."

I glance up and watch her disappear in thought for a moment, only to return with a dazzling smile.

"I wouldn't know what else to do with myself. Helping people is the best feeling in the world," She says. "Doesn't hurt that the more I do, the more people forget who raised me."

I've always wondered if that played some role in her perpetual state of benevolence.

"If anyone confuses you with Trakstull… they're an idiot."

"Unfortunately, idiots are in no danger of going extinct… just us."

We continue down the hallway catching up on what's new. As if there's ever anything new in my life. I live miles from anything resembling civilization and have constant supervision; I might as well be a pet. Miku's life, on the other hand, is everything but boring. Of the eight of us, she's by far the most beloved. She's the Princess of Groga for fucks sake. *Daughter* of the Regal. She's an icon.

"Well, Victor fought again this weekend..." She looks down at me.

"So, let me guess. Fargo threw a *Fargo Party*?" I chuckle.

"You know it. All out as always. The man has his niche, I will give him that."

"I do miss those parties." I haven't been to one since we've moved to Su Hoz. I used to be allowed to leave our lab in the Capital once every thirty days. But the testing has ramped up more and more since Emoss'ss death, and this new lab in Su

Hoz lets Qwillow double and triple her workload. Which means I spend more time in a medically induced coma.

"I'm sure, but these have gotten out of control lately... some really sketchy guys showed up, Victor and Fargo got into it, it was a mess. We left and stayed with Dansro," She says. I can see the legitimate concern on her face. It seems like more than typical Fargo bullshit, but I don't want the time we have to be spent griping over him, so I don't push the subject.

"Well, you know how those two can be," I say.

Miku can sense I don't want to talk about it, so she changes the subject.

"Hey, why don't you come spend a week with me? This place is depressing," Miku says. *As if I'm allowed to just leave and take a vacation.*

We pass a sealed door with *Restricted Access* etched across it, and finally see Qwillow sitting at her workstation, going over the test results.

"Why hello there, Q. How's my favorite super genius?" Miku asks. She has such a genuine nature to her. She loves people, and people love her. People love me like they love getting sick. They're miserable and wish it never happened, but at least they don't have to go to work.

"I'm great. I was telling Tanya earlier that we're getting really close!" I can see the optimism in her eyes, but she's said that many times before. She really believes she can find a cure. "Before you know it, you two will be galivanting around the world, and they'll be no need for me and this dumb lab." Her smile is so soft and tender. I know it's what she truly wants for me. It's times like these I feel guilty for hating her. But then I look down and see my med gown. Feel the ache in my nose. And remember what my life has become because of her.

"Yea, I'm not going to hold my breath." I can be too cold sometimes.

I walk into the kitchen and search for something to eat. Through the door, I spy on Miku and Qwillow talking. They glance at me periodically; I know they're talking about me. Qwillow is filling her head with the same hopeful bs she feeds me, and Miku is so pure she believes it.

"Q said you were *very* cooperative today. So, you get a treat. Good girl!" She pets my head and holds out a piece of candy in her other hand.

"Give me that," I snatch the candy away from her as we both laugh. "That's not funny." I try to snarl at her, but I can't keep a straight face.

I don't know what I'd do without her.

We plop down on the oversized cushions of a glass nook along the far wall. I lay my head in her lap, and we stare out at the Su Hozi countryside.

"Did I tell you Gwinn visited a few days ago?" I ask. Miku stops chewing on her candy, an eyebrow peeking up.

"She came here?"

"Yep," I say, my glance sharing in her disbelief. "It was so weird." I chuckle just thinking about it. "She came in, pretended to be friendly for about five minutes, recorded some nauseating campaign ad about ending the Rotting, then asked Qwillow for a tour of the restricted area of the lab." I grab another piece of candy from Miku and pluck it in my mouth. "It was bizarre. I could tell Q didn't want to, but you know how intimidating Gwinn can be." I shake my head, replaying that day.

"I'm positive she pulled the Russa card because Q doesn't allow anyone back there. I mean, not a soul."

Miku doesn't respond right away. She stares out at the tall grass that sways back and forth in the wind, curling my hair around her finger.

"I feel bad for her," She says.

I sit up. "Feel bad for her?"

"You know how much she loved Emoss."

"Miku, that was almost 10 years ago…" I say. She can't be serious.

"Yea, but losing a parent has to change you," She says.

"Adopted parent."

Her expression flattens. "All eight of us have adopted parents Tanya. Does that make them less of parents?"

I glance over my shoulder to Qwillow, who continues to work diligently at her station. I don't know the answer to that question. Sometimes, I genuinely think it does matter. That maybe if Qwillow was human and my cells made of the same substance as hers, that she'd rescue me from this nightmare and all the pain it causes me.

"Well, I didn't even get to the worst part. When she finished the tour, she just rushed out of the lab and didn't even say goodbye. Just blew right past me lugging a metal case with High Council emblems all over it." I rifle through the bag of candy to find a piece I want. "I'm almost positive she stole it, but I could give two shits if she did. She can steal everything from this Godforsaken place for all I care." I hike my med gown up to show Miku the knot along my shin. "I was just pissed because she nailed me in the shin with it and left a huge bruise. No apology, no good-seeing-you, nothing." I shake my head. "We've all been through shit. I don't feel bad for her."

We sit in silence for a moment.

Why do I always do this? Why do I ruin every chance at happiness I get? Miku traveled across the world to be here with me today, and here I am dragging us into awkward silence.

"...Candy?" Miku asks with a smile. I fight off a tear and smile.

"Sorry..."

"Stop, you're fine," Miku smirks and leans in to whisper. *"She can be a bit of a bitch sometimes, can't she?"*

I snort and rest my head on her shoulder.

Our moment is interrupted when the High Council agents show up like clockwork to receive the test results in person. Too sensitive of information to be delivered any other way.

An armada of armed soldiers escort two Heplin agents dressed in sharp digs. I assume they dress fancy to compensate for the fact that they're glorified errand boys. The soldiers, on the other hand, aren't your run of the mill High Council grunts like the ones who stand guard at the gate of the lab. These are specialists. I guess when a disease is tearing through a fifth of your population, it's vital to ensure the safety of the potential cure.

The guards stand at attention as the two agents approach Qwillow, firm, and trained. They're disciplined, but they can't help be distracted by Miku. They glance and try not to stare. They're here for me, yet I might as well not even be in the building. Miku smiles and toys with the guards, flirtatiously batting her eyes at them. Her bike suit is tight against her curves, and the guards nearly drool themselves looking at her. She loves to make men feel uncomfortable. I wish I was as confident in my skin as she is. But she never comes off pretentious or vain, just comfortable who she is. I admire her so much for it. Maybe if my arm wasn't full of needle marks and my ass didn't have my med gown designs pressed onto it, I'd feel sexier. Or maybe it's the bloating from the cleansing fluid. Regardless, whatever discomfort Miku causes the guards, I double it, just in the opposite direction.

"Med Doc, I shouldn't have to repeat myself. The High Council has given you every resource imaginable; they expect progress…" I overhear the two agents badgering Qwillow about something. I walk over and stand next to her. The two agents take a step back from me as if I'm radioactive.

"Qwillow is working her ass off, you pencil-necked twats." The two agents stare at me, annoyed, and take the results from Qwillow.

"People are dying Qwillow, don't forget that." They turn and signal the guards to follow them out. Dicks. Of course, she knows people are dying, who says that? Miku waves as they leave.

"Those guys are assholes," I say.

"Tanya you didn't need to interject. They were just messengers. But thank you." Qwillow puts her hand on my shoulder, and I remember that I hate her. I toss her hand off.

"Yea, well, they weren't wrong." I respond and plop back down on the cushions. Miku gives me a disapproving look. It stings Qwillow. Dammit, I can't help but be a bitch sometimes too. Miku keeps looking at me, urging me to apologize. I take a deep breath and make amends.

"Q, I'm sorry. I know you're working as hard as you can." I murmur and give her an embarrassed smile.

"No, you're right. Something does need to change. It will soon. I promise. I..." She starts to say something else but stops. Something weighs on her. I can see it.

"What is it Q?" Miku asks. I can see the wheels of her mind turn, but she dismisses it.

"... Nothing. It'll get better, I promise," She says and turns to quickly leave, shielding her face from us as she goes. I catch a glimpse of a tear stream down her cheek. Miku and I look at each other puzzled, as we pick up where we left off.

We spend the next few hours enjoying ourselves, but soon it comes time for her to leave. My stomach begins to sour. Back to my miserable existence. I give her a long hug.

"Love you, Mimi."

"Love you too... Hey, go easy on Q, ok? You know she loves you." Miku's eyes poke at the only soft spot left on my heart.

"I know." I give her another hug. "I'm gonna take you up on that week-long vacation, by the way! Soon!" I lie and smile at her as she hops onto her bike and starts it up.

"You better!" She flips her visor down and speeds off.

I watch her bike disappear out of sight, and my world instantly turns grey again. Bland and meaningless. I wish this disease would kill me or leave me the fuck alone.

5

LEO ABERNATHY

Paradise

Gravel crunches under our boots as we cut through the darkness toward Paradise. My stomach twists as I inhale metallic, disorienting heaves of recycled oxygen. I *loathe* recycled oxygen.

My suit's air-pump cycles in a steady rhythm, contracting then releasing. I've heard that maddening mechanical hissing so many times, it's been seared into my mind. The beat follows me into my nightmares.

Few things make me feel less human than the taste of repurposed air. Russa is certainly one... Paradise is another.

We reach the outer limit of the quarantine zone and push open the rusted barricade.

It moans a haunting melody that reminds me of the sorrowful chorus played at Emoss's funeral. Each harsh note of Dykamo's world-renowned quartet, scratching against our hearts.

I'd expect nothing less from a place that's witnessed such atrocities.

Time seems to crawl as we creep through the outer zone. My mind continually drifting back to the lab and the last images of that failed experiment. It was right there. My entire life's purpose, just at the edge of my grasp. Some would've crumbled under disappointment so catamount. But my father endured sixty years of failure to bring us life. The least I can do is show a fraction of that perseverance through my adversity.

We move in a diamond formation, Patawa and Spri trail me on either side, and Bryl itches for action in the rear.

The world is a shaken snow globe, the glass on the outside smudged with oil. Crystalline flakes spew from swollen grey masses hanging in the sky that stare down on us with venomous wrath. I *wish* they were clouds. I'd much prefer the torrential storms of the Opora Sea to this. This is something far more... abhorrent.

Light desperately tries to squeeze its way between the looming formations in the sky, but they're too dense. The dimness sneers at us.

Flakes land on Patawa's visor, and the vents on the top of her helmet activate and blow them off before they coagulate. She sticks out her hand, catching a few, bringing them closer to her face.

"Leo... what is this?" She asks over her comms, her tone not confident she wants the answer.

I don't turn around.

Words aren't meant for all moments. Some things must be seen. Or better yet, never seen at all.

Are they prepared for what lays beyond the outer ring?... I know I wasn't.

Past the mutilated military rigs and temporary barracks of the outer ring, we can vaguely make out the entrance to the town.

"Sharpen up. We're here," I say. Our formation tightens.

"*Boss...*" Bryl calls out as he kneels down and wipes the grey ash from a metal plate on the ground. Scarred and scorched, but still legible, the sign reads:

Welcome to Earth Beyond:
Valenia's own slice of Paradise

Bryl pulls an extra ordinance clip from his belt and reluctantly jams it into the alt chamber of his cannon. He switches his headlamps off for a moment so I can see his face. All I can muster is a solemn nod, and the brute shudders. He looks to the sky at the heinous formations that cry out the ash and soot, and his jaw clenches as he understands what they are.

"Lamps off..." I say. "Tactical only, Russa's orders." My crew prime their silent rounds and reconfigure the diamond formation. "Move together. Move slow. Maintain your line." I take a moment to look them all in the eyes. "Let's get in, find the salvage, and get the hell out of here."

I debate whether to warn them or not.

I don't.

It's not that I don't want to, it's that I don't know how...

My fist taps twice on Spri's shoulder, signaling I'm ready.

"Prime," I say.

Spri taps Bryl, who then taps Patawa, and once I feel her fist against my shoulder, we move.

Military-grade synthetic webbing wraps the town. A ten-foot-high womb of interlocking yellow fibers, harboring the catastrophic spawn of the High Council's failed experiment and the unspeakable action they took to resolve it.

Nothing in, nothing out.

If only that were true.

Gashes line the webbing in both directions as far as I can see until the webbing bends around the town and disappears. My throat tightens. Before we step through a tear in the webbing, I glance again at the readings on my rifle. Armed.

Heavy inhale through my nose, ignoring the recycled air, I wedge the rifle into my shoulder and step through the slit.

Paradise's remains are nothing more than a sea of petrified dwellings that line, what I know, are cratered streets. Though, you'd never be able to tell.

The white picket fences, green artificial lawns, quaint replica suburban homes, and manicured street tops are nonexistent. Replaced by an inches-thick sheath of greyish purple ash and soot. Structures that still stand are horribly warped and bend as if desperate to flee from the town center's massive crater. Flickering light dances off the façade of a building to our left as an inextinguishable chemical fire glows, neither growing larger nor dying off. Just burning. Coughing thick plumes into the sky.

Fires like this freckle the obliterated town. Snickering.

Patawa clicks her headlamps on, the beams rigid on a bundled heap just a few lengths ahead. I try to grab her shoulder before she strays too far, but she's beyond my reach.

"Pat..."

Her breathing quivers over the comms as she kneels down, dropping her weapon, ash dusting up in all directions.

A horrified sob sucks into her chest.

Melted into the steel beams of a scenic view tower are the bones of a Reyllion mother and child. Their skeletons, scorched black, their skin, incinerated so quickly their frames remain behind intact. Melded into the mangled structure that slopes away like all the others do.

The mother's spine curls around the child as if her last moments were spent trying to shield her loved one from the unthinkable devastation heading their way.

Patawa gently reaches out and touches her glove to the mother's arm. It dislodges, spilling to the ground and dissolving, instantly becoming indistinguishable from the grey storm of flakes that swirls all around us. She yanks her hand away, mortified as she turns to the sky, the realization unbearable.

"Leo..." The word barely escapes her lips, her eyes incapable of moving. That abominable awe sparks tremors through my soul as I remember seeing this for the first time myself.

This place meant so much to me as a child. To the natural Valenians, Earth Beyond was an attraction. A theme park. A glimpse into the world lightyears away from here where my alien ancestors originated. But to me, this place was a sanctuary. I don't know if this is what Earth truly looked like, but I didn't care. Here I could imagine. Imagine a life far different than this. Here, I could play in the yard with parents who'd exist, maybe even a brother or sister. We'd have a pet. Everything I've read said many humans did. I think I would've liked a golden retriever.

Life would be as it was meant for me. Earth and humanity and all the typical experiences every other generation was fortunate enough to experience.

Not this.

I scan the destroyed remnants of my cherished memories and fight away the creeping hopelessness that lurks in the shadows of my mind. This place was only a museum, but it might as well represent all that remains of humanity. Destroyed beyond recognition. We last eight humans will remain, just as this place does, but only until the last of the fires burn our ashes into the cosmos, and then we'll just be a memory. That is unless I can solve the DNA formula...

I rest my helmet on hers, wrapping my arm around her,

but flicking off her headlamps. She needs a moment to process, and I'll give her that, but we also have a job to do.

The imprints of our footsteps only last minutes before the steady rain of debris fills them in again, and any trace of our presence vanishes with them.

"Anything Spri?" I ask as we pace with caution, pushing deeper into the town. Spri examines his dataplate, reading the different wavelengths being emitted from nearby sources.

"Heavy interference from the debris field. Readings unreliable." He tampers with settings along the dataplate's face and reanalyzes. "Seems to be a surge northeast of here, but that is just an approximation. Level of certainty is below my standard for formal recommendation."

Spri, always hedging his bets.

We push northeast, ignoring the viscid disgust that attempts to root our feet to the ground every time we pass a melted corpse. I hate that life was thrown away so callously, but I hate that we simply ignore it even more. If my father's journal has taught me anything, it's that life is precious. How easily it can be stripped away at any moment, and all that you are ceases to exist. Your fears, your hopes, your dreams... meaningless as a pile of ash.

I raise my hand, signaling my crew to halt.

"Do you hear that?"

At the far end of the museum town, atop the highest hill, a stone building sat for thousands of years. Polished and grand, peering down on the entire obedient realm. It was a beacon of hope and order. A paragon of virtue. Now, all that remains of the High Council's Consulate is a meager scattering of crumbled walls, deep cratered holes, and the rubble of the statue, *Trakstull the Righteous Regal.*

Just beyond the crest of that hill, within the depths of the crated lot, drones a chanting, low and steady.

I gesture without a word, and we fan out, ascending the hill, armed and ready.

The half-demolished archway of the main entrance lies in shambles, frowning at me as I pass under it. My crew disappears around the corners of the building, and I'm alone inside the Consulate.

The chanting builds.

With my rifle scanning the dark corridors for threats, I step over the head of the fallen statue of Trakstull, his stone face scorched black like all the rest. A stew of anger brews in my stomach as I pass him. Paradise was the closest to a home I ever had... and he destroyed it. Self-serving leech.

A dune of ash builds against the stone leader.

For a moment, I consider swiping the soot over his face, but I leave it. I want him to watch this place erode. He doesn't get to forget the horrors he committed here.

The deeper into the broken Consulate I push, the louder the chanting becomes. Words drip from the walls, racing down the labyrinth of corridors and scrambling their origin. I follow an echo; it lies.

Another hall ends abruptly, a hole punching into the imposing grey sky like some gargantuan monster bit a hole through the stone.

Bryl's voice clicks on over the comms in a whisper.

"Boss... package located. You need to see this."

My path west is blocked on the first story. I backtrack and scale the body of the statue, vaulting to a second-level terrace. Here, the chanting isn't warped. The word "Jah" rings true, over and over. Getting louder as I approach until the chanting suddenly stops.

My boots against the stone seem loud as rig engines in the heavy silence.

A voice begins to fill the void.

I move through the second level until the Consulate ceases to exist, and all that remains is a crater. The stone floors and walls and roofs all chewed off around it, I peer down into the crater as if I'm watching a play from the mezzanine decks of the prestigious theater halls in the *Ivolo* province.

"What the..." My voice trails off.

Surrounding the crater on the Consulate's second deck stands dozens of zealots, no suit or protection guarding them against the chemical residue that hangs over the town. Instead, they wear nothing. Stark naked, their bodies acid-stained, their faces mangled from surgical alterations in an attempt to appear human. They don't...

Each one has the divine star of the *Proselytes* branded on their neck, chest, and back. Holding ropes with nooses tied around their throats as one among them begins to preach with a fiery passion. By his side, another nude cultist grovels. Yet, he roams free. Scurrying about the group, ensuring the ropes they hold are secured to their anchors.

In the center of the crater sits a reflective satellite panel of the *Redemption*. Our mission.

I crouch behind the remains of a railing as the leader continues his sermon.

"... and we can be one with the Starborn. The Chosen. The miracles, sent from the sky to serve as our masters in the grail beyond. The world thinks them beings of flesh and bone, like us..."

The Proselytes laugh.

"... yet we know. We know the Jah consist of a purity unlike that which our mortal minds can comprehend. The shells of skin and hair they wear, just another of their flawless gestures to us."

Many of the cult members begin to weep in gratitude.

"They fell from the sky in a ball of fire, scattering their remains across the planet so that *you* could Witness their glory in every corner of this world... Witness the flesh."

The Proselytes all touch the brands along their neck and answer in unison.

"Witness the flesh."

"And what did the world say, when the heavenly transport opened, and nothing waited inside?"

The Proselytes murmur amongst themselves, growing uneasy.

The leader calms them with a gentle raise of his arm.

"They said 'this vessel was once filled with life.' Well, where was it? Life does not disappear. Bone and scales and hair and skin are steadfast. They withstand. Yet, nothing..." The leader lets his pause baste his worshipers.

"For decades... nothing. Yet, *you* believed. *You* knew *life* was not aboard that colossus of screaming metal, 'twas something divine. And despite their inability to explain the absence of life, you were shunned. Ostracized. Mocked.

"And yet you remained loyal. Dedicated to our creators. Confident in their holiness until the day they revealed themselves to the world. The day your loyalty was rewarded."

I peer past a pillar to my left and watch the emotions overwhelm a young female cultist. Tears stream down her face as she relives the day we were born. Such gratitude in her eyes.

"Tell me, what life can spawn from nothing? Do you know of beings that can materialize without interaction? No... because they do not exist."

I dart back behind the railing; did he just look at me?

The leader's tone shifts. He no longer preaches, he states. The words quiet, so his disciples must listen.

"Eight Gods revealed themselves that day. We are the only ones who know this..."

I peek over the railing once more, and the leader's eyes are fixated in my direction. But if he does see me, he doesn't bother reacting.

"And now has come the time to join our Gods in the realm of their origin. We have recovered a piece of their divine creation, and with it, you will leave this shallow world and rejoice in their perfect dimension... Are you ready?"

The leader smiles, holding his arms out to usher his faithful crew to their ill-advised deaths.

"Witness the flesh!"

Wild fervor fills the eyes of the cult. They hang on every word. What sick creatures they are... though there's something admirable about having such devotions. How many can lay claim to such passion? It's misguided, but a life lived with misguided zeal is far better than one of utter apathy.

Through the darkness, I can make out the edges of Bryl's suit on the ground level as he positions himself across the crater. Patawa and Spri must be somewhere above or below because I can't find them in the traffic.

"What's the play, boss?" Bryl whispers.

"Hold."

I scan the faces of the warped minds that stare at the satellite panel like a portal to the afterlife. These are poisoned minds. Did this man poison them? Or did the proof of alien life break their sanity? It's so hard to accept the role I played in shattering the world these people have known. But how do you reason with such fanaticism?

"Leo, we have to do something?" Patawa says, making a tiny gesture from the roof across the crater. "We can't just let them die?"

I roll onto my stomach, wedging my rifle into my shoulder and focusing the scope on the leader's forehead. If I kill him, would they stop? Is killing him better than letting the other's die? Maybe this man was poisoned by another?

My mind speeds up as their mass suicide grows ever more imminent.

I consider revealing myself to them. If they worship me as they claim, would they listen if I told them to stop? Or would my presence prove, in their twisted minds, that this satellite panel actually *is* a portal that made me appear and push them over the edge?

"Spri, what's my exposure if I pop my top?"

He mumbles to himself as he formulates my calculations.

"Boss, you're not going out there with no helmet on. End of

story," Bryl says. "Let me slug this nut case, and we can talk them down."

"No, hold!" Sweat begins to bead down my spine as the moment builds. "Spri, numbers!"

"Exposure increases with elevation, yet the crater is still too high. Risk is above recommendation. Under two minutes is..."

Before I can decide, the leader touches his brand along his neck and shouts with all his might.

"I WILL SEE YOU IN THE BEYOND. WITNESS THE FLESH!"

The last words that rattle from the Proselyte's lips are 'witness the flesh' and the dozens of cultists launch themselves from the balconies and slam to a stop as the ropes around their neck snag.

Those whose neck's break are the fortunate ones; they already dangle like windchimes made of altered flesh. The others struggle. They kick and squirm and claw at their necks. Instincts overriding their zealotry. They don't want to die. No matter how much they convinced themselves otherwise, life refuses to give itself away.

We skid down the face of the crater, meeting at the satellite panel.

"Spri and Pat, you two secure the package, anyone else approaches, you're green for all conflict. Bryl, you're with me, hurry!"

We hustle up the arch of the crater as one last Proselyte struggles for his life, the chemically-stained skin around his neck bruised and dark. All the rest hang limp, swaying back and forth.

"Hoist his legs up."

Bryl grabs the man's lower half and steps up onto some rubble as I climb the side of a crumbled wall to shear the rope with the knife from my leg. The tension snaps, and the full weight of the man comes crashing down onto Bryl.

I hurry to remove the noose from his neck and check his breathing.

"He's alive."

His eyes slit open just enough to see, a word barely escaping his damaged throat as he sees me.

"...Jah?..."

The man faints, and Bryl collapses to the ground with him.

I pat Bryl on the shoulder, and he nods with tired eyes.

"Pat, we got one alive over here. Bryl will take him back to the rig, you two get that panel latched up and get him out of here ASAP."

I scan the horrible scene as bodies droop, greyish purple ash already beginning to build along their shoulders and head.

"Are you not coming?" Patawa asks.

I meet the eyes of the young girl I watched during the speech, and they strain, frozen in death. What could her life have been if just the wheels of fate had turned ever so slightly different?

"No. Leave me the rover. I'm going to stay and cut them all down." She glances to the dozens of bodies and back to me, a muted expression on her face.

"There was nothing we could do, Leo..."

I give her a half-hearted smile.

"I know. Now go, get this man some help."

My crew nods and hustles off, leaving me sitting upon the broken stones of a graveyard inside a graveyard.

My back aches from carrying bodies to the crater and yet, a dozen or so still hang. Their faces petrified in agony. It's a disturbing sight.

I couldn't reach the ropes on the south of the crater, so I scaled the levels to the third story and had to cut the ropes from their anchors. Every heavy thud of a lifeless corpse hitting the ground makes my heart twist. I try to treat them with as much respect as I can, but there's only so much I can do. Some may find glory in their death, but few things are more indignant than the disposal of death.

The last few bodies don't hang over the crater, but the Consulate's interior, just a handful of meters away. They dangle over what was the Throne Room, where Trakstull would conduct his business. His Regal throne sitting perched on a slightly elevated platform, with ramps leading up to it on either side of a seemingly bottomless pit. How many who opposed Trakstull lay mangled at the bottom of that pit? Times may have changed, and the savagery gone, but people don't.

From the elevation of the top story of the Consulate, I gaze out over the bombarded wasteland that remains of Paradise, and it's all too obvious that the evil hasn't evolved, just the methods.

I peer over the edge and try to find a solution. If I cut these three down, they will plummet into the pit. But I can't pull them up by the rope either; they're too heavy. I go over the possibilities in my head when the crunch of rubble startles me from behind.

I whip my head around. The beams of my headlamps slicing through the darkness, but nothing is there. I shoot a nervous glance to my rifle on the bottom story and pull the knife from my leg.

Again, the echoes play tricks on my mind. Footsteps bounce off sharp angles and clatter all around me. I don't blink. Eyes darting from hall to hall, but nothing comes.

Then, there's nothing but stillness.

I take a step back, but my heel breaks debris from the chewed floor, and I dart forward, my eyes shifting to the ground.

When I look back up, a metal pipe speeds its way toward my face, and my visor shatters.

Glass erupts and sends shards digging into my skin. Pain sears my temple.

I stumble back and catch the slightest glimpse of the psychotic minion that hunched by the leader's side, sprinting at me, a noose tied around his neck.

I swipe clumsily at the charging man with my knife but miss and feel his shoulder plow into my chest as we're launched off the ledge. My knife is knocked from my hand and plummets into the darkness of the pit. I fall, weightless, until the very air from my windpipe gags from a noose, and I snap to a stop.

The world instantly begins to blur.

The vessels in my head want nothing more than to explode as blood pools at the chokehold.

I can't tell if it's me who is gargling for his life or the lunatic who swings helplessly beside me, but a manic smile breaks across his face.

Our eyes meet.

He enjoys watching the life seep from mine.

A blood vessel breaks, and black liquid floods his mouth. Snaking into the corners of his rotten smile.

"Take me to the beyond..." He gargles.

I already feel the chemical burn singing the top layer of my skin.

I claw at the rope, but the more I squirm, the tighter it gets.

I plead for air. My mind spasming. This can't be it. This

67

can't be it!

A piece of shattered glass on my visor pricks at the fibers of the rope. One by one, they fray. I grab ahold of it and saw the twine against the shard. Desperate. The minion lets out a suffocating laugh and wheezes "Witness the Flesh" as his body quits, and he goes limp. And just as the world closes in around me, the rope explodes, and I plummet into the darkness below.

6

RILEY HOLT

Three For One

The Forest is still. Quiet. Bugs chirp their low pitch songs. Branches and twigs crack under our feet as we slowly creep along. A narrow path in the grass is worn from beastly paws and hooves. We follow it. The brush is thick around us, but low, only hip-high. The trees stretch skyward and fold over one another. Their bark a soft purple shade and rock hard. Rays of sunlight scatter through the tight cracks in the canopy and spot the Forest floor like paint splattered onto a canvas. Our eyes don't blink; they search. Remmy treads to my right, a few paces behind. Always cautious. He steps into a ray of sunlight, and the blue myrite paste we dye our hair with shimmers and gleans. The light is so bright contrasting with the sun blocked Forest, it's nearly impossible to see him when he steps out of it.

I've always tended to move with more urgency than he does. He's too calculated for my tastes. Sometimes you aren't going to know what's around the corner, but what's life without a little surprise?

Bug guts make a slimy paste against my hand as I smack the insect trying to make a snack of my neck. I wish the myrite paste worked to keep them off our skin like it does our hair, but unfortunately, it doesn't.

I smack another bug along my leg, and I wipe the mixture of guts and sweat on my shirt.

It's so damn hot...

Remmy continues to lag behind as usual. I don't know if fear is the right emotion to describe it, but something inside pulls at him. Keeps him cautious to a fault. He wants us to "farm". As if that's a realistic way of life for us. I tell him farming requires land. Land needs to be tended. To tend land, you need time, consistency, and stability. I glance back to him as he fusses with a vine that's snagged a strap of our pack and laugh at the proposition. Our entire lives are in that pack, and he wants to play house. We are nomads; we have none of these. Sometimes, I think he forgets why we left Okotall in the first place. That awful house with those dreadful people. Not one person in the entire province would take us in. Not one. Left us to rot in Archler House with those maniacs after Emoss died. Valenians will never accept us. Never. Gwinn is a fool for staying. They're all fools for trusting the people of this planet. Creatures are threatened by what they don't understand, so as long as we're alive, they'll always view us as a threat.

The moment we plot out a chunk of land, grow some Tullie or Red Root, get a herd of livestock, and play happy farmer family, is the moment we stop moving. The moment we stop moving, the world knows where to find us. And the moment the world knows where to find us, they will. I'll take my chances in the woods with a spear and my brother.

Remmy clicks his tongue, signaling me to stop. He points his fingers to his eyes then down at the grass next to him. Another track pressed into the soft edge of the brush. Deeper this time. Fresh. It's a good find; I don't know how I missed it.

He shoots me a little victorious smirk. Always relishing my rare moments of error. I roll my eyes and poke the blunt end of my spear at him. He bats it away and grins.

I nod my head forward and mouth, "They're *close.*"

We follow the tracks so deep into the woods, I no longer recognize the landscape. It's a corner of *Berban* so remote, Sentinel teams don't even bother patrolling it. Or maybe they're scared to. Either way, it's one threat we don't have to worry about.

The farther we go, the less distinct the trail becomes. The thin thicketed trees of before are replaced with scattered behemoths of trunks. Their vast girth stretching so high into the sky the canopy seems in the clouds. And the cluttered Forest floor opens into pure wilderness. Untouched by intelligent life. A place where beasts rule.

We have to be sure of what we're doing. We only have one chance at this. I don't remember the last time we caught a trail of a Tyko. Just one of their horns would trade for a months' worth of the usual scores.

The soft trail ends and with it our tracks. But I know we're close. I push forward quicker; I don't want to lose it.

"Easy, Ri..." Remmy whispers the warning. Even his hushed voice startles me. My mind so consumed with tracking this beauty. He can tell I'm getting antsy. He thinks I want this too much. I think he's crazy for not wanting it more!

Bits of his boring lecture from earlier rattles around in my brain. "... we'll be fine without it... deaf ears... visions of grandeur... not grounded in reality... you're bored... rather be bored than dead..." I love him to death, but I need more adventure in my life than picking berries and selling myrite dust to envoys.

We continue to weave through the Forest, investigating every rustle we hear. The frayed strap of the huge backpack Remmy lugs is digging into his shoulders. It's tattered and patchy.

"We need a new one." He whispers to me. No shit, why do you think we're chasing this thing.

"We get these horns... you can buy whatever you want."

Remmy quickens his pace, striding shoulder to shoulder with me.

"Yea, don't need it *that* bad."

A powerful snarl roots our feet to the ground, sending a jolt down my spine. We snap our weapons to attention and hurry toward the ridge ahead that obscures our view.

"That's it!" I whisper. We crouch, peering over the edge to spectate a pocket of grass that cuts a hole in the Forest, a rough line of trees encircling the field. Without any canopy above, the circle bursts with light. It almost looks like a stage with the audience around it hidden in darkness. Facing off at center stage are two majestic creatures. Beasts unknown to the rest of the world, confined to the unexplored pockets of this alienated province. One predator, one prey.

The Tyko's gorgeous chocolate coat whips in the wind that tunnels its way into the grassy bowl. His fangs arch out over his bottom lip, strong and powerful. His body is lean. Quick, strong, stealthy. A machine of death. On top, the prize. His spine is lined with nubby, dull, ivory horns. The Tyko's best line of defense.

"He's perfect, Remmy. It's not an alpha. Too thin, his tail is too short. This is our shot."

"What about the Luta? He's fully grown."

"Don't worry about him."

Apparently, that's not an acceptable answer.

"Riley he's massive... He could trample us. We have nothing to pierce his hide, and we can't take our eye off the Tyko." He looks at me, waiting to hear how I plan on handling both these creatures when we're barely prepared for one.

"Well, we can't just sit here. They could run off, the alpha could show up, anything could happen. We have tracked this thing for weeks. I'm not letting it get away." I vault over the ridge and slide down the other side, mud and dirt spilling down with me.

"Riley!" He tries to grab me, but I won't let him ruin this opportunity. "Shit." He grumbles and follows me down the slope face. We skid to a stop behind a fallen tree trunk that's so big it looks like the shin bone of a God.

The beasts remained locked in their stalemate, just a rocks-throw in front of us. Predator and prey readying themselves for battle. They slowly circle one another, tempting each other to make the first move.

"What's the plan?" He asks, sounding half sincere, half skeptical.

I inspect our surroundings. My mind working quick. Formulating plans, playing them out, and picking the best scenario.

"We split up. We have to contain them in this clearing. Push them closer together. How many rounds do you have?"

His rifle is an antiquated piece of junk by current standards. A relic. Literally. A weapon of Earth. Scavenged from a piece of the Redemption wreckage with a huge depot of ammunition. We... acquired it... from a traveling caravan that had been overtaken, by someone or something. When we came across it, its cargo was scattered about, but not much was taken. The merchant was dead well before we stumbled across it. Only seemed right that we put the cargo to good use.

It may be a relic, but it's reliable and steady. And when he shoots, he doesn't miss.

"I've got plenty, don't you worry." He pats his belt, which is lined with bullets fatter Red Root stalks.

He's a conservative shot. Fiercely accurate, and he doesn't waste rounds. Our ammo is finite. I'm not sure what the plan is when we run out, but thankfully that won't be for a while. Who knows, maybe if this works and we survive, I can barter my way into a more suitable weapon for him?

"Ok well, get that trigger finger loose; I'm gonna need you."

"When do you not?" He winks at me and sticks his tongue out.

"Please... it's really hard standing back and shooting stuff when I'm running around getting mauled and swatted at." I love him, but he wouldn't last a day out here without me.

"Here's the plan. We're gonna take the flare packs from the bag and plant them along the edge of this clearing. You go left, and I'll go right, three on each side. See that rock formation on the other side? Plant your flares and meet me there. Be quiet though, we don't want to startle them until we're in position. Hopefully, they'll start fighting, and they won't notice us. Ready?"

He knows he's got no say in the matter, but he nods in agreement anyway.

We take off in opposite directions.

I plant the first flare and glance across the field. Remmy plants his and keeps moving. I should've grabbed something from him before we left. He moves clumsily carrying so much. I can't help but laugh, watching him fumble with all our stuff.

He plants his second flare and continues on. The stupid backpack keeps slipping off his shoulder. His rifle is strung across his chest and bounces uncontrollably as he runs. He moves to plant the third flare, and the stock of his gun jams into his groin. I snort. He buckles and lets out a muted welp, as he sees me snickering from the safety of the rock. He freezes, worried he's alerted the beasts, but they circle each other slowly, their attention solely on one another.

"This plan sucks so far," He says as he reaches the rock. "Ugh... that made my stomach hurt."

As Remmy tends to his issues, I glance back out over the clearing. The Tyko and the Luta still haven't engaged. The Tyko toys with the passive beast. Pawing at him and growling. He knows the Luta is dangerous. It's nearly three times his size. Two tons of sturdy bone, muscle, and scaly overlapping hide. One kick could break the Tyko's jaw clean. The devastating power of its short and stocky hind legs.

The Luta's forelegs, though, are long and hooved. Built for speed and quickness. He sits back, perched up at an angle from the difference in length. A wide tail curls its way into a ball on the ground under him. The back of his neck has four fin-like appendages that fan out behind him and pulse in and out as he breathes. His skull bones protrude and create a type of shield encasing his facial features from predators. He's not an aggressive creature, but he's trapped and poses a huge threat when cornered.

"Now what?" He asks as his tender parts have apparently survived.

"We're gonna use the Sonostick." I don't look at him when I tell him. I know he's not going to like that idea.

I can feel him staring blankly at me. "You can't be serious. How exactly do you plan on using it?"

"I'm going to stick it in the ground and detonate it. It's going to let out a massive sound wave incapacitating everything with ears. Exactly how it's supposed to be used." I keep looking straight ahead. He may need me, but he's not an idiot.

"It's SUPPOSED to be remote denoted. As in, don't be anywhere near it when it goes off. Manually detonating could kill you!" He scoffs. "My God Riley, you wouldn't last one day out here without me." He concedes when I don't offer another solution. "Well, how exactly do you plan on killing this thing when you're unconscious?"

"I won't be unconscious." I reach down and scoop a massive heap of mud from the ground and push it deep into my ears. Too deep. This can't be good for me. But it works, I can't hear much. "I wouldn't have to do this if you didn't lose the remote." I cram more mud into my ears and pull the Sonostick from the pack on Remmy's shoulder.

He tries to wipe the mud from my ears, but I swat his hand away.

"Riley stop. I'm serious. That isn't going to work. Was this your plan the entire time?" I ignore him and go to hurdle over the rock, but this time he snags my arm. "Riley!"

"Sorry can't hear you. You know what to do!" I smack his arm away and jump down from the rock, and sprint full speed ahead.

"What the hell?!"

My eyes bounce as I watch him scramble into position, laying down, readying his rifle, making sure his sights are zeroed in. I do a quick glance at each flare, so I remember where they are. They're harder to see in the grass than I'd like. Hopefully, he can see them better than I can.

I'm full stride like a maniac. Sonostick in one hand, spear

in the other.

I let out a loud whistle and signal Remmy. At my signal, he fires a round at the Luta. It doesn't hurt him, but it startles both the beasts, and they lunge at one another. The creatures growl and snarl as saliva and dirt are slung through the air. The Tyko bites into a leg of the Luta, clamping down hard. The passive beast screeches in pain, convulsing until the Tyko is thrown off. The Luta panics and tries to flee.

He barrels to my right and nearly stomps on me, but I roll out of the way, just in time. Remmy swivels his rifle, taking aim at the middle right flare. *Wait... Just a little closer.*

The Tyko roars, aggravated. Its explosive legs catapulting him to full speed in the blink of an eye as he pursues his prey across the field. From my knees, I signal Remmy to fire, and the rifle rocks against his shoulder. The flare pack explodes, sending a bright red flare streaking into the sky. Red smoke blooms from the flare and the Luta lets out a shriek and turns back.

The Tyko charges. He dives and turns, slamming his horns into the Luta as it recoiled from the flare. The Luta topples over, and the Tyko's momentum sends him rolling past.

While the two are on the ground, I scramble to my feet and make a mad dash for the center of the field, ready to dig my hole. The Sonostick needs to be sturdy in the ground when detonated.

The Luta struggles to stand, one leg clearly injured. It begins backpedaling away from the Tyko.

My finger-tips begin to bleed as I claw at the rough top layer of the ground like a mad man. I rip chunks of grass from the soil until the cool sensation of mud begins to soothe my aching digits.

I freeze for a moment when I hear the next gunshot. It sounds like a small pop my ears are so clogged. A jolt of anxiety rattles through me. I could still hear it, though. I glance up and see the fireball scream toward the sky. The smoke follows and scares the Luta back toward the center. I keep my eyes on the beast as I continue to burrow.

The Luta streaks across the far end of the clearing.

Remmy loads another bolt and fires at the far-left flare. Another explosion and plumes of dense red smoke. The Luta skids to a halt again. The Tyko pursues just behind, leaping onto the hindquarters of the Luta. Its talons and fangs dig deep into his tough hide.

Blood begins to drool from the back of the Luta. He

squirms and shakes, but the Tyko won't let go this time. The two are tied together, wrestling through the grass. They stumble and groan toward the edge once again. Remmy fires at the middle left flare and pushes them back toward the center as my hole continues to cave in on itself.

The wind that tunnels and swirls in the bowl doesn't let the smoke escape to the top. A veil of red smoke begins to swallow the clearing. I have to dig with one hand while I cover my mouth with my shirt. My coughs are violent and hard, and the smoke is agony to my eyes. Almost there.

The Tyko slips off and as the Luta is bucking and twitching, kicks him with its hind legs. The predator is thrown across the clearing, skidding to a stop just in front of me. The smoke continues to build.

The Tyko shakes off the kick. But for the first time, his eyes meet mine. He roars and lunges for me.

"O SHIT!" I roll out of the way once again and spin to my feet. Smacking the Tyko in the face with the blunt end of my spear.

His eyes stare through me.

Murderous and primal.

But the beast is beautiful. The most beautiful creature I've ever laid eyes on. I almost feel guilty wanting to kill it. Then he parts his jaws, and as the eager saliva drips from the points of his deadly fangs, any guilt that ever existed in me zaps away by a mortal fear I've never known before.

The smoke continues to drift, and I almost lose sight of Remmy in it. I glance back over, and the Luta is trying to escape. The remaining flare packs erupt as Remmy improvises, small explosions bursting around the circle. Smoke bellows out and makes visibility go from difficult to almost nonexistent. I take my bandana from my hair and wrap it around my face. The last I see of Remmy before the smoke consumes me is his shadow vaulting from the rock, his hatchet in hand.

The smoke is so thick now, it's hard to work my spear. My eyes flood, and coughs overtake my lungs. The Tyko seems bothered as well. He paws at his eyes and shakes his head. The smoke sticks to his coat, turning him red. He looks like a creature pulled straight from hell. The Luta blindly stumbles by and nearly tramples us both.

The smoke fills my lungs, and I drop to a knee. I can't breathe. The Tyko sees me defenseless and pounces. He knocks me over and pins me to the ground, my spear wedged

76

in his mouth. Every cough makes me weaker, and the Tyko's fangs inch closer and closer. I can feel the spear bending under his powerful jaws.

"REMMY!!!" I scream. Terror fills my body as I can feel the whiskers of the beast. Feel the heat of his breath.

"RILEY!! I'm coming!" I think I hear him shout.

"REMMY!!!!" I cry out again. Tears fill my eyes as I see the end happening. This was so stupid. Remmy was right. We didn't need this. I don't need this. All I need is him; our life was fine without. How could I have been so ungrateful? The talons dig into my arm, and blood rushes from it. I scream.

For a moment, the world stands still. I feel the tension of the spear give, and it snaps in half. Nothing stands between me and the carnal beast. My last seconds play out in slow motion.

The Tyko snaps his jaw wide and tilts his head. His fangs brush against my hair as he prepares to bite down and erase me from the world. I close my eyes and think of better times. Times when Remmy and Gwinn and Emoss and I were still a family. Times when Leo looked at me like I was the only person in existence. Times when the eight of us would meet at the beaches of the Litopi and dive into the cresting waves, being thrown about by Victor as we tried to wrestle him to the ground.

Those were simpler years when people loved us. And we loved people. Memories from when Emoss was still alive. And we still had a home. Before the moment came where we fled Archler House, and Remmy was all I had left in this world.

I think of it all.

I feel a catastrophic pain in my head, and I assume it's the sensation of death. Of life leaving my body and my skull being crushed by the devastating bite of a Tyko. But I open my eyes. And the sun is so bright I have to squint. I'm looking right into it.

The smoke is gone, and the Tyko lays draped over me.

I strain to push the beast off and roll out from under it. My head pounds, pure misery. Maybe it did kill me? I fight to my feet and look around. The red smoke whispers its way through the Forest in all directions, but the bowl is completely clear. The Tyko and the Luta are strewn on their sides, unconscious, blood still trickling from the Luta's wounds. What happened?

I study the field until dread sharper than any Tyko bite claws at my chest.

Remmy!....... I turn and see Remmy's body lying sprawled out in the center of the clearing.

He detonated the Sonostick.

7

GWINN DEMARCO

The Fraud's Burden

"Three more, let's go. Push it. Push it." My muscles burn, and sweat pours from my forehead as my trainer barks orders at me. "Keep going. All the way down, you got this!" My body wants to quit, but I refuse to let it. My arms are nearly numb. It takes all the force I have just to push myself up inch by inch. I get to the top and collect my breath as I hold myself straight. My body quivers in exhaustion. I gather my breath, grind my teeth, and start down for one last push up. Down and up. Everything I've got. I reach the top again, and my body collapses to the ground. I roll over onto my back, gasping for air. My lungs can't expand fast enough.

"Great job, DeMo!" My Brushu trainer reaches his hand out and helps hoist me up. There's a starfish of sweat imprinted on the ground where I laid. "Hell yeah, you killed it today." He tosses me a towel as I bump his knuckles and head into the cleansing room.

I pull a lever, and a river of water pours from a hole in the wall. Running my hand under the water, I back out as I let it heat and peel out of my sweat-drenched clothes. My reflection on the steam clouded glass glares back at me.

So much has changed over the years. I barely recognize myself sometimes. My muscles are firm and defined, and my body has lines that carve out every angle. My face has matured and has an aggressiveness to it most are intimidated by. My body is full and complete, the awkward, clumsy form of my childhood long behind me. Any innocence of youth I once had is gone. A woman stares back at me, not a girl.

The days of timid, weak Gwinn are gone too. The woman who looks back at me is hardened. Mentally, physically, emotionally. I will never be that scared girl who got Emoss killed again. I'll never again be the girl who loved so wholly, she broke when he was gone. My walls are thick and high, and no one is ever allowed back in.

I open the door to the gym, and steam coughs out from behind me. I step out and walk toward my trainer. He double-takes, then looks away, embarrassed as he sees my bare body.

"O... Sorry... I..." He stays turned away from me, trying to respect my privacy. Apparently, he doesn't understand. I say nothing. I grab him by the hand, turn around and pull him into the cleansing room.

"DeMo.. What are you..."

"Shut up." I take his shirt off and pull him into the water.

The steam evaporates away and leaves behind two people drying themselves off in the silence of a damp cleansing room. I can feel him glancing at me. Unsure of how to proceed. I don't have time for his insecurity and bashfulness. I change into my work clothes and finish drying my hair. He must feel awkward because he can't handle the silence.

"Gwinn." He stops changing, and I give him a look through the mirror.

I don't respond. There's nothing to say. I'm changed and dry, then I finally speak.

"Can't work out tomorrow. I have more meetings, so the day after. Same time?" I don't bother looking at him; I'm trying to gather my stuff. I have everything and walk to the door. "Hey!... Same time?" I stand half out the door, looking at him. Emotionless.

He doesn't know what to say or how to react. He tries to speak a few different times, but can't find the words. He's still confused. He's uncomfortable, and I'm sure he's attaching meaning to it when there was none.

I give him another moment to answer.

"Uh.. Sure."

I was hoping he could make me feel something. He couldn't. Simple. I walk out the door and leave him in the shower room half-naked and used.

The world's eyes meet me as I step out into the bustling city. They pierce me like angry thorns, malicious, and spiteful. The people don't bother being subtle. They stare and gawk. I'm a sputtering neon sign in the dark, they can't look away.

Two stubby Reyllion men part me on either side as they walk by. One spits at my feet, the other nudges me and mumbles something in his backwater jargon. I stare back at them... *yea, that's right, keep movin'.* This place doesn't like me, and I don't like them. The Hated Human.

I have a meeting with the High Council tonight. My third in as many days. A serious of questions and tests determined to evaluate my legitimacy as a High Council member. Since Emoss passed, the Okotall province has been without proper representation. We've had temporary stand-ins and people unwilling to take on the daunting responsibility of running a province. I intend to fill his shoes. Continuing the legacy my father built.

The city buzzes. Motion swarms all around me. You become accustomed to the pace of life in Dwaul Fir, but coming from the serenity of Okotall, speed has been a learned skill.

But learn I have.

I glide through the crammed masses with ease. Perpetual noise rattling through the air as common as oxygen. It never stops.

My skin itches as the hairs along my arms stand at attention from the constant vibrations in the air. That, I'll never get used to.

The source of the vibrations are massive poles that act like oversized antennas. They spike up from the streets, just beyond the boundary of the traffic above, and are piled high with *Surgs.* The disgusting bug-like beings, nearly as old as Ancients, communicate with one another through these tremors. These "buzzer" poles are their only means of long-distance communication.

I grab a *Surg* by the back of its smock, yank it from the pole and toss it to the ground as I walk by. I don't bother looking back at it.

I scratch at my arms as it clearly is yelling something at me, but the only people who can understand *Surgs* are other disgusting *Surgs*. And that's perfectly fine by me; it seems like they never shut the hell up.

I step onto a slidewalk track heading west and have to brace myself so the momentum of the speeding floor doesn't sweep me to the ground.

A small Heplin child hops onto the howling track with ease and giggles at my difficulty. *Little shit.* Many things on the planet still aren't exactly user-friendly for humans.

These tracks snake through the city carrying bundles of people to every corner. Endless styles of rigs roar by in the air, their engine thrusters spitting out vapor trails behind them. The trails create a mist that hangs over the city indefinitely and weaves its way into every nook and cranny.

Some hate the haze... I, for one, love it.

The bright lights of the buildings glare in the mist and create a soft fuzz around them. But high above the fog and commotion, the glass towers glisten and shine in the moonlight, pristine and spotless.

I can't think of a better metaphor for how we live our lives. On the surface, we look clean and tidy, yet underneath, we're all nothing but ugliness and chaos.

My stomach sours from the smell of rig exhaust and Surg feeding troughs, but overall, I don't mind the frigid wind that pricks at my face as I ride the track. I enjoy numbness.

The endless buildings cease for a moment as the track carries us over a shallow river that cuts through the city. The opening allows us to see the shanties of the Valley flickering far northwest in the distance.

Next to me, the small Heplin child desperately strains to see over the handrail to watch the dilapidated town blur by. She glances at me for help. Apparently, she's not old enough to understand we don't get along. I glance at her briefly and turn away.

It's for the best.

She should want nothing to do with that place. She can take my word for it.

The child groans in frustration, endlessly whining until I reluctantly turn back around and pick her up to let her rest along the handrail.

"Thanks," She says and runs her hand along my neck. I recoil a bit. I don't know if it's a species disconnect, but I've always been uncomfortable with how Heplins express gratitude. The child doesn't notice and continues staring at the Valley.

"My mom said only bad people live in the Valley."

I can't help but smirk at a statement like that.

"It's complicated," I say.

"So, the Vipers don't live there?"

"No, they do. But other people live there too. For instance, my friend Fargo lives there sometimes," I say.

"So, he's a good person?"

I laugh.

"Not really. That was a bad example."

"So, it's only bad people then?"

"Like I said, it's complicated."

"Doesn't sound very complicated."

I like this kid. Got more backbone then half the twats I deal with on the High Council.

"You'll learn this when you're older, but we're all bad people. Some of us just don't try to pretend that we're not."

She doesn't know how to comprehend that. I suppose most people don't. But it is fun to watch her sort through a concept of that magnitude.

While I study the child, thoughts of Leo flood my mind. The smile that had creased my face just seconds ago vanishes immediately, and I drop the kid from the handrail back onto the track.

"Hey!" She contests, but I've already hurried away. A tear welts in the corner of my eye, but I shove it away and look for anything else to focus on.

Trakstull Tower is three blocks ahead. The center of the city. Lodged between dozens of other skyscrapers, it peaks just beyond all of them. The High Council awaits me on top. A dramatic, arrogant building.

A portrait of Emoss and Trakstull painted along the façade of a building speeds past as I settle into my new spot. That's plenty distracting. How I would give anything to see that man one more time. I squeeze the handrail as hard as I can when my eyes meet Trakstull's, though.

Exploitative bastard.

How Trakstull has maintained control during his reign is beyond me? The war with the Gaz, a ship from another world crashing on your planet, a ravaging disease, the introduction of an alien species...

His tenure as Regal of the High Council has been tumultuous, to say the least. But just like Emoss, he's an Ancient. He hasn't been hamstrung by his impending mortality, blessed with the luxury of patience. Of foresight. A man who lives for 1000 years does not fret over the prospect of tomorrow's future. He's concerned with the next decade. The next millennium.

But only a handful of Ancients remain. And as their numbers dwindled and the voices around him changed, so did his policy. The inevitably of his death soon became a somber realization. The patience he had has evaporated as his light draws ever closer to the end of his tunnel. His motivations became blurry and convoluted. The good of his people at ends with the fleeting years of his legacy.

My father's death was the catalyst of this decline. Of all the Ancients, Emoss was called upon the most to advise Trakstull. His level headed, calm demeanor always kept Trakstull poised. Confident in the direction of his leadership. When Emoss passed, he left a void that Trakstull was never able to fill. I surely won't be able to. The other Ancients who remained on the High Council were Lyrell and Russa. And neither commanded the same respect Emoss did. Russa too brash and loose-lipped, too unpredictable. Lyrell too apathetic and disinterested.

My thoughts of the past are interrupted by vibrating inside my pocket. I pull my comm out and glance at the face. It's encrypted. Oh shit... I look up, and I'm only a block from the tower. This conversation is the last thing I need before heading into this test. I silence the voice request and wait for a message.

"Gwinny, darling. Pleasure doing business with you. I must say, I'm quite impressed with your... tenacity. If you ever grow bored chasing the validation of daddy's overlord buddies, I could use an advisor of your caliber. Food for thought, darling. Anyway, I am in your debt, use it wisely."

I shove the comm into my pocket. Just hearing his voice makes my skin peel.

Psychopath.

I close my eyes and take a long, slow breath to settle my nerves. These are the distractions I can't have right now. I open my eyes and glance back to the small Heplin girl. I push away every horrible memory that claws at the gates to my mind and exit the slidewalk.

The bottom floor of Trakstull Tower is a fortress. Swollen Brushu guards posted all hours of the days. The best security tech the High Council can create adorns the walls as a guard immediately halts me. He stands a rod up in front of me with a small sphere on miniature rails attached to it. The sphere emits a barely visible green beam. It moves down the rod, and the beam scans my body as it progresses. It reaches my feet, and I'm cleared to move along. I get that it's protocol, but it's pretty obvious who I am; this is always ridiculous.

Another checkpoint.

An old *Savron* woman sits at a desk hunched over. I double-take as I approach. She looks somewhat familiar. Then again, all these vagrants look the same to me.

She's decrepit and wrinkled. So soft she's nearly putty. A permanent scowl scratches across her face. She grunts at me to continue toward her, not looking up.

I smile at her and stick my hand out. A manufactured gesture. The woman grabs my wrist and flattens my hand against the desk. Her skin is cracked and rough to the touch. A compact contraption lays on the desk in her other hand. She places the device on my finger, and I wince as a needle pricks it. She turns the device over and allows a droplet of my blood to splash into the funnel on the other side. The tool spits out a small crystal with my blood embedded within it. She places the crystal into a bracket, and a series of lasers and beams scan the crystal. She glances up at me, unenthusiastically waiting for the results. Clear. No signs of the Rotting or any other biological threat. She ushers me off to my next stop.

I continue through a gauntlet of security checkpoints. As thorough as they can be. Once I'm upstairs, there will be no guards, so they ensure safety for the High Council below. One by one, I clear the checkpoints until I reach the lift that will take me up to the new "Consulate". It's an insult to the true Consulate, really. The Trakstull Chateau had no security. No lasers scanning people, or armed brutes patrolling about. It was a place of and for the people. This place couldn't isolate the High Council from their constituents any more. But then again, the old Consulate is in ruin. The inevitable result of human interaction with *anything*.

The door to the lift opens, and I step inside. Before the door can close, the old Savron woman sticks her bony arm in and stops it. She stands there, straining. As if standing is a major physical task for her. Her voice is so raspy I'm not sure she's used it in years. And she very well may not have. I'm not even sure how a Savron woman got a job here.

"Gwinnett." The words coming from her throat are painful and hoarse. "I didn't realize it was you earlier. My eyes move slow these days, but my mind moves slower." She drops her head for a moment, ashamed. But she gathers herself and speaks again. "I see him in you." She looks up at me, and I see tears welt in her eyes. "He was the sweetest man I had ever met." She speaks slow. Every word is a battle to get out. "He found me when I had nothing and no one. I was living just outside the building, in the alley. He brought me to your home; you all were just kids. Let me bathe myself and got me clean clothes. He offered that I have dinner with you four. But I was too embarrassed, so I left. The next day, there was a small box of food from your dinner with a note on it, left in the alley. He offered me this job, and I've worked here ever since." She chokes back harder tears, and the ones that do fall instantly prune her withered cheeks. "If it wasn't for your father, I would've starved in that alley. He saved my life." She can no longer fight the flood of emotion that pushes against her, and tears spill from her. "I wanted you to know that. Wanted you to know how special Emoss was. And I want you to know that I see him when I look at you. How you treat people. I can see it in your eyes. Emoss would be proud of you. We're all rooting for you." She smiles at me, and for the first time, her scowl softens to something else. She's lived a harsh life, but Emoss gave her purpose.

I am stunned. She caught me completely off guard. She looks at the rest of the room, and they all stare back at me with the same look. The look I watched people give Emoss for years. Hope. Inspiration. Purpose.

"Thank you." I reach out and clasp the old woman's hands in mine, the vague memory of her beginning to crystalize.

"Go get 'em. We all believe in you." She smiles once again and heads back to her desk.

The lift door closes as I watch her limp away, and a heaviness buries into my chest. I press my eyes shut, forcing back my own tears. Thoughts of my father chip away at the walls I've built. They crumble even more when I think of what she said. *Emoss would be proud of you.* This woman doesn't know me. She knows my persona. I'm a politician. Everything on the outside is a mask. A façade. Emoss would be so disappointed in who I really am. Of who I've become. The thought of that strikes to my core. My eyes beat red, lips irritated from biting them so hard, I fight the urge to collapse onto the floor of the lift and sob. The way those people looked at me... I'm such a fraud. An imposter. I rub my eyes, trying to scrub their image from my mind. Those people are so desperate for someone to care about them, the way Emoss did. I don't care about anything. I'm empty and blank. I smile at them and treat them the way he used to, but he acted from his heart. I do it to honor him. But witnessing how those people see him when they look at me, I realize I couldn't be insulting his legacy any more.

I've been an emotionless, distant zombie for months and today's the day I choose to have an emotional breakdown. Cowering in the corner of a lift that's climbing to the most crucial interview of my life. The lift reaches the top, and the doors pry open. I stand to the side so they can't see me as I corral myself. I can see my warped reflection in the metal of the lift. I look into my eyes and, for a moment, can see that girl who was sweet and kind and generous at her heart.

But in an instant, my face straightens.

The pitiful self-loathing is flushed away, and I stand broad and cold. That girl in the reflection is the reason Emoss is dead. And that sweet girl died with him.

I will get this title, and there's nothing that will stop me. I step out of the lift and into the room. Around a crescent-shaped table sit the High Council staring at me, Trakstull in the middle.

Two seats are empty, A'gorr's and mine.

8

FARGO SHEPHERD

Brotherly Love

"It took some time, Sir, but we've finally gathered a list of all known party guests." The servant hands me a dataplate with a scrolling list of names and addresses.

"This is everyone?" I don't look up as I scroll.

"Yes, Sir. All known guests." His voice is timid and squeaks. A feeble man.

"You keep saying known guests. Were there unknown guests?" I stop scrolling to look up at him.

"Um, yes sir.. five guests were either unknown, uninvited or were present under false names." He knows he's not to blame for this, but he also knows I don't care.

"Well, which was it?"

"Excuse me, Sir?"

"Which of the three was it? Unknown, uninvited, or here under false names?"

"Um... uh.. all three, Sir. If they were here under an alias, they would be, by definition, both unknown and uninvited."

Little shit. Maybe he's not so feeble after all.

"Well. Get me images of these unknown guests immediately. I need to know who this Zina woman is who stole from me!" I hand the pad back to him.

I yank back on it as he pulls away and jerk him closer to me.

"And don't ever speak to me like that again... do you understand?"

Before he can answer, Victor grabs me by the neck.

"Hey! Why are you terrorizing this poor man?" He peels my hand from the pad, and I give the servant a look to ensure him I was serious. "What's your name?" Victor asks.

"Fallon, Sir." The servant replies to Victor.

"Fargo, apologize to Fallon." Victor clenches down harder on my neck. Giant prick. The apology oozes out from the cracks in between my teeth.

"Fallon... I apologize for my tone with you just now. I know you were just doing your job. Poorly, but doing it none the less. If you could, please get me those images... I would greatly appreciate it." I give Fallon a manufactured smile and nod my head to Victor. "Happy?"

"Thank you, Sir.. right away." Fallon scurries off to whatever nest hole he came from. Victor, let's go of my neck.

"What the hell was that about?"

"None of your business, you Neanderthal." I punch him in the chest, and my wrist feels like it breaks against his pec. "Goddam... what the fuck are you?" I shake my hand and turn to walk away.

He grins and follows me.

"Why are you such an asshole to the workers?"

"I'm not an asshole. They're servants. That's the way you speak to servants."

"Dude... When did you become such a pretentious douchebag?" He shakes his head, chuckling to himself.

"I guess around the same time you became a self-righteous pussy..."

"Ha. Ha. I'm telling you, man, keep it up and one of these nights your gonna wake up and ole Fallon is gonna have a knife to your throat. And then you'll cry out to me, and I'm gonna have to come in there and kill the poor bastard, and all because you're a dick."

"If people aren't trying to kill you, you're not important enough..." I smack him on the ass and turn the corner.

"All hail King Fargo!" Victor mocks as he bows and tries to kiss my ring. "Hey, your highness, can I get a ride to training? My streamer is in maintenance, Miku isn't back from Su Hoz, and I don't have ten vehicles like you?"

I pause, trying to display my annoyance without words.

"You can just take one, I don't care."

"C'mon man. You're so anal about your rides. I'm not touching those without you in it. I learned that lesson the hard way. I'm not dealing with another temper tantrum."

Temper tantrum?! He wrecked my favorite speedster. Totaled it. Just took it out without asking, couldn't handle it, and ended up in a ditch. But shame on me for being furious!

"I'm busy. Just take it, I got some things I gotta do."

"Nah, I'm getting in." Victor opens the door to my hauler and shoves himself in.

Fucking. Prick.

I get in my luxury hauler, and the door hisses closed behind me. I shoot an aggregated glance at Victor. The vehicle roars to life as I push the initiator. Lights sprint their way from front to back across the ceiling, and the gauges across the dash illuminate with dazzling rotations of colors. The hauler pushes off the ground, and we take off, kicking up dirt and grass behind us. We cut through the sky and plunge over the edge of the floating Grogan island.

Victor lounges in the passenger seat, soaking in the skylines as we fly past. Life is carefree for him. He wants things, he gets them. Simple. Straightforward. He has a gun and a target. Shoot it, he accomplishes his goals. It's that easy. My life is far more ambiguous.

I built my life. Victor and Miku were born into theirs. The world loves Miku. She thinks they have to as the daughter of the Regal, but that's not why. She's beautiful and charismatic and charitable and genuine. Easy to love. She's what the world wishes we all were.

Victor is a brute. Something these people usually wouldn't care for. But he's a champion. He's a phenom. A once in a generation talent, who also happens to be a foreign species. The world has always been enamored with skill and dominance.

Then the world saw me.

I wasn't beautiful. I wasn't a dominant fighter. I wasn't a muscle-bound specimen. I didn't have some fantastic talents or abilities. I was average. Painfully average. An alien, yes, but compared to the others, unimpressive. And, in the eyes of the world I was born into, invisible.

Groga is not like the rest of Valenia. It's more superficial. Wealthy, pretentious, judgmental, and mostly delusional. Some islands more than others, but these people live in the clouds, literally and metaphorically. So many people here inflate their own worth, their own importance, and influence. So, to them, average is a disgusting word. Insulting. I repulsed them.

It wasn't until I met Cyto that I realized what my true potential was. He showed me that I was anything but average. My skill set was just... less mainstream. That's an odd way of putting it. They were... not as surface level as the others. A talent that could only be maximized in the shadowy part of the world. A world less judgmental. More result oriented than superficial. A world where the slimmest, most despicable slice of the population conduct business. And what I learned about myself is how naturally that world comes to me compared to the one I live in.

Well, the world I used to live in.

What I also learned was those two worlds, the aristocratic Groga and the dishonorable world of Valenia's black market, weren't so different after all. All you needed to be successful in either was a simple trait. The trait I had.

The art of shamelessness.

"So, what do you have going on today that's so important you weren't going to give your big brother a ride in his time of need?" Victor is tired of the sites and turns to me, a dumb grin on his face.

"You have GOT to stop it with the big brother thing. Hatched four minutes before me, spend the next twenty years, giving me *older* brother advice." I roll my eyes. "The only thing bigger of yours is that Gaz looking head you got."

"Come on, that's not the only thing bigger." He laughs and winks at me.

"There it is! You can't go five minutes in conversation with Victor Bells without him bringing up dicks." I shake my head. "Be careful, brother, people may get the wrong idea about their beloved champion." I raise my brow at him.

"My conquests out of the Arena are just as well documented as they are in the Arena."

"Some would call that compensation..."

"I call it an appreciation of the female form and the requisite *tool* to garner appreciation back."

I stare blankly at him.

"Spell requisite..."

"R-E-Q-U-I-S-I-T-E. Requisite. Suck it bitch."

"You're unbearable," I laugh. "What would your fans think if they knew what a piece of shit you actually are? Not some noble saint, bound by honor or whatever BS you pull off?"

"Probably the same thing your *fans* would think if they knew you were actually a filthy drug dealing low life."

"Fuck you!" I snap at Victor. That pisses me off. He always takes it too far. Always making sure I'm below him somehow. Maybe it stings more because I know he's right but fuck him for thinking that. I do what I have to. He doesn't know that part of my life. He has no moral high ground to stand on. He's a lunatic. "What if your fans knew about Hades?!"

Victor jolts his head around and glares at me, anger stretched across his face.

Dammit. I shouldn't have said that. The silence in the hauler is thick. I need to apologize, but he's hard to apologize to.

"Victor... I'm.."

"Don't!"

"Vic, I'm sorry, man. You know I didn't mean it."

Victor doesn't face me. His eyes stare out blankly into the cloudy sky. The whistle of the wind against the visor of the hauler seems louder through the awkwardness.

"Vic." I reach my hand out and place it on his shoulder. I tilt my head to its side to try to catch his eyes. "I'm sorry. That was uncalled for and messed up. I'm sorry, ok?"

He turns his head and glances out the corner of his eyes. He nods and sticks his fist out toward me. I bump his knuckles and fall back into my seat.

"Yea, I'm sorry too," Victor says softly.

Some time passes before I speak again.

"So... how has he been?" I ask. The elephant is in the room, I have to address it as much as I don't want to.

He looks at me for a moment before answering with a sigh.

"I don't really want to talk about it."

"Vic, come on. I didn't mean it, you know you can trust me." I feel terrible about the comment. I know he insulted me first, but I went too far this time. I'm the only person he confides in about it. Outside of some of the competitors in BoW, I'm the only person who truly knows about it. The other warlords don't dare say anything because they're terrified of what he'd do to them. I don't say anything because of how much it tears at him. How much he struggles with it. I'm such an idiot.

He hesitates again and finally opens up.

"I don't know. I feel like it's getting worse. I can feel him itching at me all day now. I get angrier for no reason; my patience is thinner. When he's here, he's here for longer. And it's harder to get back control." I can hear the pain in his voice. He tries to hide it, but I know him better than anyone. It hurts me to hear his pain. "Sometimes, it's hard to tell when he stops, and I begin."

He keeps his face away from me. This giant ball of muscle and testosterone is embarrassed. Insecure at times. It's hard to believe, but sometimes I have to be his rock. A lot of times, I fail. He deserves better from me, but I give him what I can. I'm not built for sympathy. I'm certainly not one to give life advice. But in these times, he needs me to be less of myself and more of Miku.

"Listen to me, bro. You are not him. You understand me?" I try to put on my best therapeutic voice without being patronizing. He just wants his brother, not just someone to say it's ok. "You're a good person. You're not a monster. Got me? Look at me, dude."

Victor turns toward me. He hears me, but I don't know if he believes me. He drops his head briefly, struggling with himself to get something out. He finally gathers his thoughts and speaks again.

"I've been thinking about it. And you gotta promise me something," he says.

"What is it?" The tone of his voice worries me.

"If the day comes where he takes control for good, you take him out." Victor implores.

"Take him out? What are you talking about?"

"I mean, you have to get rid of him. For good. It won't be me anymore, do you understand?"

"That's not gonna happen." I don't like the way he's talking about this.

"Fargo. I'm serious. It's getting worse. If that day comes, you cannot let him assume my life. You don't understand how dangerous he is. I mean it, you have to promise me." His face is cold. Deadly serious.

"Vic... I... uh... I promise..."

The hauler rips through the sky as we pass over top of the city. We cruise for a while, letting the tension of the prior moment bleed away. We pass over the towering skyscrapers and over a vast warehouse district where a grid of massive metal warehouses dot the streets like sand on a beach. On one corner is a blue-roofed warehouse with a sprawling painting of the High Council on it. They sit around a large oval table, and one seat is empty. A grotesque portrait of Gwinn is on one side of the table, and a perfectly manicured portrait of a Heplin man named Wylk is on the other. In large letters, a slogan is smeared across the roof, *A Hound or a Heplin, Your choice.*

"Vic, you see this shit..?" I point down to the warehouse.

"Yea. Why does she want to deal with this crap? I don't get it?"

"I don't get it either."

We finish flying over the warehouse district, and the city begins to unravel into small clusters of buildings. Ancient infrastructure littered in between, unintentional monuments to the past. Left untouched.

"Hey, so really, what do you have going on today?" Victor asks.

We're almost there; I was hoping he was going to drop it. He didn't.

"Got some business with Cyto," I answer but try to keep it vague. I really don't want to answer more questions about it. Victor's face says all I really need to know.

"Fucking Cyto. That old croak gonna get you into more shit you have no business being in?" Victor never sees the big picture. He has tunnel vision. "This *business* have something to do with whatever his name is and the rest of his Viper goons?"

"Don't worry about it. Just meeting up with him to get some information on someone." I continue to look ahead. My life requires me to keep everyone else in the dark. They can only know what I let them. For all our sakes, the less they know, the better.

"Oh, I get it now. It's about that redhead from the party. The one you were cupcaking with all night," he smiles and crosses his arms. "Don't even waste your time, you'd never stand a chance with her. What's your obsession with women out of your league anyway? First, Geeva, now this girl... just stick with your skeezy Heplin women."

Zina. The thought of her again swarms my mind, and I ignore Victor's jab. But this time, they're not thoughts of infatuation or lust, just business. Her pheromones are no longer pumping up my nose, so the spell she held over me earlier is gone. She took me off my game for long enough to take advantage, it won't happen again.

"No, it's not about her; she left me her contact," I answer, but it's only partly true. There's a lot I have to discuss with Cyto; she's only part of it. "And for your information, Geeva and I mutually agreed to no longer mix business with pleasure."

Victor shoots me an incredulous look and runs his fingers through his hair.

"Surree. But really, man... I know you said you've got it under control, but just be careful. That shit was sketchy at the party. They showed up at our house Fargo... And I promise you, if you get Miku or I mixed up in whatever shit you got going on and we'll have problems. Got me?"

"You won't." At least, I hope they won't.

"Just be smart, man."

He looks at me with honest concern. If he only knew the half of it. I wish I could tell him about everything, but I can't. Wish I could ask him what to do about Zina and the Vipers and the missing case and everything, but I can't involve him. So, I lie.

"Thanks, but I got it under control."

We finally arrive.

"Hey, remember which one it is? Grey building right there by itself." Victor points the way, and I begin to descend. As we approach, two humongous men lumber out the door. The golden grain is pushed in all directions as the hauler inches toward the ground. The buildings look closer together from the sky than they are. An isolated pocket of yellow Golden Grain surrounds an Ancient era dwelling. Out in the distance, the skyline of the city sparkles. In the opposite direction, elevation and a dim tint of orange spread across a thinly wooded hillside. The two men eyeball Victor as they move past to their vehicle. He matches their leer and sticks his fist out to me. I bump his knuckles as I help him with his macho staring match. As if I bring any level of intimidation.

"Alright, bro. I'm gonna hang in the city for a little after I'm done. Maybe see if Leo and those guys are around. Wanna come?" Victor asks, still staring at the two men.

"Eh, I do, but I gotta see how long I'm gonna be. I'll let you know. If not, tell them I say what's up."

Victor climbs out of the car, his chest puffed out, and posture rigid. The hauler nearly shakes with his weight leaving. The two men finally turn toward their vehicle and take off. He glances back in and winks at me as the men speed away.

"Everyone wants a piece of the champ 'til they actually get one." He flexes his bicep at me. I roll my eyes and laugh.

"Alright ya ogre, I'm out of here."

"Peace." Victor turns and heads into the building. I watch as the door shuts behind him and breathe a huge sigh of relief. I got off easy there. Thank God for his abysmal communication skills.

The moment he's gone, I pull out my comm.

No messages from Deterro, thankfully. Doesn't seem like word has gotten out about the heist yet. That won't last long. I give it until the end of tomorrow before I'm strapped to a table, and some brainless Viper grunt is pouring acid over my back.

The thought makes me need a smokewrap.

I pull one from my jacket and light the end, sucking at the dry butt. The smoke only mildly helps. What I could really use is some venom.

I check my comm once more to see if Fallon has any updates on our unwelcomed guests, but that's a dead end. I knew that runt would be worthless.

What the hell am I going to do?

The rig rumbles to life once more as I suck in as hard as I can to finish the smokewrap and toss it out the door.

If Cyto can't help... we're all fucked. This old hag better have a trick up his sleeve. I take off and head toward the Valley and pray a miracle is waiting for me when I get there.

9

LEO
ABERNATHY

A World Below

My eyes crash open. Water spewing from my mouth in violent, convulsive coughs. Sand coated thick on my face. I'm a beached carcass. Water soaked so deeply into my skin, I think my bones may be soggy. The hair that dangles over my face still drips to the ground.

What the hell happened?

I've washed ashore, laying half submerged in frigid water, and half burrowed in sticky, damp sand. It's so dark I can barely see my hands in front of my face. The type of blackness that plays tricks with your mind. "Hello?" The yell sends a twinge rifling through me. Cracked ribs. Add it to the list. I grab my torso and roll onto my other side to avoid the pain. Breathing is a nightmare. My lungs wheeze as if the heel of Bryl's boot presses upon my chest.

The yell seems to echo indefinitely. Rattling around so often, I'm not convinced it isn't just in my head. I battle to my feet. The darkness disorienting. It's hard to gain my balance, but I do, probing the unknown with my hands. A rock ledge scratches at my palms about shoulder high. The top is flat and wide. Dry. Dry is all I care about right now. I try to pull myself up, but my ribs remind me I'm human. *Holy shit....* A groan that sounds like a dying *Garpo* involuntarily squeezes from my throat.

I eventually slog up the rock face and flop to the ground.

Laying here until I die doesn't sound so bad. There are worse ways to go.

My suit looks like molted insect skin after I moan my way out of it.

The rock face is freezing, but the irritation on my skin from the air in Paradise needs soothing, so I don't mind it.

How the hell am I alive?

I must have fallen 100 meters... At least.

Thank God for modern suit technology.

I stare up at the pit's entrance, which is no more than a greyish spec in a sea of blackness punched into the ceiling of this massive cave I've fallen into.

My throat kills.

Damn noose.

I run my fingers along the raw skin of my neck, and my mind instantly sends me back to that moment.

The twine squeezing tighter and tighter around my throat. My vision beginning to blotch. The image of the Proselyte who attacked me as I was disposing of the hung bodies, fading away. I can still picture the horror as my life flashed before my eyes. All the mistakes, all the memories, all the moments. Everything. But one memory lingered. Flashing over and over. That heartbreaking night with Gwinn. How empty and hopeless and betrayed and...

I press my palms to my eyes and shake away those devastating thoughts. I can't go back there again.

Instead, I need to figure out where the hell I am?

The screen of my comm stares blankly back at me as I tap it. Nothing. Water and electronics, still mortal enemies. Calling for help is out of the equation... I close my eyes and let out a weary sigh. I should've left with the crew. The poisoned air would've feasted upon the cultist's bodies, and I could've gone back to the lab to scan the Redemption salvage for traces of human DNA before we had to report it to Russa.

I sit up and try to scan my surroundings.

No... I did the right thing. Life is too precious to let rot at the end of a rope.

From the rock's vantage point, a faint twinkle of light pierces the darkness, reminding me of the lone stars that are bright enough to be seen through the haze of busy nights in the Capital. Thankfully, my eyes begin to adjust enough to see meters in front of me, and I'm no longer floating inside the pitch-black bowels of a beast, yet standing on the jutting fringes of a cave.

The rock I stand on is actually a ledge. A ledge with a path that continues beyond my vision in both directions. The water below gently knocks as a dull current pulls it in the direction of the light, its shore swallowed by rocky ledges in the shape of a horseshoe. It's quite beautiful, honestly. I haven't seen rock formations like this outside of Berban. They're fascinating. Yet, as much as I'd love to stay here and inspect these exotic stones, I can't risk Russa growing suspicious of my extended absence from the mission. The less he looks into our business, the closer I get to solving the formula. I power to my feet and begin in the direction of the faint lights, hoping it's a way out of the cave.

I'm not sure how long I've walked, but the blister on my heel that formed what seems an eternity ago now admits defeat and tears open, squeezing out blood into my sock with every step. They'd just gotten dry too. But on the positive side, it does help me forget about the rubble I used to call a ribcage.

Why isn't this damn light getting any bigger? Am I not getting closer?

The path continues to run parallel to the water. Pebbles occasionally splashing into the stream as I kick them from the ground.

My pace slows. I can't quite make out what's ahead.

What is that?

The path stops flush against a massive wall that consumes the entirety of my vision of the cave. As I get closer, I see the light is actually an illuminated window of a bunker door carved into the wall. Why or how there's a door inside, what appears to be, an unexplored cave is beyond me?

I try to wipe the sludge from the window with no luck. This muck has built up for years; it has completely stained the glass. I pull on the handle, but the door doesn't budge.

It's either locked or hasn't been opened in ages.

Hmm...

I turn around and am met with unrelenting darkness. Well, I'm not going back that way.

Mounted on the wall next to the door is a small box with a dataplate attached to its side. I press the screen and hear the soft hum of the device turning on. Thin white digitized lines streak across the screen. Nothing happens. I press the screen again, and a symbol flashes for a second, only to be instantly replaced by the white lines. The same thing happens each time I press it. Some symbol, which looks to be a word in a language I don't recognize, appears then disappears, followed by stale white lines.

I press the screen once more to see the word. It flashes across, and I realize I vaguely recognize it. I don't know what it means, but I've seen it before. I press it again and again, searing the image into my brain. Then, it finally hits me. I've seen this on the walls of the Consulate. The old Consulate, the Trakstull Chateau, the one I just fell through. Not the monstrous tower in the Capital that Gwinn spends her days in, lobbying for power she doesn't want and seeking validation from people she can't stand. No, they don't use the Ancient's native language there. Only in preserved historical sites. This place must be centuries old... But this technology isn't? What is this place?

I continue to search for clues around the door. I find nothing. Tugging at the handle unsurprisingly doesn't work either. It doesn't budge. Maybe this pad is some sort of bio scanner? That's why the door won't open; it needs someone with access? But why put a window in a door that only certain people can enter? There must be a way in.

I fiddle with the dataplate over and over again, and all that happens is the same sequence. White lines, flash word, back to white lines. Maybe the thing doesn't work anymore? Those lines do make the screen look busted underneath. I try repeatedly, but nothing happens.

Stupid thing!

My ribs begin to groan again, and I need to sit down.

So many body parts have joined the coalition against me, I'm not sure what allies I have left. I have to stop making enemies of them.

I ease myself down on a jutting chunk of the wall and lay my head back. I use the side of the small box for support as I rest my head against the dataplate. I close my eyes to rest. Think. What is the screen saying?

Gwinn would know. Honestly, she'd be upset with me that I don't. How many times did she eagerly share Emoss'ss lessons with me? Teaching me the history of Ancient culture she had learned from him that day. I listened because I love her, but I was always more interested in the mysteries of

Earth. The origins of our species and the connection to my father. I wish like hell I would've paid more attention now.

I rack my brain.

Those conversations are still in there somewhere; I just have to find them. But allowing thoughts of Gwinn in is like navigating a minefield. At any moment, I could step on the one memory that breaks my heart all over again and sends me spiraling.

Scan!

That's the word.

I painfully climb to my feet and run my fingers along the edges of the dataplate and box, searching for a scanner bead. The smooth reticle of a bead runs along my left index finger as it probes the bottom of the box.

That's it.

I place my left hand under the box and press the dataplate with my right.

Green beams that were imperceptible before, scan over my left palm.

The dataplate chimes, and another word flashes across the screen.

Success.

Wait? I figured this was a scanner, but why the hell did my hand grant it access? I was just wondering if the scanner existed.

A long low rattle begins all around me, and a quiet hissing builds intensity. I take a cautious step back. A thin light built into the wall starts to flicker with life. The bulb fills and steadies.

The light from the wall shoots in both directions, filing bulbs that run in a single straight line. They reach the wall's corners and dart down the sides. The darkness flees from me as the light plows its way farther down the corridor until it follows a bend and disappears.

I have to squint to give my eyes a moment to adjust.

The cave I'm in is actually a massive tunnel. Running as far as I can see.

A thin river flows through its center, rocky ledges skirting it on either side. Occasionally an arching bridge connects the two sides. They look retractable as if to make way for something much larger coming downstream. A small dock rests on the opposite side of me, and rickety ladders are peppered periodically downstream.

What is this place?

The river's tide softly rolls in just shy of the wall in front of me and ends in a small sandy beachhead. I can see the entire wall now. It stretches the tunnel's width, and the ledges on either side of the river stop flush against it.

A colossal disc consumes the majority of the wall. Motors, hinges, wheels, and gears speckle the disc. This is a massive door. What could possibly need a door that large?

I turn back to the screen. Somehow, I've been granted access to this device, and a menu of options is listed in Ancient writing.

Activate
Bridge
Disengage

I have no idea what I've stumbled upon, but my mind is seizing with curiosity.

I press *Activate* to see what it does, and the ground immediately begins to rumble. The intricate parts of the disc begin to twirl and spin and crank. The rumble continues, and the disc begins to pull apart from its core.

Oh. My. God.....

The disc continues to split apart, and I ignore every ache and pain that floods my body and hustle my way down the ledge onto the shoreline as it finishes opening. The disc tucks away into the walls, and the rumbling stops.

I stand there in silence. Frozen. My head slowly tilting up so I can see the entire thing. It's incredible. The most beautiful sight I've ever laid eyes on.

"... a flying city made of metal and hope." I whisper.

Those are the words my father wrote to describe seeing the Redemption for the first time. What an understatement.

Inside this chamber rests a fully intact hub of the Redemption. The crest of Earth blazon across its side. It's massive. By far, the largest piece I've ever seen.

I run my hands along the cold metal. Amazing. The engineering is beyond flawless. My damp fingers slide across the bolts and screws along the seams. Its beauty nearly brings tears to my eyes. I can picture it all now. The entire ship. Each hub. The crew flowing through the halls. My father at the helm. The sun beaming off its curves. The last hope of humanity clinging to life in this metallic arc.

"My God Dad, would you look at this?"

My admiration gets interrupted by less glamorous thoughts. My mind begins to race.

What is going on?

Why is this here?

Five years I've worked for the High Council at the Alien Artifact Recovery Service. Five years. I've found satellite panels, engine coils, antennas, airlock motors, you name it, but nothing like this. Never even heard a rumor of something of this magnitude existing. This could've been sitting here for a century, and I've spent half a decade scouring every corner of Valenia looking for ship scraps when a complete, intact hub was under my feet the entire time. Undoubtedly, the High Council would want its top researchers knowing of this, right? First, they don't let us study Tanya in Su Hoz, and now this? I don't understand.

My stomach twists. What if the High Council knows that my crew and I are trying to reverse engineer the wombs instead of working to cure the Rotting? Trying to rebuild humanity after they explicitly voted to destroy us? They could've hidden this away because it holds the key to solving the womb formula. *Oh shit, they know...*

I can sense the conspiracy theories beginning to overwhelm my brain, and I have to take a deep breath.

No.

If the High Council knew, they would've just detained me. Or hell, maybe even killed me? Plus, if they were hiding this from me, why did the scanner grant me access? No, this is something else.

I work my way around the hub until I reach a patched hole in the exterior. This must have been where it dislodged from the rest of the ship. But it's been sealed shut. The evidence is in a crudely welded seam of the patch.

Why would they do that?

On the opposite side of the hub is an airlock door. One that Redemption crew members would use for maintenance or whenever they would need to access the outside of the ship. I pull on the lever connected to it. Nothing happens. A panel connects to the airlock. My dad wrote about these in his journal, I remember reading about them:

Damn finicky airlocks. The lever never worked; we always had to open the panel and override the system. I'll never forget that stupid code. You'd think with the fate of humanity on the line, they would think of everything, but the buttons were too small. It was so hard to punch in the right code with gloves on...

Damn, I can picture the code in my mind right after that sentence, but I can't remember what it is.

Huge power lines drape from the ceiling and connect to the ship. Something is clearly powering it. I try to follow the power lines to find the source, but the thick cords vanish into the floor. They rattle with energy. Their buzz fills the Vault, echoing throughout. A distinct, unpleasant scent is in the air as well, indistinguishable. My nose searches for the culprit, but it can't find it. Like a mixture of mildew and harsh chemicals. The smell makes me lightheaded.

I circle the hub; any urgency I had before to return to the lab has been sucked away by a vacuum of curiosity. A mesmerizing sense of wonder at the greatest discovery of my life and the closest I've ever felt to my father.

Stationed on the opposite side of the hub is an army of machines. Chairs are tucked neatly under desks that rest adjacent to them. I approach a desk with a tri-paneled dataplate at its head. It's an older model. An original, maybe? A thick film of dust coats the entire setup. A small glass case rests on the right side of the desk. Some kind of mechanical arm hanging over it, an unrecognizable device attached at the endpoints down into the case. I wipe the dust from the glass; it's empty.

I press a button on the dash of the desk. The chair slides out from under it. Dust billows as I clean off the chair and take a seat.

It's frustrating that this laboratory chair, in what appears to be an abandoned Vault, is still more comfortable than my rig's cockpit, but that's a complaint I'll keep to myself for the time being.

It seems obvious to press the button on the dash again, so I do, and I'm tucked neatly back under the desk.

Can't tell if that's lazy or convenient?

The dataplate croaks to life.

The screen sputters briefly, then lights up. Another Ancient symbol gently rotating in the center. This one is more complex. I can't make it out.

I press the symbol, but nothing happens. Not this again... I fiddle with the dataplate for some time before giving up and continue exploring the Vault.

It'd be fair to assume the place is abandoned until I reach

a desk on the far side. It's clean. No dust. I press the middle screen, and it boots right up. It's been in use. I inspect the Vault closer, and it makes sense. This place has been maintained, if not minimally. It clearly isn't serving its original purpose, but someone is keeping this place functional. More questions rifle through my mind.

What was this place, and what is it now?

Where is everyone who worked here?

Why is it essentially empty?

None of this makes any sense.

On the wall adjacent to the clean desk hangs a large diagram of the exterior of the hub. Labels and notes littered across it, all in Ancient Valenian. Next to it is a space that looks like another diagram would hang, but nothing is there. A jagged corner of a film-like sheet is all that remains of whatever hung here. Inspecting the small piece left, the logical conclusion would be that a diagram of the hub's interior was displayed here. It's ripped from the wall, only the top corner remains, dangling like a flag in the wind. My hands inspect the area where the diagram should be. It seems out of place. I look around the Vault, everything else seems so tidy, so organized. Unkept, but organized. Then there's this. As if ripped from the wall in a hurry, it doesn't match the rest of the room.

Above the diagrams, a staircase leads to a type of glass observatory overlooking the entire Vault. I climb the stairs and enter. Florescent lights flickering on as I stride in. Thick glass encases the cylindrical room. The buzz of the power chords drowns out as the door seals behind me, soundproof.

Silence.

A dataplate hangs from the ceiling in the center of the room. I tap on the plate, and the glass all around dims. This room has a presence to it. Palpable. It feels like the type of room where important men make decisions about the lives of less important men. The type of room where the fables of conspiracies live. Conspiracies where the shadowy legions who control the world turn the cogs of the machine, while the ignorant citizens look elsewhere.

Or maybe it's just an office, and I need to stop reading those forums that Spri writes on? Either way, it's eerie.

Just below the dataplate rests another control panel.

It opens by way of a simple latch and hook. There's no dataplate this time. No bizarre Ancient symbol. Inside, a small slot with a unique design has been built into the panel. The slot design looks like a ladder with pointed spokes that lead to a diamond at the bottom. And just below that, a hand lever, rigid in place. I run my fingers over the slot. I have no idea what this could be? My confusion boils over, and I slam the panel shut in frustration. What the hell is going on? What is this place? I need answers.

I storm out of the observatory. The sounds of the Vault rush back into my ears as I press through the door.

Searching the Vault for something to reveal its purpose has proved futile. Every corner is just another dead end. Just more questions and no answers. I search every inch for hours, but there is nothing more I can learn from this place.

I walk back over to the hub. This ship has answers to questions I've searched my entire life for. I can feel it in my bones. If I'm to ever successfully replicate the womb formula, there is no better resource than what rests in front of me right now. Yet, I've never known of its existence. Someone has hidden it from me. But why do I have access to something so secretive? I don't understand!

I press my palm against the metal once more. Closing my eyes and trying to picture the life they intended for us.

My father and I walking through a busy market. Humans of all ages and races, living in harmony to renew our mark on history. A happy, healthy community that slipped through the fingers of death to live on and prosper. Paradise.

My eyes snap open.

The slot in the observatory... I've seen that shape before. I don't know how, but the memory shoves its way to the forefront of my mind. It was the night Emoss lost his battle with the Rotting. Riley refused to stay out of his room, and I refused to let her go through that alone, so together, we slept curled up in a chair next to him. Just two kids clinging to each other for strength.

It was deep into the heart of night. I stirred awake, stiff, and thirsty. A hushed conversation was being held in the kitchen as I approached. I could only make out bits and pieces of what they were saying, but Russa and Qwillow were arguing about Tanya. I hid around the corner, still terrified of Russa at this point, and watched as he tried to yank a case from Qwillow's hand. She only let go when Russa slammed her against the wall. Tears streamed down her face; she was terrified. He snatched the case from her hand and opened it on the counter behind him, pulling out the containments.

And that's where I recognize the shape from.

Because wedged in between Russa's cord ends as he inspected it against the light was a vial filled with an orange glowing fluid, shaped exactly like the slot in the observatory panel.

10

GWINN DEMARCO

Psychological Warfare

My chair is deep and cold and built for someone much larger than me. I sit atop a boost they've provided, a bit demeaning, but no more demeaning than having to answer questions with just my brow peeking over the table.

The new Consulate is minimalist, yet somehow pretentious. A massive crescent-shaped table, forged from minerals all but exhausted, is erected from the same material. Retractable glass wraps the entire floor in all directions. The glass is down tonight, and the breeze tiptoes its way through the room. Cool at first, chilling, raising the hair on my skin, and waking up my senses. Then a warmer breeze creeps in. Cozy and comforting. Back and forth, it goes. The others aren't as sensitive to the temperature; they don't even notice.

Power consumes the other chairs that surround the table. High Councilors from each Province. I'm not one to be intimidated, but if there was ever a time...

I can't tell where I feel more unwelcome, the streets of the city, or in this room. Not that I care either way. The show of support by the Savron in the lobby was surprising, to say the least, but the goodwill earned by Emoss only extends so far to me.

A hologram of Valenia flickers in the middle of the room, the table curving around it. Aside from the table and the hologram, the room is barren.

Each seat at the table has a dataplate built into the smooth stone surface and their own smaller personal hologram projecting Valenia. I press on my datapad, and the screen illuminates.

Okotall High Council Candidate #2
Name: Gwinnett DeMarco
Organic Age: Youth/Prime+
Race: Human
Province of Origin: Unknown - "Okotall"
Council Experience: None
Lineage: Unknown - "Emoss"

A picture of my face is displayed next to my bio information. My features look softer, more welcoming than they are. The work of Tolla, no doubt. It's a full-time job to keep me appealing to the public. She works night and day to make me more approachable. Intimidating. Aggressive. Provocative. All words attached to my perception we've had to fight to counter. Tolla was a Low Councilor under Emoss for years at the end of his tenure. When he passed, she bid for his position, but the High Council deemed she wasn't qualified for all the opposite reasons I'm being criticized for. They felt she was too compassionate, to the point where she couldn't enforce policy effectively.

They wonder if I have a heart...

She was also too passive, allowing other voices to influence her decision making. They worry no one can sway my opinions, even if they're better informed. And she wasn't physically appealing enough. Almost boring. Plain, simple. Not beautiful, or ugly, just ordinary. They worry people can't relate to me because I'm too attractive. As if anyone on the planet can relate to the alien. The hypocrisy is maddening.

I tap the screen again, and my scores from the previous tests appear.

Physical Health: Prime+
Mental Stability: Prime+
Cognitive Aptitude: Prime+
Communication: Sufficient-

History: Prime
Economics: Sufficient+
Foreign Relations: Inferior
Military Strategy: Prime
Vulnerabilities: Prime+
Leadership: Prime+
Electability:

This last test today is the most important. Electability. It's a more subjective test than the others. The grade is not based on how you do, but how the High Council perceives you did. It's a game of cryptic questions and convoluted answers. A game of stroking egos, tough skin, and asserting your place. Whatever this test has become, I can't imagine it was the same when Emoss was alive. It's become slimier. A game of arrogance and petty pissing contests. It's almost less about the candidate and more about validating the power of the current members. Play the game and win the favor of the High Council.

When all candidates have gone, the High Council will be giving their unofficial endorsement to the candidate they give the Prime+ grade to. It's against the High Council's policy to directly influence an election, but only one candidate has ever been elected without the Prime+ electability grade; Russa. And that was hundreds of years ago. The election might as well be ceremonial because the High Council chooses its own members.

The Regal of the High Council, Trakstull, stands and addresses the room, his voice still powerful and firm despite his age and deteriorating body.

"Listen." He quiets the murmuring, raising his arms. "It's time to begin Candidate Two's final test. As I call your name and Province please signal you are ready to begin." Trakstull looks down the table in both directions, the ends of his fibrous cords squirming and wiggling like bloom algae being tossed around by the rip currents of the Lotopi. When he's captured the attention of his council, he begins to list off names.

"Meelo, Groga *Canter*?" Meelo gives a firm nod. A stern, brooding man. A Brushu with a square jaw and the personality of a rock.

"Lyrell, Groga *Du Col*?" Lyrell lifts a finger, barely picking up his eyes from his dataplate. It's hard to tell if he's genuinely disinterested or just trying to make me think he's disinterested, but regardless the Ancient looks unenthused to be here.

"Russa, Groga *Oilsterr*?" Russa looks to me with a wink and smile and signals to Trakstull. His wily demeanor is one of the few sanctuaries I have here. No matter what, I know Russa has my back.

"Bhugon, Groga *Ivolo*?" Bhugon signals dramatically. Raising his frail hand, legs crossed, and hair manicured perfectly. Russa rolls his eyes, and I try not to smirk at his pretentiousness.

"Hesh'ka, Dwaul Fir?" Hesh'ka has his misshaped Reyllion head buried in his dataplate. Mind always going a mile a minute. He's preoccupied with something. He doesn't hear Trakstull.

"Hesh'ka, Dwaul Fir?" Trakstull asks again. I tap him on the shoulder, and Hesh'ka nearly jumps out his chair.

"What?" He looks up at me, his face the usual mix of thunderstruck and restless energy. I point to Trakstull, whose expression lacks patience. "Oh. Ready. Sorry." He shoots me an embarrassed glance.

"E'Zuu, Su Hoz?" E'Zuu nods. He's the youngest of the current members. Cocky, handsome, ambitious. He's on the far side of the table from me. He gives me a sly smile. Disrespectfully flirtatious in this setting. His confidence drips from him. It's both nauseating and alluring. I match his gaze, match his level of seduction. My eyes crawl all over him. He's no match. I overwhelm him, and he finally looks away. The others notice, but don't acknowledge it. They just quietly take notes in their mind, some caring more than others. The games have already begun.

"A'gorr, Berban?" Trakstull looks to the empty seat to his left. "Make note that the High Councilor from Berban is absent once again." Trakstull taps something on his dataplate. The rest of the members seem unfazed by his absence. I supposed I should be too. A'gorr hasn't been to a High Council meeting in years. His inclusion in the High Council was more a show of good faith than his desire to be in it. Berban has always been isolated from the rest of the world, but ever since the treaty was signed, Berban might as well be another planet.

"And finally, Candidate Two, Gwinnett DeMarco, Okotall?" Trakstull looks to me, waiting to see if I am ready to start. As if today's evaluation didn't begin the moment I walked off the lift. I nod my head confidently, and the test officially begins.

The hologram in the middle of the room shifts from an image of Valenia to a list of pictures of each High Councilor. Trakstull sits down and explains.

"Rank the members of the High Council from most competent to least competent." Trakstull stares blankly, matter of fact. Such a simple mundane task, yet the implications could be severe. Each High Councilor now has their full undivided attention directed toward me. Their eyes all say the same thing, be careful.

I feel a tightness swell in my chest. I didn't know what to expect, but this surely wasn't it. Tolla tried to prepare me as well as she could, but these electability tests are all unique to the candidate. There was no preparing for this.

I look around the room, and the men who stare back at me all genuinely believe they're the most competent. Even the zany, soft-hearted Hesh'ka is a proud man, one who would be very insulted to be called incompetent. There's no way of answering this question without alienating half the room. Maybe that's the point, to demonstrate that in politics somebody will always be angry with you. Or perhaps it's just a game to fluster me. Either way, I need to think this through.

The way I see it, I have a few ways of answering. The first is the truth. Which is how I want to answer. I've never been one to shy away from frank conversation. I speak my mind. I'm insulted if they think they can intimidate me into compromising my principles. If I were to answer truthfully, I'd say:

A'gorr
Trakstull
Russa
E'Zuu
Hesh'ka
Meelo
Bhugon
Lyrell

They would all be disgusted at me for claiming A'gorr to be the most competent. A Gaz savage in their minds. Backward and primitive. But A'gorr has accomplished everything his people wanted and more. Berban has been closed to nearly all other races, he technically has a seat on the High Council to affect policy around the world if he chooses, and his people are thriving well beyond the means they ever have. He's realistically accomplished more from his improbable position than some of these men who were born with silver spoons in their weird alien mouths.

I consider him a genius.

But I might as well walk out the door and not come back if I answer A'gorr as number one. Not to mention, I have an Ancient in last. It's hard to claim a man whose led for 1000 years is incompetent, but he's so apathetic he has no idea what the people of Groga *Du Col* want anymore. So, as much as it pains me to do, the truth is out. Plus, Tolla would kill me if I answered like that! I have to play the game. That's what she stressed to me over and over. *Play the game DeMo, play the game!* That's why I'm here.

The next way I could answer would be the order in which the men would be least offended. The most arrogant to the least, with A'gorr at the bottom. That's essentially where I have to rank him, no matter what.

Trakstull
Bhugon
Lyrell
Russa
E'Zuu
Meelo
Hesh'ka
A'gorr

The Ancients all at the top with the unbearably dramatic Bhugon sandwiched in the middle. Then E'Zuu and his vanity, followed by the silent mountain of a man Meelo, and finally the spastic sweetheart Hesh'ka. This would be the path of least resistance, but I worry my motivations in that answer would be too transparent. Also, I need allies. People who will fight for me. I know Russa will. But even though he wouldn't confront me about it, I feel Hesh'ka would be hurt by my lack of confidence in him. I need proponents. Guys like Lyrell and Bhugon could care less to align themselves with me; they just want to be petted.

"Gwinn. We're waiting." Trakstull's voice breaks my concentration. It startles me. He's a man of little patience.

"Oh. Sorry. You are all so unthinkably incompetent; it's hard to narrow it down." I don't look up, nervous my joke won't land. But it does. The room bellows with laughter. Though, I worry they laugh because they're all convinced they are a lock for the top spot. It may sting worse when they realize they aren't!

I cycle through all the possible sequences and the pros and cons of each, but time has run out. I have to answer.

I press on A'gorr's face and drag him into the bottom spot. The hologram in the middle of the room mimics my screen. The men mumble amongst themselves, mostly in quiet, obvious agreement. I mull over the next options and get the list formulated in my head so I can quickly put it out all at once. I want to avoid drawing each position out and facing the backlash that will come with each. Put it all out at once and have the room be one big bag of mixed emotions.

I take a deep breath, and my fingers twitch over the dataplate. The names flash onto the screen, and for a moment, the room sits still as the men digest the information in front of them.

Trakstull
Hesh'ka
Russa
Bhugon
Lyrell
Meelo
E'Zuu
A'gorr

The room crumbles into a commotion as the men project their insecurities onto me. I sit there poised and sturdy, wearing insults from the petty leaders of the free world. Trakstull stands and raises his hand.

"Enough." The ruckus dies down slowly. A tension floats through the room. Meelo and Lyrell beam with hushed, anger-filled humiliation, as others bask in their false sense of superiority. E'Zuu inspects me with the same devilish charm as he did before. He doesn't seem insulted. He seems intrigued. He's so blindly confident of his talent, he views my ranking as a flirtatious jab. Just as planned.

"Test one is complete. Let's move on before Lyrell's head explodes," Trakstull says. He tries to hide a feathery smile as it curls its way across his beak, but we can all see it. He glances at me as if to suggest he thought that was funny, but I try my best not to acknowledge it.

A once full-bodied man, Trakstull has become frail and weak; time has never met an opponent it couldn't beat. His sheaths covering his cords are dry and loose. A tall, slender frame, some of his silky white hair sits upon his head in a bun, and the rest flows down his chest on either side of his shoulder knots like a river forked in two. "Test two."

"Next, we will show you a series of images. There will be no context, no description, no detail, just choose one. Then, the next series of images will appear, you will choose one, and so on."

Another test that sounds simple, yet I highly doubt will be.

The hologram of the list disappears in the middle of the room and, in its place, projects three images. A Jymira, the wiry pack feline perched on a tree limb, ready to pounce. An Hotógo, the gnarly beast's huge square jaw dripping with saliva, its hooves dug deep into the soil. And finally... my heart skips a beat on the last image. A Viper, camouflaged within tall, thick grass. Its eyes glowing red. I try my best to avoid looking suspicious as I scan over it. *It's not a message; it's just a coincidence.* I move on as quickly as possible, looking for hidden clues or subliminal messages in other images as well.

The Councilors sit in silence, staring at me exactly how Leo would stare at images of painstakingly boring genetic images until his eyes bled. Those nights were unbearable.

I shake the thoughts of him away immediately... that's the last thing I need right now.

Each image looks as if it could hold some underlying meaning, but I have no clue what that could be. What are they trying to see? Regardless, the only thing I know for sure is I'm staying the hell away from the Viper.

After a thorough examination, I choose the Jymira. A fierce, compact, agile predator who stalks its prey with a pack of allies and pounces at the right opportunity. Wickedly intelligent, they make no wasted movements and only strike when a kill is a sure thing. Patient, precise, capable, and far more deadly in a group. A perfect combination of traits for a leader. If that's what the analogy was supposed to be?!

Each High Councilor make notes on their dataplate. I study their body language trying to gauge their responses, but these men are expert manipulators, I don't get a thing.

The next images appear.

The first is an image of me standing above a Savron woman dressed in rags, my foot pressed on her throat. Horror is etched across her face as I gaze upon her in disgust.

I stand against a wall, blindfolded in the second image, my hands tied behind my back. A firing squad points their rifles toward me as a stadium of people cheer them on.

And the last image is set inside a dimly lit war-room. A high-tech command center, High Council grunts stationed in small pods around a floating hologram. A crosshair is juxtaposed over the hologram, resting on the sacred Gaz village Pom'do'kon. My finger hovers above a large button encased in glass.

The images disturb me. Why would I ever choose any of these? I glare at those around me, the disgust not hidden on my face. These men can't all be monsters. They can't all endorse this type of psychological manipulation. I refuse to believe Emoss behaved this way. I look back at the images, twisted and perverse. Who came up with these? They're asking me to choose between slavery, self-annihilation, and genocide. I look away to calm my nerves. These sadistic assholes. I started this journey to fill the void left by my father's death. To earn the position he coveted for so long as a way to honor his legacy. But after seeing this... These tyrants have poisoned the name of Emoss. Undermined his entire life's mission. I will stop at nothing to ensure I have a voice at this table.

I have to remember these are just tests, designed to toy with my mind. Don't overthink them; just pick one. But as the images flicker through my mind, I can't help but feel ashamed. Disgusted. It rips at my heart, but I pick.

I choose the first image. The Savrons have been relegated to the slums and ghettos ever since Trakstull has been in power. Years of attempted uprisings squashed with shows of brutality and force. A sentence handed down to them for crimes committed a millennia ago. An Ancient oppression maintained for generations. This generation quickly forgets Savrons used to run this world; they aren't the feeble-minded vagrants the world above them has portrayed them as.

No man in this room will feel any sympathy for that Savron. That's why I chose it. But all I can think about is the receptionist at the desk downstairs. The look in her eyes, the belief she had in me. If she only knew how I spit in her face now. How I disparage her and her plight for the sake of self-promotion. But I know this is how I must behave if I want access to this sanctum. She is a piece to be played, and a means to an end.

I close my eyes and wipe the Savron woman from my mind.

As the Councilors mull over my decision, the final sequence appears. They aren't images; they're videos.

Three play in loops, projected by the hologram in the middle of the room. It takes a moment for my mind to process what I'm watching. I stare at them in disbelief. Words can't describe the anger they cause. They make the blood in my veins boil so hot it may sear through my skin and melt the table. I snap a glare at Trakstull. The entirety of the High Council stares back smugly. I look to Russa for help but catch the edges of a grimace as he turns away. He can't look at me. There must've been nothing he could do... I turn my attention back to the videos, my mind a collapsing star.

On the left is a dark rainy night in a thick forest. Two beams of light split the darkness, headlights from a hauler. Steam rises from the hot rig as I dig a hole just in front of it. Lightning cracks above and illuminates the Forest. Emoss'ss dead body lies in the mud, rain sinking him farther into the muck. I finish the hole, climb out, and stand over top of him. His lifeless corpse plunges into the hole as I shove him in with my foot, water quickly accumulating inside. I fill the grave with dirt, stab the shovel into the ground and drive off in the hauler.

The middle video starts inside a habitation unit of the Redemption. Emoss walks the rows, inspecting the cryopods. He probes each one, searching for something specific. He finds it as he stops, signaling another man to come. He stands in front of a cryopod with my name on it. I rest in the artificial womb, an infant about to be hatched. Another man I don't recognize stands next to him, whispering into his ear. His face is filled with hate and fear. Emoss looks to the man and nods. Cold, emotionless. Not the Emoss I know. As he turns and walks away, the video follows him. In the background, the man left behind smashes the glass case of the cryopod with a mallet. Fluid rushes from the shattered womb pod, and the child slides out onto the ground. The man picks up the hysterical child, and the glimmer of a long knife shines as he pulls it from his belt. The video follows Emoss out of the airlock, and as the door closes, you see the man raise the knife above his head. The airlock slams shut, and the screaming of the child silences. All you hear are the clicking of Emoss'ss boots on the smooth surface as he walks away.

And finally, the video on the right. An empty warehouse. Leo is tied to a chair, his head to his chest, unconscious. Blood drips from his mouth and nose. His wild brown hair clumped together with dried blood from a wound on his head. I walk across the warehouse, dragging a heavy metal rod, sparks kicking up behind it. I smack him in the face to wake him up. He comes to as I yank his head back by his hair. I'm enjoying torturing him. The bones of his bare foot shatter as I slam the rod into it. He screams in desperation. The video pans to the left, and my siblings kneel next to him, the twins begging me to stop.

I stare into their eyes, not overjoyed to be seeing them after so long, yet disgusted with them. They reach out to stop me as I crush Leo across the face, but they're too late. The force of the blow knocks his chair over, and he crashes to the ground. Blood pools on the floor. Riley scurries atop of him, sheltering him from me. I laugh at her. *"You think he'd ever choose you over me?"* My sister pleads with me once again, but I ram the butt end of the rod into her stomach, and she rolls off, coughing. Remmy charges me, but I jab him in the throat as well. Leo looks up at me through horribly swollen eyes. No one in between us any longer. He mouths *I love you,* and I scream in fury. I swing the rod as hard as I can, and just before it connects with his face, the loop starts over.

I turn away from the table, biting the inside of my cheek until I've fought back the swelling tide of emotions. I know they're just mind games, but they gnaw at my core like insects. Because I grew up closer to the High Council then most, I forgot just how powerful they are. How connected they are. How they can learn everything about you, no matter how much you close yourself off to the world. They know my weaknesses. My insecurities. My fears. Their power terrifies me. I hadn't thought about it until now. I've been so engrossed in my preparation, in my vision for the future, that I took for granted the institution I'm trying to join. It's the first time I've questioned my resolve.

Tears welt in my eyes as the videos loop, but I force them back. They *cannot* see my pain. But as I replay these videos over and over, I don't know how they won't. The look of compassion on Leo's face as I beat him unmercifully... Even in this fictional world, I don't deserve his love. The disappointment in the eyes of the twins. The same look they gave me the night I told them I wasn't going to flee Archler house with them and disappear into the Forest. The betrayal etched so clearly across their faces. Emoss's corpse, stone-cold and stiff, discarded like rubbish. The image of his lifeless face seared into my soul. I miss him so much. Squeezing the thick fabric of my pants is all I can do to stop myself from snapping this dataplate in half.

And the child... Oh my God, the child.

I don't even allow myself a second to think of it because if I do, I'll implode into a hysterical pool of tears.

The thoughts race through my mind making me dizzy, I may just puke.

But I can't.

I've come too far. I'm not that weak, scared girl anymore. I'm not... Around the table, the Councilors anticipate my break. Wanting it. Craving it. The three options play over and over on the hologram. There's no justifying any answer here. But I won't choose the child. I can't. Never. Not again. And I won't choose Leo and the twins either. I would gain nothing from doing so. They know I broke Leo's heart just months ago and that I haven't seen the twins in years, it would look like the easy way out. No, only one answer will send the message I want. And that's Emoss.

His death is my fault. I'll never forgive myself for that. And although he died quietly in his bed with my hands woven into his and not tossed carelessly into a hole, I'm still the reason he's gone. So, I must fight for him. And if that means selecting his video to show the psychotic creatures of the High Council that I am as ruthless as they think I am, so be it.

I press the dataplate, my expression bold and undaunted on the outside, deteriorating quickly on the inside. I waste no time climbing down from my chair and hurrying to the lift. The tests are finished, I'm not spending another second here. The doors open, and I step inside, turning to face the High Council once more, letting them know I cannot be broken. Russa seems to apologize with his eyes; a pang of guilt riddles his face. I refuse to acknowledge it. Hesh'ka is sedated, his eyes down. Even E'Zuu wrestles with what happened. His pompous demeanor replaced with an apprehensive facade. The monsters ashamed of my torment. I have no sympathy for them. I press the button, and the doors close in front of me.

The lift begins its descent, silent.

For a moment, I remain strong. Assuring myself I'm ok. The lift hums, descending floor after floor. But my body begins to quiver. I grab the handrail, my legs quitting. My breath dissolves into short, choppy gasps. I slide down the back wall of the lift. Fighting as long as I can, but I'm overwhelmed. I break and end the interview the same way I start it. Balled up in the corner of the lift, a crumpled, emotional heap.

11

RILEY HOLT

Predator and Prey

I've never been so tired in my life. Blood coats me head to toe. My blood. Tyko blood. Luta blood. Remmy's blood. Streaks of it wash away from tears that roll down my face. Tears of exhaustion. Tears of panic. Tears of desperation. My body has so little energy left. My mind has even less. My strength is all but gone, yet I trudge along. The sled is so heavy behind me that Remmy will occasionally slide off, and it takes all my might to roll him back on to it. Made of tree branches and whatever I could find from the pack, the makeshift sled doesn't glide very well against the rough Forest floor.

Remmy is still unconscious from the powerful sound wave of the Sonostick. It makes poaching the Tyko feel like a worthless endeavor now. A flash of the beast's breath just inches from my face replays in my mind. I can smell it. Taste it. As if it snarls right in front of me. My life, seconds from ending.

The night creeps in faster than I can get us to shelter.

My body quits. I collapse to the ground and lay my head back against Remmy. I can feel the plants and bugs crawling all over my legs, but I'm too exhausted to care. Too exhausted to even continue being overwhelmed. My emotions wisp away. A calmness setting in.

Maybe I'm just delirious, but it feels like eyes are on me. Watching me from the concealment of the brush. If I had any energy left, I'd be concerned, but my eyelids crave one another.

I pull our canteen from the pouch, the cool liquid soothing my splintered lips. I want nothing more than to pour the entire thing over my head. A bath sounding like paradise right now. Ice cold. Washing away this horrible day. But I need this water. The next outpost is still some time away.

I stare up at the canopy. I can't see the top, but the sounds of small Koes jumping from branch to branch fill the darkness. Their eyes glow a soft yellow. The sight would be terrifying if I didn't know how adorable they are. One hops down from a tall branch and lands just next to us. He squeaks and chirps quietly as he inspects us. He sits on his hind legs, fiddling with the laces on my boots. He resembles a monkey from Earth, like the ones we've seen in books. Books we've bought from the envoys that pass through from Su Hoz. I don't spend much time thinking about Earth, but I figured if anyone should have these salvaged books, it should be us.

The shy little Ko grows more daring. He slowly crawls up my leg, carefully inspecting my face as he does. His tail wraps around my shin like it's a tree branch, and he inches along. He's fascinated by my belt loops. I let him explore. His little fingers hook through one, and he tugs on it, confused. Tugging again, then looking closer at it. Pulling it out enough to look through it.

This little critter's antics take me away for a moment. Away from the harsh reality I'm in. Away from the dire circumstances facing Remmy and I face. I feel guilty for enjoying the moment, but as the Ko climbs farther and farther up my body, I realize I need it. I let his cuteness warm my heart. A heart that could use it.

I reach my hand out slowly, trying not to startle him away. The Ko is weary of the gesture. He recoils a bit at first. He doesn't reach out yet. He just sits there, his big eyes searching for something, head tilted to the side. I stretch open a small front pocket of our pack and pull out a small pouch of Sweetberries. Ones we collect as we go. They're Remmy's favorite. Too sweet for me, I prefer the bitter bite of Fryttleleaves.

I place a Sweetberry in my palm and reach my hand back out. This time the Ko is more interested. He sniffs. Smelling the pleasant aroma of the berry. He reaches out with both hands and pulls the berry to his chest. He looks up at me as if waiting for permission to eat it.

"Go ahead... it's yours." I signal for him to eat it. The Ko pops the berry in his mouth, and his cheeks fill. His eyes lighting up with joy. He unwraps his tail and hops straight up in the air. It's impressive how high he can jump such thin limbs. He lands back down on my chest, and I let out a soft cough as he squeaks with excitement. His full personality bursts to life. He squeaks and chirps, and bounces all over me. He investigates everything. Playing with my hair, tossing the ropes of the sled around, wrestling with the sleeves of the shirt tied around my waist. He tumbles out of the balled-up shirt and reaches out once more. I place another berry in his polite little hands, and it explodes in his mouth as he mushes down on it. The juices drip down his chin, and he bounces up and down with joy.

The Ko crawls over me and hops onto Remmy. He pats on Remmy's chest to no avail. He looks to me, and the moment of joy this little guy brought me is replaced with the sobering reminder of the situation. The Ko can sense my sorrow. He looks at Remmy and pushes on his cheek.

"Don't, buddy." I reach over and scoop the Ko up. His adorable eyes now match the pain of mine. As cute as they looked before, they look even sadder now. He lets out a dull whine and buries his head into my chest.

"Hey, it's ok buddy. He'll get better." I pet his head as I console the Ko. I'm not sure why, but it helps me too. His fur is soft and smooth, much cleaner than I expected. "He's tough, he'll come around." I can hear the shaky confidence in my voice. He will get better. I know it. He has to.

As much as I want to lay here and ignore my world falling apart around me, I have to get up and prepare to make camp for the night. The darkness has moved in quick. I pick myself up and prop the pack up against a tree stump. The Ko is still hanging on me, slung over my shoulder.

I dig through the pack; there's so much junk in here.

We need to do a better job of consolidating. Remmy has no right to complain about how heavy this thing is. He's such a packrat. I continue digging through the bag, tossing junk I feel is useless behind me. The Ko jumps off my back and scurries off into the darkness.

"Oh... bye, buddy..." The Ko disappears, and I'm left alone. I liked that little guy; I wish he would've stayed longer. Any distraction from the state of my incapacitated brother is welcomed right now.

I continue to rummage through the pack tossing more and

more stuff into the abyss. I finally find what I'm looking for. A thin metal tube about the size of my arm. I unscrew the cap and wipe residue from the lip of the hollow tube. Myrite Dust. Remmy and I stumbled across this stuff years ago, exploring a cavern along the edge of the Rift. It's been a lifesaver ever since.

No bugs in our hair. No creatures in our camps.

I clear a small area around the sled, removing twigs and branches and leaves, and pour a line of the dust in a wide circle around us. I grab the snaptorch, stand back, and light the dust. It ignites, bursting into a cloud of cyan blue, streaking in both directions. A surge of light blinds me for a moment as the cloud and smoke rise into the canopy. Once the initial smoke burns off, what's left is a bright glowing circle of cyan blue. Its neon shade illuminating a small perimeter around us. The light we needed to make camp for the night.

I settle in to get some rest, pulling Remmy's head into my lap and try my absolute hardest to not let my worrying keep me awake.

I wake when the Forest does. When the sounds of trees smacking together from the wind and the morning calls of animals create a symphony throughout the woods. I groan as I roll to my side. I need more sleep. The bright sun peeking through the treetops stings my eyes.

The myrite has burned off, and a circle of ash is left in its place. I climb to my feet, stretching out the knots in my neck. Sleeping on the Forest floor always leaves me feeling stiff. It's not as hot today, thank God. I may be able to reach shelter if it stays this mild.

I bend down to check on Remmy. Running my thumb across his cheek. He's still unconscious. His face is so still, so peaceful. I reach into the pack and pull out a nutrient pen. *Emergencies only*, Remmy always harps. I think this counts! I lift up his shirt and jab the pen into his stomach. Holding it there as the pen pours vital nutrients into his body. Hopefully, he doesn't have a reaction to it. They obviously weren't designed for human needs, so there's the potential for unintended consequences. A risk I have to take, he needs essentials.

I toss the empty pen to the side, no more hoarding. I check his vitals. Pulse, temperature, hydration. All things we've had to learn on the fly. Things we didn't think about before we left Archler House. We were angry kids, scorned by a world that hated us. Abandoned emotionally by the one family we had left. The Forest sounded like the perfect escape. But there was so much we had to learn.

We were supposed to be a team. The four of us. Emoss, Gwinn, Remmy, and I. We were happy. We always felt Emoss cared for Gwinn more, but we still had our place. When he was gone... Gwinn was too. The sister we had grown with, who we loved, who we would do anything for, had become a stranger. Remmy tried and tried to keep her close, but she wouldn't let him. I wasn't as accommodating. I was so angry with her. How could she just shut us out? We're family. Not blood, like Remmy and I, but family all the same. I would've done anything for her. And she acted like we didn't exist. As if Emoss's passing didn't hurt us just as much. As if the world didn't blame us just as much as they blamed her. I shake the thoughts of Gwinn and Emoss and Okotall and all the bad times and finish with Remmy.

I run my fingers through his wavy hair, pushing it back, inspecting the fading blue coloring, wondering if I need to reapply the myrite paste for him.

"I'll get you better, I promise." I kiss him on the forehead, praying his eyes peel open and that radiating smile shines across his face. But they don't. He just lays there.

As I stand to get the day started, I hear a small clank, like metal against metal. I turn, and just beyond the perimeter of the clearing is a small mound of junk. All the junk from our pack. Stacked neatly like a pyramid of garbage. I walk over to the pile, and as I approach, the Ko pops up from behind it. He's holding the nutrient pen I tossed earlier. He's reaching out as if to give it back to me.

"Hey, you're back?! Did you collect all this stuff for me?!" The Ko tosses the pen in the pile and picks up a broken hatchet handle and reaches it up in the air.

"No thanks, bud, I don't need that." He puts it down and grabs another piece of junk, displaying it proudly. I tell him no again, and he finds another piece. I keep telling him no until he's dug through halfway through the pile.

"I don't need any of this stuff. Thank you, though. Thanks for keeping me company last night too, little buddy. But I gotta get going." I smile at the Ko, pet him on the head, and start off in the other direction.

The Ko frowns and squeaks. As much as I'd love to stay

and play and forget about all my responsibilities, Remmy's condition will get worse by the hour. I need to move.

The Ko follows behind, matching my pace. I search around, but there doesn't seem to be any other Ko nearby? Usually, they travel in packs.

"Where are your friends, bud?" The Forest is calm this morning. The canopy isn't its lively self. This little guy is alone. Just like we are. I look down at the Ko as it follows and see the same look on his face that I've seen from Remmy a thousand times. He just wants a home. I reach into the pack and grab another Sweetberry and hand it to him.

"Alright, you can come with us." The Ko pops the berry in his mouth and hops onto the sled, wrapping his tail around the front bar as he perches himself onto it. The Ko licks the sticky juice from his fingers, and together we head deeper in the woods.

The Ko has actually been quite helpful. He walks in front now, hopping along, grabbing rocks and clumps of twigs on the path and tossing them to the side so the sled can glide smoothly. We chased the Tyko so deep into the Forest the landscape is hard to navigate. I don't recognize it as much. I feel like we've been walking in the wrong direction; we should've been there by now.

I stop to get a sip of water. Sweat beads across my forehead. I take a pull from the canteen and pull out a map Remmy and I have sketched over the years. A small legend in the bottom right corner marks shelters we have, access to water, known merchant routes, Gaz settlements, everything we've come across in our time in the Forest. It's hard to tell where exactly we are, though, because we wandered into uncharted territory. And with everything that happened, we didn't have a chance to draw in the path we took or landmarks we've seen. I scan the map and the surroundings trying to get my bearings.

The Ko crawls up my body and wraps his way around my shoulders. He stares down at the map with me.

"Got any idea where we are, pal?" The Ko points. He touches just on the outside of the map, beyond where we've drawn. There's nothing there. It would be the northern ridge of Berban. We've never ventured that far north, too many Gaz patrols.

"No, bud, we're somewhere over here." I point to an area

farther west. Closer to the Rift. The Ko knocks my hand out of the way and points to the same spot again. "Don't smack my hand, mister. No wonder you're lost." I fold the map back up and put it away.

We walk until my feet are numb.

Maybe it only seems this way because I'm dragging the sled, but we've haven't made much progress. I've at least figured out where we are, but the nearest abandoned war outpost is still too far away to make it before dark.

About an hour back, I passed a perfect place to hunker down for the night. Good sightlines, fewer trees so the moons would help light the area. I won't find a better spot to rest. That's become obvious. But I was so desperate to get Remmy to safety, I pushed right past it.

Now, as the night pulls its dark sheet over the world, I'll have to make due in a rough patch of dirt, surrounded by head-high chyllo bushes.

I follow the same steps I did before. Ready the sled, pour a circle of myrite, ignite it, and lay back against Remmy. This time though, I have company.

The Ko wedges his way in between Remmy and I. It feels better to have him here. Someone to help me keep my mind off Remmy. But tonight, I do have to think about him. I have to start formulating a plan. He has to wake up soon. Or I have to find a way to wake him up. I don't have enough nutrient pens to keep him going like this.

I pull a large book from our pack. An outdated medic manual we found at an abandoned outpost near the border of Berban and Okotall. Just like the one we're heading to. Old outposts like these are scattered all over the edges of Berban, hollow ghosts of building haunting the province. A bitter reminder of war and chaos. When we first discovered one, we couldn't believe how well stocked it was. A fossilized building, frozen in time. Plates and utensils lay at spots on long tables in dining areas. Like men just stood up in the middle of their meals and left. Their medbays still flush with drugs and gauze and tools and all sorts of medicine of the time. The dorm's bunks, all unmade messes, some even left their clothes. These men couldn't have left quicker. The only thing they took with them; their weapons.

For scavengers like us, it was paradise. We found more supplies in that one trip that we did in months. We still use some of it today. Whenever we need to restock, we set out to find a new one we haven't raided. We even turned one in a shelter. One so hidden, we questioned who would even know about it. It was the smallest one we found, the worst stocked, and the poorest made. But we felt confident nobody would ever be back to check on it.

It's underneath a waterfall for damn sake.

I thumb through the manual, searching for answers. Remmy has marked this thing through and through, making notes of Valenian's early understanding of human biology. It all looks foreign to me. If the roles were reversed, he'd know exactly how to decipher this jargon and treat me immediately. But as it stands, this manual is more useful to me as a pillow than an answer to my Remmy situation.

I fold the book closed. If I ever do find those answers, it won't be tonight.

Resting plump in the night sky, the moons hum their soft glow. The sky freckled with stars. My stomach growls, startling the Ko, who is curled up on my chest. It makes me realize I haven't eaten anything all day. The piece of Luta meat I pull from our pack looks like the human liver diagram I saw in the medic manual. It's a greyish blob sealed in a pouch.

I was hoping to sell everything we claimed from that hunt, but my stomach has other ideas. My snaptorch sears the meat giving it a more appetizing color, and I chew down into the tender muscle. The meat is delicious. I wish Remmy could taste it. We haven't had a delicacy like this in some time. I tear off a small piece and present it to the Ko. He sniffs it and turns it down. Good, I didn't really want to give him a piece anyway! I lay there, savoring my meal, petting the Ko, and mapping out my treatment options for Remmy when I hear a loud crack on the edge of the darkness...

I pop to my feet and grab Remmy's rifle. The Ko jumps to attention as well. Another crack behind me, like the breaking of tree limbs. I spin to face it. The chyllo bushes blocking the myrite from illuminating the area. Something moves in the darkness beyond them. Something big. Moving with weight and power. Stalking me. I can feel eyes scouring over me. A predator lurking in the blackness. Waiting to strike. The Ko shrieks and tugs on my pant leg. Another crack. The other side this time. There's more than one. I sense them circling me.

My gun is wedged into my shoulder, ready to fire. I scan the Forest, trying desperately to see into the night. My finger is primed on the trigger. The bolt loaded. My eyes dart. Ears twitching at every sound the Forest makes. Another crack snaps behind me. I spin and fire a round into the darkness. The recoil rocks against my shoulder. I stumble to absorb it. The gunshot drums against my ears. The pain, unbearable. I had forgotten how damaged they were from the Sonostick.

The ringing in my ears screams at me. Did my brain rupture? Disoriented and deafened, I think I hear another crack, but can't be sure. Before I can regroup, a splitting pain shatters across my back. I'm launched forward. Pain jolting up my spine. I try to move, but my body screams at me to stop. My cheek is throbbing from landing on a stump. Fingers bent horribly into the dirt. I manage to roll to my side. The myrite dust out. Darkness swallowing me whole. I reach over and feel the hard bottom of the sled. My hand probes with panic.

"Remmy?... Remmy?..." My hand scours the sled, but he's gone. "REMMY?!" I wheeze as I try to yell. My head still throbs. "REMMY?!" I pat around the area in desperation. The ringing in my ears dies down, and another crack taunts me from the blackness. I freeze in place. Heartbeat pounding in my throat. My eyes are starting to adjust, but I'm looking down at the ground and don't dare move. I can barely see the sled now. He's gone! The Forest seems frozen. Suspended in time. I stay there on my hands and knees, trying to hide in plain sight. The rifle is strewn on the ground just beyond my reach. I have to try to get to it. I muster my courage and roll.

I grab the rifle. My adrenaline skyrockets. I flip onto my back and cock the bolt, readying the gun against my shoulder. The barrel spears out from my body, one eye aimed down sight, just as I've watched Remmy do a million times. I pull the rifle left and right. Nothing. My heart strains to pump harder. Back to the left again. Nothing.

Time cackles at me as I lay on my back, waiting to be swarmed by an invisible enemy.

Puke creeps it way up my throat.

I hear another crack.

Then all I feel is unthinkable force yanking me by the ankle.

Dragging me.

Weeds and plants slash at my helpless body.

I dig my nails into the soil.

It's no use.

I scream.

The ivory horns of a behemoth warrior bounce in my vision.

The rifle is engulfed by the darkness as I speed away.

I grasp at anything I can until I take hold of thick plant roots and jolt to an abrupt stop. The massive silhouette that drags me halts, and as he cocks his head back, crystal blue eyes strike against the moonlight.

There can be no mistake who has me...

The Gaz.

12

VICTOR BELLS

Nightmares

My fist slams into the pad. Over and over and over. With every ounce of energy I have. Faster and harder. Faster and harder. My knuckles pop as my punches land, one after another. A blind trance of endorphins works my limbs. A maniacal puppeteer pulling at my strings with twisted intent. The anger spills from me. I don't know if I'm breathing. If I've been transported into some other realm, where the spawn of my kind erupt from eggs like psychotic jack-in-the-boxes. I feel outside my body, spectating the birth of a lunatic, as he wails upon a practice dummy with reckless abandon. I watch Dansro call out to him, but the man is gone. Devoured from within by the dormant rage that has lurked in the shadows until now. I reach out to stop him, but he can't hear me either. His pace never slows. Uncontrollable. A group of men try to pull him off, but he swats them away like the insignificant peons they are. Dansro tackles him. The man lets out a bone-chilling scream. It terrifies Dansro. It terrifies me too. Like a screech from the pits of hell. He squeezes Dansro by the neck and holds him in the air. His eyes meet mine. I howl at him to stop. Plead. Demand. Beg. He squeezes harder as Dansro squirms desperately, life seeping from his corpse. I lunge at the fiend, but my feet are rooted in place. I can only watch. Helpless. He squeezes and squeezes until Dansro melts to the floor, and I cry out in agony! The man walks over to me, lording above, as I lay distraught among the wreckage of my father. He gazes down on me in disgust. When I look up, I realize I'm staring at myself. Into my own eyes. Spiteful. Wicked. Evil eyes. His fist cocks back and launches at me. All I can do is cover my face and cry out *HADES!*

"Hades?..." I feel a touch on my shoulder and jolt awake. I nearly fall off the bench. I look around, and I'm back in the gym where Fargo dropped me off, a young Oltish boy stands in front of me. My heart pounds, sweat-drenched through my shirt. "Sir..." The young boy gazes at me with star-struck bewilderment. I look back at him with stone eyed confusion. "Dansro said it was ok to ask for an autograph." I swallow hard as I come to, rubbing my eyes. Dansro! He's leaned against a wall across the gym, speaking with a group of young Warlord trainees. Not strangled to death by my own hands. He glances over at me. Something about my expression must concern him because he dismisses the trainees and makes his way toward me.

I sign for the young boy, and he darts off in delight, boasting to his friends.

"What's gotten into you, kid?" Dansro lifts an eyebrow at me, his posture, relaxed and carefree. A part of me is still rattled. Still coming down from the terror of the dream.

"Just a bad dream, no worries," I say deflecting.

"They say dreams are a window into our soul." Dansro spouts, attempting to sound philosophical.

"And who exactly are *they?*" I ask.

"You know... they. Them. The wise. People much smarter than you or me."

I roll my eyes and reach out my hand.

"Ah, yes, how could I have forgotten about *them? They* are truly brilliant. My apologies." I rub my hand along the back of his neck after he hoists me up. "Let's get to work o wise one."

I wipe the dream from my mind, and for the next two hours, we train. Dansro runs me through drill after drill. Conditioning, strength, dexterity, accuracy, hand to hand combat, stamina, the works. The other members of the gym flock to my workout. Watch in appreciation. Some of the more experienced Warlords keep to themselves, either jealously or indifference keeps them at arm's length. They watch and see Hades work. See him strike against practice dummies. Watch him prepare. But what they truly witness is me. They watch *me* prepare for when my body runs on autopilot. Preparing my instincts and my reactions for when I no longer control them. For when Hades takes over, and all hell breaks loose. He'd be nothing without my discipline and precision.

I'm nearly done with my workout when I hear a weaselly voice squawking from across the gym. Silva walks through the door with a band of idiots by his side. A gang of imbeciles.

"Well, what a treat. Hades and Dansro. Everyone's favorite father-son duo. We walk upon haloed ground gents." Silva curtsies as his cronies laugh.

"Silva... *Surgs*... nice of you all to join us today. If you're looking for lessons, check the sign-up sheet on the counter, I think I should have an opening after a couple of these pups." I point down to the young Oltish boy and his friends, as they snicker at Silva.

"Tempting, but I've found a mentor." As Silva finishes, a colossal man lumbers in through the door. Tattoos of heaven and hell streak down each of his four arms. His jet-black hair woven into a thick braid splits his back. His jaw as square as physically possible. It's unmistakable who he is. I can't believe it. Pyra the Immortal. My idol. My childhood hero. The greatest warlord to ever live.

The entire gym stares in disbelief. No one has seen Pyra in years. Many were convinced he was dead. A death in the Arena hasn't happened in decades, but rumors swirled that Pyra had been killed, and they were keeping it quiet. The last anyone saw of him, he was mangled beyond recognition. His suit nearly destroyed underneath the boot of Hades. The day the Arena stood still, and the day Hades and I skyrocketed to stardom. The best and worst day of my life. I knew he wasn't dead. He couldn't be. I always held out hope. I couldn't live with myself if he were.

I was younger then. Emotional. Undisciplined. Raw. It was the day Hades was born. I can replay the moment in my head as clear as if it happened yesterday. I could feel him spread through me like a virus. Taking control. And before I could make sense of anything, he was in.

I rub the scar that streaks just above my hip bone as I recall that moment from the Arena so many years ago.

Pyra and I were the last two standing. The living legend, flawless in his mechanics. Unmatched in his technique. Unparalleled in his violence. And a brash kid, nothing but reckless aggression and arrogance. Our suits sang out harsh notes of screeching metal as we clashed together. Weapons spewing their ill intentions. A crowd roaring with excitement.

We fought upon the perch of a tower. Dozens of meters

high, a death trap of detonated debris and jagged shrapnel eagerly awaiting us on the battlefield floor.

Blow for blow we went, the master wearing me down. I made a desperate play. Unleashing my shield pulse too soon, just as the rookie berserker did at the end of my last match. Pyra countered in an instant and rifled a kick into my back, launching me from the tower.

Fifty meters I plummeted.

Agony is the only word to describe what followed.

Whiplash shattered my nose against my visor as I'm impaled on a jutting spoke of a destroyed building foundation.

Pain, unlike anything I've ever experienced, consumed my mind. Unleashing something deep within me. *Someone* deep within me.

I was always an angry kid, intense, but this was something different. This was poisonous. Wicked. Profound hatred. Unfiltered Rage. I could do nothing to control it.

The pain flooded every circuit in my brain until all sensation in my body shut off. It was gone. In a flash, vanished. But so did any semblance of control I had over my body.

Hades slid our torso off the pipe and climbed to our feet, an angry machine of death. Unfazed by our mangled septum and gaping puncture wound. Pyra launched from the tower to finish the job, but he didn't realize he no longer fought me... He was fighting a demon.

I had to watch as Hades dismantled my idol. The hole in my side gushing blood the entire time. He destroyed everything Pyra was. It was mortifying. I loved this man. Idolized him. Respected him more than anyone I'd ever known. And Hades beat him within an inch of his life. There was no honor in it. No dignity. Without remorse. It was the day I received the Warlord name Hades. Somewhere the slogan, *Only the Devil can kill the Immortal,* was created, and before my next fight, the world had already branded me Hades. The Devil of Earth. I hated it, but there was no going back. Hades and I were forever one.

"Victor." Pyra's voice has a velvet smoothness to it. A deep reverb that would intimidate the real devil himself. As he comes closer, I can see a jagged scar across his chest that disappears under his deep collar. I don't know if he had that before or not. His gaze rips through me. It's not violent or spiteful on its surface, but something smolders behind his eyes. I can feel it.

"Pyra." I nod, trying to be as respectful as possible.

"Pyra was a fighter. I'm Rozza." He breaks eye contact with me and glances around the gym, speaking to me out the side of his mouth.

"You'll always be a fighter to me, Pyra," I say with reverence. I hope it's taken that way.

"Well, he still would be if it wasn't for your psychotic friend." Silva quips. Rage jolts through me. The balls on this twerp. Has some new muscle and thinks he can speak to me this way? Pyra warns Silva with a sharp glance, signaling him to mind his tongue. Thankfully no one seems to have understood the insult. Probably still distracted by the legend in their presence.

"Very well, call me what you wish," Pyra says. "You've done quite well for yourself, Victor. Congratulations." I can't get a read on him. Is he purposefully calling me Victor instead of Hades? His tone seems dismissive but direct simultaneously. I can't believe I'm actually upset someone didn't refer to me as Hades. It seems like he's insulting me somehow, but I'm not quite sure.

"Thank you. I've been fortunate. It's been a good run." Silva seems to balk when I say it.

"Where's the cocky asshole I'm used to, Vic? Don't let this act fool you people, the real Hades is no honorable saint." Silva yaps like the pathetic gremlin he is.

"I save my humility for those I respect. And a manipulative, honor-less vulture-like you, doesn't make that list." I wish I could knock the teeth out the back of his head.

"Ohhh, you respect Rozza? Got it. Couldn't you guys really feel that admiration in the Arena when he was crushing Rozza's suit into his skull?" Silva smirks with a delusional sense of accomplishment. Silva is brash, but I didn't think he was stupid. In a flash, Pyra rifles a jab into Silva's ribs. So incredibly fast. He may have quit fighting, but he hasn't lost a step. Silva whimpers like a spanked dog.

"Remember who you speak of, child." Pyra's face never leaves its stern disposition. He's a man stuck in time. The way he speaks, the way he carries himself. It's from an era before this. Before Champion Tours, and raucous parties, and the celebrification of the Arena. Before people like Fargo saw an opportunity to monetize it, profit from it, and achieve fame from it. It was pure. A time when the only prize for a Warlord was the glory of victory. They were men of honor. Revered.

Stone cold. Not like they are today. Warlords are celebrities now. Sex symbols. Icons. Those men were legends. Deities. No one dared to aspire to be them, because who aspires to be God? It was a time I was better suited for.

"We must be on our way." Pyra nods to me and leads Silva and his band of goons to a far corner of the gym.

I watch as they walk off, and the crowd gathered around us breaks up and scatters to their own areas. How could Pyra train Silva? The man is a despicable coward. He stands for the exact opposite of everything that Pyra is. Was. The thoughts cloud my mind.

Dansro and I go to finish the last of my drills, but I can't stop thinking about it. I peek over in the corner and watch them work as I do my exercises. Silva has no appreciation for the man he speaks with. But as much as I hate him, he has talent. I watch him soak up Pyra's teachings like a sponge and execute with precision. I get too distracted, and a glove racks my jaw, and I spill to the floor.

"Do not let your dinner rot thinking about the dessert of another's." Dansro reaches his gloved hand out to pick me up off the floor.

"What?" I grab his hand and hoist myself up. "That doesn't even make sense." His attempts at proverbs make me groan.

"Ok how about this, pay attention, and you won't let an old man punch you in the face again? How's that? Direct enough for ya?" Dansro puts his gloves in front of his face and throws another soft punch my way. I slap it away and smile.

"Yea, don't get used to that old man." I throw a heavy combo of punches into his body, and he submits.

"Ok, ok, ok. Stop!" Dansro coughs and moans as he holds his side. He gives me a bewildered look. "Shit." I just smile. "That's enough for today, let's call it."

Dansro throws a towel at me and climbs out of the ring. I feel bad. I shouldn't take Dansro for granted. He was a phenomenal Warlord, a great teacher, and a caring father. But he's too sweet to be insulted by my infatuation with Pyra. The true definition of a poetic warrior.

I climb out of the ring as well and glance in the corner one last time. Pyra's eyes meet mine, and I still can't solve his look. He looks at me with force, like a man staring at the bane of his existence. Like he'd want nothing more than to return the thrashing I gave to him. But he also looks at me with respect. With empathy. As if he understands what happened. As if he can see into my soul and understands I had no control over what I was doing. He breaks away, and so do I.

The hot water of the shower soothes my aching muscles. I stay under the stream for longer than I need to. Trying to clear my head of everything that happened today. Silva has finished showering as well. No surprise, he didn't work out nearly as long as I did. He tries to start with me again, but I've had enough of him for the day; I just ignore his blabbering. He follows me from the cleansing room and out the door, chirping the entire time. I walk outside and use my Comm to signal for a transport.

"Using transports, Victor? You're pathetic. What good is being filthy rich if you don't know how to spend it?" Silva crows. As he does, a luxury *Stretcher* approaches from the sky and settles just in front of the building. A rig that would make even Fargo jealous. The long bay door against its side hisses as it creaks open. "Now, this is how to travel in style, Vic." Silva displays his hands, asking me to soak in the vehicle with him. Delusional as always.

"You got safety seats for all your kids here?" I mock as I point to his posse. A couple buck at me as they walk by and pile into the Stretcher. Fake tough guys.

"See ya around, Vic." Silva winks at me and walks over to the rig. The last two seats face out toward me. An absolutely stunning red-headed Brushu woman is in the seat next to his, putting an arm around him as he plops down. She looks mildly familiar, but I can't place her. Then again, the herd of women Fargo parades through our house on a nightly basis makes it impossible to know for sure.

Wealth is the only thing a woman that beautiful could find appealing about Silva. He leers at me and mockingly waves as the door closes, and they speed off.

That rat couldn't leave soon enough.

When my transport arrives, I give the pilot Leo's address and head back into the city as I close my eyes to decompress.

I open my comm and call Miku.

My world shines when I hear her voice.

"Hello, handsome!" She says.

"I am quite handsome, aren't I?" I ask, smiling. My eyes are still closed, head resting on the window as the whooshing sound of buildings passing by hypnotizes me.

"Oh, Fargo, I'm sorry, I thought Victor was calling," She jokes.

"Ouch." I chuckle. "What are you doing?"

"Just finishing up at the rally?" She answers, her flowery tone soothing my swarming headache.

"Rally?"

"Ya know, the donation drive for the cure? Rally for the Rotting... I told you about it."

"Oh, yea. I remember. Help find the cure so the High Council will release Tanya from Su Hoz. It's a sweet gesture Mi."

"And saving countless lives... but yes, it'll hopefully help her."

I sit in silence for a moment. Almost forgetting where I am.

"What's going on, Vic?"

Her question snaps me back.

"What do you mean?"

"Something's wrong... I can always tell." She's right. I can't hide things from her.

"Just a lot going on."

"You mean with what happened between Fargo and those thugs at the party?"

"That's part of it. I know he's in some kind of trouble, but he insists he isn't. I don't know what to do with him sometimes." I don't really want to vomit my entire brain's stew of worries on her, but the words won't stop flowing out. "And you'll never believe who came into the gym today... a ghost. Pyra the fucking Immortal. He's training Silva now."

"*Pyra?*" She asks in disbelief. "Did you all speak?"

"Briefly... and now I can't shake the feeling that they're planning something." Why else would Pyra be back? And training that vermin no less. He has to be plotting some type of revenge against me.

The thought makes Hades scratch at the back of my mind.

"I'm sure you're just being paranoid," Miku says, trying to be reassuring, but it's not working.

Hades grows stronger as I think of him. Growing angry at the prospect of Pyra trying to sully my record out of spite. And using Silva of all people to do so. I slam the inside of the door with the side of my fist. It startles the transport pilot.

"Hey, I need to go," I say, hurrying off the comm so I don't do anything to upset her. "I'll see you at Leo's."

"Wait, Vic..." The comm signal abruptly dies, and I shove it into my pocket. Anger bubbling in my stomach. If they want to steal my glory, it'll have to be over my dead, lifeless body.

13

FARGO SHEPPERD

Pandora's Box

The city slowly deteriorates the farther north I go. Fractures into scattered pieces of infrastructure until you reach the Valley. Wedged into the *Elkowa Valley,* on the border of Dwaul Fir and Su Hoz, sits a crown jewel of squalor. The Valley should be its own province. There is no place like it. A microcosm of unique definition. A place of filth and grime and rust and poverty. A place of crime. A place clinging to a life before this one. A lawless, ruthless time, where a man with a gun could be anything he wanted. A time before an alien craft landing on the planet sparked an explosion of technological growth. When the skies weren't filled with flying vehicles and slidewalks didn't carry people across the city. The Valley is harsh and unforgiving. And the only place to carry out my business.

My hauler hovers to its landing, squeezing its way between the rickety buildings and onto the narrow street. The people below scatter like cockroaches under an old trash bag. I power down, and as the roar of my engines die, the melody of the Valley is born.

Many would find it unpleasant, but these are my people.

Scrappers. Fighters. A people devastated by the Rotting. People who have clawed for every inch of ground they have. Not the friendliest kind, but undeniably real.

I open the door and peel out of the hauler and onto the busy street. Shit, it's cold.

"The fuck out of the way!" A man darts by me in a hurry, shoving me to the side and chased by a heavyset repo man who struggles to keep up. The two shoot by me and blend into the frenzy of motion on the street.

"Gettin' trampled down there?" Cyto yells out from a second-story window. I glance up to find him. "Careful slick, between the shiny new hauler and the amount of grease in your hair, someone might think you're from Groga!" I flip him off and open the trunk. He mumbles something to himself and closes the window. Crotchety old hag.

I grab my pistols, their holsters, and a jacket from the back and close the trunk. The holster vest fits snugly over my shoulders, and the pistols clamp down into their magnetic slots. Once I have the jacket on, I make my way into the building, hand hovering just above my weapons. I love these people, but I'm not naïve.

I walk through the abandoned first floor of the building. Squatters have carved out their own corners of the ransacked floor, making the decommissioned drug store look like a refugee shelter. I step over entire lives on my way to the staircase. Any sympathy for these people gone. Now I just see opportunity. Exploitable, vulnerable vagrants who want nothing more than to spend their last earned *Soft* on Venom. A reliably dependent client base. Not downtrodden hardworking Valenians who've just been dealt a bad hand. These are the truly delinquent. They don't care about their lives, so why should I? Venom's not addictive, it's not habit-forming, it's purely an escape. I feel no guilt in providing them a portal to a better life.

The staircase moans under my boots. I'd fix it, but it would seem out of place considering how the rest of the first floor looks. And I'd prefer to not draw unnecessary attention. In the hall at the top of the stairs, a hybrid man's corpse decomposes from the Rotting. Spotted with gaping holes like parts of his body were simply deleted. The smell is putrid. The scent of life literally dissolving away, unbearable. I don't need to fix the stairs, but this has to go...

The smell of the corpse only disappears after I step into a small white room at the end of the hall. Inside, it's only an arm's length wide. A thin metal pipe with the diameter of a pen comes out of the ceiling and stops just before my mouth.

"Green and Gone." I speak clearly and emphatically into the microphone. A door outlines itself from within the wall in front of me as it hisses and clicks. The microphone darts back into the ceiling, and I proceed through the door and into my headquarters.

Cyto is waddling around like a madman.

My base of operations is a thing of beauty. Has to be the most luxurious place in the Valley. If it wasn't wedged down in between these mountains where the sun barely breaks through, I'd almost consider living here. But there's nothing quite like a Grogan sunrise.... Or Grogan women. So, I stash crazy Cyto here and make him do my bidding in my absence.

Once through the security door, the room blossoms into a massive space. It takes up the entire blueprint of the building. Consuming the remaining three floors. There's no ceiling until the roof, which has a crystal-clear window in the shape of a pentagon in its center. At exactly midday, the sun shines right through it and projects a gorgeous kaleidoscope onto the floor. An excessive touch, but I am a man of nothing, if not excess.

The room is a command center. The heart of my well-oiled machine. On the far wall is a dataplate that stretches the entire length of the wall. It shows everything from client lists to shipping routes, to acquisition priorities, to outstanding credits. Every logistical aspect of my black-market dealings. Venom is just the tip of the iceberg, albeit the most profitable. I buy it from the Vipers, the people buy it from me, your basic commodity economy. But as much as I love profits, pushing Venom can be boring. My thirst for extravagance has pivoted my business model over the years. I now consider myself more of an... exotic appropriator than an apothecary. When people rich or poor, usually rich (but I don't discriminate), require assets *difficult* to obtain, they enlist my services. The results have been far more gratifying.

"Slick! How are ya?" Cyto gestures toward me in passing. The man is always on the go. "What you got for me today?"

"We need to talk..." I raise my eyebrows at Cyto as I drape my jacket over a hanger that then automatically slides back into the wall. "It's not good..." I sit down at the bar and look over a hand-written ledger of past exchanges. Cyto's work. He's an old soul. Like's to write things down. My bodyguard Geeva is balled up on a couch, picking at her nails. "Hey make yourself useful and pour me a drink. I don't pay you to sit around and look pretty."

Geeva barely acknowledges.

"You don't pay me at all..." She finally glances up.

"Exactly. I don't pay you because you sit around all day doing nothing!" I reach over and grab a bottle of haze. The cloudy liquid burns as it goes down. I walk past Geeva and toss her feet off the chair. "And get your feet off the furniture." Geeva glares. She thinks she hates me. Understandably so, but I feel the statute of limitations should be up by now!

"What is it we need to talk about, slick?" Cyto shuffles over from putting away some items into specifically marked containers. He's tough on the eyes. A hybrid. Born to be an outcast. Half Heplin, half Reyllion. Two races that should never breed. Short like a Reyllion, yet thin like a Heplin. He looks like half a man. His hair is wiry and wild and streaked with different colors. His eyes are beady little things tucked too deep into his big round Reyllion head. He's all the wrong parts of two already ugly races. But the man is a firecracker. Fearless. Old school. Always looking for an edge. And has a huge heart. Despite Victor's apprehension, the man wants me to thrive.

"I was robbed." I take another pull of my drink as I replay the night in my head. "A few days back."

"A few days?! Why the hell it take you so long to tell me?" Cyto haggles.

"Shit Geeva was there, she could've told you," I say. Cyto shoots a disapproving look to his daughter. "Speaking of... where the hell were you when the Vipers showed up? Do you understand what a *bodyguard* is supposed to do?"

Geeva purrs in annoyance.

"You put me on drunken asshole duty... remember?" A rebuttal forms on my lips, but I know she's right, so I just ignore her and turn my attention back to Cyto.

"I didn't say anything right away because I was doing some recon on my own. I *am* quite capable without your expertise."

"Hog shit! You just didn't want to tell me." Cyto leans back in his chair, a probing expression across his face. "What happened? What they take?"

I pull the card Zina gave me from my pants pocket and slide it across the table.

"... Everything from the wall safe. Some cash, maybe a dozen vials of Venom, some other useless shit I had in there. But the pressing issue is the case from the Vipers. Don't even think they had any clue what it was." I shake my head thinking about it. "It looked legit too. Had High Council seals all over it. I'm talking max security type indications. No clue where they got it from." What a shit show... I want to know what her plan would have been, had Victor not knocked me out? Was she going to try to seduce me? Try to sneak out in the middle of the night with the score? How did she expect to get in the safe? The more I think about it, the more amateur it sounds. And she has the nerve to leave a card mocking me like she's some mastermind. The whole situation has me riled up.

"Shit... What the hell happened? How did she get in your safe?" Cyto is more annoyed that I let myself get robbed than he is at the theft itself.

"Does it matter? The shit's gone. How it happened is irrelevant." I try to avoid the subject.

"So basically, you did something stupid?" Geeva chimes in.

"This conversation doesn't concern you."

"Sure as hell does! Because when Deterro and the Vipers come kicking our door down for reimbursement, I'm gonna be the one who pays for it. They'll treat me like a damn pincushion, stickin' shit everywhere."

Cyto is appalled with the analogy.

"For fuck's sake, Geeva..."

"What?"

She has a point. Deterro is as callous as anyone I've ever met. If I can't get the case back, he and his entire organization will be crawling down my neck. He wouldn't blink an eye tearing down Geeva to get to me. The Vipers don't accept any excuse for a missed payment.

As head elder for the Vipers, Deterro and his family have plagued the Valley for generations, and their vice grip on the city grows tighter every day. Years ago, they began manufacturing a new type of drug in a pharmaceutical plant they extorted. It wouldn't travel through the blood; it traveled through the command centers of the body. The nerves of the Heplins, Brushu, and Reyllions. The worttle glands of Olts. Whatever the hell Surgs are made out of, it fucked with those too... It was the most intense high ever created. The drug on the street had a lot of names before the Redemption crashed. But once it did and knowledge of Earth became more prevalent, people started describing the drug as snake's Venom. And Deterro's family quickly became known as the Vipers. Extremely deadly beasts that hide in the weeds and strike with total force every time. The match was uncanny.

"She's right, slick. You know she is." Cyto is still inspecting the card. "I know of the group. Low level. Nothing too crazy, it doesn't seem. Some bookkeeping, rig theft, note fraud. Shouldn't be a problem getting the Bytrol back." Cyto tosses the card down, his concern from before seems diffused.

"What the hell is Bytrol?" Geeva picks up the card and inspects it herself.

"Doesn't even matter. What they took isn't the issue. The issue is getting it back to Deterro."

"I know, I was just curious. You can never just answer a question." She scoffs in frustration with me.

"Fine. Bytrol is... I don't know how to describe it... it's a bit of myth, honestly. We're not even sure if it's real."

"Care to elaborate? That's not an answer smart ass," Geeva says, growing more annoyed.

"I'm getting there, ya Surg!" She could use a pull of this haze, she's wound so tight. "Anyway, there was a rumor swirling around the black-market channels that the High Council had developed an experimental serum to extend the life of Trakstull and the other aging Ancients. Supposedly, this thing can morph to any genetic code and be fully programmable. So, obviously, that shit would be a game-changer... Problem is, no one has confirmed its existence."

"Ok, so why exactly do we have it then?" Geeva asks.

"Had..." Cyto corrects. Crusty old bastard.

"The Vipers have too much heat on them to have it validated. Especially if they actually did grab it from a High Council lab somehow. We can fly under the radar, get it tested, then send the case and the results back to Deterro, getting a MASSIVE payday in return." I plug the top back into the bottle of haze and rack it back on the shelf. "Happy now, cupcake?" My tone is a bit harsh, and Geeva widens her eyes at me. A little too strong, understood.

"And because it's so hard to come by, we can't just pay the Vipers if they don't get it back. It's priceless." Cyto clarifies.

"Yea, that part was pretty obvious. I'm not an idiot." Geeva scans back over the card from Zina. "Who is Z? The girl who pulled one over on you, I assume?" She points to the note on the back of the card, trying to hide her jealousy.

"I wouldn't say she pulled one over on me... She capitalized on a rare moment of weakness. She said her name was Zina." The more we talk about it, the more disgusted I get with myself for letting my guard down, but I'm sure as hell not going to admit that to her.

"Women are a lot like Venom, slick. One moment they make you feel on top of the world, the next it feels like you got hit by a rig!" Cyto snorts, his words trail off, and he grumbles to himself again, something about a woman and the devil. Cyto pulls a huge smokewrap from his breast pocket and lights it. It's funny watching him try to get his tiny mouth around it. He inhales and coughs out a thick plume of smoke. "Geeva here, is the only woman I trust. And even she's starting to stretch that loyalty thin." Cyto grins and sinks down deep into the chair. Geeva throws the card at him, and they laugh.

"I'm sure women are just devastated by your lack of interest in them," She jokes.

Cyto's confidence doesn't do much to wain my anxiety, though.

"Cyto seriously. I need you to get whatever info you can on Zina and her group. And I need you to do it quick. I can stall for a little, but if Deterro catches wind that the Bytrol went missing, we're all in some serious shit!" I plead with him. I worry my message isn't getting received, though. He fusses with me and shoos me off.

"Don't tell me how to do my job, slick." He wrestles his way out of the chair and hobbles over to a table littered with crates. "I'll do my job, in the meantime, you two still got runs to make." Cyto hauls over a crate as big as he is, fighting to keep his balance. He drops it on the floor at my feet, and the merchandise inside rattles about.

"Easy ya, old toad!" I kneel down to check to make sure nothing is broken.

"Ah, its fine. Nothing fragile in there. A couple high clearance ID's badges, a few Savron organs for some rich Olt bastard, some new microchip for encrypted dataplates, and oh yeah.... No Bytrol!" Cyto shoots me an agitated look as he turns around and climbs the stairs to a storage locker.

"You better watch your tone, ya little geriatric shit." I eyeball him as he hobbles along. I continue to take inventory as Cyto returns with a rusty metal cart. "What the hell is this?"

"What do you think it is? You gonna carry that massive crate around town all day? Put the shit in here and wheel it around." Cyto's face is matter of fact. I glance at Geeva, and she looks away.

"What happened to the Floater?..." I ask.

No one answers. I wait for a moment, but neither want to look straight at me.

"Are you kidding me? Did you two let another one get stolen?! Why the hell do I even pay for all these nice things?" Unbelievable. "It attaches to your belt for God's sake! How could you possibly lose it?"

The two don't answer again. Cyto's face doesn't lose its disposition, but he looks at Geeva.

"Fargo... you know Effie doesn't allow the Floater in her shop." Geeva tries to reason with me.

"You left it outside to get some fucking noodles?!" I ask, just baffled.

"Hey you let the Bytrol get stolen!"

"Not. The same. Thing... I didn't leave it sitting outside tied up to a light pole. Someone broke into my safe."

Geeva tries to find an excuse but can't.

"I'm tellin' ya, slick. Women, ya can't trust 'em." Cyto shakes his head in disappointment.

"Hey you're not innocent either. Where were you during this noodle pitstop?" I fold my arms and interrogate Cyto now.

"I'm an old man, slick. Sometimes old men need a nap. She was just going right down the street." Cyto stares back with conviction in his response.

"You're not that old..." I take a deep breath. It's a miracle I'm as successful as I am.

"My God. Let's go." I dump the goods into the cart and bark orders. "Noodle bitch you're with me. Senior Citizen, you stay here and find me that info on Zina." I roll my eyes. Hopefully, by the time we knock these runs out, Cyto will have some details for us. If not... everyone around me will probably have a bounty on their head.

Geeva and I head out the door for the day, an anxious knot twisting in my stomach, as I yell back to Cyto. "And no fucking naps!"

14

LEO

ABERNATHY

Blind Love

The crew is all in their usual spots when I walk through the door of our living space, filthy and exhausted. My mind still reeling from the discovery of the Vault. It's all I can think of. How incredibly gorgeous the Redemption was. The mysteries of the workstations. And the vial slot. And the memory of Russa and Qwillow that night at Emoss's. And the secret lift leading back up into the Consulate I used to get back. Every discovery leading me deeper into a rabbit hole I'm desperate to explore.

Patawa is seated at her workstation, a dataplate stretches in a ring around her. She swivels to face me and stands up, peeking her eyes over the top of the dataplate.

"Leo! There he is!" A wide smile stretches across her fragile Heplin face, and she waves excitedly. "We were starting to get worried."

"I'm fine."

Bryl stands over a long table with weapons scattered across it. He holds a railcannon, polishing the inside of its chamber. He turns toward me, raising his gun in acknowledgment.

"Hey, boss." He double-takes when he notices how awful I look. "The hell happened to you?"

"Long story..."

He doesn't pry. Never does.

Spri sits in the middle of the room on a square couch sunk into the floor. The fins along his head squirming as he concentrates. A hologram projects up in the middle, Spri examining it diligently. He barely notices me.

"Spri..." I pat him on the shoulder as I walk by.

"Not now." He flails his arm behind him, shooing away whoever he thinks is talking to him. I'm not sure he's blinked in hours.

My room is in the back corner of the first floor of our living space. Walls covered top to bottom with copied pieces of my father's journal. Notes on Redemption discoveries. Genetic formula theories. Artificial womb schematics. The inner workings of my compulsive brain spewed onto the walls like graffiti. Thankfully, few are allowed in here, so I can keep the extent of my obsessive savior complex a secret.

I melt into my chair.

Glass windows encase our three-story penthouse from floor to ceiling. We have the best view in the city. Above the bright lights and commotion of the busy streets. Nothing, but beautiful sky and the crests of other skyscrapers that make it above the vapor line. From this high up, I can vaguely make out the Valley, and Berban falls, Groga *Ivolo* and Groga *Oilsterr,* a sliver of the Rift, and the snowy edges of northern Su Hoz. We are literally on top of the world. Sometimes I'll open the hangar doors on the third floor and just stand on the landing pad, soaking in how mesmerizing Valenia can be. That is until I get dizzy from how thin the air is and come back inside.

I still can't stop thinking about the Vault. About the mysteries that lay inside. The possibilities excite me beyond containment. The crew won't believe it!

I begin to walk out to the main room, but something stops me. I don't know why, but for some reason, I don't want to tell them. I trust these three with my life. Have multiple times. Yet, a voice from within urges me to have patience. To wait. I can't reason why, but the voice grows stronger, and I begin to agree with it. I put it off for now and move on to other business.

Spri is still engrossed with the hologram map as I approach.

"Spri!" I nudge him firmer this time to wake him from his trance. He flinches and seems bothered.

"What is it?!" He turns around, annoyed. He sees me and gets slightly embarrassed, his eyes instantly avoiding mine. "Oh... Hello Leo. Didn't see you come in." He's a neurotic sort. Hyperactive and buggy, but brilliant. A tech savant with an eidetic memory stored with every historical archive we could need, and an expert geographer. The one area he lacks, social skills.

"I need you to take a look at my comm. It's fried. Can you salvage it? Or should I use my older back up in storage?" I hand it to him, and he immediately starts disassembling it. I wait for an answer but never get one. "I'll come back later."

Next, I head over to Patawa's workstation.

"Leo! Hey!" She hops off her chair and ducks under the dataplate to greet me, squeezing me into a tight hug. She's always enjoyed human gestures more than her own. I groan in pain. She recoils immediately. "What's wrong?"

"That's what I was coming over here for. Think I busted some ribs," I say to her as she motions for me to lie down on the Med Bed. She scurries back into her workstation and begins to prompt commands into the machine.

"How'd this happen?" She asks, fingers a blur across the screen.

"I... fell..." I say. She stops for a moment, looking over the top of her station once again.

"Fell?" She asks. A skeptical look on her face. I tilt my back and look at her upside down.

"Yea fell..." I answer. She doesn't seem satisfied but continues running the protocols anyway. A mechanical arm reaches over the top of me and stops just aligned with my forehead. Small green beams shoot from a ball in the center of a long rod it holds. The beam scans me from head to toe and spits out the results onto Patawa's dataplate.

"Alright, get up." She helps me upright. "Yea, six broken ribs. My God Leo. What happened? Your ribcage is a mess!" She probes like a worried like a mother. I dismiss the question and ask about recovery. She brings over a small tube with a round mouth coated in needles around its brim. It doesn't look fun.

"Take off your shirt." She orders. She still looks at me with scolding disapproval, but in a loving way only Patawa can pull off. I oblige. Purple and blue dance across my chest and side. A wicked bruise. "This is going to hurt, ok. Take a deep breath." She looks at me, and I nod when I'm ready. She jabs the tube's razor-sharp mouth in the gaps between my ribs and releases the hardening gel. I yelp. My eyes water as the gel darts into the cracks and seals them shut. The pain is maddening. And just before I blackout, she yanks the dispenser off.

I roll to my side in relief. Thank God that's over.

"You should be as good as new in a few minutes." She flashes her soft-hearted smile back at me and tucks back into her workstation.

Even though I've decided against telling the crew about the Vault, for now, the secret gnaws at me. Deception isn't a trait I employ often. I tuck back into my room and grab an old comm off my desk, signaling for Gwinn. It's not but a few seconds before I'm redirected to her message center. Still not speaking to me. My tongue can't match the speed of my brain, and I leave a message that I can only assume sounds like the ramblings of a madman. There's so much that needs to be said between us that doesn't involve hidden underground bunkers and secret laboratories. But that will have to wait for another day. Until then, she's the only person I allow myself to tell.

Maybe I'm just using it as an excuse to talk to her. That the intrigue of this secret will be enough to bridge the gap that has fractured between us. That it'll bring her back to me from whatever has her so lost. Or maybe it'll be just another of many futile attempts to reclaim the love we once had. Well, the love I *assumed* we had. Regardless, I need to tell her.

I strip from my sandy, damp clothes, and rinse off in the cleansing room. The warm water soothes the aches from the insane day.

As I change, I hear the crew talking to someone in the main room. I peek my head around the corner and see Victor and Miku conversing with them.

"Hey, guys! What's up?!" I hurry out and wrap them both in hugs. "Man, I've missed you guys! How have you been?" They both look great. It's been some time since I've seen them. It's a shame, really. I've been gone so often for work, I haven't had a chance to get out much. Miku looks as beautiful as ever. Her olive skin is flawless, and she has such a glow about her that sometimes I forget she's not *actually* a princess. And Victor makes Bryl look feeble. I can tell how insecure it makes Bryl feel. He's not used to being outsized. Victor looks like he's carved from marble. Patawa fawns over him to the point where I nearly have to close her mouth for her.

"Where's our loveable trouble maker?" I ask. Miku glances at Victor.

"Who knows. I'm sure being an upstanding citizen somewhere." Miku laughs and rolls her eyes.

"He had to take care of some business. Said he'd come by later on." Victor answers. Miku glances again to Victor, this time inquisitively.

"Defending him until the end. A true brother." Miku runs her fingers through Victor's hair.

"What about Tanya? Russa and the Council of dicks won't let me see her. How is she doing?" I hate small talk, but this is the only way I get updates on her.

"She's been better... The loneliness is killing her. I can tell. Every time I visit, she puts on a brave face; you know how proud she is, but things have just gotten bleak...twelve, thirteen-hour testing sessions. She's stuck out there in the middle of nowhere. Qwillow doesn't seem to be making any headway. I don't know. Something needs to change for her. I really worry about her." Miku's pain is tangible. Written in the creases of her forehead. I suppose I should feel guilty about using my resources from the High Council to solve the womb formula instead of prioritizing a cure for the Rotting, but once the eight of us are gone, they'll have no one study anyway. Humanity takes precedent.

She tries to quickly change the subject.

"So... we haven't seen you in a few months. What's the deal with Gwinn?" The crew discretely glance at each other, trying to hide it from me, but I see it anyway.

"... She's the same bull-headed woman she always is. She'll come around." It's not technically a lie, but I still feel fake as I say it.

"There's bull-headed, then there's mean." Patawa quips. I shoot her a glance, and she drops it. "Just saying." For as kind and gentle as Pat is, her protective claws come out whenever Gwinn is mentioned. She thinks Gwinn takes advantage of me. Steamrolls me. Plus, she insists I was happier with Riley. I tell her it's easy to be happy as kids. Life gets exponentially more complicated as you get older. Plus, Riley disappeared. Not me.

"I'd let her be mean to me." Bryl jokes. "Boss ain't really the sharing type, though." I act like I'm going to throw a punch at him, but he doesn't move. "You love me too much to hit me."

"Unfortunately, I do," I smirk. Miku leans in.

"Leo, you're the sweetest man I know. You're right, she'll come around. She's been through a lot. Just give it some time." Miku cups my hand in hers. Her compassion so genuine a part of me actually believes her.

Bryl wastes no timing hitting on Miku.

"But women don't love sweet men. Do they?" He asserts, arrogance and swagger drip from his tongue. He speaks slowly, his pace purposeful and suggestive. "They love strength. Power. They love a man who knows what he wants and goes for it." His eyes baste Miku, he never looks away. "They want a man to make them feel alive!" He leans across the table, his bottom elbows resting on his knees.

Miku plays along, entertaining his fantasy. She leans over the table and meets him in the middle.

"The type of man you're describing is fun. I won't deny that." She's nearly whispering by the end. Bryl intoxicated with her seduction. "But in my experience, when it matters the most, they never last!" She puts two fingers on his forehead and pushes him back onto the couch as she says it, and the room laughs. Bryl doesn't seem embarrassed; he loves the game. Victor, on the other hand, looks as if he could pull Bryl's head clean off his shoulders. I lean over and murmur into his ear.

"Easy big guy..." I glance at him; his jaw is clenched so hard he may crack his teeth. I put my arm around his bulbous shoulder and make a declaration to the group. "How about some drinks?!" Everyone cheers in approval, and in unison, we stand up and head to the second story lounge.

The night is filled with long memories of our youth and loosening inhibitions. Patawa throws herself at Victor, who is entrenched in guarding Miku like a bloodhound, as Bryl peppers her with innuendos and pick up lines. Spri starts down a story's path and then inevitably ends up somewhere miles from where he began. And all I can do is watch the clock melt away, minute by minute, and with it, my hopes that Gwinn will show up. It's no Fargo party, but it's still a good time.

My comm lights up, and I have a new notification.

This guy always knows how to ruin a day.

"Guys, new assignment from Russa. Check your comms." I wave my comm in the air to the rest of the crew. "Looks like... oh shit. The Rift, beta grid." Bad news. I hate going into the

Rift. We all do. I can see the apprehension wash over the room as the crew scans the assignment. They look at me like I can do something about it. I can't. I'm just as uneasy about it as they are. "We leave first thing in the morning. Better ready up."

"Ah no, don't go!" Miku pleads.

"Trust me, I'm not happy about it either, but we've got to prepare. I hate it when he throws these on us last minute." I give Miku a hug and turn to Victor. "When's your next fight?"

"A few days from now. In *Oilsterr.*"

"Perfect, I'm definitely coming! Should be easy to convince Russa into not giving us an assignment with the fight being on his turf and all, ya know."

"Shit, just tell him to come." Victor replies.

"Yea we'll see. He doesn't like going places where he won't be the center of attention!" We laugh in agreement. "Miku, you going?"

"Of course! I've never missed a fight!" She smiles at Victor and rests her head on his shoulder as she pats him on the chest.

"Ok great. We need to make it a whole trip of it. I'll tell Gwinn, and you see if Tanya can come. I don't really know what her situation is like for leaving or anything, so could you find that out for me?"

Her face tells me that was a stupid suggestion, but the High Council has kept me at such an arm's length with Tanya and Qwillow; I honestly don't know their procedure anymore.

"And I'm assuming Fargo will be there too, doing whatever it is he does! We can make it a mini-reunion!"

Patawa chimes in, her comment not as innocuous as I'm sure she meant it to be. "Well, minus the twins."

Obviously... I get she loved when Riley and I were together, but it's frustrating when she makes comments like these. The optimism I base my life around is put to the test every day I deal with Gwinn; the last thing I need is to be constantly reminded of another love lost.

Miku smiles at me empathetically. Like I'm describing some fairy tale.

"What?" I ask.

She grabs my hand again, hesitating, mulling over how to put what she needs to say. She tries to start but pauses. I understand what she's thinking now. She doesn't believe Gwinn would show up. I don't want to hear it. What's the point? I stop her before she starts again.

"I want to try, ok..." I say. She gives me a hug.

"Listen, some people are just angry to their core. Ya know? Sometimes there's just no fixing it," She says, a protective tone to her voice as if she's shielding me from heartache. And it's why she's the best of all of us. She hasn't allowed the world to change her. She's been pure-hearted since the day we were born.

Victor has an odd expression on his face as she says it, though. It's riddled with hopelessness. Empty. The look a terminal patient gives their doctor as they receive their diagnosis. The sort of disposition I've never seen on Victor before.

"I know..." I say. "But, I should fight for it." I smile. She seems disappointed I can't just move on. Patawa does too. Sometimes I get frustrated with myself as well. But we are alone in this world. There are only eight of us. And I don't know if I could've stopped it or not, but we already lost two of them... I refuse to lose another. She will not go at this life alone, no matter how hard she tries!

The distraction provided by Miku and Victor vanishes the moment the door closes behind them. And now, all I can think of is the Vault and how I have to go halfway around the world from it to the most dangerous place in existence. The Rift.

15

GWINN

DEMARCO

Widow's Wing

Miles below the tower full of sadistic oligarchs, along the belly of the Capital, Surgs huddle together in the darkness of a strobing neon lounge and squint their vile little roach eyes at me as I drunkenly stumble in. They gnaw on hallucinogenic vines that sit in planters surrounded by cushions and teeter in and out of consciousness as they hiss at me during their rare moments of sobriety. Always a pleasure to be among friends.

A particularly disgusting creature operates the dispenser at the bar. It doesn't understand a word I say, but I've been yelling at it for the last ten minutes to give me a bottle of Haze that I'm almost certain isn't there.

The world is predictably blurry.

Music pounding against my head hard enough to block out those horrible electability tests. Why couldn't one of the videos been burning down this Surg cesspool? I would've actually enjoyed picking that one. But then where would I go to enjoy my mind-numbing solitude?

I scratch at my wrist. These stupid bugs yell at me. Even through the intoxication, I can feel the constant itch of their vibrations crawling up my arms. Sometimes I scream back at them. I consider it self-help. Leo is always harping on me to be more in touch with my emotions. *Apparently...* I bottle things up.

Yet, as much as I hate these disgusting grubs, this *is* the one place I can let my guard down. I can scream and laugh and cry and kick and spit and do whatever the hell it is I please down here because they can't tell a damn soul about it. They have no written language. Comms are useless to them. And they fraternize strictly with other Surgs. Down here, you may as well be on another planet.

A single vine squirms from an individual-sized pot at my seat on the bar. It dances in the air like an amputated tentacle. I stare at it. My glazed eyes struggling to follow it wiggle. I shouldn't eat it. Things always go south when I do. But the images of those High Council tests flicker through my mind once again, and the bitter vine is halfway down my throat before I can give it a second thought.

It always amazes me how quickly my mind turns to soup.

Colors erupt in my vision. Like a paintbrush having an orgasm. They tunnel and swirl. The walls of the lounge melting away. The bug next to me transforms into the little Heplin girl I met on the slidewalk. She smiles at me. Her lips moving like she's speaking but nothing coming from them. Then the words echo in.

"What was Emoss like?" The girl asks.

"Magnificent," I answer. The world continues to dissolve into beautiful chaos as I swallow the stem of the vine. "Everyone loved him. He was more than a leader; he was a compass. He showed you the way, and all you had to do was follow." Memories speed across the surface of the bar like gushing water. I cup one in my hands and watch it. Emoss, the twins, and I walk along the rocky shoreline of northeast Okotall.

"How did he die?" She asks.

"I killed him..." I say quietly. The lounge has completely vanished, and I sit on the rocky shoreline of the memory I just watched. The little girl sitting beside me, tossing pebbles into the ocean.

"Why? Didn't you love him?"

"More than anything in the world... I didn't mean to." The waters turn black and grow choppy. "I was sick. And young. And scared. So, I ran away." Massive waves crash at our feet, yet we don't get wet. They just thunder against our ears. "I thought they would send me away like they did Tanya..." We snap to nothingness. Floating silent in an empty white vacuum. "I was missing for days. Emoss was leading search parties all over the globe. Russa was as well. But I was hunkered down in a cave I found atop Berban Falls." I blink, and we are right there atop the Falls. It pours from the middle of a massive jagged rock, more mountain than boulder, like a tongue from a mouth. Stone surrounding it on all sides, fifty meters tall and 400 meters wide. Roaring with unrelenting power. The water chews through the facade creating a gorgeous arch that connects the very western edges of Su Hoz, Dwaul Fir, and Okotall. Groga *Ivolo* perched high in the sky miles above the very peak, immaculate and flawless.

I walk to a thin slab of rock that knifes its way out from the arch, suspended beyond the break of the Falls. Staring out at the sprawling Forest.

"What is this place?" The girl asks.

"Widow's Wing," I answer. "It's said ancient Berban tribesmen, well before A'gorr united them as *Gaz*, would summit this peak and stand at the edge when their partner died. They'd wait here until sunset. If they were meant to be with their partner in the next life, the winds would howl, blowing them from the ridge, and they would plummet to their death. If the sun set and they were still standing atop *Widow's Wing*, it meant their journey was not done, and they would return to the tribe with new purpose."

The little girl stands with the fins of her feet hanging over the edge, her arms spread wide, letting the wind coil around her body.

"That's beautiful," She says. *"But what does it have to do with Emoss?"*

The sun speeds from the sky, and darkness swallows us whole. My chest tightens. "Because this is where it happened."

I begin to explain, but she stops me. *"Show me..."* She dissolves into a wisp of air and slithers into my body. Together we transport into that moment.

I'm thrust back into my teenage self. Frail, cold... weak. I stare at my hands as I rub my fingers together. It feels so real.

"Show me..." She whispers inside my head.

From the darkness of my cave, I peer out to Widow's Wing, it's gusting winds whistling through the hollow corridor just as they did that night.

The embers of the fire I'd built are slowly going dark, and

the crackling of flames have all but died out. I lay there wrapped in the warmth of a moss bed, mindlessly staring out into the star scattered sky, eyelids heavy, when I hear the crunch of footsteps outside my cave. I snap to attention. Knowing what approaches but adrenaline still pumping through my veins as if I'm experiencing this all for the first time. I scurry behind a large rock against the back wall of the cave.

I wasn't supposed to be here. This place is scared *Gaz* ground, and intruders are met with unapologetic force. Purebred warriors, born with a staff in their hands, the *Gaz* are titanic creatures. Jagged horns of ivory spear from their shoulders, then bend and drape down behind them like pristine ice sickles. Their thick rawhide is a faded blend of grey and green, and their cold glass blue eyes strike a terrifying mix of beauty and rage.

He's coming.

The face I see in my nightmares.

He'll appear in the opening of the cave any second now, and nothing will ever be the same. Time slows. I don't want to relive this moment. But the child urges me forward.

"Show me..."

I carefully peer over the edge of the rock, a silhouette of terror standing at the cave entrance. A Sentinel. Paired with a smaller, nimbler warrior, a Precursor, they roam Berban together, searching the Forest for threats to the tribe. When the pair detects a threat, the Sentinel attempts to eliminate it, and he sends the Precursor back to the tribe to warn the rest. The Sentinel before me stands alone, his warning already sent off. More will be here soon. And blood will inevitably follow.

The Sentinel ducks his head to enter the cave, the dim fire casting his haunting shadow against the wall. His staff twitches in his hands. Each step alert, deliberate. He scans the area, short, probing inhales through his large nostrils, searching for clues. The smoke covers my scent, but it's all too obvious someone is still here. He pokes the fire with the end of his staff, bending down to sniff the moss bed, grunting in frustration. I'm paralyzed. All the fear of that night surging through my body once again. My bony feet ache as I stand on the point of a rock, but I don't dare move. And it's the cries of my feet that sink my heart, silent tears streaming down my cheek as I remember how he finds me... My shoes. I forgot about my shoes. They sit atop a flat stone on the far wall of the cave, just out of the light of the fire.

The Sentinel roars so loud against the cramped quarters I have to cover my ears.

"SHOW YOURSELF!" His voice, unimaginably deep. Horrifying. My entire body trembles. Melting down the back of the rock, my head resting against its stone face, tears flooding my eyes so violently I may never see again. The pain in my throat, unbearable from muffling my whimpers. All I can think of is Emoss. How desperately I wish I could actually go back in time and let this warrior kill me right here. To spare Emoss from the fate that awaits him. To spare Riley and Remmy the spiraling life I set them upon. To spare Leo. To spare myself. To spare all eight of us.

"SHOW YOURSELF NOW!" The Gaz bellows once more as he cracks his staff against his horns. A move done to intimidate their enemies in battle... it works.

"Show yourself now, and I may spare you. If I must find you, you will not leave this cave alive." He throws my shoes out of the cave entrance and continues to rap his staff against his horns.

What choice did I have? He would surely find me and kill me. My only hope was to show myself and beg for his mercy. But how could I? How could I throw myself at the feet of a warrior, trained from birth to kill, and expect his mercy while intruding on the very lands he swore to protect? It was suicide.

"Time is up." The Sentinel raps his staff against his horns one final time and begins his pursuit.

"...Wait...." the weakness in my voice is embarrassing. I was such a coward then.

My fragile fingers wrap around the lip of the rock, and I slowly pull myself out from behind the stone. My eyes catch his through the dark, and the purpose in gaze is petrifying. Covered in think gruesome scars, this warrior is no stranger to violence. But as I cautiously inch closer, something changes on his face. Once the light has a chance to illuminate my entire body, I can see him disarm. I was clearly no threat. I was tiny compared to him and hadn't eaten much in days. Feeble.

"Girl, do you know where you stand? This is sacred *Gaz* land. Widow's Wing. Outsiders are forbidden here." His stance relaxes, and he carefully lowers his staff from its ready position. He studies me, analyzing. "Human. You are the girl the world searches for, are you not? The reason Heplin, Olt, and Reyllion soldiers walk on Gaz soil?

The reason A'gorr is allowing such direct violations to our treaty?"

I want to answer him. Tell him I have no idea what is happening outside this cave. Beg him for his forgiveness and plead for mercy. Tell him I had no idea this place was sacred, no idea I was desecrating a place of such importance. But nothing will come out. I was still so frightened, tears still streaming down my cheeks. My life resting at the blunt end of a war staff, yet I can do nothing. Barely move. My breathing still stifled and spastic.

"ANSWER ME, GIRL!" He slams his staff into the ground with such force it knocks me from my feet. I crawl away on my back, the warrior closing in on me, staff now resting inches from my temple. The piercing stare of warrior eyes returning to his face. "Answer me, or I will scatter you across these walls with one swing."

Why? Why could I say nothing? Why did I not have the courage to speak to this gargantuan?

"Very well." He draws his staff back, ready to strike. Ready to wipe me from the world without a second thought. But outside the cave, yelling can be heard, and the Sentinel turns toward the noise.

"GWINN?!.... GWINN, where are you?"

"Who did you bring here? What is this?" The Gaz warrior grows furious, spinning his staff through his hands and ending in his battle stance facing the cave entrance.

The moment I hear the voice, it's as if life is reignited in my soul. Emoss. The tears dry, the breathing steadies, and I'm able to get to my feet. It's just enough for one moment of courage.

I hesitate, searching for my spot, but then I go for it. I roll under the Sentinel's behemoth legs and sprint for the exit.

"DAD!" I scream with all the voice I have left. Racing toward the hole.

"GWINN!" He's so close.

I don't make it but a few feet before the startled Sentinel twirls his staff through the air and sweeps my feet from under me. The crack of his monstrous weapon against my leg sends leagues of pain scorching through my body. My head crashes against the floor, teeth nearly shattering. The Gaz quickly pins me underneath him, staff pressing against the side of my head. Blood pooling in my mouth, leaking out to coat the moss under me a glossy red.

"Let her go, Sentinel." Emoss skids to a stop at the

entrance of the cave. Russa and the soldiers they brought appearing just after. "Let her go now!" Emoss demands.

"Lower your weapons or I will crush her skull, then destroy each and every one of you." The Sentinel presses harder against my head. I squirm in panic. "This girl desecrated a holiest of sites, she must pay."

"You touch another hair on that girl's head, and I will burn this Forest to the ground and every Gaz in it." I didn't remember the viciousness in which Emoss spoke to this warrior. He was such a gentle soul. Threatening me may have been the only act that could birth this anger from him. Why did I ever think he'd send me off like they did Tanya?

"I say try it. I would love to wipe you mongrels off the map," Russa says, always eager for conflict.

"My name is Kan'dor, the first Sentinel of the Gaz. I have been on this planet far longer than her, and I will remain here far longer than her. I will not be disrespected on my own land. You are on sacred ground; I have every right to kill every last one of you. You threaten me? Come onto my land, break all the rules of a treaty upheld for years, and expect me to obey your orders? I should kill you just for your arrogance."

Just as he finishes, a small garrison of Gaz warriors storm the cliffside led by the Precursor. A standoff. Half a dozen Gaz armed and primed to defend their land, rapping their staves against their horns. Emoss and Russa backed by ten fiercely loyal soldiers. And Kan'dor, with me pinned to the ground, blood still oozing from my mouth, body aching in pain.

All of this because of me.

Because I didn't trust the one person who loved me unconditionally. Because I was scared and emotional and weak.

"Enough of this shit," Russa's pistol bucks, and a shell chews through Kan'dor's shoulder. Blood spills from his arm and splatters across my back. He wails. Ferocious reverb rattling my skull. The next few seconds sit frozen in time. An eerie silence washing by. But then all hell broke loose.

Kan'dor recoils. He twists his staff in opposite directions, the weapon converting into a massive metal shield. The Gaz outside all do the same. War cries spilling from their lips as they charge forward. A hell-storm of shots ring out. The agonizing sound of metal on metal, as bullets deflect against shields, shredding my ears. Gaz crash into soldiers, their staff snapping aggressively back and forth from offense to defense. Kan'dor and his Precursor fighting with impeccable synchronization. Emoss's soldiers forcing their way in front of him, guns blazing, all adrenaline-fueled heroism. Agonizing screams fill the air as war staff crushes bone. Bullets dive into rawhide. Bodies begin to crumble. The shrieks reverberate off the walls of the cave and will haunt me until I die.

The fighting rages on, rocks chipping off the narrow pass and hurling down the Falls. Both sides fighting with unwavering determination, it seemed there would be no one left standing at the end. But just as Emoss and Russa begin to turn the tide, Kan'dor activates his shield and plows off Widow's Wing, bringing four soldiers with him. The remaining *Gaz* cease fighting and immediately follow Kan'dor off the cliff. The soldiers plummet to their death while the *Gaz* pull apart their staves, opening a glider and soar to their retreat, disappearing into the misty night air.

I'm finally able to get upright, head still pounding, and limp my way to the littered battlefield.

"Emoss?" Panic begins to set in as I don't see him anywhere on the tiny battleground. No one else is left standing. The fear of this moment was more than I could handle. "EMOSS?!" I desperately dig through bodies. "EMOSS!" I call out over and over, but he's not here.

"Gwinn! Help!" Emoss shouts as he dangles off the edge of Widow's Wing. His cord ends barely hanging on. I try to pull him up, but he's far too heavy.

"Russa!" He scampers over, and his cords split into several limbs to anchor around Emoss. Two under the knots of his shoulder. One wraps around his waist. And one up near his neck. Straining, he pulls Emoss to safety. The three of us crashing to the ground, exhausted. Chest rising and falling, groaning in pain. Emoss rolls over, rubbing against the stem of his neck.

"Are you ok?" I ask.

"I don't know. Something sharp just jabbed my neck." Emoss moans. Russa stares at the moon, his composure crumbling just like mine is. I've never seen him so emotional. He sobs. Turning away as when he catches me looking at him. I don't remember him being so distraught. Why is he so hysterical? He just saved him?

I roll to my side. Heart overwhelmed with the sight of my father. I miss him so dearly. I know it's a hallucination, but I'd give anything to stay right here in this moment forever. He winces, still struggling with his neck but nestling my head against his torso.

"I'm so thankful you're ok." He squeezes me so hard it hurts, but I don't care. I get to feel him one more time. Spend just one more moment in his loving embrace.

We lay there for hours.

Never wanting to let go of one another. Savoring every second of this hybrid memory.

Russa now sits on a rock, hunched over, turned away from us. He's still upset. I've never seen him in such a state.

Emoss jolts up. Face wild. Something wrong. I forgot how quickly the sickness came for him. Just like it does for everyone else. Black bile spews from his beak. Chasms sprouting along his torso. I shuffle away from him. He calls out for Russa, who doesn't turn around. Splinters of his frayed cords shed along the stone wing as he rolls about in pain. I scream out as the Rotting eats away at my father until the world goes black.

Rain drums against the roof of our childhood home. Emoss laying perfectly still on a Med Bed, his end near. Remmy, Riley, and Leo are bundled up in a chair next to me. Somewhere scattered throughout the house are a collection of Ancients and Qwillow with a team of Med Docs.

It's quiet. Everyone in the house asleep. I kneel by his side, whispering to him. Telling him how sorry I am. How much I love him. Begging him to power through. But he won't. He can't. He slips away from this world right there with my fingers woven into his.

"That story is depressing as shit." A voice yanks me from my hallucination, and I'm sitting in a mud bath with no clothes on inside a swanky apartment. E'zuu, the High Councilor from Su Hoz, sits across from me, drinking haze from a galestone mug.

"Is this real?" I ask, struggling to settle in. I try to find the little Heplin girl, but she's gone.

"Sure is," He says.

My chest still quivers from my final moments with my father. His face already fading to black.

"How'd I get here? I was..." I stop. Seems like I've already shared more than I care to with him. Knew I shouldn't have eaten that vine. He doesn't need to know everything.

"You just busted through the door high as hell. I don't know," He says. "You were mid-story, so I had to piece some things together, but I figured it out." He sips from his mug again, face slouching slightly. "I didn't realize all that happened..." He feels guilty about the tests now. I don't want his sympathy.

"Save it." Mud drips off me as I exit the pit and dip into a small pool next to it to wash off. "I don't want your pity."

I linger under the water until I feel the last of the hallucinogenic sparks leave my body.

"Then what *do* you want?" He smirks and struts from the bath, bending down to glide his finger along my collar bone. I planned to come here after the Surg bar, just not in this state. But it seems like it's all working out. I just need to get my head in the right space.

I focus.

Pulling him closer, breath cresting against his lips and whisper.

"The electability grades." I nibble on his lip, hoping to lull him into my web of seduction. He smiles. He knows what I'm doing but doesn't care. The type of person who enjoys being used.

"And in return?" He kisses down my neck. A simple look convinces him.

"First me... then you," I say as I climb from the pool. He disappears for a moment and returns with a dataplate. He rubs along my hips, kissing my shoulder as I scroll through the scores.

Shit...

"Wait for me on the bed." I purr. Seductive on the outside, furious on the inside. "I'll be right back."

E'zuu hurries off, and I grab my comm. I stare down at the score in disgust. All that on Widow's Wing can't be for nothing. I have to carry on his legacy at all costs. I owe Emoss that much.

The comm signal rings. A velvety voice answering.

"Gwinny... darling, it's late. If this is a night call, I'm flattered, but you're not my type. I like them less hostile," He says. My heart is filled with heat. A phrase rattles through my head. *Stomach and sacrifice.* Russa preaches that to me all the time. Actions must be taken. Sacrifices made. Emoss is worth it.

"You owe me a favor," I say, those last beautiful moments with Emoss on that cliff, etching one last memory in my mind. "I have a problem... and I need it taken care of."

A subtle hum fills the line.

"Consider it done," He says. "And Gwinny... I expect the

rest now."

I click off the comm without another word, not wanting to spend another second speaking with that monster and turn a half-filled haze bottle to the sky until the last drop burns down my throat. Fuck. I want to cry. Or scream. I don't know.

I wipe everything from my mind until it's a hollow void and strut back to E'zuu, tying my hair up in a knot.

"Where were we?"

16

TANYA CROWN

Control

Wet, frigid soil squirms in between my toes as I walk barefoot through a field just inside the lab's exterior fence. It's one of the few comforts I have in Su Hoz. Naked plots of garden, stripped of their seasonal crops, dusted with a frost from the afternoon thaw. The first step upon its icy crust sending frozen bolts of lightning up my spine. Then comes the numbness. The beautiful sensation that, for once, nothing can hurt me. I'm immune to the pain and agony that's become synonymous with my life. I'm untouchable. A God.

A Savron guard barely pays attention to me atop the south watchtower. Instead, he miserably slides grey nutrient blocks into the pulsating slit of his torso. Spending every day at this hour alone in his perch, the other towers lying vacant. I know it shouldn't, but it comforts me to watch him lifelessly absorb his meal. The poor bastard sits on a stool far too short for him, wings clipped so he can't fly and galestone weights bolted to his hooved feet so he can't make use of his immense jumping ability as well. I glance down at my med gown whipping in the breeze, and the pill-sized bulge under the skin of my wrist as the tracker inside blinks green and can empathize. We're both prisoners being held in broad daylight.

I haven't spoken to him before, but Miku's lecture on helping people and its *soul-cleansing* qualities has me trying to soften my edge.

"Those good?" I yell up the tower. He glances around, realizing I can only be talking to him.

"What?"

"The block things... are they good?" I point to my stomach, not knowing how else to signal what I'm referring to. The guard's face has a reptilian quality to it, covered in prickles that look like tiny mountain ranges peaking up through his skin. They're an ugly race with a stubby snout set between two sets of staggered eyes, yet he's not entirely repulsive to look at. He inspects one for a moment and shrugs.

"You tell me." He tosses the block from the tower, and I have to lunge to catch it before it lands in the mud.

"Shitty toss." I glare up at him. He smirks.

A distant rumbling turns my attention to the east. It's low and steady like the hum of excavating bots. It wouldn't surprise me if the digging crews were getting an early start on the day. It's warmer than usual. Plenty of resources in Su Hoz. Just hardly any people.

"Can I even eat these?" I ask, lingering on the faint trembles that echo just out of sight, a puzzled expression twisting on my brow. They seem oddly close for excavating bots, though.

"Don't know. But if you can't and end up dying, the lab probably shuts down, and I get to leave, so... I say go for it." He grins as he presses another block into his torso slit. His arrogance pulls me away from the rumbling.

"You got some nerve talking to me like that." I sniff the block. No scent. I suppose that's a good thing, considering the alternative...

"What do I have to lose?" He gestures around to his pathetic perch and lifts a leg over the railing to showcase his bolts. "Plus, I figured you'd prefer frank conversation since that seems to be your native tongue with us." He pulls himself up by the railing, standing now and leaning over it to speak with me. "The guards talk, ya know?"

I glance around to the other empty watchtowers.

"Yea, really seems like you got your finger on the pulse on what's going on around here." I mock. "Tell me again, where's everyone else right now?" I don't need him to answer; I know where they are. They leave at midday and head into the only piece of civilization for miles, a tiny merchant settlement called Yerally. There they guzzle haze and get conned out of their daily pay by the envoy merchants who bring back *exotic* goods from their trade runs in Berban. And the

Savron chump has to stay behind and cover for them. Because as a second-class citizen, he can't say a damn thing about it.

"Just because they don't talk to me, doesn't mean I don't have ears," He says. "Just eat it already."

I glare at him.

"I'm gonna eat it, relax." My face puckers as I lick the block. "And for the record, you don't have ears." I chomp down until a piece finally snaps off, and I grind it against my molars. It's unbearably dry. Soaking up every molecule of liquid in my mouth. "Hey, it's actually pretty good!"

He perks up.

"Really?"

"No, it's fucking horrible." I spit the congealed paste, or whatever the hell it is, from my mouth, and the guard cackles with laughter.

"Welcome to the life of a Savron." He smirks. The nozzle of a sprinkler groans as I shut off its valve, rinsing my mouth out. That was disgusting.

"What's your name?" I ask, still trying to scratch the taste off my tongue.

"Klawka." He answers.

"Alright, Klawka, wait here." He looks around as if to say, *where would I go?* "Shut up, I'll be right back." I didn't think it was possible to have a more miserable existence than I do, but the bleakness of his life has me feeling guilty of my self-loathing. I return moments later with a trey of edible food. Nuvu filet strips. Sweetberries. A stalk of terracorn. "I'm gonna puke if I have to watch you digest another one of those. So here." The trey of food is delivered to him up a small emergency shaft used for ascending the tower quickly. The guards are so lazy, they've repurposed it for everyday tasks. "And please use your mouth. The stomach thing is disgusting..."

Klawka's snout bounces as he sniffs the filet.

"It's not weird eating living creatures?" He asks, suspicious of the hunk of meat.

"You eat their shit every day, might as well eat the whole thing." It's actually depressing to think this is the first time he's ever had a chance to eat real food. "Just eat it already."

He grins.

The stubs of his wings begin to flap as he chews, his eyes bulging. "It's incredible." His jaw snaps open wide so he can shovel the rest in at once. It's appalling to watch. Maybe the stomach thing wasn't so bad after all...

"You're not supposed to eat the bone." I chuckle. For all his quick words and witty retorts earlier, he now stands in awkward, silent gratitude. Remnants of his meal-avalanche bleeding down his chest. And with this concept of generosity being foreign to me, I don't know how to bridge the silence. But I don't mind. It's a comfortable silence. Like two invisible people being seen for the first time. Without a sense of obligation or guilt or pity. Just a shared understanding of what a life lived alone feels like.

He doesn't say thank you, and I don't want him to. I know Miku would be proud of the gesture, and that's enough for me.

"Do you not hear that?" I ask, my head snapping east once again. The feint tremble growing louder in the air. Those can't be excavation bots; there's no way the High Council would allow them so close to the lab. I can't place where it's coming from, but it gradually builds intensity.

"No ears... remember?" He jokes. But the smile on his face fades as something in the distance pulls his attention. He slides over to a dataplate in his tower, working his fingers across the screen. A hologram spits onto the weathered metal siding. His snout curls up, the trey rattling to the ground as he drops it. "Get inside now!" He yells.

"What?" His sudden bark startles me.

"Get inside!" Mud splatters against my med gown as Klawka vaults from the tower and slams to the ground. "Go." He shoves me toward the lab and sprints toward the main gate.

"What's happening?" I yell. My mind swirls too quickly to run. I backpedal toward the lab, watching Klawka stride away. Even with his hooves weighed down, he flows with ease. Each stride propelled farther by a burst of his wings. He launches over the guardhouse and onto a small platform where primes the coil of a mounted railcannon.

"Oh shit!" I turn and race toward the lab. "QWILLOW!" Mud streaks along the floor behind me. Nearly slipping against the manicured tiles. "Qwillow!" I find her up the stairs working in a soundproof pod. She jumps as I slam against the glass.

"Tanya, what are you doing!" She scrambles from the pod as she sees my state. My breath heaves.

"There's... I don't know. Something's wrong." I squeeze out. "I don't know!"

Qwillow hurries to her desk to examine the exterior

cameras. A caravan of armored rigs speeds toward the lab. The blood flees from my face. Body going cold. Through the screen, Klawka is signaling his missing counterparts over the comm.

"Who is that?" I ask, stomach acid creeping up my throat.

"I don't know." She answers.

"Are they here for me?"

"I don't know."

"Well, what are..."

"TANYA, I DON'T KNOW!" Qwillow snaps.

We glue our eyes to the screen and watch an automated barricade rise from the ground along the lab's service road. Even High Council members must stop at these checkpoints to enter. But the rigs don't slow. A searing blue light surges from a railcannon on the lead rig, and the barricade erupts into a ball of fire. The lab shakes.

We flinch. Horror painted across our faces. "This way. Hurry!" Qwillow yanks me by the arm down the hall toward the testing rooms. Her panic not helping mine. We stop at the door labeled *Restricted Access*, and Qwillow feverishly enters a code on the dataplate.

The door hisses open.

Qwillow shoves us inside. The room a haunting purple glow. Black lights transforming our skin to different colors. She seals the door behind us, and the sound of liquid rushing through tubes along the ceiling is all that can be heard.

"What the hell is this place?"

The room is no larger than the testing center I spend most of my days in. Except here, there is no Med Bed. No hissing machines reading my vitals. No glass wall where Qwillow apologetically smiles on the other side as mechanical arms shove needles into my neck. No. Here, tubes streak along the ceiling until they collide with the back wall and cascade down into a glass cauldron filled with a pulsing orange fluid. Here something horrible lurks. Shame festers in the creases of the countertops along the walls. In the indented seat of the workstation that sits next to it. In the stack of encrypted datacards that form a tower of secrets so high, it nearly topples over. Every inch of this room feels wrong.

"Hide." Qwillow orders. She holds open the tinted glass door of a vertical tank that leans in the corner. It's so dark I didn't see it before. "Now!"

I don't fight it. Fear pushing my legs forward until I'm stepping inside the tank, and the cold metal is pressing against the back of my neck. The glass sucks shut. Qwillow hurrying out the door of the lab and leaving me with the sounds of my pounding breath against the metal walls.

Time crawls through a pit of molasses. Each passing second, sinking deeper than the last.

Those were armored rigs speeding through the fields. Weaponized. High-tech. Not scrappers from the countryside, perpetually high on Venom. Those idiots try to knock off the lab's trash disposal rigs so they can pawn salvaged tech-waste in Yerally. Most of them end up scattered across the field as fertilizer. Bodies reduced to rain clouds of meat when the mine-drones that roam outside the lab's walls catch them sneaking onto the property. Detonations that echo for miles in this isolation. Jarring me from my sleep in the middle of the night. Haunting my dreams. Sprouting pits in the bottom of my stomach at the sounds of vaporized men spilling back to the soil in pieces.

Ungrateful *Surgs.*

These swarming floods of fear and anger consume my thoughts as I hide. Uncontrollable. Stress so thick there's no swallowing it down. The eternal moments that pass, driving a wedge of madness into my mind.

Then, the lab door slams open. A soldier creeping in behind it. And every morsel in my body freezes in place. Is that a soldier...? The tint of the glass is so heavy the figure looks like an inkblot smearing across the door. But I can make out the bulk of body armor and the jutting silhouette of a weapon.

I cover my mouth. Desperate he can't hear the sounds of my terrified pants.

Multiple voices crackle from his comm unit.

"Mess hall clear."

"Terrace clear."

"Entryway clear."

More must be here. Twisting through the halls like a serpent chasing a rodent down a burrow hole. Knowing its prey will eventually run out of places to hide.

The figure paces along the opposite wall. Weapon primed and scanning. It moves my way. I push harder into the back of the tank with each closing step. Praying I somehow morph through the metal shell and back out into the garden. But the figure still grows larger. Panic tightening my throat as I scour the tank for something to defend myself with. Why is it so fucking dark?!

"Med Doc secured. Find the girl."

170

Qwillow!

A tear crashes into the corner of my mouth. Lips squeezed together to avoid making a sound.

The spotlight of the soldier's rifle slices across my door. The guard still creeping my way. I dart away from it. Pushing myself farther back. Going nowhere. A knot twisting into my chest. My thumb runs along something bulky on the sidewall of the tank. It's connected to a metal hinge. I trace its outline and recognize the shape. It's a mechanical arm like the ones attached to my Med Bed. I recoil when the end of an incision blade glides across my thumb. I yelp. Slamming my hand back over my mouth, blood from my thumb leaking onto my lips. The spotlight snaps to my door. Spreading wider across the glass as it gets closer.

"Hukar, what's your status?" A voice calls over the comm.

I fumble along the mechanical arm and yank the blade from its mount. The soldier, so close I can hear him click the output button on his comm. Answering with a guttural Oltish croak.

"Investigating."

His footsteps are slow. Cautious. Plodding against the tiles of the lab. A nauseating pause between each one. Light consumes the entirety of the glass now. The tint must be so heavy he still can't see inside or else he'd have alerted the others by now.

The clasp of the tank clicks open. White knuckles squeeze around the end of my blade. Sweat slicking the broken metal in my palm. Courage swelling in my stomach.

The tank door flies open.

Harsh light blinding my eyes.

Gloved fingers wrap around my forearm and try to rip me from the tank. But I yank back. Pulling him toward me. The first stab punches into the padding of his armor. The second, the meat of his shoulder. The third, through the middle of his hand. And the fourth, clangs off the butt of his rifle.

A fist plows into my ribs. Bones surrender instantly. I flail in pain. Swiping the blade blindly until I feel it cleave through fleshy hide. His rifle drops to the tank floor as he stumbles back. Blood erupting from a gash along his face. I lunge out, but he turns, and the blade digs into the protective gear along his back. I'm stuck on top of him. Endlessly stabbing. Trying to work my way to his head. But he launches us backward. Slamming my skull into the tank wall. The bony barbs of his spine jabbing into my torso like dozens of tiny sledgehammers.

Together, we groan.

Pain swarming my chest.

I try to push him off, but he's too heavy.

Our heads dart to the lab door as a herd of footsteps approach from the hall. Others are coming.

He tries to reach for his rifle, but I drive the blade under his arm. He wails. More blood painting over the pattern of my med gown. I cover his mouth and slam the tank door shut.

More murky figures pile into the room. Dragging something behind them. They head toward the workstation.

Hukar flails, trying to shout, but my hand muffles his voice. Pressed tight to the slimy hole of his mouth. I hack off one of his antennas, and he growls into my palm as I yank him even closer.

"Not another word!" I whisper into his remaining antenna, digging my blade under the shell of his skull and pressing it against a pulsating sac that sits at the base of his spine. "You'll bleed out in ten seconds. Don't fucking try me."

Hukar stills. Our breath, crashing up and down in unison. Bodies pressed against one another. The stench of his wounds making vomit race to the top of my throat.

We stare through glass. Silent. Figures dragging someone by the fin of their skull. I almost faint when I hear her cry out.

Qwillow...

"Show me the supply manifest." Someone orders. Figures move across the lab. Qwillow's outline crashes into her workstation as she's shoved in the back. The shadow of a rifle barrel pressed to her head. "Now!"

Qwillow hunches over. A soft glow shining around her silhouette as she boots up the workstation.

"Hukar, where's that status report?"

My heart drops. I dart to silence his comm as the voice crackles out from the other comms in the room as well. Shadowy figures turn around. One direction. Then, the other.

I stand utterly still.

Hukar's steaming breath plowing against my palm once again.

The figures turn back around, and air spills from my nose as I try to conceal my sigh of relief.

"You're stalling." Someone says.

"I'm not. I swear..." Qwillow's voice trembles. A figure moves closer. She squeals. "WAIT!"

A loose, rattling noise fills the air. I shove Hukar's head to the side and try to squint through the glass. Her head is yanked back. A soldier is pouring tiny metal balls down her throat. Shoving her head forward once the bag is empty. She whimpers. Purring a noise I can't make.

"Please don't..." Qwillow cries. A distorted warbling noise radiates through the lab. Qwillow screams in agony. Hunching over in pain. Lumps growing along her shaded silhouette as the metal balls they poured down her throat now try to tear from her insides to reach the groaning magnet in the grunt's hands.

"You're stalling." He barks. Qwillow sobs. Begging them to stop. Hukar squirms as I squeeze him harder. Tears pooling in my eyes.

The noise dies, and Qwillow collapses. The grunt rips her from the ground and back into her chair.

"The Bytrol manifest... NOW!" The grunt barks.

Bytrol? What the hell is Bytrol?

I press the blade harder against Hukar's spine sac.

"What is he talking about?" I whisper. I shove his head to the side so he can see my eyes. "I'm gonna take my hand off your mouth. You even so much as look like you're going to scream, and you're gone. Understood?" He nods, face a mangled mess of Oltish features I won't try to interpret. But the one thing I know he understands is, I'm in control. The circumstances are horrible, but it feels so good to have power. For once. Even if it's just over this one hideous grunt. Life happens as I say so.

Hukar quivers. I slowly peel my hand from his mouth, blade still pressed to his spine sac. "Talk."

Small appendages flutter along his face where a nose would be. Like fingers drumming on a table. His eyes seem to narrow, but it's hard to tell.

"Don't know." He mutters.

"Try again." I can't shove the blade any harder against him, or else I'll pierce the membrane, and he'll screech to a miserable death in my arms. But he's going to answer my questions. I'll make sure of it.

"I'm secure and contain. Organic only. They point at people, I grab 'em. Got no clue about the rest." The twitching appendages on his face settle. Folding over one another. "All I know is it must be important, or else *he* wouldn't be here."

He?

I squint once again through the glass at the shadowy figure looming over Qwillow. The shapes of his outline now looking different than Hukar's as I look closer. He towers over the others. The edges of his silhouette... moving? It's only when he turns to the side that my world darkens. A sharp angle protrudes from his head, cracking open as he shouts. Like vile words spilling from a beak.

"Here." Qwillow cries, turning the screen toward the figure. He leans over, scanning whatever is being displayed. Hukar grows restless in my arms.

"Where is it!" The figure shouts, smashing against the workstation. The glow vanishes with the sound of shattering glass. "You had one job you scheming little Heplin runt. Who did you sell it to?" Qwillow shrieks as she's picked up by the throat. Legs squirming underneath her. "I made it very clear what would happen if you tried to expose this."

The desperate sounds of her chokes overwhelm me. Almost biting through my lip.

"Russa... please." She wheezes.

It *is* him...

"You thought we wouldn't notice a vial missing?" He purrs. "We see everything!"

"I didn't..." She whimpers as he squeezes tighter. "I don't know... what you're talking about."

"Lie to me one more time, and I'll shatter your neck right here and find the Bytrol myself." His voice has such venom to it. Such heat. "You're the only person with access to this room. I know you took it."

This room...

Memories flash across my eyes of the day Gwinn randomly appeared at the lab. Claiming she was shooting an ad campaign. Strong-arming Qwillow into showing her this room. Lugging a case behind her as she hurried from the lab. Ignoring me even as she bashed into my shin on her way out.

I knew she stole something that day... But my spite towards this lab let her get away with it.

Qwillow's body begins to limp. Russa choking the life from her. What have I done?

I whisper once again to Hukar.

"Listen. I'm not gonna hurt you, but there's been a misunderstanding, and I need to fix it. I just need to use you as protection. Don't do anything stupid, and we'll all get out of this alive. Alright?" I say to him, clicking open the tank door. Blood still oozes from his wounds. Drenching our clothes in cold, dark fluid. He nods, scorned but grateful. Miku would be proud of me once again.

I open the door and usher Hukar out, peering over his shoulder like a Gaz warrior using their shield. Blade still pressed to his spine sac, but no intention of causing him any more harm. We can fix all this.

"Don't shoot."

Rifles snap in my direction. Three in total. Russa balks. Guards step forward.

"Put her down. I can explain."

Russa glances to Qwillow then back to me.

"Put her down, Russa!"

His cords unwind from her neck, and she spills to the ground. Gasping for air. Sobbing uncontrollably.

"You should have no knowledge of this place." Russa purrs. "I should kill her just for allowing you inside." He steps toward me, but I retreat further down the lab, dragging Hukar with me.

"Someone took what you're looking for. The Bytrol or whatever it's called. I know who," I say, concealing myself further behind Hukar as he gets closer. His beak curls up.

"Go on."

My mind races. I hadn't thought this through... I can't just tell him. There's no guarantee he doesn't kill Qwillow immediately after. What if he kills Gwinn? Would he do that? Do I honestly care if he does? Wait, what the hell is wrong with me?

"Now, *you're* stalling," He says.

No matter what, this may be the only leverage I ever have against him. This could be my way out of here... For good. I have to be smart.

"I need something in return," I say.

"No." Russa quips back instantly. I flinch. Not expecting such a quick response. He continues closing the distance between us.

"Not another step, or I'll kill him." I bluff, pushing Hukar's head up. Russa's cords spilt into four limps. Outstretching. Darting to the pistols along the hips of the other three soldiers. Four thumps ring out in a flash. Dark fluid exploding onto my face. A heavy film of blood coating my skin. Hukar spills to the ground. Only a stump left in between his shoulders. I stand mortified. Body shaking uncontrollably. The other three soldiers crash to the floor as well. Pieces of them stained against the wall behind them.

"I don't have time for this shit Tanya."

I stare down at Hukar's body. Wiping him off my face.

Blood pooling under his corpse. I wasn't going to hurt him. I was in control...

"TAYNA!" He barks. I can't move. "No one can know of Bytrol. They were dead the moment they walked in here." My eyes flick back up. "Now tell me what I need to know!" Qwillow squeals once again as he drags her in front of me. Pistol pressed against her skull.

Qwillow stares at me with terror. Unsure if I'll save her... It tears at my heart. Of course, I would.

I push away the anxiety of the moment and think. I can't tell him. Not without assurances. Think...

He has a gun pointed at her... Not at me. I'm too valuable to him.

"Hurt her, and you'll never know!" I shout and shove the blade against my neck. He darts a limp at my arm, but I bat it away. "I'll do it!" Pressing harder until I feel a single bead of blood race down to my collar bone. "Think I got anything to live for? Don't test me. You need me!"

Russa growls in frustration but concedes. Tucking the pistol into his belt. His cords twisting back into two limps. Shoving Qwillow to me. I slam her into a hug, glaring at Russa as we do.

His comm chimes, and he glances down to it.

"Shit." He mutters. "I don't have time for this. Tell me. Now!"

"No..."

He slams his cords against the table in the middle of the lab. Glancing around the room. Shaking his head. He clicks on his comm.

"Lockdown the compound. No one in or out until I return. I need the two assets under constant surveillance. Do not let them out of your sight. And no one is allowed inside the Restricted Access room." He snarls at me. Stepping so close the stench of his torso fills my nose. "I have to go. But when I get back, you better think carefully about your next move. You will not get another chance." He shoves us out of the room, slamming the door behind him and into the arms of four more soldiers.

He storms down the hall and out of the building as his grunts drag us in the opposite direction. Exhausted tears pour from my eyes. I glance to Qwillow, so utterly confused.

"Qwillow... what the hell is Bytrol?"

PART II

FIRE

17

RILEY HOLT

The Dark Chief

My eyes slowly peel open. Vision is hazy. I'm in a dark room whose details are indistinguishable. My mind must be playing tricks on me because I see the world upside down. I go to wipe the haze from my eyes, but my arms can't move. They're bound together. I try to move my feet, and they're tied together as well. My mind clears, and I begin to feel the throbbing. Blood coursing through my skull, pounding against the inside. Eyes about to burst from their sockets the pressure is so intense. Panic begins to set it as I realize I'm hanging upside down, strung up by the ankles like a Nuvu in a chilled meat locker waiting to be butchered. I squirm and try to scream, but my mouth is gagged. My body convulses back and forth as I attempt to free myself. Mind racing. I scream out again, but muffled grunts are all that escape. I struggle to free myself until I wear out.

Giving up and allowing my body to sway back and forth as I try to calm down. It's no use.

My eyes have adjusted slightly, and I try to take inventory of where I am. It's an old building. War-era. Like the outposts scattered across the border. Eroded stone bricks stack interlocked atop of one another to create the walls. Some primitive adhesive wedged in between each, solidifies the structure. Sophisticated work for the time. Other than a heavy bolt-locked door on the far wall, the room is blank. No windows, no designs, nothing but the hook on the ceiling from which my rope hangs. Light stabs its way in from small holes chewed through the stone bricks sending bright yellow rays cutting across the room. Without them, it'd be pitch black.

I hear a mechanical hinge operating, and the door swings open, bright light rushing in behind it. When the spots and stars in my eyes recede, I'm met with the massive legs of a Gaz warrior. Another stands off to the side. I tilt my head up to get a look at the towering brute. As I do, he cuts the tension rope, and I drop like dead weight onto my neck. I groan as he flips me over onto my stomach and cuts the restraints from my hands and feet. The moment I'm free, I shuffle away to the back of the cell. A mixture of fear and adrenaline flooding my brain.

"Get up!" The Gaz commands. He raps his war staff against his horns and twirls it in his hand until it snaps to a stop inches from my temple. "Move." He shoves me out of the room and into a narrow hallway. The ceilings are far lower than my apparent jail cell. This was no structure built for Gaz. The warriors have to duck their heads slightly as they drag me to whatever horrific fate awaits me. A compact mantle with a thin lip is built into the walls, about halfway up, and stretches the entire length of the corridor. Myrite dust lines the mantle and sparks its beautiful cyan blue combustion, its familiar glow the only thing keeping me from throwing up.

The Gaz trailing behind will occasionally jab me in the back with his staff, telling me to keep pace. I want to walk faster, but my legs are spent from days of trudging through the woods.

The hallway winds for some time until it spits us into a breathtaking foyer that looks like how I'd imagine a Gaz version of Fargo would decorate a palace. It's punctuated with a spiral staircase dotted every few steps with guards adorned in ceremonial white and gold armor and erected from a material I've never seen. It's smooth and glossy, like polished grey stone, yet it gives ever so slightly as we step upon it.

Staining the walls are intricate murals of ancient battles. Battles before A'gorr unified the tribes of Berban as one. When every village fought not only those from beyond the trees, cho'wa, as they call them, but every Gaz that wasn't part of their sect. They're gruesome paintings. Bodies piled onto one another, maimed from battle, reservoirs of blood at the feet of those standing.

"Where are you taking me?" I ask. The Gaz don't answer. Glass blue eyes, steel cold, stare obedience into my tongue. I don't ask again. Atop the stairs, a landing ends in a massive wooden door carved with the Gaz crest. They usher me in with one last sharp jab, but neither follow me inside.

I stand in the mouth of opulence. An awe-inspiring throne room. Statues of hallowed Gaz warriors tower twice, three times my height, sitting upon tiered displays, one behind another. Massive tree trunks bolted together to form the trusses of a ceiling arch that connects to the floor on either end. Hanging from its center is a gorgeous contraption, part sculpture, part chandelier. Consisting of Gaz horns turned upside down with wicks aflame at their points. The room has a level of decadence I'm not accustomed to seeing from the Gaz. We've only ever stumbled across remote villages consisting of wooden huts and stone obelisks.

For a moment, I forget I was just hanging upside down in a dark cellar. Nose so close to the dirt floor, I was sucking up dust with every breath.

The filth covering my body makes me feel self-conscious in the immaculate chamber, as if I came here willingly. Another Gaz awaits me on the far side of the room. Perched atop of a pretentiously extravagant altar, he signals for me to approach.

There's no exit but the door behind me; I don't have a choice but to oblige.

A massive window that spans the entire floor frames the man just beyond the altar. As I get closer, the world below reveals itself. Shit... Rows of dwellings stretch into the distance. Gaz tribesmen flowing through the streets hauling baskets, guiding beasts into stables, sparring with one another in pockets of courtyards. This is no remote village. This is a city.

The man signals again to approach, my eyes glued to the window. A jolt of anxiety stops me in my tracks. I know where I am. And I know who sits upon that throne.

"Riley." The man speaks, his tone firm and commanding. "Come." How does he know my name? My feet inch along, arguing with my mind, which is screaming at me to run. Then I remember they must have Remmy too, and my heart twists. I reach the edge of the altar, the man pacing down the few stairs to meet me. He's wildly different than any Gaz I've ever seen. Not nearly as tall, his horns, only a fraction of the size, don't even bend down his back. His eyes lack the glass-blue beauty of the others, and his skin is far darker, barely green at all. He almost looks as if he could be a hybrid.

"Riley Holt. Sister to Remmy Holt. Adopted daughter of the late Emoss of Okotall. Human. Suspected of fleeing Archler

House to the Forest of Berban nearly five years ago." Even though he's down from his altar, he doesn't seem interested in observing me. Still, he can see the surprise on my face as he recites the information. "Yes, even *beasts* of the woods know of the creatures that fell from the sky." He paces by and wraps around the throne, gazing out the window. "Follow."

I reluctantly obey.

"Look." He points out to the village below. "Do you know where you are?" He asks. I can see it all now. Its symmetry is astounding. A straight path cuts through the middle of five bending arcs, each smaller than the last, intersecting with an avenue running perpendicular to them all. The structures that line the paths are all perfectly spaced. Old stone-built dwellings are blended with newer construction just like this building and are all propped up on stilts resting a few feet above the ground. The village is sunk within a deep crater, and along its ridge, rest trees that don't seem physically possible. They are enormously wide and twice as tall as any tree we've come across. With sprawling branches that are all the same height up the tree. Each branch has thick vines that drape to the ground and pile up, like noodles from the tongs of a utensil. Hundreds of these vines run over the canopy and are tied to a manmade obelisk in the middle of the village that reaches the height of the trees. *How did they build that?* Without it, anyone flying above would be able to see the city. But the vines block the view, while still allowing sunlight in. An ingenious invention for a people obsessed with their isolation.

"Pom'do'kon?" I answer as I try to conceal my worry. "Where is my brother?" I assert. He continues to stare out of the window as he answers.

"Pom'do'kon. The last true city of purity." He pauses, staring over the landscape and ignoring my question. "My people have seen more sorrow than you can comprehend, child. I understand the look when I see it." I thought he was ignoring me, but maybe he's not. "Your brother is here as well." Tears welt in my eyes when he tells me.

"Is he ok? Is he awake?" I plead. The thoughts of Remmy hanging like dried meat in some cramped cell fill my body with pain only love can produce. This is all my fault! We shouldn't have chased that Tyko, we shouldn't have used the Sonostick, I shouldn't have stopped before I reached shelter. The guilt drums through me.

"I understand sorrow, but criminals are not in a place of

leverage to demand answers of me." He's stoic, but not intimidating. His voice has rationality to it that I didn't expect from a Gaz. A poise. Maybe I have a warped view of these people, or maybe this is why he leads them?

"Why are you in my woods, girl? Humans are not my enemy, you did not try to burn our villages down, didn't murder our people, but you are not Gaz either. You trespass on land we nearly lost everything to maintain. Many of our people would find the disrespect a capital punishment..." He finally turns to look at me. "So, what is a leader to do? With someone who is not our enemy, but not our ally. Who trespasses on our land, yet poses no threat to our people? Do I send you across the border unharmed, telling the world Gaz threats are hollow? Do I kill you and your brother, display you along the border and justify society's perception of us as murderous savages? Do I allow you to stay, live in my Forest ordained for Gaz and lose the respect of my people? Tell me? What do I do with you?"

He's hard to read. Does he ask rhetorically? Or does he expect a legitimate response? I don't have time to answer my own questions about his inquires before someone barges through the doors shouting.

"WHERE ARE THEY?!" A mountainous Gaz storms down the walkway, screaming with all his force. A Sentinel. His body is riddled with scars. Death oozing from him. "A'GORR!" The Sentinel's voice is so powerful it triggers a horrid flashback of the Tyko roaring in my face. A shiver of terror sparks down my limbs. A'gorr walks calmly from behind the throne to meet the Sentinel. I follow tentatively.

"Kan'dor..." As he begins to speak, I finally emerge from behind the throne, and Kan'dor stops dead in his tracks as he sees me.

"So, it is true! *Ga kana su ko!*" Kan'dor is irate. "Where is the other? A'gorr... Tell me the other is dead?!" Kan'dor pleads. His anger sways from betrayal to disbelief to pride.

"The other is alive as well. He is ill. We are tending to him." A'gorr answers purposefully. His eyes command respect from his subordinate, though I'm not sure he'll get it.

My head darts to A'gorr as he says it. Tending to him? I nearly collapse with joy. Fighting back tears that swell in the corners of my eyes. I'm so grateful, but I'm too afraid to show any emotion while Kan'dor is here lobbying for my execution.

"TENDING TO HIM?!" Kan'dor lurches forward. A'gorr's poised disposition shifts quickly, stepping in between us.

"Mind your words, Sentinel! Stand down!" A'gorr barks. Kan'dor towers over A'gorr, fury burning in his eyes, but A'gorr demands obedience. "STAND. DOWN." He may look different, but he is undoubtedly Gaz.

Kan'dor disarms and backs away.

"The humans are our prisoners. They will know harm only when I say so. Understood?" A'gorr commands.

Kan'dor swallows his rage and attempts to speak calmly. "Dark Chief, please, I urge you to reconsider. These creatures from the sky are poison. They're a scourge. I showed mercy to one upon Widow's Wing, and Gaz men died because of it. Have you so easily forgotten?" Kan'dor states. "Because I have not!" Kan'dor pulls his armor over his head and reveals his trunk. Tattoos of Gaz names line the left side of his abdomen and have a jagged knife scar under each name. Clearly done by his own hand. "Then they infected their own keeper and killed him. They are rodents!"

A'gorr allows him to finish.

Kan'dor breathes heavy, his poise, short-lived.

"Who ran to her rescue when the human girl went missing at Widow's Wing? Heplin. Olt. Reyllion. Ancients from the High Council. The very men from beyond our trees who fought to eradicate us. Humans are one of them. They should be treated as such!" Kan'dor demands.

One of them?! Anger bubbles up my throat as I picture the torment those exact people put us through.

"We are nothing like those monsters!" I emerge from the background, vicious words spewing from my mouth. His eyes spark with rage.

"How dare you speak to me in this chamber!" He steps forward, but A'gorr halts him with a simple raise of his hand. "Dark Chief. You'd allow this runt the courtesy of words in your temple?"

I bark at him again, all rationality wiped away by the tidal wave of rage that crashes down on me.

"Those people shunned us, blamed us for the death of Emoss! Hated us as much as they hate you. We had no option but to flee to Berban." My fist balls so tight the tendons of my wrist may pop. "We were beaten, tormented, starved... All for something we had no control over. Had we stayed, someone would have murdered us. That I have no doubt." My chin begins to quiver as my emotions overwhelm me. "All for the death of Emoss. A man we loved as much as they did. A death which my brother and I had nothing to do with... So, no, the others may be like them, but my brother and I have lived in this Forest for years. It is our home as well!"

"BERBAN IS HOME TO GAZ AND NO OTHER!" Kan'dor roars. The veins in his neck bulge. "This was the creed you promised to your people A'gorr. Or have you forgotten that as well?" Kan'dor stares disgust through A'gorr. "Allow the dregs to claim this land as their home and watch the days of your reign..." Kan'dor steps closer to A'gorr, looking down at him, snout to snout. "...end."

The two stand inches from one another until A'gorr finally speaks. "You overstep Kan'dor." He shakes his head in disappointment. "Guards!" He yells. As he does, the two warriors outside the door rush in. Kan'dor gawks in astonishment.

"A'gorr! Have you gone mad?!" He slides back into his armor and readies his staff. "I will not be arrested like some common miscreant! I am the First Sentinel of the Gaz, I protect our people from the threats beyond our realm. But I will not hesitate to protect them from the threats within it." He preaches.

A'gorr darts back to his throne and grabs his staff as well. The two guards and A'gorr circle the Sentinel. Even with numbers, they're still outmatched. Kan'dor is a poet of death. He rotates slowly, scanning his opponents. I glance at the door. It's wide open. Kan'dor makes the first move, and the four warriors clash into a blur of madness.

The moment they do, I make a dash for the door. The grunts and growls of battle muffle the sounds of my escape. I reach the staircase and yell down.

"Guards! A'gorr is being attacked!" The Gaz warriors stationed along the staircase come rumbling up. I hide behind the door as the guards storm by to protect their leader. When they pass, I scurry down the stairs as fast as I can. Reaching the bottom and darting into the tunnel that leads to my cell. Blue cyan glow blurs past as my heels pound into the stone floor. I have to find Remmy. The guards will eventually overtake Kan'dor, and they'll realize I'm gone.

I sprint past my cell, hoping Remmy is in the next one. The door slams against the cell wall as I barge in. It's empty. SHIT! He's being looked after. I forgot! Where would they keep him? I continue sprinting down the hall and reach the far end, bolting through a door that leads to the outside.

The moment my feet hit the grass, I realize I don't have a plan. I can't just run through the middle of the village. The instant I'm spotted, I'll be cut down.

The sounds of clanking armor approach from around the corner of the palace. I jump behind a mountain of fire logs against the building. A splinter of the freshly harvested wood gashing into my arm. Two Gaz walk by, unaware of my presence. I watch them pass through a slit in the logs, wincing as I pry the splinter out with my teeth. As soon as the two brutes are gone, I dash across the street, skidding to a stop along the backside of a building. Hidden between the racing slope of the crater and the stone rear of a building, I hear a familiar chirp behind me.

The Ko from the Forest. He runs up and tugs at my pant leg.

"Shit, you scared me!" I whisper, unsure of where he came from.

The Ko's face is scrunched with worry; he points straight ahead and yanks hard on my pants.

"What is it?" I ask, nervously peering around the edge of the building. The Ko tugs empathetically at my pants, pointing over and over, insisting that's the way to go. "Is it Remmy, buddy?" The Ko takes off in the direction he points. "Shit! What are you doing?" I check to see if anyone is coming and follow the Ko. He leads me deeper into the village, avoiding the Gaz and sticking to the edges. As we approach another large stone building across the widest path in the village, the Ko stops and points at it. We lay concealed under the stilts of the dwelling across from it as a Gaz patrol strolls by. Just as he does, Remmy bursts from the doors with the help of another man wearing a long robe. A hood over his head and clearly not a Gaz. The sight of Remmy's blue flowing locks pierces my heart.

"REMMY!!!"

The Gaz patrol is startled as the men crash from the building. He fumbles for a blowhorn slung around his shoulder until a deep note bellows throughout the village. The patroller charges as he blows. Readying his staff. Remmy drops to a knee as the man supporting him charges back. It's clear Remmy's awake, but he's groggy. I scamper from under the building and blitz the warrior as well. My shoulder dives into the Gaz just before the two men clash. He barely staggers. A gnat flying into a boulder. But it's just distracting enough. Our ally tackles the brute. The two men tangling into one another. We wrestle the staff away from him, and our hooded partner jabs a needle into the neck of the Gaz. The patrol quickly falls limp. The instant the Gaz is taken care of, I sprint to Remmy and hurl myself into him.

"REMMY!" I squeeze him into a hug as hard as I can, tears streaming down my face.

"Hey, kiddo!" Remmy moans. I hug him so hard my spleen may burst. Remmy wipes the tears from my eyes and kisses me on the head. "What took you so long?" He laughs.

I laugh and punch him in the shoulder. "Shut up!" I've never felt more joy in my life than hearing his voice at this moment. The Ko runs up my back and wraps himself around my shoulders.

"Who is this?!" He asks. Remmy reaches out and pets the Ko atop its head. I hug the little guy too. My emotions swarming. But before I can answer, the man who saved Remmy barks at us.

"Come, Children, we have to go!" He orders. Something down the path gets his attention, and he starts heading for the tree line. "NOW!"

At the far end of the path, a herd of Gaz warriors rumbles toward us. "Go, go, go, go!" I help Remmy up, and we follow behind the man. "Come on! Hurry!" Remmy's weight drags on me. We move slow. The Gaz are gaining on us.

The edge of the village is in our sights, but the steep incline of the crater mocks us. "Help!" Remmy calls out to the man who runs ahead. But he disappears over the ridge. "Let go! I got it." Remmy tosses my arm off of him.

He winces as he pushes up the hill. I can't take my eyes off him. "I'm fine! Go!" He pleads. The swarm of Gaz close in.

"Where did he go?" I yell to Remmy. The Ko squeaks in fright as he holds onto my neck for dear life.

"I don't know?" He yells back. My lunges burn. Why did this man risk his life just to abandon us?

Just as we struggle to the crater's lip, a massive Hotógo snarls, bucking onto its hind legs. I fall back away from it. As it comes down, the hooded man is mounted on its back. Our pack strapped to the rear. *Where did he get that?*

"Get on!" The man urges.

"On that thing? Are you crazy?!" Remmy yells. The Hotógo snorts and stomps its hooves.

"Remmy, get your ass up there now!" I shove Remmy onto the back of the beast and sling myself onto it as well. The man kicks the Hotógo in the ribs, and the animal takes off.

My vision bounces as I collapse in exhaustion onto Remmy's back. The crater begins to shrink in the distance, and as I turn back to look at it, A'gorr stands atop the ridge staring at us as we disappear deep into the Forest.

"Thank you." I moan. The hooded man glances back at me. The tip of a beak jutting out from his hood. I lift my head from Remmy's back as I notice it. *That's an Ancient...* My stomach plummets. Oh shit... Behind us, Pom'do'kon is a distant memory. The threat of Gaz at bay for now. But I was so terrified of them, I forgot they're not our only enemy... Where is he taking us? How did he find us? A pocket of grass is carved into the upcoming tree line. I study it, then glance back one more time to ensure we aren't being followed. I wrap an arm around Remmy's chest and loop the other through our pack. The Ancient's head bobs as the Hotógo gallops. His attention no longer on us. I don't know what he wants, but I'm not sticking around to find out.

"Hold on!" I yell. The Hotógo snarls as I launch off its rear.

"WHAT THE...!" Remmy shouts as I drag him with me. We crash into the grass. The air punched from my lungs as I slam into the ground. Remmy landing on top of me. Groans crawl through the air. Sunlight burning my eyes as I stare up through the canopy in pain. Then, the brilliant rays are shielded away by a bulking figure, and I'm staring into the frantic eyes of an Ancient.

"Child, are you ok!" The cords of his arm slither around me, guiding me to my feet. "Yara must protect the Children. He must." The Ancient hurries to Remmy and helps him up as well, wiping mud from his face and obsessively inspecting him for injuries. "His master made him promise." His head twitches, then it violently snaps to me. "I found you. Yara found you." I reach for our hatchet as he lurches toward me. But he doesn't attack. Instead, he pulls a strand of hair from my face and tucks it behind my ear. "I have searched these woods for many years, trying to rescue you." The Ancient smiles. It's a manic, terrifying smile, but no longer threatening. "I am Yara. And my master sent me here to protect you."

18

GWINN DEMARCO

Crashing Waves

The morning sun yawns through the window and warms my face. I've been up for hours. My legs still tucked neatly in the sheets of my bed, my back rests against the soft quilted headrest. I don't know how long I've stared through the glass, but I realize I'm no longer looking at anything. I'm trapped inside my own consciousness. My mind and my morals tugging at either side of my soul, like pests fighting over littered street food. My mind convincing me what I did was a means to an end, but my morals sound sirens that echo weary disclaimers to my core. An alarm that warns of crumbling integrity and a slippery slope to sociopathy. But as the light warms the glass, I can see my reflection in the mirror, and as I cast a gaze into my own eyes, I can see the undeniable truth. I'm already there.

"Good morning, *High Councilor!*" E'zuu grins and kisses my shoulder as he stretches out the early morning stiffness. "How does your first day feel? How does power feel? Everything you ever dreamed of?" He whispers into my ear as his hand flutters across my thigh. His warm breath on the nape of my neck sends shivers down my spine. Tempting, but my mind is too preoccupied with fading internal arguments of right and wrong.

"I feel exactly what I felt last night, nothing!" I toss E'zuu's hand off of me and climb from the bed.

"And yet... you keep coming back!" E'zuu smirks something pompous and tilts his head to the side to get a better angle of me.

"Please... don't mistake boredom with flattery." I quip as I wash my face. The cold water soothing my irritated skin. I glance back at E'zuu, and he lays sprawled out arrogantly, sifting through traffic on my dataplate.

"You ever gonna call your love-sick puppy back?" He mocks as he holds up the dataplate to face me. "He's signaled.... A *lot!*" He scrolls through the list of calls and messages snickering to himself. I snatch the dataplate from his grip.

"Don't touch my stuff." I skim through the dataplate myself. Call after call. Message after message. What the hell does he want? Take a hint.

I walk from the room and leave E'zuu behind. Out of a heavy glass door, a balcony overlooks the city. I rest my elbows on the rail and let the breeze run through my hair as I listen to the messages Leo has left. He spouts more of his obsessive *Earth* talk, stuff about ships and secrets, and all the things that pushed us apart in the first place. His desperate need to fill a void with those relics annoys me. I barely listen. Who cares about Earth?

The city will be alive soon, but this early in the morning, the streets lay quiet, readying themselves for another day of controlled chaos. Savron city servants trudge about their miserable lives pining for a time before this. They clean the slidewalks, hang from the towers washing the vapor residue from windows, collect garbage, and shoo their own kind out of their homeless sleeping spots. They work through the night to make the city presentable to the deserving population. Then return to their slums and wait for the night so they can do it all over again. A life of no promise. No future. Futile and meaningless. Not much different than ours, I suppose. Of course, the quality of our lives as humans will be far better, our future is just as nonexistent. Much of we what we do is equally as futile. When the eight of us are gone, humans will be nothing more than fleeting memories. We've impacted this world *because* of our existence, not because of what we did during that existence.

If anything, Valenia is worse off with the knowledge of humankind, then they were without it. The calling card of our race. Death and despair. Emoss would be alive, the Rotting wouldn't be tearing through the population, relations with the Gaz would go back to its mutual post treaty civility, and these Savrons may have a chance at real life (maybe...). We are a virus, and all it took was eight germs to infect this world. It's at times like these when I question the motives of my life. Why do I even bother? What am I doing? Playing messiah to a people I couldn't care less about? Trying to make amends for the pain I caused this world when I killed Emoss? All I've wanted for years was to become High Council of Okotall, and now that I finally am, it's as if a blindfold has been ripped from my eyes and I see the world for what it truly is. I'm disgusted with myself for wanting this, and even more appalled about what I did to get it.

I'm seated at the crescent table in the Consulate as High Council of Okotall for the first time ever. Eyes lurch over me. Some with suspicious bite and others with pleading innocence. E'zuu winks from across the table. I ignore him. My stomach is twisted in knots; I have no time for his games. Russa is late. He hurries in, heading straight to Trakstull, whispering something to him. Trakstull nods, his stoic demeanor remaining intact. Where the hell has he been? He glances at me as he takes his seat, and Trakstull stands. The Regal speaks with kingly reverb as his dataplate is perched vertically on the table, recording his every word.

"The time has come to inaugurate the first High Council of the province of Okotall since the passing of our dear friend Emoss." He broadcasts to the world. "This province has hungered for leadership for years since his passing. Craved direction and order. The legacy he leaves behind is one we all hope to strive for. Love, compassion, and integrity. Our world is better today because of the actions of his past. And he made the ultimate sacrifice for those he loved." My eyes want to welt as Trakstull delivers his sermon on the life of Emoss, but my mind is still so distant. Colder than ever before. "He showed us all the true power of the soul." Trakstull continues on for some time, using the holiness of Emoss to inundate himself with sympathizers. The longer he preaches, the less I believe his words. The people still love Emoss, and that means so does Trakstull.

I can't help but notice tears in the edges of Russa's eyes.

His head is tucked ever so slightly, and his posture is one far more vulnerable than usual. The man may have loved Emoss more than I did. Trakstull finishes his state of the union and finally addresses me.

"As many of you know, today an election was to be held. As Regal of the High Council, I would have posted the electability scores, and you, the people, would have flooded to ballot boxes to choose the next High Councilor of Okotall. But the world had other plans. Last night, Candidate Wylk, along with the crew of his boat, was killed in a flash storm while sailing the Lotopi Sea. Patrols off the southern coast of Okotall spotted the submerged ship and attempted rescue, but ultimately arrived too late. After a full morning of searching, his body, along with his three crew members, were found among the sunken wreckage." The eyes from before, crawl their way back to me. Bhugon and Lyrell, of which have been my least staunch supporters, give me sinister smiles. Approving of the unspoken accusation that hangs over me. Hesh'ka looks upon me with a soft face but has little conviction behind his eyes. He thinks what they all do; he just doesn't want to believe it. Meelo's rigid view scrutinizes me. Judgmental. Even Trakstull glances at me from time to time with trepidation. The only people who don't send any relevant expression my way are Russa and E'zuu.

The crawling eyes don't help my internal struggle, but I'll be damned if I show them that. No. My expression stays flat. I don't give them anything to analyze.

"So, an election will no longer be held. The High Council has deliberated extensively on the subject and has decided in an unprecedented action. I, as the authoritative presence of the High Council of Valenia, hereby name Gwinnett DeMarco, the new High Councilor of Okotall." His words ring true in my ears as the news is made official. The moment the announcement leaves his lips, I feel the burden of responsibility weigh heavy on my back. The lives of thousands at the discretion of my will. No part of me wants this any longer. "Gwinnett scored the highest on every test and received the coveted Prime+ electability grade. She is the candidate meant for you. We mourn the loss of her competitor Wylk, but I can imagine no better person to continue the legacy of Emoss than his daughter." Trakstull signals me to stand, and I fight to wipe the pale expression of regret from my face. "I am honored to introduce your new High Council of Okotall, Gwinnett DeMarco!"

My fellow leaders pound the table obligingly. The dataplate in front me stands vertical, and my face is displayed across its screen. I address my people for the first time, as the realization of the mistake I've made claws at me like a weasel trapped in the jaws of a Tyko. My throat is so tight the words struggle to escape. The horror of my new-found self-awareness drips off every word I say.

"I was raised on the sandy shores of Okotall. I hear the gentle rhythm of its tide when I close my eyes to sleep. I went to school in the heartland. My siblings and I would pick the ripe Rupas from vines and eat them on our walk. I can still taste their sweet nectar on my tongue. I waded through the murky mangroves of the west with my friends, fearless kids wanting to test who was the bravest. My brother Remmy would always lose!" I smile for a moment, reflecting on that joyous memory. But the moment fades and I return to my speech. "My heart belongs to this land and my soul to its sea. I have watched as the province my father built spiraled into turmoil. I have watched as the love and compassion that comprised the people of the great province of Okotall become slowly replaced with discontent. I've watched this, and I understood my role in it all. I understand the anger, the blame. I carry it with me every day. But it is that burden that drives me to be here today. I will not rest until my home of Okotall returns to the glory of its past. And its people are once again looked upon with reverence. I give all of myself to you, and in return, I ask for your help. Together we can revive this great land, but only together. I am Gwinnett DeMarco, the High Council of Okotall, and I am ready for change. Are you?"

The dataplate turns back horizontal and tucks away into its slot. I sit back down slowly. The words echo in my head over and over. The speech spilled from me, as if on autopilot. So believable. So genuine. It terrifies me how good I've become at manipulation. At lying. At presenting a person to others far different than who I truly am. What have I become? My mind erases the self-doubt as the dataplate turns off, and the ceremony is finished.

The High Councilors move to leave the instant my words are done. Piling into the lift in waves, no pomp or celebratory words. Just business as usual. I board the first wave with Russa, E'zuu, and Meelo.

As we begin our descent, the lift is quiet. The four of us stand in silence. E'zuu is preoccupied, and Russa still hasn't fully recovered from his earlier moment. But I can feel the heat of Meelo's stare burning holes in the back of my head. Here comes the accusation, I can feel it. I turn to face him.

"Have something say, Councilor?" I rip, my arms crossed, stance firm.

He scans over me, unimpressed.

"You are a coward." He states. Matter of factly. It hits me harder than I expected. "And you! I should report you for tampering. I know you told the girl she didn't receive the Prime+ grade." He berates Russa. E'zuu glances up and subtly steps back from the altercation. Russa recoils and returns fire onto Meelo.

"I did no such thing! Saying shit like that was dangerous in my time. Soft ass generation now. I could've put a slug in your skull, and no one would've batted an eye for accusing me of some shit like that." His cords twist into the shape of a gun, and he presses it to Meelo's temple and gestures for it to fire.

"Nobody is scared of Trakstull's lapdog." Meelo puffs his chest out and bumps Russa. "You're a good little helper, aren't you!" Meelo's voice wreaks of condescension. But Meelo is wrong, Russa didn't tell me, E'zuu did. The pillow talk of a loose-lipped narcissist is a valuable thing.

Meelo shoves Russa to the side and approaches me. E'zuu tries to step in, *as if I need his protection*, but I cut him off. Meelo meets my eyes with a loathsome stare.

Say it... I'm begging you.

"You killed those men, didn't you?"

There it is. No tact, no nuance. What a bore he is, as predictable as they come.

He pries, eyes squinting with abhorrence. "Knew you would lose without the electability grade and eliminated the competition. Knew Trakstull didn't want to delay naming a High Council any longer. No time to find a new candidate and go back through testing, the people needed it now. And you knew you could exploit your relationship to Emoss to bypass the election. You are not fit to be a member of this Council, and you will not get away with this!" Meelo puffs.

He really thinks he has me cornered? Laughable.

"So, you believe a member of the High Council broke their oath and gave me sealed information..."

"Not any member. Russa. Your watchful guardian." He retorts. E'zuu slinks away once again.

"So, you believe a member of the High Council broke their oath and gave me sealed information saying I was going to lose the election. I then took that information and killed four men in cold blood during a violent flash storm. All so I could force myself into a position governing a population who hates me? And your response to all that is to threaten to expose me?" I ask blankly. "If what you say is true, you seem to be walking a treacherous path, Councilor."

He stares back in disbelief.

"Are you threatening me?" He asks.

You're Goddamn right I am.

"I'm not threatening you, I'm just saying if you're convinced I killed four men to earn my position, why would I stop at one more to maintain it?" As I respond, the lift doors open behind me. Russa slides his way by us, and I slowly back my way out of the lift. "Proceed with caution, Councilor. The world's a dangerous place..." Meelo glares back with utter disbelief. The lift doors close as we stare hatred into one another. I turn and begin down the concourse to my new office. Russa is glued to the floor. He's not getting soft on me, now is he? I turn back, and his eyes meet me with consternation. My flame still burns, and I bark to Russa.

"Hey! Are you coming or what?"

Russa begins to say something but stops himself. He takes a breath and follows me to my office.

God, I hate that fucking lift.

19

FARGO SHEPHERD

The Raid

Geeva and I pass under the tattered sheet metal awnings of a narrow Valley street in the fleeting hours of the night. The Valley is devoid of sunlight for most of the day, so the night seems to linger. The mountain peaks suffocate the shantytown below. The only growth that survives is the fungi and algae that thrive in the darkness. Much like its citizens.

String lights line the gridded Valley's narrow roads, flickering from the unstable power. Street urchins meet for unsavory dealings in the strobing darkness of its most nefarious regions. Shameless people who use any means necessary to improve their stock in life. As Geeva and I push our empty cart past back streets, our eyes meet theirs, and they glare back with animosity. I don't judge their hatred of us. Those who have not always despise those who have. It's been like that since the start of time. If they only knew how much *Hard* we carried on us from our deliveries today, my pistols would be in my hands, not my holsters! A double-edged sword of commerce in the Valley. Payments in *Hard* avoid Low Council digital detection but carrying that much physical currency around these parts is asking for trouble.

Geeva keeps her eyes peeled as we traverse the dark to our last client. She assesses every threat we pass and readies herself for action if the need should arise. My pistols are primed and loaded, but they're more symbolic than anything else. Geeva is my real protection.

My comm buzzes, and Cyto's name flashes across the interface.

"Got that info on Zina and her crew for me?" I ask.

"Yea, yea I got it, slick. Calm down." Cyto answers. "Small crime family from the east Valley. Known as the Rojo. Own a small chunk of the mountain line there. Just like I assumed, pretty low-level stuff, though. Either they're trying to make a power push, or they have no idea what they're holding," He says. "The girl you spoke of. She's their leader. Zina. Inherited the family business when Deterro and the Vipers wiped out three whole bloodlines about ten years back, including her parents. Don't know too much about the other members. Know she has a brother, but don't have any info on him. Then it's just your normal bandit crew. Muscle, financiers, drivers, etc." Cyto informs. "I'll send you over their last known address. Go ask nicely for it back!" He laughs.

My comm chirps and a map slides onto the screen. A blue diamond marks the location of their last known affiliate.

Great, another murderous crime family. As if the Vipers weren't enough of an issue. Images of the stolen case flash across my mind from the night Deterro gave it to me. The night Zina stole it from me. High Council seals were imprinted all across it. A thought that hadn't occurred to me yet strikes at my core. Tremors of fear racing down my spine. If Bytrol actually can morph to genes the way rumors claim it can, and that case contained it, the High Council must have had it under unthinkably tight security. If it's gone, they certainly know... And they'll be hunting for it too.

"Change of plans, we're heading East." I copy the map to Geeva's comm and quicken my pace, the gravity of our situation beginning to terrify me. "We need to get this shit back and get as far away from it as possible."

My stomach anxiously turns as we continue eastward. We've done too many extraction missions to expect this to be easy. There will undoubtedly be blood... I just hope it's theirs.

We go on foot for many reasons, but mainly discretion. My

luxury hauler was suspicious enough in the south where the Capital and the Valley begin to blend together, but in the east, all eyes would turn to the sky as we approach. We don't want to announce our presence, not just yet!

As the night grows thick, the temperature plummets, and frosty crystals float down gently from the blackness, crowding our sight. The snow sticks and turns soot-black, absorbing the grime of the dirty street. The crunch of snow under our boots echoes off the sheet metal of poorly constructed towers. And the chaos of the day has melted away, replaced with an eerie stillness as people fight to shelter themselves from the elements.

We pull our ThermHoods over our faces, and the feeling returns to my cheeks. The edges of our coats drag along the snow as well, and we creep through the haze like frozen phantoms. It's easy to tell which buildings are controlled by crime families and which aren't.

The tower we approach glows with stable light as the surrounding buildings sit in silent, frozen darkness. The only light that breaches through their hollowed-out window frames are the flickers of small garbage fires. Huddled masses crowd around the flames and their stretched shadows cast against the walls. The tower controlled by the Rojo, though, brims with light and heat and the loud laugher of privileged poverty. Proving a life of crime in the Valley is not only preferred, it's almost necessary!

Geeva and I stand across the corner to case the tower. Two Brushu grunts are stationed in front of the building. The glare of smokewraps burn on their lips. They lean lazily against the wall, the butts of their rifles wedged into the snow next to them. Two young recruits just trying to earn their stripes. My heart is heavy knowing their fate. More bystanders who will pay the ultimate sacrifice for the actions of those well above them. Violence still never sits well with me. But I am nothing if not a survivalist, and if I must kill to survive, so be it.

I tap Geeva on the shoulder and signal our plan with my hands. Stealth for as long as possible, brute force if need be.

Geeva pulls her ThermHood off, and her black hair spills from it in a wild mess. Her gorgeous emerald eyes are a sight to behold among the dreary grey landscape. A hybrid as well, but thankfully, for her sake and mine, she doesn't resemble Cyto in the slightest. Full plum lips and ghostly pale skin. A trendy tattoo of some primitive Earthly text cascades down her forehead, to either side of her nose and down to her neck in two thin columns. She has an exotic beauty I'm drawn to and a sharp aura about her that few others have matched. She briefly glances with soft affection and a sigh. I return the look and half a smile. We're too similar, too self-indulgent, too unique in our makeup to enjoy the tension that wafts between us. We put on a good show for Cyto, but for a moment, she was more than my gorgeous bodyguard. There was a time where I fell under the spell of her devilish grin, but neither of us was capable of the self-sacrifice required for love. Even so, she still can peel back layers of the mask I wear and begin to expose the warmer, deeper emotions that have been repressed from years of promiscuity. The type of feelings that blinded me from the ruse of Zina's doing. The feelings that lead me to the circumstances of now. It's the thoughts of Zina that spark my concentration again. No time for the regrets of love lost or embarrassing mistakes made of the heart. It's time for business.

Geeva tosses her hair and unbuttons her coat, nearly exposing the delicate parts of her. She struts her way toward the guards, weapons all hidden behind her, as I flank secretly to the side. A laughably cliché plan that works with calculated precision. The men a slave to their biology.

Geeva whistles as she approaches, as gusts of frigid wind whip her hair and coat. She's hard to ignore! The guards step out from their post under a rattling awning, one totting his rifle, the laziest leaving his behind. Both are portly men with coarse amber beards that stretch down their chests. Their bottom arms are far shorter than they should be. The unarmed guard yells out something in a wild Brushu dialect that's rarely ever used. I've never heard it before. Geeva puts on a desperate face and calls to the men.

"Have food? A bed? I don't have *Hard*, but maybe we can figure something out..." She's a wonderful actress, and the guards consume her performance.

"*Ch'oy!*" The unarmed guard removes his hat and tidies his stringy hair as his eyes disgustingly baste Geeva. "It's our lucky day Grimdu." The guard laughs to his partner as he circles her.

"*Ch'oy.* It. Is!" The armed guard replies with an arrogant smirk.

"Shall we then?!" Geeva gestures for the door. The three of them crunch through the snow and disappear through the doors to the tower.

I sit patiently around the corner of the building, listening to the rumble of the wind through the alleys and hollow structures. Snow builds on the edges of my shoulders. My ThermHood covers all but the edges of my eyes, which water in the chill.

"*Fargo!*" Geeva whispers from the doorframe. The sound almost gets lost in the symphony of the weather.

I peer my head around the corner and Geeva signals for me to follow. I hug the face of the tower and duck my way under the door cameras that Geeva has tilted upright. I trail her through the double doors and reset the camera's viewpoints as we enter the building. Warmth wraps my body as the door seals us inside the insulated complex.

The bodies of the two guards are piled atop one another in a heap of silently executed flesh. Geeva glares at me with agitation. She hates the seductive stranger bit. I roll my eyes and mouth, '*I'm sorry,*' but she knows I trust her with much more than the deception of despicable men. No matter how hard of a time I give her, I can't do this without her. She's the needle that breaks the skin, and I'm the virus that infects the blood.

Inside the doors is a blank entryway with a tight stairwell that leads to the levels above, eight in total. The cold grey walls from the outside, replaced by red-stained paint. I pull my pistols from their holsters and prime them into silence mode. The hum of their discharge chambers dips an octave, muted machines of pain. Geeva sheds her coat. Under her thick hided jacket is an exoskeleton of weaponry. She's an angel of death. A spine harness is lined with three sets of dual-chamber pistols like mine, just decorated with feverish designs. Thin metal slats connect at hinges in the shoulders and elbows and trace her arms, cuffing at the wrists. Stun tipped throwing daggers are cranked onto their magnetic locks, four on each tricep. Non-lethal sonopulsers and blinders line her belt. Meager ingredients in her stew of agony. And finally, the main course she will serve to her unsuspecting victims is connected by a compression hose that attaches to a valve on her exoskeleton's chest. Her rapidrifle screams out tiny balls of time-delayed ammunition, no bigger than a drop of rain, that fire with such force from the chemically compressed hose, they can shred through any material.

She's a terrifying metallic deity of contraband.

She turns her ThermHood inside out and pulls it back over her face. A white skull is woven into the design, and she looks at me with wild excitement, ready to tear through the building.

She smacks me on the ass and darts up the stairs, leaving me standing there incredulous.

Wow, maybe I do love this woman? I laugh to myself and follow her up the stairs.

Geeva leads quickly, but stealthily. The first floor is quiet. A hallway is lined with crammed bedrooms like a dormitory. Each dark room has a ragged door that closes it off from the lit hallway. It's the only thing separating the sleeping souls inside from the reaper who awaits them. Geeva carefully slides open the first door on the right as I creep behind. Another amber bearded man slumbers on a small cot against the back wall. She stalks her way toward the bed, pulls a dagger from her arm, and in one motion, covers the man's mouth and jabs the dagger up through his jaw.

I have to look away.

The aftermath of death is far more digestible than the raw, guttural act itself.

Geeva lurks room to room, only half are occupied. She moves with lethal grace and speed. This environment suits her far better than the gopher routes of typical days. I stay near the edge of the stairwell, looking out for incoming threats. Geeva returns to my end of the hall, the blood of her victims fresh on her sleeve. She starts up the stairs to the next level without hesitation, but I turn back to look down the hall. The playfulness of the moment before vanishes in an instant as I stare back at the silent hallway. We morphed this dorm into a crypt. I balk at how easily we just wiped eight lives from the world. The gravity of our undertaking hadn't set in until now. And for a moment, I fear Geeva. A wave of uncertainty rushes over me. What are we doing?! This is supposed to be an extraction, not a massacre. I grab Geeva by the harness and pull her back down to the first level. Her manic eyes now frighten me.

"What are we doing?!" I whisper. Insecurity plagues my voice.

"What?" Geeva is confused. She glances back to the stairs, anxious to continue her tirade. Why are all the people I'm closest to so eager for violence?

"We just murdered eight people..." I whisper. "How is this part of the plan?"

"*I* murdered eight people! You stood there and watched." She corrects. "Fargo, this was *your* plan..."

"We're here to get the Bytrol. Not kill these people."

"Fargo, there could be dozens of armed Rojo in this tower; if any one of them warns the others, we're fucked!" Her brow is firm and commanding. Determined to shake the doubt from my bones. "We can't risk leaving them alive."

"I know, I know." I guess I hadn't thought about what exactly I was directing her to do.

"If we don't get the Bytrol back to Deterro, he'll hunt us down and slaughter everyone we've ever known! Our deaths will be nothing like theirs," She says, pointing down the hall. "It will be merciless and agonizing. They'll tear the limbs from our loved ones before our eyes and break us like wild dogs." I know all this, but there has to be another viable solution. Killing everyone can't be the only way.

"This is not like anything we've been in Fargo. I understand your reservation, I do. But I will not let my family and my friends be snuffed out like insects because you can't stomach survival! This is your mess! Clean it up!" Her words are harsh but true. My ego is bruised from the scolding, and I have to recover. At this moment, she's my subordinate, not my friend.

"I can stomach survival! I've clawed through the mud for everything I have! Don't talk to me as if I don't know struggle." My eyes signal pseudo-anger as I whisper yell at her. "But how are we supposed to find the Bytrol if we kill every person in the building?" I point out, trying to make her reconsider her murderous rampage. "I gave you these weapons for *defense*, not *offense*."

She looks to me with more conviction than I to her.

"Offense *is* our only defense Fargo." She states. "They brought this upon themselves. This is kill or be killed! Nut up!" Her eyes overpower me. I feel in my gut that there has to be a better way, but right now, I can't think of one. All that rolls through my mind are nauseating images of the repercussions of failure here. Vipers using their favorite torture methods on her. Torturing Victor and Miku and Cyto as well. Dipping their arms in the acid vats they use to make Venom. Carving away their eyelids, so their eyes painstakingly dry out and disintegrate. High Council soldiers dragging us to detention cells. Locking us away in cells at the bottom of hell. Screams no one can hear as we rot away in isolation.

I concede.

Violence it is.

"...Fine," I say, disappointment dripping from my tongue.

It's the weakest I've ever felt. "But if we find Zina... we need her alive!"

We sweep through the floors of the tower, like fog overwhelming the sky. Few even see us before they are struck down. Pistol's thumping their muted tone and daggers silencing throats before they can call out. Men and women slurping down broth as evening meals. Reading old print copied books. Washing in communal showers. We slice through them all.

The barrels of my pistols steam with vengeance, but my mind still fights itself with every life we extinguish. A tumor of horror swelling in my chest. We've been a silent plague. And it tears me apart.

The top two floors abandon their dorm hallway design for large open shared areas. A filthy kitchen is littered with used cooking pots and utensils. The rusty hull of a first-generation *Speedster* is overturned and acts as a table in the common area to the side. Ten Rojo members sit in a circle around the hull, playing games and getting drunk on haze. They laugh and yell at one another, their weapons strewn casually about the dilapidated lounge. The dire conditions make me question our tactics even more. These are not people who live a life of luxury. They are the exact type of people who I claim to be one of. Those who have to use the cloudier side of righteousness to create opportunity. Those who create purpose where there was none. Whether they stole the Bytrol on purpose or not, I empathize with their plight. And yet I cut them down without thought like Gold Grain for harvest. This will be a scar that may never heal.

We scan the area from the concealment of the stairwell, no Zina.

Geeva looks to me, tapping her rapidrifle. Essentially asking for permission to go loud. I signal with my hands to try the top level first and see if we can avoid direct confrontation. She strains in frustration but obliges.

We sneak up the short set of stairs to the landing in between levels, avoiding detection. The top level is one large bedroom. The penthouse of the impecunious.

Colorful beads drape from the entrance to the room and block our line of sight to the far corners. A polished wooden table rests in the middle of the room. The nicest piece of furniture we've seen in the building. Something gleans in the light on the table. I recognize it. It's an ignition key for a high-end rig. Maybe a luxury *Stretcher* or *Hauler*, like mine. Regardless, it's far too expensive of a vehicle for anyone in this building to own. I signal for Geeva to hold as I carefully pull apart the beads to the room. I peer in, ever so slightly.

There she is...

Zina's fiery locks are tied into two tight braids that run from her forehead to the back of her scalp. Her powerful legs, carved with angles of seduction, silk smooth. She stands in front of a dirty mirror, removing the sweat of the day from her face. Her eyes sparkle with amber and gold, just the way I remember them. Her beauty strikes me, and a pang of anger dances its way through my heart. Why do I feel so betrayed by someone I do not know?! Before I can signal Geeva, our eyes meet. Her face contorts like a Tyko lurks in her living room. Terror floods her eyes as she comprehends who I am. She darts across the room, and I lunge in after her. But I'm too late.

Sirens wail and warning lights strobe throughout the tower of a breach. Geeva comes crashing into the room as I pin Zina to the ground.

"They're coming!" Geeva yells. She slides behind the heavy table, flipping it onto its side. She mounts her RapidRifle onto its ridge and aims at the stairwell. It will be a slaughterhouse if they storm up those stairs.

I drag Zina behind the table as well, kicking and screaming the whole way. She's stronger than I am, but I have positioning. I grab a dagger off Geeva's arm and activate its stun-point. Zina nearly kicks free, ramming a heel into Geeva's shoulder. The impact causes her to clamp down on the trigger. A hailstorm of bullets shreds through the compound. The stampeding footsteps in the stairwell grind to a halt. I carve the stun blade into Zina's thigh deeper than intended. Her body convulses until she collapses. Temporarily paralyzed.

Rojo grunts gather in the stairwell. Panic and rage in their voices as they learn the rest of the tower is dead. Most of the beads still block our view out of the room, but a small section is missing. I scramble to change my pistol settings to burst and join Geeva mounted on the edge of the table.

Her breath is steady and poised. She doesn't fear death. My breath, though, is erratic and paced. Anxiety rifling through me. Maybe we're not as similar as I thought.

We can feel rifle barrels peering over the stairwell's edge at us, like trench warfare of the famous Earth battles. They stare

203

at us with rage and retribution for their fallen comrades. Our No Man's Land is about twenty meters but feels far closer. I swear I can hear the pulse of my enemy, drumming against his veins. Smell the sweat that beads from his forehead in angst. Feel the fright that stifles his breath.

The stillness is pure terror.

Nobody moves.

Geeva keeps her finger on the trigger as she pulls a Sonopulser off her belt. She nudges me and tilts her head to the right without taking her eyes off the invisible enemy. I leave one pistol on the table and grab a Blinder on the other side of her belt. She holds up all three fingers and then points one straight ahead. I understand the plan. I nod, and she begins the count down.

3...

2...

1...

We lob our Non-lethal at the stairwell. The orbs seem to float for an eternity before clanging against the hard floor. The world is still for a moment before the explosions of sound and light consume the stairwell. We try to rush the soften line, but as the orbs detonate, the thugs blindly squeeze their triggers in fear. Bullets scream past us. Ripping into the table and shredding the thin sheet metal behind us. I cower behind the table, flinching at every round that snaps just above my head. Frigid wind howls its way in through the bullet holes in the exterior wall and whistles a haunting song. Adding to the groans of deafened men and the shriek of rifle muzzles.

Geeva slings her RapidRifle over the table and blindly returns fire. Roaring with intensity. It takes all her might to control the recoil of the gun with just one hand. The RapidRifle's lurid death note strikes dread among the defending gangsters. A voice screams out over the gun's dirge. You can barely hear it.

The bullets cease in our direction, and I grab ahold of Geeva, who was lost in a trance of violence.

The silence is marred by the sound of smoking guns and injured Rojo and the rhythmic bouncing of beads torn from the wall. A voice calls out to us again.

"Don't fire! Don't fire!"

I peer my head around the side of the table. Four hands extend upward over the staircase, showing us he's unarmed. His head peeks over the top as well. The beads have all been shredded from the wall and scattered about the room. Our view of our enemy, no longer blocked.

A small beady-eyed man calls out to us. His hair, dark. Absent of the amber flairs of his partners. His voice is high pitched, nasally. His tongue moving with a different rhythm than the rest, though you can hear the root of his accent. He calls out, but his voice lacks the fear I would've anticipated. He's confident. Arrogant almost.

"Where is Zina?" He yells out. I crank my neck around even more to get a better view of him. He looks familiar... "Where is my sister?" He yells out again. *Sister*? Well, we found her brother...

"She's here. She's fine... For now..." I yell back in between breaths. I rest my head back against the table, pulling the ThermHood off. My heart nearly burst from my chest. Buried bullets lodged into the thick wood of the table freckle the once smooth underside. The frozen draft from outside pricks at my steaming skin.

"Let her go, and we'll let *you* go!" He offers. I laugh.

"Or how about I kill all of you instead and take her with me?" My bravado is far more intimidating than the reality.

"Well, we can't have that. Now can we?" He chirps with a smug tone. As if he holds the cards. Something's not right. "I know why you're here, Fargo." I shudder when he says my name. I peek my head around the corner once more. I know him.... Who is it that? I stare desperately from behind my cover, trying to decode his face. "Now I think we can help each other out here, Mister Shepherd. You do something for me, and I'll give you back the money my sister took from you." I scrunch my brow in confusion and breathe a sigh of relief.

"I don't care about the money, you fucking moron!" I laugh hysterically as I realize he has no idea what he has gotten himself into. "I need the Bytrol. We're all dead if I don't get it back. You, me, your sister." I can't help but laugh in hysteria, surging in mania from the bout of trauma I just experienced.

He doesn't respond. I can hear the wheels in his head turn as he realizes he doesn't know as much as he thought.

"What is Bytrol? What are you talking about?" He asks cautiously.

"You idiots..." I still can't catch my breath. "In my safe. The night Zina and you goons stole from me." I hiccup in shock, breathing a bizarre, unhealthy pattern. "I received a package. Bytrol. From Deterro himself, that was supposed to be tested. Tonight, mind you... Once it was tested, I was supposed to return it." My hiccups subdue, and my mind begins to calm. I can see the pure horror on his face when he hears Deterro's name and plays out how the rest of the exchange will go. "When he doesn't get it back, he'll send a legion of Vipers after me. And when they catch me and torture me, whose name do you think will fly from my mouth as quickly as I can spit it out?" I close my eyes exhausted, spelling out the bleak reality he's stumbled into.

He pauses. Overwhelmed by the thought of Viper mercenaries slithering through his world once again. But he's brash and foolish. I can see ignorant pride veto his rational thoughts.

"Well, I have a proposal then." He walks his way from behind the stairwell and into the entrance of the room, standing just ten meters from me, unarmed. I spin and ready my pistol on him. He raises his hands to pacify my threat.

"Why should I not rip a hole through you right now?" I ask, one eye closed, the other sighted on his forehead.

"You really think you can take all of us by yourself?" He asks. "Even if you can, I don't think your partner has that long." My head whips to Geeva. Blood pools at the base of the table. She lays in a crumpled heap on top of it. I was in such shock I didn't notice she hadn't been moving. I frantically pull her ThermHood off and check her pulse. She's alive.

"Geeva!" I whisper. Dangerously dark blood soaks her abdomen.

"Accept my offer, and I'll let you leave here with her. Don't. And you will have to fight your way to freedom. You may kill us all, but she will surely die." The man remains standing in the middle of the room with his hands up, the other men watch on anxiously from cover.

My mind races. Panic clutters my thoughts. I glance over the table once again.

"What do you want!" I yell. My heart cringing, watching the blood continue to pour from Geeva.

"There's a Battle of Warlords fight in two days. I want to win, and I want to eliminate Victor. You get the ogre to agree to that, and you'll have your Bytrol." He smirks with the callous of an insane man.

The words seem so ludicrous as they leave his mouth. My mind is still so tangled in the fate of my friend that I don't fully comprehend his request. But as I look up once more at the man, I now understand why I recognize his face. It's plastered all over Groga next to Victor's. In advertisements for the Arena. In marketing ploys where they push narratives of

Warlord rivalries. The vulture. The rat. Silva stands before me. I stare at him in utter disbelief.

"You'd jeopardize all of our lives for an Arena fight?" I ask, dumbfounded. "Your life? Your sister's life?" I stare at this hollow creature. The realization of Silva and Zina's relationship making me wondering if he set this whole thing up? "Vipers have already torn through your family once; you'd let them do it again?"

"The Arena *is* my life! Defeating Victor would not just change my life, but every Rojo under our mooned crest! They could leave the Valley. And my sister could give up this exhausting pursuit of reestablishing our family's legitimacy." Silva drones.

He preaches noble intentions, but I see nothing but selfish motivations behind his eyes. The ignition key that rested on the table earlier now lays by my feet. The pieces of that puzzle now coming together. It must belong to Silva. Who else here could afford such an expensive rig? Seems like he already has the means to help but chooses luxury rigs and high-end clothes instead. Regardless, I don't have time to decipher his true reasonings, nor do I care. I grab the ignition key and shove it in my pocket. An escape plan beginning to formulate in my brain. Geeva's skin is losing warmth. I have to act quick.

"Deal!" I grab the RapidRifle and spray bullets in a circle at the wall behind me. Silva flinches. I stand up, backing away toward the wall behind me, gun now primed in his direction and kick out a hole in the weakened sheet metal where my bullets outlined. The panel rips off and hurls toward the cold, dead streets. Wind gusts its way in. The frigid breeze scratching at my cheeks. I reach into my pocket with my free hand and press the locator on the ignition key. We stand there like frozen monuments until a sparkling luxury *Stretcher* appears outside the open hole. Hovering in place, eight stories high. Silva lunges forward in protest when he sees his rig. But I buck my gun at him, and he backs down. The long side door hisses open and exposes its gorgeous stretched interior. I grab Geeva as I keep my eyes on Silva and the grunts, and gently place her onto the floor of the rig.

The other Rojo have advanced beyond the stairwell and now fill the room. Anxious fingers wrapped around rifle triggers. I glance at Zina's body crumpled up behind the table, then back to the grunts. Another bad idea forms.

"I'm taking her as collateral!" I dart back in for Zina, grab her and dive into the *Stretcher*, slamming the mechanical door behind me. Bullets shred into the rig. I scurry into the cockpit as Silva screams something at me, but I can't hear him over the roar of the engines. The rig punches into the night sky as I set course for the nearest MedCenter and the glowing Rojo tower begins to fade into the distance.

I put the rig on auto-navigate and rush back to attend to Geeva. Overwhelmed tears begin to crest along the ridges of my eyes. I shake violently. The rig cuts through the snowy sky as I hold Geeva, my fingers running through her blood clotted hair. Zina lays incapacitated to my left, white foam accumulating in the corners of her lips from the stun poison. I stare at the two mangled women with silent traumatized sobs, and all I can think of are the words I said to Victor over and over again in my naïve tantrum.

I've got it under control.

My body quivers. Nothing could be farther from the truth.

20

LEO

ABERNATHY

Death From Above

News of Gwinn's inauguration cycles everywhere. We've been traveling for hours, and I've seen it sourced from dozens of publications on my dataplate. I don't know how many times I called last night. It was too many. I know that. But when I saw the news of Wylk's death, I feared the worst. I had to hear her voice. I had to know she couldn't have done this. I needed to know she hadn't done something you can't come back from.

I scroll through the stories. Pundits scream atop one another about the legality of Trakstull's actions. Those supporting the Regal praise him for his decisiveness in such a tumultuous time. Stabilizing a province that desperately needed it. Those opposed to him drone on and on about the overstep of power and cry the warnings of Ancient atrocities committed centuries prior.

Our rig soars through the clouds as we course for the Rift. My cockpit is quiet. I've had enough propaganda pedaling for one day, so I switch over to the sketchpad of my dataplate. The files here are littered with sketches of the Vault. Crude drawings of the Redemption hub. Incomplete traces of the workstations. The observation deck. The key slot in the control panel with the diamond-ladder-shaped insert. The massive disc wall. Everything I can remember of that place. It festers in my mind. The obsession spreading through my head like an unstoppable ivy.

I thumb through the drawings until I reach the chaotic notes of my womb formula work. Rough lines twist into a double helix. Notes of how human DNA is structured and how it operates scatter the page. Missing genetic information, marked in red. Endless sequences of attempted womb accelerants cascading down the edge of the page. None of them correct. File after file of failed attempts to resurrect humanity. I hurry back to the sketch of the Redemption. My mind heavy with the weight of the world. The answers are here. I can feel it. Or maybe I'm so desperate I've convinced myself they are. Either way, the moment we get back from this mission, I'm returning to the Vault.

The crew is busy with their prep work in the cabin behind me. Nervous energy hangs over us. I stow the dataplate and let the whistle of the wind against the windshield clear my mind. It's times like these when I close my eyes and try to picture what my father would be thinking in *his* pilot's chair. Floating through the empty vacuum of space. Hauling the hope of an entire species. Staring into blank nothingness and praying answers lay on a horizon that's yet to come into frame. The weight of existence chewing at the strands of optimism that have held him together. The sheer impossibility of faith in those circumstances. How badly do I wish I could've met the incredible man.

But today I don't think of him. Don't think of our ancestral voyage or the chronology of humanity. I think of Gwinn. I contemplate the absurdity of her situation and can't comprehend why she insists on forging through that slog alone. Why she refuses to speak with me? Where along the line I lost her? And what I can do to get her back. She needs my help right now, more than ever, but how do you help someone who refuses to accept it? The body is only as strong as the mind allows it to be.

My thoughts scatter as our rig quakes from turbulence. My focus tightens. Patawa darts through the airlock to check on me.

"You ok?!" She asks, eyes wild with concern.

"Yea. We're here..." I answer, throat tightening. I flip a

switch on the dashboard, and a red light pulses softly underneath it. "Director. Bird R8 entering Rift Anomaly Zone, Grid Beta." My hands work with fluid grace along the rig's interface as I signal our entry point to the Rift. Fingers gliding over the cool glass of the dataplates.

"Understood R8. Patching you through to High Councilor Russa." The Air Director replies.

Russa answers through a grainy comm signal. The Rift beginning to interfere with its clarity.

"*Leo, I'm warning you now, today is not the day for your normal shit.*" Just the way you want to be greeted. But I'd bet my left hand his attitude is a product of whatever is going on with Gwinn. Why won't she let me help her? "*Got everything straight and tidy?*" He continues, far less professional than the Director or me. Sometimes I wonder why he insists on being so directly involved. Seems like a job for delegation, or at least some chain of command. But knowing Russa, I think he enjoys personally seeing to it that my days are as painstaking as possible.

"Entry point located, exploration zone mapped, and exfil locations A, B, and C locked." My palms sweat as the mysterious grey chasm approaches into our view. We've only come to the Rift once, and none of us ever wished to return. Russa's cavalier tone frustrates me.

"*Sounds good.*" His voice is distant. Tense. He signaled me, yet all of his focus is light-years away. Focused on something else.

Anxious energy builds in my throat the closer we get.

"Clearance level for engagements?" I request restlessly.

Russa doesn't answer.

"High Councilor?" I repeat. Nothing again, but I can hear the commotion of him adjusting awkwardly from an uncomfortable position. My frustrations boil over, and I snap.

"RUSSA!" I yell into the comm. This finally gets his attention.

"*Excuse me?*" He replies, insulted. He pauses. I can picture the scowl on his beak as he lets the silence remind me of my place. "*...Green for Environmental. Green for Synthetic. And Green for Organic. Clear for all engagements. Prime+ Priority level for the asset.*" His tone shifts as he issues explicit and severe instruction. I let another moment pass in silence to act as my apology.

"R8 acknowledges Green for all engagements and Prime+ Priority level." I respond conservatively. I don't know how

Gwinn likes Russa. She doesn't like anyone but clings to him for support? I'll never get it. I can't stand the guy. Maybe it's the boss, subordinate dynamic? I don't know... "Breaching Anomaly Zone in three."

"Carry on R8," Russa says.

"Oh, High Councilor..." I blurt out before he can click off. He doesn't respond but allows me to continue. "...will you tell Gwinn... I mean, High Councilor DeMarco, congratulations for me. I know how much this position means to her."

We sit in awkward silence for a moment, then the comm clicks off abruptly. Patawa glances away quickly as I catch her eavesdropping behind me.

"I don't want to hear it." I grumble to her as I turn back.

The Air Director is redirected back onto our clearer regional comms.

"Director, going dark in two. Request Zone Entry signal signature and full cargo activation." I request.

"Green. Copy, going dark. Uh... Good luck, R8..." The Air Director adds informally at the end. She does a poor job of masking her uneasiness.

"Thank you, Director. Comm out," I say and flip the switch back off, the pulsing red light dying with it.

"Suit up!" I yell back through the opened airlock doors. "Full Green, Bryl... Load it all." I nervously bark back to the rest of the crew. As I do, the Director's authorization signal activates our High Council controlled gear. Our four suits illuminate and commence their rapid boot sequence. The exploratory equipment flickers to life as well. I turn my attention back to our destination. The warped air ahead of us looks like the heat rising from a scalding hot stone.

I take a deep breath to calm my nerves, and our comms scramble as we pass through a warped veil of light and enter the Anomaly Zone.

The Rift lurks thousands of meters below.

It's bizarre magnetic field tugs at the seams of our vessel. Gravity thick and heavy, the metal panels groan under pressure. Our gauges seize and contort uncontrollably. The warped field parts the clouds on either side, like an invisible wall billowing smoke from an inferno. The Rift's crack stretches from pole to pole like a hatchet wound, separating the Eastern and Western hemispheres of the planet. Its harsh terrain contrasting with nearly every biome the world as to offer. In the Western hemisphere, the Lotopi Sea to its south weakly penetrates the force field and dribbles down the sides of the fault. The trees of Berban all curve slightly away from the Rift along the central grids. And the Opora Sea acts much the same in the north as the waters do in the south. In the East, the fault line conflicts with the frigid northern regions of Su Hoz, creating massive snowbanks along its border. The ridges of Dwual Fir, where the Old Consulate ruins lay and the lowest elevated Grogan Island *Canter*, run along the central grid. And the Savron Slums line the southern grids of the hemisphere.

Electrical static sparks violently between ultra-charged particles suspended in the air. Bright light from the midday sun wrenches in absurd ways and doesn't reach the floor of the Rift. All that lays below the distorted Anomaly Zone is darkness. Patawa, Bryl, and Spri all meet me in the cockpit and stare out into the schism with silent reservation.

"I was hoping we'd never have to come back here..." Patawa murmurs.

"You knew we would." Spri answers. Even the ice-veined Bryl has to take a moment to compose himself.

The jagged steel-grey rock splinters open and expose the intestines of the planets. Chaotic spontaneous combustions rattle our vessel. We flinch with each burst of energy. Our rig chews through the Anomaly Zone as Spri tries to locate our landing sector.

We slug through the turbulence for some time, rig bucking and rattling continuously. The chop of the air shakes our wings, our headlights off, worthless in the fractal. The cockpit is silent as the tension of our journey squeezes our mouths shut. If there was any other way to our location, we'd take it.

"Bank left ten degrees." Spri directs. I strain as the manual controls combat my efforts to navigate. The ship violently bucks once more, pulling the rig nose down. We desperately cling to whatever we can hold as our magnetic harnesses fail. I yank up as hard as I can to correct course, but the gravity drags us farther and farther down. Raging debris swirls with menace the deeper into the suspension zone we dive. The gravel and ice and vegetation pulled into the Anomaly Zone pelts our ship with a deafening barrage. Like hail shot from a railcannon against a tin roof. The debris blinds our approach as static cracks just meters above our wing.

"BANK LEFT LEO!" Spri yells over the thunderous noise. He points as he fights to stay grounded in his seat. "BANK LEFT!" I lean on the controls with all my weight, and the rig begins to yaw. The cries of the ship intensify. I glance at

Patawa, who is frozen in fear. Her knuckles white as she grasps her harness for dear life. Bryl's jaw is clenched, vice tight. His swollen arms wrapped through the harness, and his heel presses firmly on the back of Patawa's chair, wedging himself in place. Spri's eyes flicker with frenzy. I have to regain control, they're counting on me, the rig can't take much more abuse.

I prop my foot on the control board to prep myself and yell to the crew with as much confidence as I can muster.

"YOU GUYS TRUST ME?!" I scream to them, false conviction on my face. They return worrisome looks and nod. "THEN HOLD ON!" I take a deep breath and dive the rig straight down.

We plunge.

I shield myself from the drop, but the crew whiplashes, and the ship croaks with disapproval. We plummet straight down, rocks, and debris smashing into our windshield, but it holds. The crew battles to stay in their seats. Gravity begging them to come crashing to the helm of the ship. Our speed builds and builds. The g-force intensifying. My mind focused, ignoring the surrounding signs of destruction. We free-fall deeper and deeper. The darkness hiding its horrid secrets from us. My neck strains as I pull with every ounce of strength I have on the elevation throttle. *Just get it to twenty degrees...* The ship begins to obey. Lifting its nose. Our velocity slowing. But before I regain control, the windshield shatters. A large rock smashes through the hull, fracturing the glass, shards exploding in all directions. Patawa screams in terror. I can't see. Debris filling the cockpit. An ice chunk hurls into my arm, knocking it from the throttle. The ship bucks again. I frantically search for a lane of visibility until the endless swarm of debris suddenly stops as we punch through the Anomaly Zone.

My nerves settle as breath finally explodes from my lungs. We descend smoothly. The rig's headlamps clicking on. But my comfort was premature as Patawa screams out once again.

"PULL UP! PULL UP! PULL UP!" She points in horror through the clear side of the windshield and braces herself for impact. The now visible headlights illuminating the rapidly approaching Rift floor.

"Oh shit!!"

I pull up as hard as I can and Spri pounds on the emergency landing rails release valve. The ship's nose begins to climb, but it's not enough. We scream for our lives, but the horrid clamor of steel against rock drowns out our cries as we impact the floor. My head slams against the console. Warning sirens wail of ship damage and we grind against the rugged surface of the Rift. Our wing clips a stacked formation and shears from the hull, flipping the rig end over end. The roof caves as we skid and roll through the chasm. Bryl clumsily yanks at the back of Patawa's seat and shatters the reclining hinge dropping her into a horizontal position. The roof crumbles under the weight of the ship just where Patawa's head was. Bryl lurches over her, both bodies jerking back and forth chaotically, shielding her from the shrapnel of the shredded roof panels. My hands no longer hold the controls, and I slip from my harness. I slam into the ceiling and then back down to the floor as the ship rolls. Spri reaches for my hand as I fall again, but his head jerks viciously from another impact, and I watch his body go limp. The rig doesn't ever seem to slow. We crash for an eternity. We hit another stack formation, and my body is hurled through the open airlocked doors and into the back-cargo bay. I grasp ahold of a twine cargo net and wrap my body around the ratcheted down equipment.

A crack breaches the hull of the ship along the floor. With every hit, I watch it widen and widen until the vessel's cockpit rips from the rig in a violent burst and is launched into the darkness. I cry out to my friends who speed into the unknown, trapped within the crushed cockpit. Wind explodes into the hull, the darkness outside only a blur of madness. The change in pressure nearly knocking me unconscious. The rig slams into a sidewall of the Rift, lodging the only intact wing into a crevasse and jarring the ship to an abrupt halt. The stop yanks my grip from the net, and I'm hurled against the rig's metal panels and drop to the floor.

Silence.

My lungs wheeze in agony. My bones crying for help. I squirm involuntarily in pain against the filth covered floor. My entire being fraught with misery. The deafening roar of our doomed vessel finally plays its last note. And all that's left is the noise of wind sucking against the once pressurized cabin.

I roll to my back. Eyes squeezed shut in exhaustion. The dirt and the air are one and the same here. Heavy hacking coughs try to eject the soot from my lungs as each inhale draws more and more in. My abs may tear from my torso if I keep coughing this hard. Where is my suit? I palm my way around the cargo hold, desperately scanning for my suit stand. Every cough, worse than the one before. I move so slow, my body still jarred from the crash. I pull myself along tethered ropes and clamped equipment crates until my hands recognize the shape of a suit leg. Violent coughs endlessly pounding against my sinuses, desperate for clean air. I crawl to my suit, thankfully undamaged, and weakly glide my way inside. Legs first. Trunk second. Arms third. The activation button on the suit's dataplate compresses the seals along the suit spine, and I collapse to the ground.

The suit's visor spits images of current systems in front of my vision. Oxygen, power, integrity, etc. I signal for our crew's local comm. The global signal doesn't escape the Anomaly Zone, but I pray our suit-to-suit waves can still connect underneath it.

"Guys!..." I gasp, still trying to catch my breath. "Anyone. Bryl. Pat. Spri? Can you hear me?!" I plead for the sound of their voices. Static fills the other end of the comm. I click it again.

"Can you hear me? Are you ok?" My eyes close. Body limp against the warmth of my suit's insulation. "...anybody..." My voice trails off. Again, just static.

I allow myself the chance to recoup. Eyes still glued to the backs of my eyelids. I check my body. Arms, legs, back, ribs. I miraculously avoided any serious injuries. It gives me hope that the others are alive too. Then I remember the final moments of our crash. Spri, unconscious. His body being tossed back and forth, just barely strapped into his loose harness. Patawa laying parallel to the floor, Bryl hunched over top of her, a crushed roof panel inches from them both. The only thing that gives me hope is that they were all in their suits. I have to believe they survived. Even as the images of the cockpit tearing from the hull and catapulting into the abyss cycle over and over in my mind. I have to believe.

Fighting to my feet is a chore. Nothing seriously hurt, but everything mildly hurt. I flick on my helmet lights, and two white beams slice through the dark. My lights scan over parts of the hull, and my optimism waivers. The ship is destroyed. A crippled mass of steel and ultra-panels. Wrenched metal curls around jagged rock. Glass from busted running lights scatter across the ground, and dirt from the Rift floor muddies the white of the hull. I carefully weave my way through the catastrophic mess. A trunk clamped down by ultra-steel ratchets thankfully remains intact. Dented and bent, but still here. I toss the net off the trunk and pry its bent frame open. Bryl's arsenal rests inside untouched. I grab a railcannon and all his weapons, a few of his fanciest gadgets, and a *Floater*. I clear a small area of debris from around me and place the Floater on the ground. I sync the Floater with my dataplate, and its interface wedge appears. The thin rectangular box sputters to life and lifts off the ground, about hip-high, hovering in place. I load the Floater with medical supplies from Patawa's gear and GeoSonar equipment from Spri's. My stomach turns when I realize they're out there without any of this. Stranded with no resources. My pace quickens.

Dirt crunches under my boots as I take my first steps in the Rift in years. Darkness surrounds me. The sound of my breath against my visor fills my ears, heavy and broken. My helm lights probe the unknown. Sharp rocks protrude from dull stacks of minerals. Bizarre vegetation snakes its way all over, growing untamed even without the help of sunlight. Brown and flecked with silver. The occasional flare of myrite bursts with colorful streaks at the very top of the Rift. Static from the Anomaly Zone igniting the potent dust. It makes no noise but startles me as it flashes across the chasm. The Floater follows just behind me as I creep through the haunting canyon.

A blood-curdling screech crackles in the air, echoing off the towering walls of rock. I swing my railcannon around, and the green laser attached to the barrel darts into the abyss and eventually vanishes. My helm lights can only expose so much. I stand frozen, hair pricked along my skin in fear. *Dystrogars*... Nearly mythical creatures of death that lurk in the pitch blackness of the Rift. Said to have been the first living organisms on the planet. They fell into the Rift and were never able to get back out. They evolved for millennia without any viable threats. They feast on the blind slugs, rodents, and vermin who comprise the extreme conditions. Feral, ghastly, prehistoric creatures who were bred to kill beasts far larger than anything still alive today. Massive winged creatures with six razor-sharp talons, one per each bony appendage. A perforated armored tail with a stinger the size of a Gaz staff dangles freely under it as they stalk from the height of the cliffs. Their terrorizing clicking screech sends sonar pulses out into the darkness and sends them back the locations of its prey. Eyeless serpent birds of death swoop from the air devouring everything in their path. Swift death from above. If they find my crew before I do... I shiver at the thought and push on.

I stride quickly with hushed feet. The screeching of Dystrogars sending indescribable fear rifling through my nerves. Their sonar waves rattle off the walls, disorienting me. My human ears, not built for echolocation. I need the light to see where I step, but I occasionally search along the heights of the Rift wall line. Another thought horrifies me as I see the size of the cliffside. If I find my crew, and they're alive, how the hell do we get out of here?

My light shines over a white ultra-panel among the Rift floor. I sprint ahead. Mind racing with promise. It's just a piece of wreckage, but at least I'm moving in the right direction. The piece of ship restores a sense of hope, and I charge deeper into the darkness.

Chunks of the cockpit shimmer in my lights more and more frequently. Guilt weighs on me the closer I get to my crew. I shouldn't have accepted this assignment. I knew how dangerous it was to come here. Though, Russa did too. I should've told him we wouldn't go. Whatever is here couldn't be worth the risk. But my mind was so consumed with the Vault. The mysteries that lay within that Hub of the Redemption. Why didn't I tell them about it? I asked them if they trusted me as we were crashing. They all said yes without hesitation and let me plunge our rig into the ground. They trusted me with their lives. Yet I didn't trust them with the most amazing discovery I've ever made. The Vault drug my brain far away from this planet, to the world I never lived in, with the people I never met, and to the planned life I never had. But even though I'm not the same breed as my crew, the longer I sprint through the Rift begging for them to be ok, the more I cringe for betraying my true family for my biological one.

I promise myself if I find them, I will tell them.

Up ahead, I see the faint signatures of lights dancing off the Rift walls. My heart leaps. I click on my comms, winded lungs, chopping my words.

"Guys!" I yell, sucking wind as my legs burn from lactic acid. "Can you hear me!" I urge my feet to move faster, but the uneven terrain makes pace difficult. Their headlights are now visible, oscillating in the pitch blackness like spotlights at a luxury nightclub in *Ivolo*. They're alive! I rejoice, fighting tears of joy from clouding my vision. I climb over a pile of minerals and twisted floor roots in my way to get a view of them. The death rattling screech of Dystrogars pierce my ears, and my stomach drops. I can vaguely make out Patawa, Spri, and Bryl encircled in a bright glowing ring of myrite dust, their headlights occasionally flashing over my visor and blinding me. Pinned by three Dystrogars who stab and chomp at them from the perimeter of the ring. I scream out to them as I scale down from the mound.

"HEY!!!" My voice is hoarse. The comms static and crackle, but the distorted voice of Bryl slips in between the broken signals.

"...BOSS!...Hel.. We' r.... down..." The little of his voice I can make out is nothing of the stone-souled Bryl I know. It's filled with horror. As if he stares at mortality itself and realizes it's here for him. Yet he still stands draped over Spri and Patawa, a meat shield standing between them and the grotesque creatures of death.

My legs churn faster than they ever have. My heart pounding so hard against my chest it may bruise. I bound over jutting roots and awkward rock piles. Sliding under protruding mineral spires and continue to race toward them.

A cliff fast approaches, my crew trapped meters below. I don't hesitate. I plant my foot on the lip of the ridge and launch myself off the cliff. Time slows as I glide through the air. I tilt my head down to illuminate the ground below. A jagged rock formation sticks straight up, waiting to impale me. I roll in the air to avoid the spike and crash to the ground. My railcannon spills from my hands and slides meters ahead, the Floater crashing down with me. Its remains ejecting from the enclosed basket. I scramble for the railcannon, my crew within reach, but a debilitatingly loud screech immobilizes me. I tilt my helm lights up. A Dystrogar towers over me, its six talons dug into the ground on either side of me, one buried into the pant leg of my suit. It's razor-sharp barb whipping violently back and forth, desperate to skewer me. It stretches its wings wide, and screeches, a death call, its teeth all pointed daggers, ready to tear my flesh from my bones.

I can't move. I'm too late. I'm dead, my crew is dead. My father counted on me to preserve the legacy of humanity, and this is how it ends. At the pointed end of a prehistoric monster, at the bottom of hell, following the orders of a species completely ignorant to the struggle of my race. I've failed. I close my eyes and accept my fate. All the optimism in the world isn't for shit now. I just pray it's quick.

I hear the Dystrogar howl and flap its wings, aggressively pushing away. I open my eyes, and a woman stands in between me and the beast, violently waving a glowing cyan myrite torch. It can't see the illumination, but something about the dust disorients the monster. She growls at the Dystrogar. Screaming so loud the muscles of her calves contract. A crude oxygen mask covers her mouth and nose while greasy goggles shield her eyes. Blue hair spills out the back of a ragged bandana. I stare in disbelief.... It can't be.... I mutter to myself.

"...Riley?!..." I ask. My voice soft, as if whispering to a ghost. She turns and reaches a hand out to me, still fending off the creature with the other hand. It *is* her! She looks so different from when I last saw her; a woman now. No longer the wily teen of my memories. She's extraordinarily lean and fit as if she's been a castaway on some forsaken island. Her skin riddled with scratches and scars. Where has she been? But I can see her eyes through the smeared the goggles, and those haven't changed an ounce. Still a zealous relentlessness to them. The type of vigor that nobody can compete with. The sight of her startles me so much I forget to take her hand. The creature screeches in rage, and I snap out of my trance.

"LEO! GET UP!" She yells. I grab her arm and climb to my feet. I roll to the railcannon, pump the primer, and unleash a devastating eruption. The burst tears through the Dystrogar's torso, and it crashes dead to the ground, purple blood scattering the Rift walls. The force of the launch knocks me to my back, and as I do, I disconnect the Floater from my synchronization and shove it toward Riley, waiting for my railcannon's cooldown. She opens the crate and pulls out what weaponry is left from inside, angrily firing rounds into her dimly lit targets. I try to shine my lights onto the flying beasts, but they move too spastically to keep entirely in sight.

I hustle to my feet and sprint to my crew. Two tall thin men wearing tattered body length trench coats accompany Patawa, Bryl, and Spri, both covered with similar breathing apparatuses and filthy goggles. One with stone grey hair tied into a knot waves a myrite torch viciously as Riley did. He emits an absurd squawk as he does it, disturbing the Dystrogar's sonar. Cord-like fibers wrap around the torch instead of fingers... *Is that an Ancient?*

The other has wavy blue locks resting on his shoulders, a bandana tied around his forehead. He fumbles through a massive bag, searching for something in the low visibility. My light shines over his face, and he turns toward me.

"REMMY?!" I yell incredulously. A Dystrogar swoops in

from the right, and I fire my railcannon into its body. It explodes, and pieces of carnivore scatter. This time I brace myself from its unbelievable recoil. Riley still lays on the trigger, gunshots reverberating endlessly off the cavern's walls. I want to look again at Remmy, but my lights scour over a pool of blood on the ground.

"LEO!" Bryl wails to my side. I turn, and Bryl is frantically tending to Patawa. She reels in pain, holding her leg. Blood drains from a fist-sized hole in her suit. I rush to her side. Spri sits half kneeling to my left, just coming to.

"What happened? Patawa, are you ok?" I ask, I drop the railcannon and lift her head slightly to see me. Riley's shots cease, and her clip empties. The Dystrogar uses the moment and dives for her. I double-take as I helplessly watch the creature descend on Riley. I scream out to warn her.

"RILEY LOOK OUT!" I clamor. An unGodly concussion booms from my left, and I flinch. The Dystrogar twitches in pain and crashes into a mineral stack just as Riley dives behind it. Remmy holds an Earth weapon aimed at the beast. Thin steam dances off its barrel in my helm lights. I stare at it, stunned. The creature shrieks, still alive, snapping and stabbing at a pinned down Riley.

"REMMY!" She calls out in terror. Her legs try to push as far away from the feral monster as possible, but she can barely see it in the darkness. Just feel the heat from its breath as it snaps at her.

"Leo, Pat's losing a lot of blood!" Spri says, his voice frenzied as he's waking up to a nightmare. He reaches his hands to her in an attempt to help. He looks to me, unsure of what to do. Panic plaguing his eyes. Her blood coats his hands. Patawa cries in agony, fidgeting uncontrollably.

"REMMY!!!" Riley screams out again. The mineral stack crumbling under the weight of the massive beast. Remmy fumbles to load another bolt. He fires again, and the monster wails in pain, but the small round doesn't stop the Dystrogar's pursuit.

"Leo, do something!" Bryl pleads with me. Tears stream down his cheeks. Time slows as my mind short circuits. The world moves too fast. The Dystrogar screeches and wails, stabbing with its barb. Riley screams in terror. Spri and Bryl beg me for help, as Patawa sobs in despair. The edges of my vision begin to close in, and I feel like I'm going to pass out. But just before the thin tunnel of vision folds into itself, a hand grabs me by the shoulder.

"Here, Child!" The other man with Remmy and Riley hands me his bandana. I stare at the man in astonishment. The leathery, navy skin of an Ancient gazes back at me. I have no time to revel in the mysteries of this man. I take the bandana and wrap it around the leg of Patawa.

"Brace yourself..." I warn her. She glances at me, barely conscious, and nods. I crank the wrap as tight as I can above her wound, and she groans in misery. I glance up to the unknown man.

"Can you get her to help? Can you get her out of here? Quick?" I ask. He nods and points to the far wall. I shine my helm lights on a small gap tunneled into the rock.

"But I will not leave the Children!" He says. I stare back at him, confused.

"I need your help! Please."

"A Child is in danger! We must protect her!" He points to Riley. I glance over my shoulder, the beast getting closer to her.

"Take her now!" I demand.

I dart my eyes back to Riley as Remmy grabs the myrite torch and sprints to his sister's aid.

"Remmy! Don't!" I reach out to grab him, but it's too late. "Shit. Shit." I look to Bryl and Spri. "Spri, Bryl, get Pat to safety! He knows the way," I point to the Ancient. My crew doesn't flinch. The unknown man does.

"We've got Riley! Get her help, now!" I shout. The man's eyes twitch, and he reluctantly concedes.

Bryl hoists Patawa over his shoulder, while the Ancient helps Spri hurry ahead to navigate. I turn back and grab my railcannon as the four disappear into the tunnel.

Remmy desperately swings the torch at the Dystrogar. Flailing menacingly. The beast is furious and wounded; it doesn't seem affected by the burn any longer. I aim at the monster, but Riley is too close, the blast could kill her. I aim again, desperate for an angle. Remmy screams with all his force and heaves rocks at the beast, trying to divert its attention. But the abomination is determined. The mineral stack crumbles even further, and the creature loses its balance and nearly falls. It fans its wings and pushes up into the air to reorient for another attack. When it does, I have the tightest window of opportunity and squeeze the trigger. The nightmarish howl of the beast silences as its body disintegrates into a purple mist.

I drop the railcannon, and the Rift finally silences.

Remmy and I sprint to Riley and pull her from the rumble. She's distraught. Eyes a flood with trauma. She wraps her arms so tightly around us. I think she may never let go. Remmy strokes her hair and comforts her. Riley sobbing into his chest. Remmy fighting back tears of gratitude himself. My helm lights shine harshly in their faces, so I turn them down.

Her eyes meet mine.

Emotion swarming through my mind.

We look to one another with a million things to say but no words capable of expressing them. I take her hand and muster all I can get out at the moment.

"I never thought I'd see you again..." I say, tears beginning to pool in my eyes. Feeling her skin on mine opens portals in my soul that I thought had closed forever. A warmth swelling inside me. She smiles at me as her face melts into an overwhelmed, sobbing mess. Her voice chopping between snot-filled sobs.

"Can't get rid of me that easy." She snorts.

Remmy smiles at me, and I wrap him in a hug.

"I missed you guys so much." I squeeze both of them harder.

"We missed you too..." He replies. Voice so incredibly full of love. He strokes Riley's head, and we hunch together, crumpled in a heap against a pile of rocks. Her nerves finally settle, and she looks to me with the same intensity I always remembered from her and speaks with downright exhaustion.

"Let's get the hell out of here!"

21

VICTOR BELLS

Collateral Damage

Miku orders the Green Root as always. A vegetarian for moral reasons. An absurd thought, but fitting for her. I order the Nuvu filet, seared, rare. She glances at me with a devilish grin. I can tell she wants to jab at me, but she doesn't. All the reason why she is better than us all. Both righteous *and* tolerant to her core. The hologram menu between us sputters away, and nothing impedes my view of her. Her chocolate eyes scan the pristine arboretum just outside our restaurant. Gorgeous manicured grass and rows of exotic imported trees share the space with glossy walkways that connect the various boutiques and restaurants. Miniature automated RotoBikes haul the most pretentious of passengers along the spotless avenues in shaded AirCarriages. Though most walk.

Celestial City epitomizes wealth and class. The epicenter of Grogan prosperity. It's surprising that Miku enjoys coming here as often as she does, though, in her defense, she has a naively optimistic delusion of the people who populate this sanctuary. I watch her smile at passing strangers, most of whom respond to her gesture with snobbish reproach until they comprehend who she is and quickly recover from their rudeness. That's always been the issue with Miku. She sees the best in people because people only show her their best. It's a never-ending cycle of genuine compassion returned with false kindness that validates her view of the world. But I shouldn't be too harsh. I know she's not naïve. She's exposed herself to the depths of this world. Raised by a man who's committed unthinkably horrific acts. Seen the terrible ways people treat each other. What separates her is that she understands these deficiencies of the world and the limitations of living beings and chooses to look beyond them. Thrusting herself into the eager arms of life. Meanwhile, I go out of my way to avoid encounters with people like Fargo avoids contraceptives.

It's an odd personality type to explain. On one hand, I crave acknowledgment. Demanding recognition for the mastery I've obtained over my craft. Basking in the validation of not only other fighters but the fans as well. When an Arena begins to chant, and the name *Hades* thunders in unison against the walls, and the eyes of the world lay upon me in awe, no feeling in existence can compare to that moment. Yet, when the fight is over, and I walk the streets, and those eyes *still* stare upon me, a piece of my humanity disappears. I become an object. What I do becomes all I am. My being defined by the passion I pursue. And all I want is to be treated for my worth and not my ability. But for me, one cannot be had without the other. So, I keep to myself. And find comfort in the few people who find joy in my company and not my achievement. Like the beautiful creature across from me.

The brisk air gently swirls at our high elevation, nipping at our skin. A pleasant sensation. The afternoon sun shines, unobstructed, today's low hanging clouds all below us. Today *Ivolo* earns its name as the most beautiful place on the planet. Floating peacefully in the pure air.

It's rare that any circumstance can rinse the putrid rage that churns inside me, like the belly of a furnace, but the serenity of this place, the beauty of Miku, the perfection of this moment, allows me to forget. I savor these moments because I know they will be short-lived. We will leave this place and return to our normal existence, and the extinguished embers of my spite with flicker back to life once more, and the ceaseless battle for my soul will return. I shake those negative thoughts from my mind and turn my attention back to Miku, who's been talking this whole time.

"...what do you think?" Miku asks. I stare blankly back at her. "Are you even listening?!" She smirks and sips from her mug, steam rising from its hot contents. My eyes widen in embarrassment as my brow scrunches.

"Sorry. I got distracted. What were you saying?" I ask. She rolls her eyes innocently and repeats herself.

"I was saying, I think Tanya should refuse testing. She doesn't owe the High Council any more than she's given. She deserves to have a life too!" Miku states. I was really tuned out; I didn't hear any of that.

"What about all the people affected by the Rotting? They'll never find a cure without her?" I say. "Plus, it's not like she's there by choice, she can't just get up and leave." I understand her struggle with it because I wish she could be here with us too, but her life became government property when she survived the Rotting.

"You don't know that! Who knows what will lead to a cure? They've been researching her for years and are no closer to solving it. So why are they so sure she is the only answer?" She asks, the confliction on her face manifesting in the form of heavy, sagging eyes. She knows her thoughts are biased. Maybe even selfish. For how amazing she is, she's still human.

"Miku, I know you want what's best for her, but there's nothing that can be done. She's the key to a cure, you know that." I try to smile at her, but she still stares down into her mug. "Didn't you tell me Qwillow said they're getting closer..."

"Yea, but she always says that." A soft sadness drifts over her. A foreign look for her gentle, joyous eyes. Seeing pain on her face tears at my heart. This woman is an angel; she deserves nothing but happiness.

"It'll all work out. They'll find a cure, and you and Tanya can catch up on all the time you've missed." I grab her hand and smile. My face doesn't present compassion like hers does, though. It's too rough, too sober. I try, but I can't erase the grief that weighs on her. Our food arrives from automated serving bots, and we eat in silence. I hate myself for not being able to comfort her. The heartache permeates across the table as she chews on her meal in silence. My filet is perfectly cooked, the precision of the meal prep bots, unparalleled, but the meat's flavors are dull on my tongue. Life seeming bland without her happiness in it. We spend our meal watching bystanders stroll by, all secretly as miserable as we are right now. Wealth and privilege meaningless without the warmth of loved ones.

The serving bots remove our plates when we finish eating, and I transfer *Soft* from the signal of my comm to the restaurant. My eyes lock onto Miku, who stares longingly out the open breezeway. I have to do something; I've never seen her like this.

"Hey! Follow me!" I pop out of my seat and extend a hand to her. She glances up at me, and reluctantly takes my gesture. I pull her out of the chair and tug her along. "Come on. I want to show you something!" We push out of the restaurant and into the arboretum. Everyone walking about wears the mandatory attire of the Celestial City, cream-colored linens. The loose fabric whips in the wind, making everyone look like beautified spirits.

"Where are we going?" She asks, the woe of her mood slowly turning with curious anticipation.

"You'll see." I answer.

We hurry along the marbled walkway, under the limbs of exotic trees, and through the mazes of synthetically cloned Earth hedges. We approach the only sector of Celestial City that permits user-operated rigs. A small strip that allows access in and out of the exclusive walled city. In the center of a gloss tiled circle sits a rig storage unit. No larger than the shipping containers that are stacked in columns on automated *Transport Freighters* and *AirBoats.* A dataplate is attached to the sidewall, and I enter in our information. Under our feet, a colony of stacks, slides, trams, robotic arms, and platforms house the rigs of the citizens and guests of Celestial City. The gears and cogs work with astounding technological ability and deliver our rig to the access point. Miku's RotoBike appears as the metal door to the storage center opens. I climb onto the driver seat.

"Get on!" I pat the seat behind me.

"Excuse me? This is *my* bike! Why are you driving?" She asks, her hands on her hips.

"Because you don't know where we're going." I pull the RotoBike out of the container and hover there, waiting for her to get on. She playfully glares at me as she climbs aboard.

"You better not mess up my baby..." She says with a grin.

"I'd never! Now hold tight," I say as the engine roars to life. She goes to slide on her helmet, but I stop her. "Don't. We're not going far. It's a beautiful day out. Enjoy the fresh air!" She shoots me another menacing look. She doesn't like being told what to do.

Miku holds tight, her arms wrapped around my torso, and we speed off, out Celestial City's gate.

Celestial City is the crown jewel of Groga Ivolo, but the entire island is breathtaking. Sparkling mansions hang along the cliff sides overlooking the less fortunate world below. Like Gods staring down on their minions. Sprawling estates are isolated by beautifully constructed gates and fences. The roads are few. Thin and unimposing. Most Grogan citizens have rigs capable of total air travel, not hover travel. But we enjoy the view from the ground. High in the air, the details of the world can be lost.

We soak in the gentrified landscape, the wind breathing life into our cheeks. I think the grace of the ride itself cheers up Miku but where we go is somewhere special. Somewhere we haven't been in years. I know it will revive her spirit.

The residential sectors of Ivolo begin to give way to a High Council protected conservation sector. The ruins of the Ancient city of Nykallo are contained within handmade stone walls. Nykallo rests on the westernmost tip of Ivolo and sits protected by High Council preservation efforts. It's the most intact Ancient City left. The Grogan islands sat so high in the sky, they were completely isolated from the world below before the invention of air travel. And there was no more splendid Ancient city than Nykallo. Hidden from the destructive force of war and strife, the city lay a pearl inside the protective shell of a clam for millennia longer than any other. It wasn't until the first air rigs discovered life existed on the floating islands that Nykallo was exposed to the eroding force of assimilation. But the wars had all been fought. Society grown. And the species of Ancients dwindling in massive numbers. The newly founded High Council decided Nykallo must be protected to eternalize the lost city. Nykallo was deemed sanctified land and was to be preserved in its final decommissioned state.

Large signage warns of the repercussions of rig use within the walls of the city. I turn my head back and watch Miku's eyes light up as she sees the impeccable stone archways.

"I know where we're going!" The excitement in her voice brings me joy. We pull over and park the bike just outside the entrance. We walk under the welcoming arches of the monument city, and the moment we cross the threshold, we can feel the history under our feet. Stone pillars line narrow walkways with unbelievable hand-carved detail. Miku runs her fingers along the artery of a stone carving. Tall, smooth grains twist around unthinkably old trees. Green and yellow vegetation share the soil with colorful flowers and plants. Pinks and reds and violets freckle the earth-toned ground. Endangered birds sing their shrill notes as they coast back and forth between the indigenous trees.

Miku gleefully leads the way. She knows where we go now.

I watch her bubble with joy as she picks a flower from the ground and slides it behind her ear. She hurries ahead.

Stone huts pepper the surrounding area, and the walkway cuts through it all, leading to a tall thin building at the end of the island. A staggered, glorious Pegshu temple rests along the ridge of the very Western point of Ivolo, breaching high into the sky. Miku reaches the bottom of its staircase and turns to wait for me. Her eyes meet mine, and her smile lights up my world. She reaches a hand out to me.

"Come on, slowpoke!" She says playfully. I don't know if she reaches out as a friend or something more, but I don't question it. I interlock my fingers through hers, and we start up the staircase. I watch her as we climb the flight of stairs. She digests the temple with such passion. We used to love to come here as kids. Back when Fargo didn't spend so much time in the Valley, and Tanya wasn't trapped inside a laboratory, and Leo and Gwinn would visit Groga all the time, and the twins hadn't disavowed the entire world. Back when times were simpler, and we didn't have a care in the world. Back when we were naïve to just how alien we were to this planet. Back before Hades and the anger and the fear plagued my life. A time before I realized I was in love with my best friend.

We reach the top of the temple and walk through its hollow chamber. A small bowl filled with water sits in its center atop a trimmed pillar. We walk barefoot to it. The typically unforgiving stone floor now cushioned with a layer of Heoul pedals that have fallen from the branches of nearby trees and scattered along the ground.

Eyes incapable of leaving one another, we cleanse our hands and feet and, together, approach the *Holy Spire.*

Piercing into the sky, the Holy Spire spikes up from a plank of rock that extends from the edge of the temple and over the rim of the island. Nothing below it for 1000's of meters. We step along the narrow foot planks that twist their way up the outside of the spire, watching wisps of clouds roll by underneath us. I reach the plateaued surface of the top first and help pull Miku up behind me.

Her smile stretches wide across her face. The stone, cold against our heels. The wind swirls, so we have to hold onto one another. She cups the edges of her mouth and shouts out in exhilaration. Her voice seems to travel forever as we stand, literally on top of the world. The highest elevation on the planet. I sit on the edge of the spire and let my heels rest against the stone. Miku sits down next to me and rests her head on my shoulder.

"Thank you," She says, glancing out the tops of her eyes at me.

"When's the last time we've been here?" I ask.

"I don't know... It's been years. I nearly forgot how much I love this place." Her voice purrs with delight. "Victor... why are you so good to me?" She weaves her fingers through mine, resting our hands on her knee.

My heart cringes as she asks.

Her eyes lift to meet mine. Our bodies drawing toward one another.

She's inches from my lips now. Strands of her hair dancing against my cheek. The heat of her whispers, sending shivers down my spine.

"What would I do without you...". The gentle crest of her lips against mine now. Her skin is made of the far reaches of heaven. I run my thumb along her cheek, and we surrender into one another.

The universe shatters.

Could I possibly have been this blind? So consumed with the hatred of my demon, I've not noticed the love of my angel? The realization engulfs me. Time seems to hang as the clarity of my life spills before me. As if a fog that drifts over a serene pond is blown away in a gust, and all that remains is a perfect oasis. I want nothing more than to run it. Dive headfirst into its crystal waters, but something still lurks within it. And as I approach, I see his demon eyes prowling in the weeds. Stalking me. Waiting for the moment I let my guard down. And when I do, he lurches out and strikes me down. He consumes my being, and I have lost all control. Now Miku lies in his path of destruction, and there is nothing I can do to stop him. I try to reach out to her, but he is in total control. I'm a spectator on a nightmarish roller coaster. Looking down on Miku's body and knowing I'm to blame. I let her in too close. Where *he* could get to her. I should've protected her! I love her!

I violently rip away from my horrid reverie. My mind a panic. Despair rifles through my soul as I picture it over and over. I peel from her touch and scramble to my feet, hustling down the spire. It startles Miku, and she calls out to me as I flee her warm embrace.

"...Victor?!" She hurries down the spire behind me,

confused as to what happened. "Calm down! What's wrong?"

My mind devolves into madness. The more she cries out for me, the sharper the pain of my nightmare gets. I look psychotic. Shoving my feet into my shoes and sprinting down the temple's stairs. Miku struggles to keep up. She cries out again, and I yell back to dismiss her.

"...PLEASE... DON'T!" Mania shreds at my sanity. She'll never be safe around me.

I reach the bottom of the stairs and sprint through the Ancient city. Insane, rage-filled tears choke their way past my defenses. I'm almost near the entrance of the city when I hear it. The steady warble of rig engines. An entire fleet of them. I watch them hastily land as I approach the entrance. Something's wrong.

Armed men in jet black tunics and pointed hats stream from the rigs like water bursting from a geyser. I skid to a halt, frozen. The men stampede toward me, guns primed in my direction. Terror slices through my gut as I recognize their distinct outfits. *Vipers*! I don't know why, but they charge directly toward me as fast as they can. Each armed to the teeth with high-powered rifles. Miku finally catches up, furious with me.

"Victor what the hell is going on?!" She punches me in the shoulder. Only relenting when she sees the horror on my face. She turns and witnesses the wave of death barreling down upon us. I grab her by the hand and take off back in the opposite direction.

"RUN, RUN, RUN!!!" Miku stares back starkly, a blend of confusion and panic.

"Are those..."

"Yea, just run!"

"Why are they..."

"I don't know! I don't know! Just run!"

We sprint back through the walkway once again, a crew of Viper thugs storming behind us. A stone pillar to my left explodes into a powder as a rifle round destroys it.

"Oh shit?!!"

Rounds explode around us. Ripping through vegetation and stone. Hurling debris in all directions. My heart pounds through my chest. Miku's eyes overflow with fear. There's nowhere to go. There's nowhere to go... My mind desperately tries to formulate a plan, but there's no escape. We're trapped within these walls and the edge of the island. They're too close, we'll never be able to hide. I glance down at Miku and watch her run for her life. My heart beats for this woman. I yell to her over the commotion, my words, broken, as my lungs search for oxygen.

"Listen to me... Do not stop running... Do you understand?... You run, and you hide..." I look at her with solemn eyes. Full of all the things I should've said to her, but couldn't. Eyes that say I love you without a sound. "... Miku...."

She looks back up to me, body shaking as she sprints. She doesn't contest it. She understands. Her eyes are full too, but I don't know what of. She stares back to me for a moment as if to say something, but I don't give her a chance. I let go of her hand and slide to a stop. She runs ahead, her sorrowful eyes locked onto mine until I turn with my hands up to face the Vipers.

Bullets pop along the ground at my feet. I flinch. My hands stretching to the sky.

"Don't shoot! Don't shoot!"

The closest Vipers grind to a stop as I do. The two men prime their weapons in my direction. Four more run past them, clearly not tasked to me. They're going for Miku! I'll never allow that. As the last of the four attempts to sprint by me, I lunge for him. The speeding mass of flesh snapping to a stop as I wedge him into a chokehold. I whip his body around as a portable shield. Swiping his weapon and two sizzling rounds erupting from the muzzle. One round tears through a grunt's back, and he spills to the ground. I miss the other, and he rolls to the cover of a building. The third continues his pursuit of Miku. I back my way toward the balcony of a terraced stone hut. The Viper in my grasp tries elbowing my side, but I'm far too trained to let him escape. I fire a round into his back and hurl myself over the stone wall, rounds peppering the thick ledge. The two Vipers trained on me scattered to defensive positions. I watch them signal the one behind the building to go search for Miku. He hurries off deeper into the city as I blindly fire at him from around the corner. Two Vipers lay slain along the Ancient pathway, two pursue Miku, and two stalk me. I have to dispose of them quick; the others will surely find Miku soon.

I feel the heat of my body rise, the anger boils. Hades itches to shred the skin from their bones. But this isn't the Arena. I can't lose control. I fight him with every ounce of strength I have. Rounds scream over my head and tear chunks from the facade of the building. I return fire, pinning them behind a small well. The moment is just long enough to reposition inside. My enemies take the bait. Assuming that I've retreated. They don't speak the language of war. Unaware of my native tongue.

They swing around to get an angle on the door but don't realize they crouch walk into a chokehold. I race through the building, up the second story, and back to a window port overlooking their location. They slowly creep their way up the landing, darting from cover to cover. Patience. The right moment closes in. They disappear under the balcony, and I know they're in the trap. I vault out window and land squarely on the other side, slugging rounds into their chest. The two men crash against the walls, and their life seeps from their bodies. I have to take a moment to remember this is no game. Those men wear no suits, their blood coats the walls. I stare down at my hands as I succumb to the realization. I've taken life! The spark ignites Hades' fire, and he roars to life.

Hades sprints down the pathway in search of his next victims. He craves pain and anguish. He doesn't care Miku is in trouble; he just knows two more souls lay waiting to be plucked from their husks. His legs move faster than mine. His muscles stronger. His eyes frantically dart the landscape, teeth snapping, and a manic smile scratches across his face.

A Viper sifts through tall brush just off the path, scanning for a hiding Miku. Hades ignores his rifle and blitzes ahead for a more personal conflict. The Viper doesn't hear him in time. A shoulder already buried in his chest. They tumble to the ground, and Hades ends up mounted on top of him. Fists chewing into the man's face. Over and over. The Viper's merlot skin cracking and splitting against Hades' rock-hard knuckles. Dark blood oozes from the gashes. The punches trained for maximum damage. The Viper flails in panic, trying anything he can to get away. But Hades is a black widow, and this man is caught in its web. There is no escaping this creature. He roars as he hammers the man across the face one last time, and the thug goes limp. Snapping his teeth at him and continuing his onslaught, the blood of four different lives coating our body.

Miku screams farther north. Hades follows the noise. The screams get louder until he reaches their source. Hades barks out in a feral voice. A chaotic smile on his face, eyes narrow.

"HEY!"

The Viper drags Miku from her concealment. The thug's rifle pressed against her head. Panic smears his face as he sees this blood-soaked demon. I scream out, but my voice doesn't escape the expanse I'm trapped in. Hades has his rifle aimed. The thug barely exposing himself enough to see. There's no shot, but Hades doesn't care. He craves flesh. Like a shark in blood infested waters, he's incensed. Miku cries out for me to put my gun down, but she doesn't realize I'm not in control. The thug barks orders as well. But Hades is still. Waiting. He just wants an inch. I pull at him with all my might, but he's strong. The taste of blood empowering his manic episode.

I can see the fear in Miku's eyes as she looks at me. She may be more scared of me than the gun pressed to her head. Her expression nearly rips me in half. I can feel Hades getting anxious; he's going to act with or without her safety in mind.

Miku calls out to me again. Voice calm, soothing. Tears roll down her cheeks, but she maintains her poise. Her voice is so soft.

"...Victor... put the gun down..."

The sweet ring of her voice emboldens me. Hades will not get her killed!

I love this woman.

I fight with every fiber in my being. Hades struggles back. His rage courses through me, but I have a new weapon I've never had before. Love. I wrestle with myself until I push the monster back into his cage and come to.

I toss my gun to the ground and drop to my knees, pleading with the thug.

"Don't hurt her! Please!" My eyes don't leave her. The Viper shuffles his hostage around me, eyes still cautious. He points his gun to me, and I stare my goodbye to the love I never told. Miku screams out as she tries to wrestle herself free.

"NOOOO!" Tears consume her eyes as the Viper takes aim. But just before he pulls the trigger, another man appears from beyond his position.

"Stand down, Chyra." A shorter man walks earnestly toward us. "He's needed alive." He wears the same black tunic as the rest, but no hat. His head is bald. Dark tattoos cover his burgundy skull. His eyes, cloudy and yellow. Deterro... He walks by Miku and his grunt and stands over me. My lungs still heaving in stress.

"Victor Bells. In the flesh." He scans me up and down. "You are even bigger in person, I must say." He laughs wickedly to his subordinate, who nervously mimics Deterro's behavior. He bends down and tilts my chin up so our eyes meet. "Do you know why I'm here?" I stare at the man without answers. Only one thought cycles through my mind. Fargo. "Your brother is a... reckless man." Fargo! I won't need Hades to kill him. "How do you collect collateral on a man that cares for nothing? He's an enigma. A leech sucking the life from everyone around him. A cancer. And the only way to exterminate a cancer is to destroy everything around it." He looks back to Miku as if he regrets having to tear my everything from my world. My fist clenches in the dirt. It takes all my will not to crush his windpipe. "Cooperate, and she will not be harmed. Don't... and well, I think you understand the consequences." He stares firmly into my eyes. Through me. He is not a man of hollow threats.

"What do you want from me? I'll do it, just don't hurt her!" I say. My eyes shoot back and forth from Miku and Deterro. He answers with a villainous smile, amused by my confusion.

"Find your brother. He'll explain. I'm sure you'll have some things you want to say to him anyway!" Deterro stands up and signals his grunt to take Miku away. She screams out for me as the grunt drags her away. Her shrieks fall onto traumatized ears, muted ringing. She reaches out, screaming, the thug tugging her farther away and out of sight. Deterro starts off and turns back one last time.

"Four days, Victor. Four days."

They pile into their rig and vanish over the cliffside.

22

LEO ABERNATHY

Children of the Clouds

"**F**antastic, isn't it?" A voice calls out behind me as I stand leaning against the ledge of an open spiral staircase gazing upon the magnificent well we use as a refuge. Gorgeous hand-crafted stone bricks intertwine the entire depth of the well. At the very bottom, crystal clear water rests undisturbed, a kaleidoscope of colored tiles paint a mesmerizing design under it. Stories above me, the Forest floor peeks its green head over the edge of the well, and its vegetation crawls its way down the walls. The single helix stairs are dotted with sanded pillars and beautifully arched viewports, starting from the well's opening, all the way to the water floor. A labyrinth of corridors and narrow rooms maze their way around it. The stones change color the higher up the well you go, eroded and stained with sun and weather. Green vines snake their way along the walls, and small bird nests clump in the crumbled nooks of rock. I turn, and the Ancient who saved us last night approaches and admires the architecture with me. I give Yara a conservative smile and greet him.

"Good morning Yara." He smiles gently back at me, the

very edges of his uneven beak tilting. He is a peaceful man. Calm. Patient. He didn't press us for information last night, opened *what I am assuming is his home* to us without hesitation, and even helped treat Patawa's wound with his own supplies. And not once did he attempt to pry into who we are, why we were where we were, or what happened. He knew we had been through hell, so he just introduced himself and let us decompress for the night. Yet part of me can't help but feel he didn't ask questions because he already knows the answers.

"Where are we?" I ask. Yara strides to my left, slow and soft. He's a meticulous man. Long square jaw. The knots of his shoulders confidently postured, as if he was once built far sturdier. But now he is a man afflicted with age as any organic creature becomes. His eyes have bags under them, a weary sag pulling at the skin. The look of a man who is exhausted both mentally and physically. But his spirit is still palpable. Sustaining the grace he carries himself with. He looks beyond me when he speaks. With drawn-out, precise wording, cryptic, pausing in between thoughts to ensure he delivers the message he wants.

"We are where no one is. Where no one will be and no longer comes. You are safe here." Yara rolls a pebble between the crooked, bent cords of his fingers and tosses it off the ledge. The pebble silently falls into the well, and a small ripple radiates from the impact. Yara stares at it, rubbing a finger along a rough patch of navy skin along his neck.

"Safe? You mean from the Dystrogars?" I ask. I assumed that was obvious. The tunnel we used to escape was far too tight for a creature that size to come through. Plus, those beasts would be terrorizing the world if they could use it, not trapped inside the Rift.

Yara speaks as if we share common knowledge. He doesn't address the pronouns he uses, and his words register as a coded language that I don't have the legend for.

"There are far more dangerous things in this world than blind beasts, Leo," He says. He dismisses those monsters as if they were garden rats chewing on plant stocks. I'm not sure how, though, the sight of those creatures will haunt me 'til my last days. "And yet, you are far more dangerous than them all. They know that." His head twitches slightly as he speaks. The longer I look at him, the more he resembles a robot operating on low power. His posture is rigid and firm, presentable, but his limbs and head twitch occasionally. His facial expressions struggle to match the words that come from his mouth and create a difficulty comprehending what he's trying to say. One moment he speaks with eloquent, proper poise, conducting himself in the manner of pompous Olt households. Then he'll appear nearly punch drunk, his face drooping, and an awkward smile will form where the sentence doesn't require one. It resembles an artificial intelligence failing at trying to recreate organic emotions.

"Are you ok?" I ask. Yara stiffens up, perching his head like a crane.

"Why, indeed, child." I give Yara an unconfident look. He doesn't seem ok. I try to ignore his ticks and attempt to address some of the odd things he's said.

"Who are they? And why am I dangerous?" I ask. The question confuses Yara.

"Do Tyko's understand why their prey are scared? Do they comprehend the fear of death? For nothing kills them... So how do you fear something which cannot happen to you?" I stand baffled by his questions. I haven't the slightest clue the point he is trying to make.

"Let's back up... Where are we?" I ask. "Actually! Not metaphorically..." I glance back up the well. I know we are in the Forest somewhere, just not sure where. It's obviously close to the grid we were supposed to be searching.

"The Forest is a vast mystery," Yara says. *Oh boy...* I rub my eyes, tired and unamused. Thankfully Riley clarifies.

"We're in the northwest corner of Berban." Riley stands in a doorway with her arms crossed. "And things do kill Tyko's..." She says as Yara slinks past her.

"As I said, child, there are far more dangerous things in this world than eyeless beasts," Yara says, disappearing around the corner.

"...Wait, where are you... Forget it," I say as Yara abruptly leaves.

Riley approaches and replaces where Yara stood. Her guard is up, I can feel it. An awkward silence lingers between us. She stares down into the water, eyes frozen as if the horrors of last night play out in front of them. Speaking was easy in the direct aftermath of the rescue, the fear of death pushing aside the awkwardness and the gratitude of life, bringing forward the sincerest of emotions. But since the dust has settled and we have to exist in the reality that it's been five years since we have seen each other, finding where to begin seems an impossible task.

"Riley... where have you been?" I ask. My voice trying as hard as it can to not be angry, but I am. She abandoned all of us. Abandoned me... They both did. I know they had it rough, but we were supposed to be in this together, *all* of us! She seems to have just as much difficulty trying to start too.

"Here, in the woods," She says, maintaining her gaze into the water.

"...How?... Berban is..." I stop. Everything feels so forced. I want to know five years' worth of life in five minutes. It's not fair to ask, I know, so I change course. "How are you holding up?" The question seems to lift a small veil off us, and I can see the relief of not having to discuss everything right now on her face.

"I've been better... been a hell of a few days." She finally looks at me with a tired smile.

"Yea, that was a close call, huh?"

"You don't know the half of it!" She says with a laugh. "A Tyko almost bit my head off, Remmy nearly killed himself, we got captured by Gaz patrols, was held prisoner in Pom'do'kon, got interrogated by A'gorr, escaped on the back of a Hotógo with some crazy Ancient who lives in a well, then when I finally thought I could put my head down and go to sleep, we watch some lunatics try to fly a rig into the Rift and fail miserably." She laughs as she glares at me. "You're lucky Remmy is a great person because I had no interest going down in that hell hole to save whatever idiot was trying to go in there. But sure enough, it turned out to be you, and we had to save your ass, yet I'm the one almost mauled to death by some prehistoric monster."

I let myself laugh. It feels good. I know there is so much that needs to be said, but laughing feels needed more right now.

"Pom'do'kon, huh? So, it's real?" I ask.

"Very! I wouldn't recommend a vacation there," She says. Her fiery charm beginning to break through again. "Have you ever met A'gorr?"

"No. The extent of my High Council relationships stops at Russa and Hesh'ka. Well... I guess Gwinn now too," I say. Riley perks up when I say her name.

"Gwinn?!" She asks. "What does she have to do with the High Council?"

"She's the newest High Councilor of Okotall... There's a lot that's happened, Ri..." I can't stop myself from sliding right back into the awkwardness. Her face is conflicted. I can tell she doesn't know how to process that information.

"Wow. I guess some forgive easier than others." She turns away from me, what little of her guard that was torn down, climbing back up. "There's no way I could stand in the same room as those people without trying to tear their heads off. Selfish pricks." She shakes her head. Face turning a dark red. "They never stood up for us when Emoss died, and everyone turned against us. Never publicly denied that Gwinn was responsible, never urged the public to stop the wave of hatred that was spewed onto us!" I can tell how deep the hurt runs for her. Her voice becomes raspy and stifled as she tries to fight back tears. "Do you think I wanted to go to Archler House?" A tear breaks through, spilling down her clenched jaw. "You think I want to live in these woods like an animal? I don't! Well, I didn't... But people were so horrible to us." Her emotions begin to overwhelm her. "They would throw things at us, shove us on the streets, swerve their rigs and try to hit us, scream at us until no end! I was fifteen! Sixteen! I honestly believed one day someone would kill us." She drops her head and sucks in hard, trying not to sob. "And when Remmy finally agreed to leave, we tried as hard as we could to get Gwinn to go with us! We tried for weeks! Did she even tell you that? Or does she say we just left? Abandoned her there at the orphanage?" I stare sympathetically to her; she understands she's right. "Psh... I should've known. She wouldn't leave. She was so gone, she would barely speak. Not to me. Not to Remmy. Not to Russa. Not to anyone. Part of me thinks she *wanted* someone to kill her. She had given up... I tried so hard to get her to come. So hard..." Riley breaks down as she turns away from me, draped over the ledge of the stairs. I put my arm around her to comfort her.

What about me? You just left and never said a word? I want to ask but don't. Even though the answer gnaws at me, now is not the right time. Things are still too raw. Too new. And I don't know if I'm capable of handling her explanation anyway.

We don't speak for some time. The grave truth of the past weighing on our hearts. I want to ask why she didn't just come live with me? Or with Miku? Or any of us? But I guess I understand. She thought her life was in danger. And would be anywhere people lived. She felt her only option was here.

"The world's changed, Ri. It has," I say. "No one cares anymore!"

She stares at me, a semblance of hope glinting in her eyes.

"I guess... I mean, if Gwinn got elected, I supposed

anything is possible."

"Exactly..." I say, my voice hopefully sounding confident. I don't plan on clarifying the technicality of her election. "Come home. I have a big place in Dwual Fir, my crew lives with me, we have plenty of room for you and Remmy."

She glances at me like the consideration of leaving the woods has never crossed her mind until now. The words came out quicker than I could think, but I still meant them. The thought of her disappearing from my life a second time is unbearable.

"Remmy wants a farm," She says softly. "Wants to grow terracorn." She laughs with a light sigh. "This life does get old."

"Then go! Do it! Live your life," I say. "But where ever you go, I better be nearby!" I smile at her. A taxed, weathered smile. One built on nostalgia and heartbreak. "Ri, the last time I saw you, I was telling you I..." I cut myself off, catching the conversation trending back toward the topic I don't want to stress yet. She can sense it too. A fraction of a grimace on her face. Possibly guilt? Maybe it's sadness? Whatever she's showing, I don't want to go rehash my sixteen-year-old self confessing my love to a girl who disappears without a word, days later. That's a conversation for a day when Gaz tribesmen don't scour the woods for us. "...we were kids, Ri. Regardless of what happened, the point is, I'm not going another five years without seeing you." I pull her in closer, her head nuzzled into my chest, unable to contain the intimacy of my words. "I'm not spending another night staring at the ceiling, wondering where you are. Wondering if you're safe. If you're alive. It's not happening. So, live with me, go buy a farm, I don't care, I just need to know where you are. I need you near me."

Her sleeve wipes at her face, glancing up to me as fragile as the frozen crystals that hang from the antlers of hibernating Boswyls. As if one touch could send her cascading to the floor in a million pieces. She carves through that tenderness with a strained smile.

"...maybe..."

Just as she says it, Remmy shouts out and thankfully neutralizes the heaviness growing between us.

"Well, I'll be damned!" He says. "I beg for five years to get a farm, and you always shrug me off, and this handsome devil shows up and mentions it in passing, and you're all 'hmm, maybe we should.' Unbelievable!" Remmy walks his way through the opened doorway, his huge smile stretching across his face. "Hey, brother!" He spreads his arms wide, and I wrap him in a firm hug. We growl as we embrace each other. Remmy is such a warm, affectionate soul. There is no awkwardness between us, even after all these years. He doesn't allow it. His arm is slung over my shoulder, his smile infecting all three of us. He's the best type of friend. Always sees the best in you, and no matter how long it's been since you last spoke, he has this uncanny ability to make you feel like you've always been on his mind.

"Don't be too insulted my man, you know Ri could never say no to me," I say with a wink trying to defuse the tension from earlier. Riley appreciates it. She plays into it and shoves me.

"P-lease... If I wanted some buttoned-up, romantic sop, I'd have stayed in Okotall with the *sea-carver* boys." She rolls her eyes. "You don't have enough grizzle for me, sweetie." She laughs and looks past me. "Now him on the other hand..." Bryl walks through the hall across the well, his shirt off, all swollen muscle and brands. "I will say we don't have that in the Forest."

"We don't have a lot in the Forest." Remmy chirps, trying to reiterate his point.

"I know!" She barks back. A reaction that tells me this has been a point of contention for some time now. Remmy holds his hands up, surrendering. I've never met anyone else who can go from an agitated snarl back to light-hearted joking as quickly as Riley can. She wears her emotions on her sleeve, no matter what they are. "... I'll think about it," She says.

We spend the earliest parts of the morning trying to bridge the gap of five years between us. Remmy's sunny disposition playing a vital role in the transition. They look even more similar now than they did as kids. Both trimmed by the rough demands of life in the wilderness. Their blue hair matching shades, Remmy's features a touch softer than Riley's. Every time I see them, it still amazes me of the randomness of life. Out of the thousands of cryo-frozen eggs, one that actually managed to successfully reanimate, also duplicated in the process. I'll never understand the sheer improbability of it all, but one thing I've learned is life always finds a way.

"So, what exactly do you know about Yara?" I ask. My voice weary of the odd man. Remmy and Riley look to one another with befuddled expressions.

"Honestly, not much," Remmy says. "He showed up out of nowhere. One minute, I'm lying on some primitive Gaz medicine table, and the next, Gaz healers are on the ground, and I'm being ushered out. Apparently, he'd been following us through the woods after he heard the battle we had with the Tyko and Luta. She told you about that, right?" He asks.

"Um.. sort of. Bits and pieces. I didn't realize there was a Luta involved too?"

"Well, long story short, we tracked a Tyko through the woods for weeks, and when we finally found it, it was locked in a standoff with a full-grown Luta. Big ole' thing! So, our fearless leader decided it would be a good idea to try to take them both out, with half working equipment and half a plan!" He chuckles to himself. Riley not nearly as amused. "I ended up having to manually detonate a Sonostick, Riley had to drag me through the woods, apparently letting us get kidnapped, it was a mess!" He finishes, glancing subtly at Riley as he does. He seems a bit cavalier for such a traumatic event, but with all they've been through, it wouldn't surprise me in the least if he's downplaying the severity of it for Riley's sake.

"Damn, that's wild! It's been a pretty insane couple of days for me too," I say.

"Outside of crashing your rig and almost being eaten alive, you mean?" Remmy asks with a snort.

"Well, yea, since you all have been gone, my crew and I have been working on something that could change the world..." The twins glance at one another, intrigued. "We've been gathering human DNA off of Redemption wreckage we find while on duty for the High Council and are using it to try to create synthetic humans in the womb-pods we were born in."

Remmy leans back, running his fingers through his hair.

"Shit, the High Council is letting you do that?" He asks.

"They don't know. You two are the only ones I've told. Gwinn doesn't even know. I knew she'd never approve of that... I was going to tell her about once we solved the formula." The more I think about it, I'm still not sure I'd tell her then. Yet, I've already told her of the Vault. I don't know, she makes my head hurt.

"Leo, that would be... I mean, incredible," Riley says.

"It *would* be if we could solve it. But we need the formula to be able to mutate to any gene sequence to be viable. We'll never gather enough DNA to individually build out the number of humans we need to create a sustainable population. The formula has to be able to take the bit we give it, and finish the rest." The stress of that puzzle grinds against my temples. "And we just can't figure it out..." Images of the failed solution dripping down the microscope in my lap mock me. "But, *another* recent near-death experience led to the most remarkable discovery I've ever made, and one that I'm convinced holds the missing link!" I turn my head down the hall to see if anyone else is around. Guilt stabs at me as I do. I don't know why I don't want the crew to know about it, but it just seems like something that belongs to us. Humans. The image of Patawa's eyes rolling into her head as she faints from blood loss flashes into my mind. The hole in her suit coated a deep shade. She could've died. And I kept something so massive from someone who'd easily give their life for me. Maybe I'm making a mistake?

"Wow, I thought *we* were your most remarkable discovery," Riley says with a joke.

"Well, to be fair, you found me!"

"True." They laugh. "But honestly, Leo, that's amazing. What'd you find?"

Before I can tell them about the Vault, Bryl approaches from the opposite side of the hall.

"Mornin' boss." He nods to Remmy and Riley as well. "Patawa is awake if you wanna go see her?" He says. I glance back to the twins.

"We can finish later..." I say. "Do you all want to come with? I'm sure she'd love to see you." I ask. Riley is hesitant, I'm not quite sure why, but Remmy tugs her by the arm as he starts toward the room.

"Of course, we would," He says with a smile.

Patawa lays on a stone block covered with soft moss. Yara and Spri stand over her, talking amongst themselves, as the four of us enter the room. Patawa rolls her head to see us, a gentle smile on her face.

"Hey there... How you feelin'?" I ask. Patawa rubs her leg. A makeshift patch covers her thigh, where the Dystrogar punctured her.

"Lucky... Grateful... Sore!" She laughs. She looks to Remmy and Riley. "Oh my gosh! I wasn't hallucinating! It was you two." She laughs. She extends her hand to them.

Riley doesn't know how to act around her. She fidgets awkwardly, but it doesn't bother Pat. She wraps Riley's hands in hers, eyes swelling with joy, glancing at me incessantly. I roll my eyes at her doting.

"We're glad you're ok." I chuckle.

"It's Riley... it's really her," She says, a tear rolling down her cheek as she says it to me. "Oh, and come here, I love you too, Rem." Reaching out and pulling Remmy to her as well.

"I thought..." Riley composes herself, fighting back emotions. "I thought you might be angry." Pat props herself up slightly, shooing me away as I try to stop her.

"Stop that. I'm just so glad you're ok. Both of you." They hug, and Pat stares at me over Riley's shoulder.

"I am Yara..." Yara chimes in. All eyes shift to him.

"I know you introduced yourself already..." Patawa says, giving me a worried glance. "I can't thank you enough for rescuing us. I don't want to think about what would've happened if you didn't show up." I shudder at the thought as well.

"I did not rescue you," Yara says. We all look to him, puzzled. "The children of the clouds were heading into danger. I must protect the children. I have to protect the children."

Nobody knows what to make of his ramblings.

"What?" I ask. Yara turns his neck to look at me, body stiff, heading twitching, answering with bizarre, cryptic speech.

"Had the children not gone into the dark, Yara would not have either."

Patawa laughs nervously.

"Well, it's a good thing they did then," She says.

"Yes, it is... For another child of the clouds was found. I must protect him as well," Yara says. Face freezing into a stoic gaze.

We stand there in the awkwardness of Yara, Patawa bandaged and recovering, the twins and I still getting comfortable around one another, and Spri and Bryl looking on helplessly. I try to ignore Yara.

"Well, I'm glad you're ok, Pat. I'm going topside, and I will try to figure out how we will get home. I'm sure Russa will send search parties for us when we never respond, but they won't come here. Can't. You rest up, and the guys will come with me to scout a path home..."

"No!" Yara barks, startling us all. "You cannot walk among the woods in the light. The Gaz search. The children must be safe." In the middle of his rant, his posture snaps to a change, and he lifts his chin with the poise of an aristocrat. His voice becomes smoother and velvety, his sentences cleaner. "I swore to protect you, Leo. To protect you all. He entrusted me with your safety. I will fulfill my duty. I have found the two children lost to the trees; they are now safe. I have found you. You are now safe. I have found your metal home that fell from the sky; it is now safe. You will not walk through these treacherous woods without the shield of the moon."

He faces me now. Head twitching.

"If you head into danger, Yara must be your guide."

I glance at the others, unsure of how to process everything that was just said.

"The hell are you talkin' about?" Bryl asks.

"Don't bother, it's all gibberish," Riley says.

Something he said strikes me.

"No... go back. What did you say about a metal home?" I ask. My mind begins to race.

"I'm telling you, Leo, don't bother with..." I cut her off.

"What do you mean by metal home that fell from the sky?"

Yara looks at me. His expression, unreadable.

"He told me your home fell from the sky. He told me no one must know. Only the children of the clouds."

I step in closer to him.

"What is it? Who is telling you this?"

"My master. He made me swear to protect you, protect your home."

"Your master?... Who... What is it you are protecting?"

"Leo... seriously, you can talk to him in circles. We did it for hours." Riley insists.

Yara stares with a blank expression.

"Yara... the metal home you are protecting. Where is it?" I ask. My mind going a mile a minute. It has to be the Vault. Or maybe I just want it to be?

"Only the children of the clouds may know it's location," Yara says frankly. Yara's twitches intensify.

"Leo, the man is clearly deranged, please don't provoke him anymore..." Riley says. She pulls at my sleeve.

"My master knew the truth. He said I couldn't know the truth, or I would die. So, he said, 'Yara, protect the children, and they will know the truth,' do not, and they will also die. So, when two children went missing, Yara had to find them. I found them, now they are safe. So, do you know the truth?" Yara asks. The six of us stand in complete befuddlement. He speaks as if his voice is a prerecorded message. Playing on a loop.

"What truth?" I finally ask.

"I do not know. My master said I would die as well if I knew the truth. He said the children will know." Yara repeats himself.

"What the hell..." Bryl rolls his eyes. "Leo, are we done with this yet?" He stands unamused by Yara's ramblings. "There is so much we need to do before the sun goes down." I look to my crew, and to the twins. Without the knowledge of the Vault, his words would seem like the manifesto of a lunatic. But I can't shake the feeling that it involves the Vault. And the hidden ship. It's all just too convenient. I have to tell them.

"There's something I should've told you all about when I stayed behind in Paradise..." I want to look at them, but I realize just how ashamed I am for deciding to keep it from them at all. "It's a long story, but under the Old Consulate, I discovered a Vault..." I say. "For some reason, I had access to the dataplate connected to the entrance. And inside the Vault is a fully intact hub of the Redemp..." The words punch from my lungs as Yara spears me to the ground. His cords slithering over my mouth.

"ONLY THE CHILDREN OF THE CLOUDS MAY KNOW!" Yara screams. His voice cracks as he screeches it again. Eyes set aflame with mania. His cords frantically squirm like grub worms under an overturned rock. His head snaps back to the crew. Yanking a pistol from his leg. I flinch. Trying to shove away from him. Bryl lurches in front of Spri and Pat. The twins shouting in panic. Yara bellows out again. A horrifying growl. Broken and chaotic. "THEY ARE NOT CHILDREN OF THE CLOUDS. THEY CANNOT KNOW! MASTER SAID SO!" I shout for him to stop, but they muffle against his gag as I peel the cords from my lips one at a time.

"Whoa, easy! Put it down!" Bryl yells. Pleading hands stretching to the sky.

"Yara, stop!" I yell out as I finally knock myself free. Remmy vaults over the table and positions himself in between Yara and my crew. Voice calm and poised.

"Put it down."

"Remmy, don't!" Riley cries out. She darts out of the room.

"Move child. I must protect the children. You must move," Yara says. Gun primed. Head twitching violently.

"I'm not gonna do that... I need you to put that down."

"I cannot. Because those three know. And they may not know!"

Remmy is still confused.

"Wait, know what? They don't know. I don't even know?" Remmy tries to reassure him.

"Yara, they need to know! The *metal home* you spoke of, I

know where it is. I found it. But now I need you to take me there, and I need their help when I get there," I say, watching the man devolve further and further into madness. Yara snarls, his head shaking as he smacks the butt of his gun against it.

"Master told me... master TOLD me." He crows. "He made me swear that no one but the children of the clouds know of its location. But *they* know," Yara says, shoving his gun to my crew. His face wild. The old withered features of a thousand-year-old man, growing a deeper shade of brown. Riley skids to a stop in the door frame. A rifle wedged into her shoulder. She barks orders at Yara.

"Drop the gun, old man! Now!"

"Shit. Whoa. Riley, no!" I step in between Riley and Yara.

"Leo, what the fuck are you doing, move!" She yells.

"We need him, Ri."

"He's gonna shoot Remmy!"

"I will not, I must protect the children of the clouds," Yara says.

"See, he's not going to shoot him."

"But he's going to shoot us!" Patawa cries out.

"No, he won't! Nobody is shooting anybody!" I yell. I order Riley to back down. She doesn't.

"Leo, this lunatic has a gun pointed at my brother," She says. Her posture's ready. "Get the fuck out of the way!" Her words are harsh. Panic dripping off each syllable.

"Riley, stop!" Remmy calls out to her now. A hand pointed at both gunmen. "Put it down." He begs. She glances at Remmy. Desperation scratched across the creases of her brow.

"Remmy get out of the way, and I'll put the gun down."

"Ri, you know I can't do that!" He yells back. "If I move, he'll shoot them."

"No, he won't. Yara, no, you won't." I plead.

"Yes, I will. I must," He says. "Master said only the children. You are not safe if they know the truth!"

"Yara, no, we are not."

"Riley, fucking shoot this psycho!" Bryl yells.

"Shut up, Bryl. Riley, put it down. Yara, you too."

"No! Not until Remmy is out of the way," She says.

"He will certainly attack us if Remmy does not intervene." Spri drones. "Is that your wish?"

Riley's eyes flood with tears. "Remmy is all I have."

"Ri, we have *all* of them now!" Remmy says. "We're not

248

alone anymore... C'mon." His eyes are so soft, begging Riley to see the future in us. She looks away. Knowing his gaze will beat her if she lets it. Then our eyes meet. A life playing out before them that never was. Lost to these woods. But Remmy is *not* all she has, not anymore. She has me again. And I know she can see that. I know she *wants* that. I'm realizing I want it too.

"Just put down the gun, and we can talk it out with Yara," I say, inching toward her. I have to disarm her. Yara clearly has answers I need. He could be the key to solving everything.

For a second, she considers it.

"I don't see why we can't settle on discretion as a viable option?" Spri quips. My heart plummets. *Oh no, Spri...*

Yara launches into a final rage. Trying to shove past Remmy. Every spastic, flailing movement he makes tempting the trigger to go off.

"Child move, now! They cannot know." Yara demands. "NOW!" He yells. Riley's gun darts back into her shoulder.

"Leo, move."

"Riley, don't!"

"Leo!"

"Riley!"

"Put it down."

"Move!"

"Shoot him!"

"Remmy!"

"SHOOT HIM!"

"MOVE, CHILD!"

"NO, DON'T!"

The tension of the moment explodes. Gunshots erupt. They echo throughout the cramped room. Sharp ringing drills against my ears. It's all I hear. Chaos swirls around me. I crumble to the floor and watch the ceiling speed away. Bodies swarm. Madness consuming the tiny quarters. The ringing fades and voices scream, and the last thing I see before my vision fades are empty shells that bounce on the stone floor. Once. And then twice.

23

FARGO SHEPHERD

So Shall You Reap

Geeva lays resting on a Med Bed in the Capital. Eyes closed, vitals monitored and controlled. The lights glare on the glass casing, but I can still see her. Her frosted skin is smeared with dried blood, her black hair knotted and tangled. But she still looks beautiful. Guilt chews at me. I rest my head on the observation glass and fight back tears. What the hell is wrong with me?

I rushed here as quickly as I could, I just hope it was quick enough. I don't think I could ever forgive myself if I got her killed.

After I dropped off Geeva here at the MedCenter, I hurried Zina back to my base of operations. She probably needed medical attention as well, but I couldn't afford to have her out in public. I have Cyto looking after her back at the base. Cyto... the look in his eyes when I told him Geeva had been shot. I never want to see pain like that again. He wanted to be here instead of me, but I told him it was too dangerous. The Rojo could decide our deal is off, or maybe I broke the deal the moment I took Zina, I don't know? But I had to stay here to protect Geeva, just in case.

The hours melt away, and the uncertainty is maddening. Med Doc's check on her periodically, but none have concrete answers for me.

Another hour passes. Still nothing.

The more I sit here, the more I think about how I will pitch this deal to Victor. He'll never go for this. The more I'm thinking about what I'm asking him to do, the worse I feel. But what choice do I have? It's one match compared to my life! He couldn't possibly choose the Arena over me... Could he?

My thoughts are interrupted by the sound of Geeva's voice.

"Fargo?" She says. Her eyes creak open, and she turns her head away from the light. "Fargo?" She calls out again. I rush to the Med Bed and lean against the glass.

"Hey... Geev... Yea, I'm here," I say. Her face contorts in pain as she wakes from her unconscious state. I press a button on the side of the Med Bed and Med Docs swarm in. They surround the case and begin to administer tests and medicine that needed her to be awake. The Med Docs make me back away so they can get in closer, and her eyes follow me as I do. I cover my face with my hands and press them firmly against my eyes and cheeks, relief washing over me. The Med Docs operate for some time before finishing their work and clearing the room. As they do, I grab one by the sleeve.

"Is she going to be ok?" I ask. My eyes glancing back and forth between Geeva and the Med Doc.

"Well, she lost a large amount of blood, and her Orulla levels plummeted, but we got it under control and stabilized some of her organ failures." The Med Doc says. "She'll recover... but it will take some time. One of the bullets hit her Vynal system, so toxins are spilling into her bloodstream, but we're doing everything we can to filter them out."

"So, she'll be fine though, right?"

"Yes, as long as she rests and lets our systems do their jobs, she will."

I squeeze my arm as I hold back tears of joy.

"Thank you."

The Med Doc leaves, and I collapse back into my seat, propping my feet up on the stand next to it, the weight of Geeva's death lifted from my shoulders.

"Feet off the furniture!" Geeva says with a playful smile. Her voice, soft and weak. I look up at her.

"Hey, I give the orders around here. Not you!" I say, a trembling smile stretching wide across my face.

"And yea, look where that led me! I told you we should've cleared the mess hall first."

"Yea, well, you've just got all the answers, huh?" I laugh, getting my breath under control.

"I've been saying that for years, you just don't listen," She says.

"Oh, really? Do I need to remind you of the giant shipment of *fake* synthetic silk you bought? Or what about the *awesome* deal you got on those newly released rail weapons? Yea, they were manufactured about fourty years ago!"

"In my defense... the guns did sell well as antiques."

"Ha. Yea, you got lucky!" I grin at Geeva, who smiles back. "I'm glad you're ok, kid!"

"I bet you are."

We sit there as she recovers while as I explain what happened when she passed out. She shakes her head in disbelief.

"My God Fargo, you can get us into some shit, can't you!" But before I can answer, the door to the room bursts open. I nearly fall from my chair.

"FARGO!" Victor stands in the doorframe. Face blood red. Anger spills from him. "YOU MOTHERFUCKER!" Victor sprints and heaves a massive punch toward me. I barely get an arm up. It glances off the top of my head. Pains sears my skull. I topple to the ground and scuffle around the Med Bed. He charges after me again.

"Victor, stop! What the hell?!"

He catches up and shoves me, sending me flying into a prop stand that shoots medical equipment in all directions. Geeva shouts out something for help. I crash to the ground and feel the force of Victor's massive boot slam into my back. I wail in pain. Victor keeps kicking me as he screams.

"WHAT THE FUCK DID YOU DO?!" He kicks me again. I curl up to protect myself. "WHAT DID YOU DO FARGO!"

"Vic, what are you talking ab.." He rifles another kick into my side, and pain shoots down my back. "Please! Stop!" He reaches down and turns me over. His fist pummels into my face. I nearly blackout. I can feel the blood gushing from my nose. The MedCenter guards come spilling into the room and pull Victor from me. I can barely see, eyes already swollen, but I can hear him struggle with the guards to get free. I roll to my side and spit huge clumps of blood from my mouth. My body aches. Victor is pinned to the floor by five guards, but he's looking right at me. He's winded, and his words are chopped from exhaustion and fury.

"Deterro... the Vipers... he took Miku! She's gone!" Tears begin to pour from him as he quits resisting his restraints. He goes limp onto the floor, and his chest quivers with sobs.

My entire world shatters. My heart shreds to pieces, and I'm frozen in time. Oh my God... Miku... No... How did Deterro...? It doesn't matter... She's gone. I look at Victor. Sorrow spewing from his massive frame. I've never seen hatred the likes of which he bores into me. They may very well *both* be gone.

"Fargo... what did you do?"

24

RILEY HOLT

Heartbreak

I didn't know sadness of this depth existed... I have no more tears. They all lay pooled at my feet. A devastation beyond words. I feel so light. As if my soul was the only thing keeping me grounded against this stone, and it's been ripped from my chest, so there is nothing to stop me from floating into the heavens to be with him.

I haven't moved in hours. Remmy's head rests in my lap. His gentle blue eyes gaze up at me. Mine look back down into his. Begging for forgiveness. My fingers run through the cyan locks of his hair that are beginning to fade and show the dark brown roots. An emptiness swallows me. Suffocating. My mind is blank. A vast hollow void.

My brother is gone. My best friend.

My world.

Gone.

A small knock on the stone door frame breaks my bleak trance. Leo stands in the frame, blood just beginning to soak through a bandage wrapped around his left shoulder. I thought I didn't have tears left, but when I see him, the salty drops begin to wet my eyes again. Leo fights back his own. At first, I was furious at him. Hated him. Blamed him. Then I was terrified. So incredibly sorry. Heartbroken. Traumatized. I shot him. I could've killed him. He could be lying here next to Remmy, erased from this world, and I'd truly be alone. He sits down next to me and wraps his arm around me. I rest my head on his good shoulder.

"I'm so sorry, Leo..."

He pulls me in closer, planting a kiss atop my head.

"I'm sorry too..." he says. His breath struggles. "I'm so, so sorry, Ri." He's not Remmy, but I need him all the same. I don't want him to let go.

"What do I do, Leo?" My voice drifts. I feel so helpless. My life was Remmy. My purpose. Without him, I feel a ship with no captain, sailing aimlessly about unknown seas. I smile because he'd laugh at me saying *he* was the Captain. I wipe a tear from my eye as I picture his laugh. But the truth is, every decision I made for us, I made knowing he had my back. No matter what it was. He would be there to fall back on in case things didn't work. And they didn't work plenty of times. But he was always there. I don't think I've ever felt so vulnerable as I do right now, knowing I'm on my own.

Leo doesn't respond. He just holds me as we mourn the loss of my brother and his friend.

Remmy's blood has hardened on the fringes of my pants. Stained my shirt and fingers as well. It doesn't seem real, like a prop on a theater stage. If only that were true.

"What happened?..." I ask. I slide from under Leo's arm and meet his gaze. Desperate for clarity. How did we get here? Everything happened so fast. "Did I... Did... Is Remmy dead because of me?" I don't know if I could handle that being true.

"No, Ri. Absolutely not," Leo says. "Things got out of control. Yara... He..."

Yara!

I glare at Leo as he says his name.

"He what!" I bark.

"He... was just trying to help."

"Help!" A bubble rises in my throat. I might puke. "He killed Remmy!"

"He didn't mean to. You know he didn't. You heard him; he's spent years trying to protect us."

"Didn't mean to.... Are you fucking serious, Leo?" I could punch him in the face right now. "Listen to yourself."

Leo drops his head. He knows that didn't come off right. "Listen, the Vault I was telling you about. The one that could change everything..." His eyes light up like he's speaking of a mythical paradise. "He knows about it. That's what set him off when I mentioned it... It has to mean something."

I stare back, dumbfounded.

"Leo, I don't give a shit about some ship parts!" I don't

understand what he's even trying to get at. "My brother is dead! Because of you! And because of him!" I stand up, now infuriated. "How can you talk to me about literally anything else right now?"

"Riley, that's not fair! You know it's not!"

"Not fair?! You know what's not fair? What's not fair is the most genuine, caring person I've ever known being gunned down by some lunatic, protecting people he hasn't seen in five years, after saving their lives." Tears overwhelm me. "And then someone he considers to be a true friend trying to justify it. How dare you talk to me about fair!" I can't believe what he's even trying to say.

"...Riley... I'm not trying to justify..." I cut him off.

"Just stop, Leo." I stare at him. "I need you to leave."

He stares at me. His eyes seek forgiveness, but his words continue their rant.

"Riley, I'm sorry, I truly am. If I could've stopped it, I would've."

"Bullshit! You could've moved out of the way and let me shoot him in the head."

"Ri, I couldn't do that. He has answers. I know it."

I shake my head in total disappointment. Completely exhausted with this conversation.

"Answers to *what* Leo... Whatever they are, I hope they're worth it because you chose them over Remmy."

I don't let him answer. I hold my hand up, begging him to stop talking as I head out the door. Just before I'm gone, I turn back to face him once more.

"Make your peace with Remmy, and then don't go back in that room."

My mind is twisted in a million directions. I have to wash this blood off me. Every time I see it, stabbing pain scores through my stomach. I circle the stairs down to the well.

The moonlight funnels through the deep reservoir, sparkling off the minerals and smooth rock. Wall torches covered with tree wax crackle with flames and glow softly against the grey walls. I shed my blood-stained clothes and step into the pool at the bottom. The water is unbearably cold. My skin instantly tightens as I descend into the frigid water. The chill nearly sucks the air from my lungs. The colored tiles of the floor are smooth against the calloused soles of my feet, what little feeling they have left. I work my way to the center of the pool and wade there softly. Slowly dipping my head under the water so the frozen pool will jolt my body back to life again. Every memory of Remmy comes flooding into my mind like an avalanche of heartbreak. Our entire lives flicker in front of me.

The first years of memories as children in Okotall. Jumping through the murky mangroves and how much he worried about his sisters getting hurt. Archler House and the assholes who would try to steal my meal tickets because we were so small back then. Remmy would fight them for his instead. The sweetheart couldn't fight to save his life, but he'd run through a wall for Gwinn and me. Our first night in the Forest. I was so terrified. I know he was too, but he acted like nothing was wrong. He stayed up all night on lookout so I could sleep in his lap. He was always my protector, even if it looked the opposite.

I sink to the bottom of the pool, staring up at the moon through the rocking waters. The silence of the depth is maddening. I scream as hard as I can! Air bubbles spew from my mouth and race to the surface. The scream dissolves instantly into the water, and I lay back against the tile. My eyes folding shut. I don't want to come up. I want to drown here and be with Remmy again. Tell him I love him one last time. Tell him I'm sorry for everything. He protected me, my entire life. And the one time he needed me, I failed him.

I feel myself slip away. Letting the water rush into my nose and mouth. My eyes spring open at the pain of my first breath. But I force myself to stay at the bottom. I can't tell if I'm crying, but it feels like I am. Each sob sucking more water into my chest. My vision begins to close in when I hear his voice. Remmy calls out to me.

"STOP!" I can hear it like he stands just next to me. "Please! Riley, stop!" His voice becomes a whisper as I give my body to the well. "*..Forgive the world... Forgive Yara... Forgive them all...*" I go limp, and the world around me stills. I hear his faint voice once more, urging me back to existence. "*... live Riley... Live for me... for yourself... for humanity...*"

There's nothing but darkness now. No sound. No light. Remmy's voice has been swallowed by the hush of death. I'm so eager to see him again. But I'm robbed of my agonizing farewell before I can. My eyes explode open. Water erupting from my lungs, as life is thrust back into my body. The reaper denying my entrance to the afterlife. I turn to my side, and I'm laying nude on the stone just outside the well, water hacking from my lungs in violent coughs. I blink uncontrollably as I adjust to the dim light. Yara kneels over me, clothes dripping wet. His eyes wild with angst.

"The Child is safe!" Yara sits back against the wall, relief washing over him.

Anger spikes in my soul when I see him, but Remmy's words echo through my mind. *Forgive him...*

He looks at me in utter ruin. Tears of his own streaking down his beak and dripping from the tip. Head twitching.

"Yara has failed you... One of the Eight Children is dead. I am so sorry, Child." He pulls on the stringy hair atop his head. "I've broken my oath. I will never fail you again. I swear it." His face is so broken. I recognize the pain. But I want him dead. Want him erased from this world instead of Remmy. He shouldn't be here when Remmy isn't. But I hear Remmy's words over and over in my mind. *Forgive...* How am I supposed to do that? Every time I look at Yara, I see the gun, see the flash of its muzzle, the madness of the room. See the blood bursting from his chest. His last look to me, a desperate cry for help. But I couldn't. Patawa on the ground, soaked in his blood, trying everything she can to stop the bleeding. See Leo fall to the ground in agony. Blood spilling from his shoulder as well. How can I forgive him? Remmy asks too much of me. I'm not him. I can't possibly be near the man who took my world away from me. But I hear his whisper again. It begs me to live without resentment. Without anger. So, for him... I try.

Yara sits quietly next to me. He refuses to leave. Leo rushes into the room as well when he hears what happened. His forehead is wrinkled and strained.

"Riley, what the hell? Are you alright?" He asks. His hands scanning over my face and body, searching for injuries like I was in a rig accident.

"I'm fine, get your hands off me." I toss his hands to the side, but I'm not angry. Not anymore, at least. Just annoyed. My throat does ache from the coughing, though, and my head pounds. I avoid his eye contact, slightly ashamed. But I can feel his awkward sympathy burning a hole into the side of my head. "Stop..." I say. He wrenches. Confused.

"Stop what?"

"Stop looking at me like that!" He backs off.

"Riley... I'm sorry again. Ok? I didn't mean... it didn't come off the way I meant it, that's all," He says. I know it didn't.

"Doesn't make it less hurtful..." I say, a quick spiteful

glance stabbing at him. He recoils a bit. Guilt poking at me over and over. I don't mean to hurt him. Everything is just so raw.

I swallow my pain and try my best Remmy impersonation one more time. "Sorry. It's alright... We're *all* clearly not thinking straight right now," I say with an overwhelmed chuckle that flirts with the verge of an emotional collapse. Leo shares in my mental exhaustion. Smiling at my acceptance of his apology.

"Yea, it's a good thing the ole kook can swim," He says, his brilliant white teeth flashing in a grin. I may have forgiven Yara, but I still don't like how endearing a tone Leo takes about him. I glance at Yara, his face weary. But his manic episode has seemed to die off. What's left is a once-elegant man, who now seems to struggle with the fact that his mind and his body no longer agree with one another. His words tidy, and he speaks once again without the spastic idiolect I've come to expect from him.

"Words cannot describe my sorrow, Child." He looks up at me. Eyes wanting to say a million words, lips only able to say a few. "I do not deserve your forgiveness, but I am grateful for it." I turn my head away, choking back resentment-filled tears. "My entire purpose was to protect you all. My master made me promise. I was honored he chose me. I love all eight of you like my own children." His voice now so delicate, it's difficult to maintain anger toward him. I can see his true pain now. It's as heavy as mine. "I've searched these woods alone for years looking for you. Life in the Forest is harsh." He doesn't have to tell me. "And when I finally found you both, I don't think I've ever had a more joyous day in my life." His lips bend into a crooked, awkward smile. "Nor have I had a darker day than today." His head hangs, buried in his aged, warped cords.

For the first time, I sympathize with him. It's almost a foreign emotion for me. I can see the hardship of this man's life and how everything he's devoted his time toward has crashed upon him. He has kinder eyes than I gave him credit for. And at this moment, between his lunacy, I attempt to forgive him. Maybe it's the clarity in which I can still hear Remmy's voice whisper to me, but I see the light that he urged me to strive toward. I begin to see a life in which he envisioned for me. One where I was at peace with the hardships this world has dealt me and begin to enjoy the bounties of this life, instead of rejecting them. Yara's head twitches aggressively, and he slips back into his psychosis.

"Child. We cannot stay here longer. The Gaz search. They will find this retreat, and Yara cannot protect you from the horde," He says. A sliver of guilt drips its way down me as I comprehend just how lost the man is. Remmy would never resent someone so incapable of controlling his functions. No matter how heinous a crime he committed. But the hole he left still scraps at my heart, and there is nothing that can be done to fill it.

Yara isn't wrong, though. The longer we stay here, the greater chance the Gaz have of finding us. I can still picture A'gorr's face shrinking in the distance as we sped off on the back of the Hotógo. I shudder at the thought.

I go ahead and ask, so Leo doesn't have to. I know it itches at him.

"You're right, Yara, we need to go. But first, we need answers." Leo glances at me with surprise. He reaches as if trying to tell me I don't have to, but I stop him. "Who is your master? Why did he tell you to protect us?" I ask. Yara stares back in confusion.

"My master is the father of the Children of the Clouds? The Children do not know their own father?" He asks.

"Father? What do you mean? All of us?"

"The Father brought life to the Children. He protected the Children."

"Leo and I have different Fathers? Biological and adopted..."

"There is only one Father. Who without, the Children would not have life. My master."

I glance at Leo, who looks back without answers. I think about how to phrase my question to get the answer I need. I pause for a moment then ask.

"What is your master's *given* name?" I ask. He looks at me, surprised. As if I ask a question I should know the answer to.

"Well... Emoss, of course."

The words seem to hang in the air as we process them.

"Emoss? Emoss is your master?" His name echoes in my mind. Leo's eyes spread wide like blooming flower buds. "You're saying Emoss told you to protect us?"

"And Emoss found the ship you spoke of earlier?... The 'metal home'?" Leo jumps in.

"Master gave the Children life. He found their home and hid it from those seeking to destroy it. He said the truth lay within. I must protect the Children because they know the truth. Yara may not, for he could also die," Yara says. I look to Leo, astounded. I don't know what's happening. "Master told me, 'Sir Yara, take the Children to their home when I pass. They know the truth. It shall be theirs to bear'." His gaze stretches beyond us. The reel of that memory cycling over his eyes. "But they took the Children too fast after Master passed. The children sent to Archler House. And no one was to know that I was protecting you. So, I could not take you from there. But I thought maybe you would be safe. Until I found out you were gone. Then Yara set out to the woods to find you..." He looks up at Leo and me. "But now I have found you. So, I must take you to your truth. For master gave his life to protect your truth. I must honor it."

My mind buckles yet again. Memories of my father's final days fighting over the scraps of my heart. There's too much to comprehend all at once. Leo is floored as well. He doesn't know what to make of the mad man's ramblings. But then something he said at the end pulls at me.

"What do you mean, 'he gave his life for your truth'? Emoss fell ill..." I ask, the implication of his words squeezing on my heart.

His expression grows cold. His eyes narrow, and his voice lowers as if even now he doesn't want to speak it.

"No, my Child... He did not."

25

GWINN DEMARCO

Impasse

Russa stares at the colony of projections that flicker over every tile of my office as he enters. Employment manifests, Province Budget Algorithms, Outstanding Liabilities, Capital Flows, on and on it goes. The paralyzing slog of government minutia. I sit helpless at my seat, no idea where to begin. Tolla sits neatly in the corner of the room, her legs folded under one another. She doesn't seem as intimidated with the mountain of work as I am. A lifelong politician. I flick my finger across my dataplate, and the wave of translucent images evaporate. I am in no mood to start this today.

My office feels larger without the projections clogging the floorplan. Sleek and minimalist, akin to the rest of the building. A miniature version of the crescent-shaped table from the Consulate rests in the center of my office. The ninety-eighth floor will be my new home away from home for the foreseeable future.

"Tolla could you give us a moment?" Russa asks. Tolla glances at me, and I nod to her.

"Councilors…" She nods respectfully as she leaves the

office and shoots me a cryptic look.

"Come on, let's hear it, Russa." I roll my eyes. He's acted off ever since the inauguration. I can tell the accusations against me dig at him. I already know what this conversation will be about.

"Don't be like that, Gwinn, I just want to talk," He says.

"I'm not stopping you, say what you gotta say."

He takes a deep breath and prepares his words carefully.

"Gwinn. You know I love you like a daughter, right?" I nod and gesture for him to get on with it. "But I need to know." He stares at me frankly. His posture a mixture of concern and fear.

I fold my hands over each on the table and gently reply.

"Know what?"

He's annoyed by that. I know what. I just want him to say it.

"Gwinn..."

"Know what, Russa?" I toy with him. I know he can't maintain this genuine fatherly persona he's put on for long. It's not in his nature. Nor is it in mine to have deep intimate confessionals.

"Dammit, Gwinn!" He smacks the table. "You know damn well what I'm asking!"

"Did I kill those men!" I bark at him. "Is that what you want to know? Huh?!" My gaze pierces him. What do these men not understand? I AM NOT INTIMIDATED BY YOU. I'll say these words and watch his *ruthless* heart flinch. Honestly, it feels good to say aloud, and I couldn't care less what he thinks anyway.

"Yes. I did."

His beak flinches. Every cord in his body beginning to vibrate and twitch. He begins to nervously pace around the room, murmuring to himself. I roll my eyes. How predictable?

"Gwinn, Gwinn, Gwinn..." He looks at me as if he doesn't recognize who I am. Disappointment, bordering on disgust, riddle his face. For a second, I think I feel shame. Russa is the only person left who can still *almost* elicit emotion from me. But I'm no longer desperate for my pseudo-father figure's approval anymore.

"Save the theatrics Russa." I moan.

"Theatrics? Gwinn, you killed..." He stops and lowers his voice as he gets closer, a hushed whisper yell. "... you killed four people, Gwinn!" He looks around the room. "For what? For this?!" He balks. "I promise you; this isn't worth it!"

He has some nerve telling me what to value in my life. If I want this stupid job to honor my father's legacy, I'll damn well do it.

When I don't concede, something changes in him. His cords snap stiff. Twisting tight into themselves. His eyes narrow.

"You think you can just take matters into your own hands?" He says. "You have any idea what you're doing? Did you make sure there were no witnesses? What about your loose ends? You take care of those? What about evidence? Did you even think about any of this before you acted? Or are you just a sloppy child with too much power?" A purr rolls from his beak. His cords twisting even tighter.

It's no surprise that he doesn't think I can handle my business properly. The entire High Council has underestimated me since I stepped foot in their Consulate. But I laugh at their condescension.

His words try to cut into me. But I'm made of stone, cold and hard. Except when he uses the only ammunition he knows can penetrate me. "Emoss would be beside himself if he were here." My stone façade splinters as he says it. He's right.

"Well he's not here, is he?!" I say. "And whose fault is that?" I bite the inside of my cheek, so Russa can't see my pain.

"No, no, no! You will not use Emoss'ss death again as another excuse to act like a horrible person." His face is flushed with anger. "He's gone! Ok… it wasn't your fault. Get over it! Your father dying isn't an excuse for murder, Gwinn. That's not how the world works." He closes the distance between us, towering over me. "Grow the fuck up. You want to murder people? Murder them. But don't blame it on dead daddy issues. That's pathetic."

I stare blankly at him.

I'm not going to sit here and be spoken to like a child.

"Russa, if you want to help, then help. If not… get the hell out of my office," I say, cold.

There's a palpable shift in his demeanor like he realizes some charade he's grown weary of, is no longer worth his time.

"You want the truth, kid…" He says, the anger from his eyes bleeding away. Replaced with… I'm not sure, exactly? Annoyance? Exhaustion? "All the money in Groga couldn't get me to care about those four worthless sacks. I don't even care you killed them... Don't care you rigged this election. Hell, I don't even care that you've become some unbearable pain in the ass." He inches closer. "But what I will *not* accept is sloppiness." He's so close now I smell the rancid stench of his breath. "You've made a mess. A brash, ill-thought-out mess. And if Emoss hadn't left me in charge of you, I'd make you clean this mistaken-laden bullshit up yourself."

My eyes begin to dry out I've stared so long. *Brash?* I have everything right where I want it. He just can't accept that I'm capable of getting shit done without him.

"So, tell Emoss he's welcome for saving your ass once again. Because for his sake and his sake *only*, I'm helping..."

We stare at each other at an impasse.

"Fine."

I spend the next few hours explaining everything that happened. How I coaxed information out of E'zuu, how a man approached me, offering a *solution* to my problems, and how I established an alibi by visiting Tanya in Su Hoz. I tell him everything. The more details I gave him, the more entrenched he became in this mess. The only thing I don't tell him is what I offered in exchange for all this to happen. I can't tell anyone that.

The longer we talk about how to handle the situation, the more normal the tension in the room becomes. Russa's temper fades, and my combative badgering dissipates. I like him better when he's not trying to be my life coach.

Russa checks his comm, an odd expression on his face.

"What's wrong?" I ask. He leans against the doorframe, something else clearly weighing on him.

"Have you heard from Leo lately?" he asks.

"Leo? I mean, how recently? He left me some messages a few days back. But not since then, why?"

"He hasn't reestablished contact since deploying on an assignment," Russa says.

"Well you know Leo, he's always a thorough one. I'm sure he's fine. Where was the assignment?" I ask, my legs kicked up on the table as I lean back in my chair. Russa hesitates.

"The Rift..."

My stomach drops.

"The Rift?!" I swing back upright. "Why the hell would you send him into the Rift?" My pulse quickens.

"Salvage acquisition," He says, nonchalant.

"Well why'd you have to send him? You could've sent

anyone." He glances up from picking at a small fray in his shawl.

"Why does it matter to you? I thought you don't care?" He asks, now slightly annoyed at the criticism. Residue of our awkward confrontation still lingering in the air.

"I don't... But... Seems a bit irresponsible, don't ya think?"

"Irresponsible?"

"I mean sending one of eight humans in existence into the most dangerous place on Valenia just sounds like an ill-advised plan?"

He rifles an agitated sneer my way.

"Oh, spare me, Gwinn. You don't give two shits about *humanity* or preserving your race, or whatever it is you're implying."

"True. But that doesn't mean it still wasn't a foolish decision."

He ignores my comments and moves on.

"Check the dates on his messages. They were all before he went in, right?" Russa asks.

"Yea, I'm positive they were. He left one while he was in the air. Didn't say *that's* where he was going, though. Just kept yammering on about some *secret* Vault he found under the old Consulate and a hidden hub of our ship, I don't know. All the normal Leo shit that he obsesses over that no one else cares about."

Russa stops what he's doing.

"What'd you just say?" He asks. Tolla taps on the window, and I signal her in.

"Sorry to interrupt, but everything is set up for tonight in Groga," She says.

"Give me your comm," Russa says, ignoring Tolla. I hand it over to him.

"Oh, shit, I forgot that's tonight." I rub my temples. A few days back, Fargo and Miku invited Russa and me to attend Victor's fight in *Oilsterr*. One would think I'd love watching brainless oafs bash each other over the head. It's shallow and desperate and wreaks of insecurity and pleas of validation, yet... sitting among hundreds of thousands of pitiful souls trying to fill their lives with purpose, by leeching on to these romanticized fighters, is enough to make me vomit. Plus, if I have to listen to one more history lesson about Earth's Roman gladiators from Leo, I may just shoot myself.

I suppose that won't be an issue tonight...

Yet, as much as it pains me, I have business to attend to

there.

"We need to get going soon, so we're not late," I say to Russa, but he's completely preoccupied with my comm. "What are you doing?" I ask. He hands it back to me.

"Pull up that message from Leo for me." He requests. I slide open the messages using my thumbprint and hand it back to him.

"Why?" I ask. Tolla hands me my High Council Id datacard.

"Now it's truly official!" She says. A proud, radiant smile on her face. A twinge of guilt tries to peek its way in as she looks at me with reverence I don't deserve. But I push it aside.

I look down at the datacard. My face floats in the left-hand corner. A manufactured smile splitting my cheeks. My title and information stream across the bottom in an endless loop. She's right; somehow, this does make it feel more official. Also, makes my stomach hurt.

"I've arranged transport for you both, and it's waiting on the landing pad whenever you all are ready," She says. Russa has walked to the corner of the room, intently listening to my messages.

"Hey!" I call to him. "What the hell are you doing? Are you ready to go?" He twitches toward me as if caught off guard. A bizarre expression on his face. He heads to the door as he answers.

"Yea. Let's go," He says, voice trailing off. Distracted. "Let me pop down to my floor to handle something really quick, and I'll meet you up there."

"Business, this late?" I ask, still staring down at the credential with my face on it.

"Just something in Su Hoz I needed to finish, but it can wait now."

I freeze. My face goes pale...

"Su Hoz?" I pry, trying to read his expression out of the corner of my eye. What business could he have in Su Hoz other than the lab?

"Not important." He dismisses me and hurries out the door. I stop him before he's completely gone.

"Hey!" Russa stops and turns back toward me. "Can I have my comm back?" I ask. He glances down at it and then looks up at me with an awkward expression.

"...Oh... yea... here..." He tosses it to me, then glances at Tolla and me before hustling to the lift. *What the hell has gotten into him?*

26

TANYA CROWN

Scapegoat

Locked inside the testing room, Qwillow and I sit with our backs against opposing walls, the gap of only a few feet between us feeling miles wide. High Council brutes stand guard just outside the door until Russa decides to grace us with his presence again. Apparently, he's decided he can wait to deal with us. I'm not sure what's changed since he left, but if I have to sit in this room with Qwillow any longer, I may kill her. I can't look at her. She grovels and begs for my forgiveness, but she won't get it. There is no world where I absolve her of what she's done to me. To think I stuck my neck out for her when Russa was on his warpath... I should've let him squeeze the life out of her. Not that I don't want to peel him apart as well, but I trusted her. Loved her. And she's been lying to me every second of every day for my entire life.

"Tanya..." She tries to start again, but I immediately cut her off.

"Don't."

My fingers have been stroking the scars on my torso since she told me. Lies. The entire foundation of my life, built on lies. When I demanded an explanation for Bytrol, I suspected something sinister. But what she told me... there's no preparing for darkness of that magnitude. The moments after the words left her lips are hazy, but I remember laughing. A horrible, hysterical laugh that melted into uncontrollable sobs. What she was describing seeming so unthinkably ludicrous. Those sobs quickly ignited into a rage so intense the High Council guards had to rip me off of her or else I may have clawed her eyes out. There's enough of her skin under my nails to cool that rage for now, but once this numbness passes, I have no doubt I'll want to hurt her again. Because her lies didn't just cause me pain, they robbed me of a life. Deprived me of freedom and love and friendship and, most importantly, control.

I am not a savior. Not the key to a cure. Not a medical anomaly. Not a noble sacrifice. I'm a farm.

I don't have some miraculous immune system that fought off the Rotting.

I *am* the Rotting. The source. It was built from me. Designed. Extracted. Constructed from the genetic harvests they performed on me while searching for a way to extend the life of their precious Regal. They were searching for immortality. What they found was the answer to overcrowding and the perfect scapegoat.

The narrative that I contracted the Rotting as a child and survived... fiction. These scars along my torso, precisely crafted lies. Imitations planted there to avert suspicion. I don't want to know how they did it. Maybe they had mechanical scalpels carve a tiny child? Maybe they used searing torches? I don't know. But there's not a single method I can think of that isn't horrifically morbid.

And she watched every moment of it.

Told me every day *just* how close she was to finding a cure. Lied to my face for over two decades and dares to claim she loves me. To label me as her daughter. What kind of sociopath can do that?

"Russa, he forced me..." Qwillow grovels.

"I said don't!"

"Tanya, please... You have to let me explain." She begs. There's no explaining this away. She watched me suffer my entire life. Farmed my body like the plots of soil outside. And forget what she's done to me, what about her role in the death of millions?

"You are a murderer, a sociopath, a coward, and a liar," I say, rage-filled tears welting in my eyes. "I trusted you. I..." She doesn't deserve another breath of mine. I stand and power to the door, banging on the inside, smearing my tears against my palms. "I need to use the cleansing room," I yell through the door. Qwillow is balled up on the floor below me, quivering next to the door. If she was any more distraught, she may melt into the creases of the floor tiles and disappear into the foundation. Pathetic. The door yawns open.

"Make it quick." The guard mumbles.

The hall is quiet. My eyes are still red. Hunched over grunts along the wall double-take as I approach. They sneer at me. Probably holding me responsible for Hukar and the three other dead soldiers in the restricted lab. Hopefully, they aren't that naïve. If they are, it won't be long before Russa disposes of them too.

Hukar's blood is still dried and clumped in my hair. The nauseating sounds of his head erupting still twists my stomach. His death feels even more needless now.

Three other guards are huddled around a hologram in the common area, watching a news outlet flash the breaking stories of the day. A digitized mockup of Miku's face shines into the air. My feet screech to a halt...

"Keep moving..." My escort grumbles. A news informer regurgitates a prepared statement on the hologram.

"...and while details of the incident are still unclear, it has been confirmed that two of the Eight of Earth, daughter of the Regal, commonly known as the Princess of Groga, Miku Hayashi, and wildly popular Battle of Warlords champion, Victor Bells, who competes under the moniker, Hades, were involved in a violent altercation in the Ancient Memorial city of Nykallo. Authorities suspect the Valley's notorious Vipers to be responsible for the skirmish. Victor Bells was admitted to a nearby med center with minor injuries, yet the whereabouts of Miku Hayashi remain unknown. Regal Trakstull has issued a message to the public to come forward with any pertinent information..."

My heart plummets. Miku...

"I need to use a comm." I snap at my escort. He croaks and yanks me toward the cleansing room.

"No," He says, then points to my temporary prison cell. "You go here or there, that's it." The world begins to spin. This news, far worse than any I could ever receive about myself. All the morbid truths of my life mean nothing compared to the thought of Miku in danger.

"Please, it's urgent," I beg, eyes trembling. The guard just ignores me. Dragging me back to the testing room as his patience runs thin. A smug voice calls out from behind us.

"Just let her use the comm you Surg..." A Savron jeers from the cushions of the common area. It's Klawka, the watchtower guard from earlier. A High Council brute looms over him, keeping him obedient with the barrel of a railcannon, his hands loosely bound. My escort glares back, then glances at me. "Come on. She just wants to check on her friend. She ain't going nowhere." Klawka says.

"Fine." He lets go of my arm. My eyes shoot Klawka a quick thank you, and I dart to the comm on Qwillow's desk. The comm signal rattles for an eternity. Mocking me with every passing second. I just want to hear her voice. *Please...*

A voice answers the signal, thick with mucus and regret.

"Tanya..." Fargo says. The word limps through the speaker.

"Tell me she's with you, Fargo?" I plead. Only his muffled breaths answer my question. Shame coating each staggered exhale.

"I'll get her back. I promise," He says. My hearing snaps away. His words swallowed by a shrill ring swelling in my head. The edge of the workstation keeps me from collapsing to the ground, but my body has quit. My heart shattered. Guards ready their weapons as Klawka springs to help me up. I watch his mouth move as he yells something at them, but my world is consumed with this piercing ring and the image of my best friend.

But in an instant, the overwhelming despair flushes away. A fire streaks through my veins. The only person left I care about needs me. I'm taking back control of my life.

I tug Klawka close as he helps me up, so only he can hear me.

"I'm leaving tonight. And I need your help."

27

VICTOR BELLS

The Solemn Truth

I find no solace in the peace of the tunnel tonight. The heat of my anger an inferno inside my suit. I don't bother trying to settle my nerves. Don't bother going over my game plan. I don't care who the opponents are. I don't care what they will do or how they will do it. I just care about Miku.

The sounds of her cries haunt my soul as they tear at the fibers of my being. My sanity, two unfathomable masses, held together by a string. Frayed and splintered, the string agonizes as it stretches to keep me whole. But every second that passes, the masses gain weight. Every second Miku is with that monster, the weight grows and grows, and the string's cords rip one by one. It *will* break. It's not a matter of *if*, but *when*.

My breath fogs my visor, and I can hear my heartbeat thundering against my ears. It's the only thing that blocks out Miku's screams. Silva stands to my left. An arrogant, nasty smirk on his face. I cannot look at him. He doesn't badger me like most nights. He's not in my face, hurling insults at me. He just lingers there. Basking in the joy of his moment. He's neutered me. There is nothing I can do. He'll get his first win tonight and, in the process, dismantle my immortality. He has no honor, no dignity. He doesn't care how it comes because no one else will know. To the outside world, the weasel Silva will have defeated the mighty Hades. And that is all he needs. I close my eyes and remember this is all for Miku.

No fight or fame could ever match the ecstasy of your love.

I only pray I have the strength to contain Hades until then...

Silva approaches from the side, metal feet clapping against the floor. I tilt my head in the opposite direction. I cannot look this man in the eye, or I may split his skull in two.

"Put on a good show for everyone, Vic. If anyone even sniffs a flop, the deal is off," He says. I can picture his rodent mouth moving even though I'm not looking at him. I say nothing.

"And remember I have to win too. So, you come help your old bud Silva out if he's in trouble, you got it?" He snickers, soaking up every moment he has me by the balls. I remain silent.

"This should be fun!" He nudges me and walks back to his place in line. I clench my fist so hard the hinges of my knuckles may break. *Keep it together, Victor.*

The roar of the crowd grows as the announcer begins his final invocation. I hear his words, but I can't comprehend them. The blur of life swirls around me. I'm water circling a drain. Spilling into an unknown chasm. Dark and hollow. I see the burst of fireworks and the seizure of lights and know it's time to go.

But my world falls silent.

I know the crowd roars because I can see their mouths writhe in jubilation, but I hear nothing. I look down to ensure my feet are moving because I do not hear them against the metal floor, either. Time slows. The very essence of my world around me sparkles with a clarity I've never seen before. It's beautiful. What started as an outlet for the demon who lives inside me became the very definition of my being. My two worlds blended together in marvelous, gruesome harmony. I wish it were another way, but it isn't. And it is at this moment, I realize I will never be enough for Miku. No part of me can exist without the monster. I cannot give myself to her without the threat of his wrath. The realization cements a sadness into my heart so heavy a thousand men could not lift it. But my love for her is still thick in my veins. And she deserves better than the fate Fargo has brought upon her. The fate I've brought upon her. I will get her back if it's the last thing I do.

The stillness of my moment comes crashing onto me as I see his maroon skin. I stop dead in my tracks. Deterro descends a set of stairs toward a large viewing suite at center arena. His black tunic contrasting sharply with the high fashion of Groga's wealthy. He walks past mothers and fathers, children, completely inconspicuous. The sheep have no clue a wolf prowls among them.

He reaches the suite, heavily guarded for some reason, but not by his men. The guards let him pass, and he enters the luxury suite, plucking a small snack off a silver tray. He strolls casually about the empty room, not a care in the world. Rage ignites inside me as I watch him. A door on the opposite side of the suite opens, and my heart stops. Just as it does, I drop into the tram under the floor and into pure darkness.

My mind spasms. I think I may be having a heart attack. What I saw cannot be possible. From the other side of the suite entered three people. Russa, Gwinn, and Fargo.

28

FARGO SHEPHERD

Glass Houses

"I told you... Miku said she wasn't feeling well... You know she'd be here if she could," I say to Gwinn as she harasses me as we walk into the suite.

She reads right through my lie.

This woman is a robot... a sexy... terrifying robot... but a robot nonetheless.

She shoves past me, and the harsh fragrance she wears punches me in the nose. Twisting my stomach in that bizarre way that something only frightening and erotic can, like the night Geeva put those Sparkers on my... My smile evaporates in an instant when I see him.

He's flesh and bone, just like I, yet behind his murky eyes lays something sinister. A tormented spirit who thrives on the despair of others. Wicked and vile. Deterro looks pleasantly surprised to see me, a jagged smile relishes the moment. My blood thickens to a coagulated paste, crawling through my veins when I see him.

"Gwinn, you didn't tell me we'd have company." He grins. "I would've gotten more dressed up for the Prince of the Night." Gwinn knew he'd be here? Russa falters at his presence.

Seems he was in the dark as well. I hurry back toward the door.

"Fargo... stay." His words root me to the floor. "Good boy." I slowly turn as he tosses me a Sweetberry from a serving tray, mind immobilized with fear. Gwinn pauses at our familiarity.

"I didn't realize you two were acquainted..." She says to Deterro.

"Oh, yes, I've had the pleasure many times."

"Should've known. Roaches tend to live in packs."

"Ouch Gwinny..." He says as he slides another berry into his mouth. A treacherous smile teases us. "Glass houses my darling." She glares at him. I'm too unnerved to address her insult.

"Fargo, my good man, come. Sit." Deterro motions toward a cushioned seat in the first row of our suite, the box's glass barriers drowning out the frenzied crowd around us. I reluctantly sit, thankful for the soothing texture of the plush furs I comb my fingers through. Russa giving me an apprehensive look. "Don't be shy, my friends, come join." Deterro motions to the others.

"A word." Russa pulls Gwinn to the side, my eyes begging them not to leave me alone with him. Russa looks angry. I can't make out what he's saying, but they're clearly arguing.

I flinch at a sharp snap in front of my face.

"Let the happy family have their privacy Fargo, you shouldn't pry, it's improper." I slither back to face the Arena, pushing hard into the cushion of my seat, hoping it will transport me far away from here. Deterro, by contrast, lounges casually, legs tossed over one another, just another day in his demented world. My body trembles. I can't control it.

Deterro scoffs in disgust with me.

"Where's your spine, good man?" He rolls his eyes. "If my intention was to kill you, do you not believe you'd be dead already?" He speaks of death with such ease. The words stroll leisurely from his lips. "I am nothing if not honest. You and your brother have two more days. I'm sure you've thought of something!"

Yea, we've thought of something... I just pray we can pull it off.

I gaze down onto the battlefield as the fight has begun, but Victor doesn't move. Instead, he stands perfectly still, staring up into our booth. His eyes are shielded behind his visor, but I know they're painted with rage. I just hope the target of his wrath is Deterro and not me. Seeing us together must be jarring.

He holds a fist into the sky, beckoning his loyal followers to join in their favorite call.

"TO HELL YOU GO!"

Then, he rips his bolt pistol from his leg and fires at us. The slug compresses into the indestructible glass. The crowd roars. He slowly holsters his weapon then disappears into the bowels of the Arena.

Deterro enjoys the performance.

"Your brother is a... ferocious one, isn't he?" He's enamored with Victor's valiance. "A man willing to face his demons is a man I respect." He turns toward me, critical of my crumbling composure. "Survival is not always an admirable trait, Fargo."

I look back nervously to Russa and Gwinn. Deterro notices again, he's had enough of my skittish behavior.

"Just go. Say what you need to say, you're embarrassing yourself," He says sharply. "When you come back, have some poise about you, my goodness."

I hurry to the back where Russa and Gwinn still argue.

"What the fuck is going on, Gwinn?" I whisper. I glance back at Deterro, who is hypnotized by the fighting. *"What the hell is he doing here?"*

"I could ask you why you even know who he is?"

"Why do I know who he is? Why do YOU know who he is? You're a High Councilor hosting a ruthless crime boss..." I pull the three of us farther toward the back of the suite, so we no longer have to whisper. *"...crime boss of the Valley to a night on the town?"*

She dismisses me.

"I made a pledge to begin to bridge the gap between the High Council and the underprivileged communities. Deterro is a prominent member of a heavily populated underprivileged neighborhood."

She clearly underestimates the extent of my knowledge of him.

"Yea... in Dwual Fir. That has absolutely nothing to do with Okotall." I glance to Russa for help, but he just shakes his head. "What is really going on here? Because you know how it looks, right?"

Gwinn stiffens up.

"Your opponent and his staff die in a tragic *accident,* and days later, you're seen lounging with a notorious crime lord...

Do you not see the implication here?"

Gwinn bites down on her lip in anger, brow stern.

"What implication is that Fargo?!" She steps closer, her gaze painted with a poison so wicked, I'm worried she can actually kill me with it. I glance at Russa, who avoids my eyes yet again. She doesn't let me answer, shifting the interrogation onto me. "Actually, we should be asking you to explain your affiliation with a, how'd you put it, *notorious crime lord?*" She studies the room once more. "And where is Miku? I didn't buy that sick excuse for a second. What are you hiding?"

Reality sets in the more defensive she gets. I step back from her, not wanting to believe it.

"...Gwinn... you didn't?" I say. Russa interjects himself before she can answer.

"Let's tie that lip up, kid, before you say something that makes my trigger cords itchy..."

I back off, but can't help mumble under my breath.

"Daddy Russa to the rescue again..."

"What the hell did you say?!" Gwinn barks.

We continue to bicker. Accusations and implications, thrown about carelessly. Gwinn tightens harder and harder as I change my mind and press her for answers.

That doesn't go well.

I have quite the knack for making bad situations worse.

Russa continues to passive-aggressively threaten me with imprisonment. And all the while, Deterro watches the fight intently from the seat we left him in. But he's grown weary of the disturbance behind him.

"ENOUGH!" He yells, silencing the three of us. "I am trying to watch my fight." We stand awkwardly, huddled in such a tight mass that the horrible perfume Gwinn wears makes my eyes water.

"Gwinn hired me to kill her opponents for her because she is just miserably unlikeable, and she was never going to win the approval of daddy's gang of Ancient tyrant friends." He pauses for an aside. "Darling, you do need an attitude adjustment." He continues on.

"And in exchange, she offered me the cure to the Rotting. A little serum you High Council cronies call Bytrol."

The word racks against my chest. *Wait, what? Bytrol is the cure to the Rotting?*

"I, of course, required proof that she could produce said cure, so she stole a sample from your science-slave friend in

Su Hoz and promised me she knew where more was."

The Bytrol case... it was littered with High Council emblems. I knew it had to come from somewhere with insane security. Tanya's lab makes sense.

He speeds up his cadence as if annoyed with the entire situation. "The only issue was, I couldn't be certain what she gave me was actually Bytrol, so that's where this despicable coward comes in." He picks at a berry stem stuck in his teeth with a knife, then points it at me.

"Fargo works for me on a contractual basis for a myriad of different purposes. All he needed to do this time was have the Bytrol tested and return to me with the results. Couldn't have been simpler. Yet, somehow, he botched that and lost arguably the most valuable asset on the planet, so I had to take your Princess friend for ransom until I get it back. If she was supposed to be here tonight, that is why she is not." The heat in Gwinn's eyes nearly melts me. I obviously feel horrible about it, but how she thinks she has any room for judgment is beyond me. "If he doesn't return it to me in two days, I will skin both big brother Victor and the precious Miku alive in front of him before I eventually pick him apart as well. That's why he's acting like a petrified child because he's a coward who fears death." His words shrink me into a tiny ball that sits in the palm of his hand. And if he were to snap it closed, it would smash me into a million pieces.

He reloads another deep breath.

"Obviously, I'll be forced to kill Gwinn as well if she can't produce what was promised. You all understand how this works."

My knees want to give out. Palms drenched with sweat.

Light shines off the blade of his knife as he sets it down on the snack tray. I glance at it. Heart squeezing with every beat. I should just lunge for it. We could overpower him right now. The three of us. End it right here. I don't think anyone would see.

"And the old man is, well... just an old man. I may kill you just for fun!" He finally turns around and winks at Russa.

I don't go for the knife. I just stand there like the coward he calls me, convincing myself he has kill orders in place on Miku if anything happens to him. "Now will you all please just shut up and come watch the fight, our boy Hades has never looked more vicious!"

Russa, Gwinn, and I stand shell shocked by the airing of our secrets. *My* circumstance is unfortunate, at worst negligent, but I never intended any of it. Gwinn, on the other hand, has apparently completely lost her mind.

The tension between us sits thick and coarse. We try to untangle it all, but our thoughts are fractured.

"The High Council has the cure to the Rotting?" I ask. "And you gave it to *him*?"

"You were the one testing it." She barks back.

"I thought it was some fountain of youth drug for Trakstull. I didn't realize—" She cuts me off, folding her arms into one another.

"It's both."

"What?"

Russa steps in, horrified.

"Gwinn... We don't have the cure for the Rotting...?"

She glances at him with stone eyes.

"Russa..." She pauses for a moment as if allowing him the opportunity to come clean himself. He says nothing. "I know the High Council made the Rotting from biological elements on the Redemption."

Russa balks at the claim, face ripe with a poor attempt at denial.

Wait, what? That can't be serious?

"Don't try to deny it for my sake, I agree with the decision."

My God, you are serious... and of course, you agree.

She continues.

"I know the High Council created Bytrol to prolong Trakstull's life, then realized they could program it to do the opposite."

Russa uncomfortably purrs under his beak. Gwinn doesn't stop.

"You're asked to make impossible decisions when you're in power. Population control is just one of them." Russa's eyes fill with the sorrow of a man who has carried a burden for decades, finally able to unload it onto someone else. "You never could've known it would spiral like it has. Sometimes mistakes are made."

Mistakes? Leaving your rig ignition on is a mistake... Genocide is fucking calculated!

I feel like I'm listening to a conversation I shouldn't be a part of. The type of conversation that kills you if you overhear it and you're not meant to...

"Emoss told me about Paradise..." She says.

Paradise? The replica Earth town?

"All those infected Savrons flooding the streets.

280

Threatening to overthrow the Consulate. Demanding treatment. What choice did you have?" Her face shows absolutely no signs of discomfort with what she's describing. It's horrifying.

"I also know that nearly all of the supply housed in the Consulate was destroyed with the rest of the city." She pauses as she looks at him. The magnitude of her words rattling through my core. Is she saying the High Council bombed their own city? The public was told it was a power center explosion.

Russa looks to her as if his entire life is crumbling.

"The Vault," She says. "That's why you were so interested in my messages. Some of the cure remains in that hub of the Redemption under the floor of the old Consulate. Doesn't it?" Russa sits still, wide-eyed at the level to which Gwinn has apparently unraveled years of kept secrets.

The finale siren wails, startling us. Deterro, who has remained entranced with the fighting this entire time, stands up in excitement.

"This is it! It's just down to the final four!"

I glance at him, then return my attention to Gwinn.

"What Vault?" I ask. Gwinn glances at me dismissively.

"Don't you have your own problems to worry about!" She says. "How exactly do you plan on getting Miku back? I hope you weren't planning on using the High Council to aid in your criminal debt?" Even with the knowledge of Miku's life at stake, she's as cold as ever.

I peer down feebly into the Arena and can feel the compounding weight of my actions strain my bones. I've made a mess, and there is nothing *I* can do to fix it.

"It's all up to Victor..."

29

VICTOR BELLS

To Hell We Go

Hades kicks the Wraith in the chest, launching him off the high ledge of a tower, and he plummets to the floor as the elimination siren wails. He sticks his fist into the sky, his hungry tribe crying out their approval. I live for these moments. The violent intimate juncture of two warriors, surrounded by the spectating worlds, but alone with themselves. Locked in their dance. Brutal. Chaotic. Perfect. These defining moments.

Tonight though, they bring me no satisfaction.

My mind is numb.

Hades tears through the Arena like a storm along the Lotopi shoreline, all uncontrollable force, and power. Yet I have no will to contain him. My mind is worlds away, in some far dark corner of the Valley where Deterro keeps the love of my life. I spend too much of my energy fighting the images I conjure of what he has done to her to combat the demon who lives in the trenches of my soul. Tonight, he runs free.

Hades rumbles through the Arena searching. His body trembles, high on the rush of violence. He craves more.

The deafening roar of a bullet barrage crackles in the air beyond a narrow one-story building near the centerground. Hades pushes towards it. He runs full speed ahead, scaling a ramp that leads to the building's roof, and vaults atop. Silva and the Behemoth are fully engaged in an open area scattered with waist-high steel barricades surrounding a small gunner tower. Silva is heavily overmatched.

The Behemoth is perched atop the tower, his stationary Gatling glowing bright red as it spews metal carnage. The tower he sits on is built from thin wooden stilts, but Silva isn't equipped to destroy it. All he can do is hunker for his life behind a steel barricade, its skin chewed and mended from the onslaught of superheated bullets.

The Behemoth's chain gun hisses empty.

Silva uses the moment to reposition. He rolls and slides to the next barricade, ten meters to his left. But the Behemoth still has the angle, and his gun is reloaded and raining bullets upon him once again. They scrape against the very top of the barricade and dig into the tiles behind him. He shoves himself against the steel as hard as he can, heels desperately slipping against the ground.

Hades loads two grenades into his under-barrel, and they lob from his rifle with two muted thumps. Destruction will soon follow. He darts into position to capitalize, jumping from the roof and pushing toward the tower. Concussive waves stall our assault as the grenades detonate. A fireball engulfs the tower. The crowd erupts with it.

Debris explodes in all directions, the tower crumbling to the ground. The Behemoth is launched from his balcony. Chain gun wildly spraying, bullets shattering against the glass ceiling. Hades regains his balance and storms ahead, the Behemoth's heavily armored suit now a detriment as he fights to get back to his feet.

Hades rips a burst of his rifle at the Behemoth, missing any vulnerable areas. The rounds deflect harmlessly off his shield. Hades stows his rifles, choosing the Hammers instead. He closes the distance. Legs churning with rage-filled power. He rears back to smash into the Warlord when something jolts against my shoulder and sends me flying to the side. I slam against a steel barricade, my head rocking the inside of my helmet. Pain belches from my arm. Bullets begin to pound into my shield, and it takes all my strength to pull myself over the barricade with my good arm. I crash to the other side in agony. Projectiles endlessly screaming into the barricade.

An arrow juts from my shoulder. Dug clean through the plated armor and deep into my arm. Silva! That fucking rat.

I can feel the blood oozing down my bicep and pooling in the fingers of my gloves. It's in deep. I brace myself, taking short quick breaths, for I know the pain that's to come. I wrap my right hand around the shaft of the arrow, jaw clenched, and try to pull it free. The moment I yank, a mechanism in the arrowhead triggers, and a surge of pain sends bile erupting from my mouth. I nearly pass out as the arrow's edges violently expand into a star formation, slicing through muscle and tendon until it lodges into the bone. A *Serpent Arrow*! Illegal for decades.

I recognize this pain. Paralyzing, unthinkable agony. The last time I felt it, I was impaled on a metal beam, and a demon was born. Black dots blur my vision as the world around me becomes hazy. I try to fight it. I must stay awake for her. But the darkness closes in on me, and then there is nothing but silence.

I don't know if I'm conscious or not, but thoughts rattle within my mind. A Serpent Arrow? Those have been illegal since the days of... My thoughts spasm as the revelation shudders against my soul. Pyra.

It can't be. Pyra is a man of honor and pride. He'd never advocate this. But I can picture the cold steel in his eyes that day at the gym. The gaze of a man destroyed by tarnished legacy. The immortal flame, extinguished by a careless child. And I know now the undecipherable looks he gave me that day were ones of callous. It was naïve arrogance to think they were anything but. Yet, I can't help but feel betrayed. By a hero who I sought to shape my life after. Who inspired me to pursue the very defining feature of my person. I know it's not fair to feel anger toward him, but I do. And now it bubbles, the steam of rage building inside of me. Higher and higher. The sounds of the world around me begins to fade back into existence, and I can vaguely hear the chanting.

HADES. HADES. HADES.

The sounds of life flood back into my ears with full force, and the chanting isn't the faint murmur as I thought. It's a thunder! Rattling against the glass, beckoning me back to this dimension. The fire spreads, sparking and crackling through my nerves. I can feel my heart slamming against my chest, its rhythm somehow paired with the crowd. My spirit growls from within, clawing back to the surface. And then, in one frozen moment, my eyes snap open.

The lights of the ceiling are bright through my vomit-stained visor. I feel outside my body. A spectator inside my own mind, and I shudder in fear. Something is wrong. Horribly wrong. My body springs from its back onto its feet and roars with a ferocity beyond creation. I didn't do that... I try to look to my right, but can't. My body turns left. I try to kneel behind the steel barricade, get my bearings, but my body hurdles over it, pacing with menace toward the two battling Warlords. The ground seems to tremble under my every step, the crowd surging into pandemonium. My body loads another explosive into my under-barrel, and I realize the terrifying truth. Whatever dam that separated Hades from me has exploded into a powdery mist, and he has taken full control. I am a prisoner inside my own flesh.

Hades launches an explosive at the feet of the two Warlords. The round detonates, birthing a fireball that envelopes the two. Silva is thrown to the left, the Behemoth to the right. The crowd roars.

Hades drags a hammer along the ground, pacing sadistically toward the downed Behemoth. A massive blow to the legs cripples the heavily armored fighter. Hades bends down and scoops the Behemoth over his shoulder. Pain sears agony into my mind, but Hades doesn't notice. How is he picking up this mountain of metal? The crowd's exhilarated from their champion's heroism, but I am terrified. This blind rage is unrecognizable even from Hades.

"TO HELL YOU GO!" The crowd bellows, and Hades slams the massive Warlord to the ground. A siren wails, and he raises his right fist into the sky.

Another arrow slams into his calf, and I think the nerve centers in my brain may overload with misery. Hades doesn't flinch. He stares down at the arrow jutting from his leg and then fixes his gaze upon Silva. Terror consumes my mind as I read his thoughts. HADES, NO! NO! He marches toward Silva, hammer dragging hauntingly along the floor. I scream at him to stop! NO! I try to stop his feet, but he shoves me farther into the depths. Silva is injured, just a few feet ahead. He sprays his light SMG pistols, but Hades uses his Hammers in a cross block to absorb the move. He doesn't slow. Silva retracts his visor shade.

"What the fuck, Victor?" He yells out. Hades retracts his shade as well. "...Victor...?" Silva can see the craze on Hades' face, and he knows. "Oh fuck...fuck... Hades!" He calls out to him. "Hades, stop!" He sprays another cluster of SMG rounds, but Hades doesn't even bother blocking them. They destroy his shield and dig in the metal armor. *Silva, run!*

Silva attempts to back away, one his legs badly wounded from shrapnel. I fight with every ounce of strength I have to stop him, but he's locked me out. I sob uncontrollably inside and feel tears leak from Hades' eyes, but his face shows no sorrow.

I beg him to stop! Grovel.

Hades hammers Silva across the head with more force than I've ever hit anyone. So hard his helmet actually detaches from the rest of his suit and rolls to the side. The crowd gushes from the impossible sight. Hades places his boot on Silva's chest, as the pinned Warlord shouts at him. The chant of his name hushes the moment he pulls his bolt pistol from his hip. Silva's face goes pale.

The entire Arena is frozen.

It's so quiet I can hear the Arena's air ventilation fans humming inside their metal ducts. *Dear God Hades no... you can still fix this. Please.... Please!*

Off in the distance, I hear someone cry my name.

"Victor!" Hades turns to see Fargo screaming my name along the glass in the first row. "Victor! My God! Don't!" The fear in his eyes breaks my heart, just as it does to know there is nothing left I can do. "If not for me, then for Miku..."

When I hear her name, a sliver of strength crawls back into my soul. I have to fight. I MUST!

The light of my body begins to rise from the cage Hades tried to shove me in, love the new weapon I've yet to understand. I claw and claw, but I was so far gone, I pray there is time. Hope begins to fill my heart as the waves of love begin to wash away the fiery storm that has decimated my soul. I can feel it! Her eyes sparkle in my mind, and the delicate kindness of her smile consumes my thoughts. I've never loved anything with the weight that I love this woman. She is my world. And for the first time, I realize that my existence is not defined here in this Arena, but in the warmth of her arms. And for a moment, I believe I've won. Stifled the demon who has hijacked my body. But then the booming echo of a gunshot shatters my illusion, and every ounce of hope I've ever had in my life dissolves in an instant.

I watch Fargo melt to the floor, devasted.

The Arena fills with shrieks of terror as people flock to the exits. Hades finally looks back down to Silva, and any shred of hope I had of ever seeing Miku again lies splattered in a pool of blood on the floor. Silva's lifeless eyes stare up at me, but I feel nothing. A numbness beyond repair.

Miku is doomed. I've killed her.

If I could, I would put the pistol in my mouth and pull the trigger to wipe my plague from the world. But I can't. Victor is gone, and Hades is all that remains.

PART III

ASH

30

TANYA CROWN

Salvage

Qwillow won't stop spewing her explanation of betrayal to me. I grew so tired of looking at her that I've climbed atop the Med Bed and now stare at the ceiling. I've completely lost interest in anything she has to say. Miku is my only concern now. I used to think there was a fine line between love and hate, but I realized that's because I never truly hated anyone before. This feeling is far different than love. I hate Qwillow. I hate Fargo. I hate Deterro. I hate this Godforsaken planet.

Time chews away at the clock.

My mind is scattered with fragments of escape plans. I don't know what I'll do, but I know I can't just sit here and wait for Russa to come back. Miku needs me, and she needs me now.

"... and I know you don't believe me, but I love you. I've spent years working on a way out for you. I just hoped I was able to do it before you had to learn the truth..." Qwillow finishes whatever nonsensical story she's been telling me, but that last part catches my ear. I sit up. Qwillow stands as she notices the subtle acknowledgment. Our eyes meet for the first time since she's told me the truth of my life. Hers are vast and dark and wet like the smooth, glossy stones of a riverbed. I want to hate her. Every fiber in my body wants to hate her. But the longer she looks at me, the more my eyelids quiver.

"...How could you do this to me?" I whimper. A storm of tears waits to pour down my face, but I fight them with all that I have. The fin on her head curls, her body hunching like she's been stabbed in the heart. And I'm sure that's what it feels like. I can only imagine the guilt. *But I hate her. I need to hate her.*

Yet, as I take in her slender frame once more and witness the sheer pain that is etched across her face, I know I don't... I love her. And I hate that I love her, but I do. She's my mother. And no matter how hard I try, I can't fend off this primal yearning to love her. To be loved *by* her. To share in that bond of unconditional love that only a parent can provide. Maybe I just have an unhealthy dependency on her, or perhaps I'm just terrified of the loneliness that would follow disowning my parent? I don't know. But even though it's become abundantly clear I have almost no self-awareness of my genuine emotions, I know I need her.

We rest our foreheads on one another. Bearing our souls. She strokes her hand along the back of my neck. I'm not sure I've forgiven her, but I let her do it anyway.

"I'm so sorry." She whispers.

"I know..." For once, I believe myself. I just watched Russa murder four of his men without a hint of remorse over this secret. And he won't suffer a single repercussion for it. Qwillow's actions under the thumb of power shouldn't be held against her. I realize that now. It doesn't absolve her of the pain she's caused me, but Miku always stresses to me the importance of forgiveness, and right now, that seems to be the only thing that can lift me from this pit of misery.

"What did you mean, you've been working on a way out?" I ask, shoving aside her betrayal. She peers up at me, still desperate to explain. I need countless answers from her about the past two decades, but we simply don't have time for them. Her day of reckoning will come, and when it does, I will not be gentle. But if she truly wants my forgiveness, it starts here. She can prove her true loyalty by helping me get the hell out of here.

A struggle outside the door steals our attention.

It's a grin-inducing ballad of fear and retribution. Highlighted with painful groans and bodies crumbling to the floor. A song that soaks up the wetness from my eyes and sparks a flame within me.

It's time.

Klawka casually enters the room, dusting at his uniform's fringe. Qwillow stares at him, confused. He points back to the entryway where the High Council guard lays unconscious and shoots me a smirk.

"For the record, he was being kind of rude." His prickly face watches her, wondering how she'll react. She glances between us as I join his side, beginning to understand that I expected this. A moment of contemplation settles over her as she stands at the junction of two wildly different paths. She can help me and become a traitor, or stop me and lose any chance of reconciliation.

Timid shoulders brush against mine as she leans down to gather the unconscious guard's weapons, slinging the rifle over her shoulder, then offering me the pistol.

"I'll have to stay behind," She says.

I stare down at the gun, slowly wrapping the slick metal into my palm.

"They'll kill you..." I say, meeting her eyes once more. I'm so relieved she chose me. Yet, horrified at what that choice will cost her. A soft smile rolls onto her lips as she points to the green blinking light under the skin of my wrist.

"The tracking signal... it has to be deactivated from here."

"Then, we'll do it before we go."

"Not enough time."

"Then I'll cut it out."

"Can't."

"Then—"

She cuts me off, placing her hands on my shoulders.

"Tanya, this day is well overdue," She says. "I owe you this."

Tears flirt with my eyes, but I push them away.

Klawka cranes his head out into the hall to scan for patrolling guards and hurries us along. "As lovely as this is, we need to go." He double-takes back at Qwillow and scoffs. "And give me that rifle, you look ridiculous." He inspects the firing chamber as she hands it over, and I share one last look with her. I wish we had more time. What would our relationship look like in this new world where secrets didn't drive an invisible wedge between us? Where I didn't resent her for circumstances beyond her control? Where she wasn't burdened with the cancerous responsibility of deceit? We'll never know. I run my hand along her neck, and together, the three of us push into the hall.

Silence greets us on the other side.

A trail of bodies to our left shows the way Klawka came from. Qwillow nods in the opposite direction.

"We have to get to the restricted lab before you go. When I

said I've been working on a way out, this is what I was talking about," She says. My puzzled look doesn't receive an answer. But she knows we have limited time, so I trust that this is important.

Klawka leads. He breezes around corners. Rifle tactically positioned along his body. I can't imagine I look any more ridiculous with this pistol than Qwillow did with the rifle, but at least it isn't half my size. I follow just behind him.

We lurk past my bedroom. I hustle inside, strip out of my med gown, and dive into real clothes.

Klawka signals for us to stop as we reach the corner of two intersecting hallways. Footsteps lazily echo through the air. Without much pattern or rhythm to them. As if someone wanders aimlessly. Bored. Unassuming. A rifle butt rudely interrupts his meandering. The guard crashes to the ground, and Klawka drags him around the corner.

Miku hurries ahead as we reach the restricted lab door. She enters the code, and the rancid stench of death punches me across the face as the door hisses open.

I have to pull my shirt over my nose to keep from puking.

Ripe bodies still lay in shambles along the floor. Dark internal fluids stained against the walls. Hukar's frame rests at my feet. I can't even look into his eyes to apologize because they aren't there. Chunks of his skull litter the ground like hail balls. The smell and the sight and the memory of what happened here pump bile up my esophagus. Qwillow's voice is just distracting enough to keep it from spewing out my mouth and adding to this horrid scene.

"Here it is." She shuffles through a slog pile of datacards that Russa scattered along the ground in his fit of rage and shoves one into the workstation's slot. The churn of tiny motors begins as she activates something along her dataplate and a hidden compartment rises up from the countertop next to the workstation. From it, she removes a ladder-shaped vial filled with an orange glowing fluid and hands it to me.

"This... this is what you make," She says. I stare at it, confused.

"Is this the Rotting?" I ask.

"Kind of." She shakes her head. "It's much bigger than that, though. At least it can be. If it escapes with you."

"Guys, we have to get moving." Klawka urges as he surveys the hall. Qwillow redirects my attention back to her.

"Listen to me, this right here can change the world. But it's only been used for harm. We can change that. You can change that. Everything you went through here, all of this Bytrol built from you..." I peer up at the tubes that streak along the ceiling and flow with the same orange liquid, "... it can all be worth it."

I admire the creation of my torment. *Worth it?* Getting Miku back would be the only outcome worth two decades of torture.

"I'll get it out," I say. Her breath shakes as I do.

"Good." She scrambles back to the workstation and hands me a datacard. "And this is, well, this is your way out." Elaborate plans flash across the datacard. Years of preparation. She really has been planning a way out for me.

Qwillow nervously glances at the door, then leans over to rush me through the plan.

"The salvage rigs are automated and leave the same time every night for Yerally. They're the only rigs not inspected on the way in or out—"

"We need to go. Now!" Klawka barks. I slide the vial and datacard into my pocket and hurry to the door. Qwillow blurts out the rest as High Council guards turn the corner.

"Take the salvage rig to Yerally. Keep your head down when you get there. They'll be looking for you. Find a merchant named Pox. He'll get you out of Su Hoz..."

A rifle shrieks. My startled yelps following behind it. Two guards spill to the floor as Klawka's body rocks from recoil.

"Let's go!" He orders and pushes out into the hall. Qwillow glances back one last time.

"... once you're out of Su Hoz, you're on your own. You were supposed to have somewhere to hide out, but I didn't have time to—"

I cut her off with a hug.

"I'll figure it out." I squeeze her knowing this will be the last time I'll ever see her. The fin on her head curls back. A sharp double-breath stuttering as she pushes away a sob.

"I love you." She whispers.

"I love you too."

We pull apart, share one final moment, then Qwillow takes off to deactivate my tracker.

Klawka is already at the next corner, peering around the edge. The gunshots have alerted the drowsy guards, and now, activity stirs within the lab. The comm on the downed guard next to us crackles with questions from his comrades. They won't get answers. We push down the hall as I study the schematic map on my datacard.

"There's a service stairwell about 100..."

Holes rip into the wall next to me. Metal ammunition screaming overhead. Klawka tackles me into an adjacent room as guards stampede down the hall.

We spill into a climate-controlled hydroponics lab. Frost billows from my mouth. Skin prickling against the frigid air. Klawka slams the metal door shut, icicles breaking off of experimental plants when he does.

"Move!" He shouts. Frozen leaves crack against our bodies as we storm through rows of plants. Clouds of chemically treated air plume from vents in the ceiling. Freeze-burning patches along my neck. We plow through a rear door just as the guards reach the freezer.

Blood rushes back into my fingers. Throbbing.

Workstations line the connecting room. Quietly humming. Laying idol. We blow past them and burst into the next hallway. Flanking guards ambush us. Gunfire roars. Klawka snatches me against his chest, howling as the barrage dives into his back. Blood smears the ground as we skid to a stop against towering storage racks. I scramble back to the door, shoving just my pistol out the frame, blindly squeezing out shots to halt their advance. A guard wails. The pistol spits empty. Blank clicks responding to my trigger pull. I dart back inside. Body trembling. Breath pounding against my chest. I try to scan over my datacard, but I shake so violently I can barely see it.

"Get up." I groan as I pull Klawka upright. His eyes are cloudy. Distant. Fading in and out. "HEY!" I shout. He snaps to. "Keep it together! I need you."

There's only one door to the storage closet. Guards spill down the hall it leads into. Our only option is the window. Glass shatters as Klawka kicks through the pane. Biting Su Hozi wind pours in. I climb atop him, wrapping my arms around the stumps of his wings, and he launches out the opening.

Mud pummels us five stories later.

Pain wrapping me in its warm embrace.

Coughs hack up blood and dirt. Klawka digs himself out. Limping to the exterior wall of the lab. His rifle snaps to the busted window, clapping out, and a guard drools down the building façade. Returning fire rains down on us. I claw through the mud. Scurrying around a dead tree stump. Burying my head between my knees.

Gunshots echo in the silent night.

People shout. Fear and pain and panic ripe on their voices. A rumbling mixes into the skirmish. I lift my head. The lab's bay doors spread open, and the giant salvage rig embarks on its nightly trek.

"Klawka!" I shout, pointing to the rig. I peer over the splintered edge of the tree trunk, and bark explodes the moment I do. I'm pinned.

The rig chugs through the fence interior. Heading to the main gate so it can follow the service road around its bend and onto the main channel for Yerally. Klawka glances at it, then back at me.

"Get ready!" He shouts. I scramble to a knee, keeping my head down, Klawka taking a deep breath and spinning around the corner of the building. His rifle sings. I dart from cover. Bullets trace across the courtyard. Subsonic rounds warble by my ear. Kicking up dirt as they chew into the ground. I dive around the corner of the building. Klawka peels back, and we take off across the open lot for the rig.

High Council grunts have commandeered the main gate. The salvage rig is already too far down the entry to board it now. The guards would easily see us. More soldiers pour from the building entrance.

We're so close. There has to be a way.

Klawka nods to the watchtower. The hatch at the bottom can feed me up the tower. I climb onto his back, and he darts off. Each stride storms ahead. His legs exploding with force. The stubs of his wings churn, the joints nearly hitting my face. The gate guards make out our figure slinking across the field. Rounds crack past us until their leader notices I'm on Klawka's back. He screams out an order to the swarming platoon, his voice carrying across the empty night.

"NON-LETHAL, YOU FUCKING IDIOTS! THAT'S THE ASSET!"

Bullets cease. Panicked soldiers gathering their wits. They should've never been shooting at me. I'm too valuable. But scared men make irrational decisions. And hired guns, make selfish ones.

We skid to a stop at the watchtower. Klawka shoving me inside the hatch and activating the lift. I hug my knees to my chest. Neck craned to fit inside the pitch-black box.

Weapon fire has resumed. Except now, static charges seize against the tower wall. So close, their intensity pulls at my hair. Something pounds on the surface I climb toward. Rifle shots bark out above me. Light pouring into the box as

294

Klawka peels open the lift hatch. What the hell? Did he jump—

My body contorts. Jaw seizing shut. Collapsing as electricity pulses through my nerves.

"Tanya!" Klawka shouts. He throws me over his shoulder. Body a limp mass. My eyes staring at approaching guards through a bullet hole in Klawka's torso.

I somehow become weightless. Wind whipping through my hair. The guard disappearing. Then, Klawka's shoulder jams into my stomach as my weight returns. I now stare at the stone face of the fence's exterior. Tall grass tickling my dangling forearms. He jumped over the edge.

"The road bends. We can cut it off!" He shouts. My head bounces against his back as he takes off sprinting.

Through the bouncing hole in his torso, I watch the lights of the salvage rig carve through the darkness as it plods away. Our plan disappearing into the night.

But he's right. The service road ends in a sharp curve to the left. If we cut across the field, we can beat the rig to the bend before it punches onto the main channel.

Feeling begins to return to my toes. It creeps up my legs, to my torso, up my spine, and down my arms. I can turn my head. Propping up slowly to watch the lab speed away. Grass grazes against my arm once more, and my stomach plummets when I realize where we are. Memories of darting awake at the sound of vaporized men flood my mind. I squirm. Panic building in my chest when a red beam flashes across my face. Stalks of grass bend as a mine-drone speeds toward us. I try to scream out, but my tongue still won't move. I pound on Klawka's back, but he moves too fast to feel it. My throat strains. Desperate for the words. A rolling ball of death closing in quickly.

"K... KLAWKA!" I point. He spins, tripping as he does, and I'm launched into the air. From his back, he fires his rifle, and the drone births into a ball of fire. I tumble to the ground. Two more fireballs erupting as mine-drones begin to swarm.

Klawka is already on his feet. Rifle snapping in all directions. Fireballs detonating.

"GO!" He yells, hustling my way.

I sprint. Powering through tall stalks of grass that smack me in the face. Flinching at booming explosions that spew into the night. Klawka catches me quickly. Hoisting me onto to his shoulders as he glides by.

The end of the restricted field grows closer. Klawka storms

ahead. Rifle pinpoint accurate, even on the move.

The salvage rig starts onto the bend to our right. Its lights illuminating the service road ahead. We can make it.

A trail in the grass bends in the distance to our left. Klawka tries to shoot it, but the rifle clicks empty. A silence swallows us. The sounds of his hooves pounding against the soil fill the terrifying void.

"I want to thank you, kid," He says. My eyes shoot to the trail that snakes toward us and back to the road.

"We can make it," I say. His breath heaves as he shakes his head.

"Nah, we can't." He runs his hand along his torso and shows me his blood-coated fingers. I glance down. The entire right side of his body is soaked dark purple. My heart sinks.

The mine-drone plows toward us. Getting closer and closer by the second. "You gave me hope," He says. "And I never thought I'd have something like that." My vision blurs as tears begin to pool in my eyes. "Just wish I would've met ya sooner." I suck a sob through my nose as the mine-drone is nearly on us. "You ready?" He says. I nod, biting my lip, and he winks at me. "Good luck, kid." I leap from his shoulders, and Klawka veers left, tackling the rolling drone as it detonates. I spill to the ground, scrambling to my feet, as the drone and Klawka erupt into the sky. Tears pour down my cheek as I sprint ahead, watching the smoke drift away into the night.

I finally push through the thicket and tumble onto the service road. Sobs overwhelming me. The salvage rig slugs by, and I climb aboard, watching the sizzling field and my sterile prison cell shrink in the distance.

I check my pockets as I climb into the rig's cockpit and pull out the Bytrol and datacard. They're still in one piece. A sigh spills from my lungs. I pull them to my chest, curl up into a ball on the rig's seat and watch the blinking green light fade away under my wrist as Qwillow deactivates my tracker.

The salvage rig merges onto the main channel and punches toward Yerally, and I spend the rest of the night thinking of those who sacrificed themselves for me, and the loving friend this is all for.

31

LEO ABERNATHY

LifeBlood

We've walked for three days with Riley as our guide, although Yara strides afront. His last words before we left about Emoss falling ill, echoing ominously in my mind. *No, my child, he did not.* I can tell it disturbs Riley too; she's been quiet. More than I remember her to be. Frustratingly so, but then again, we all have. The wake of lives lost and shattered realities still hang thick over our heads. We walk in a single file line, but the space in between each of us feels far greater than the few feet it actually is. The seldom words spoken among us, forced.

Patawa lags behind, her leg still recovering from its wound as Bryl trails behind with her, making sure she keeps up. Spri wanders in between us at a sporadic pace. Stopping and starting, absorbing the landscape with every step. He's supposed to be mapping the terrain, but I worry the Forest's exotic scenery is too much for my easily distracted friend. He reaches down to the thin, wiry stalk of a plant that climbs waist high and runs his finger along its tip. The plant retracts into the ground, spritzing out a cloud of mist as it does. He stares down, puzzled at the plant's sprout, the fins along the back of his head fluttering with curiosity. Bryl nudges him with his bottom arms as he passes by, telling him to keep up. But it's difficult to not be mesmerized by the portrait of the woods. No one's been this deep into Berban in decades; we lay eyes on places few have or will ever see.

I allow myself brief moments of awe as I stare at the canopy, but I quickly wipe the wonder from my face if Riley looks my way. I still feel guilty experiencing any emotion other than sorrow around her. More my insecurities than it is her actions.

My crew doesn't move as gracefully through the Forest as Riley or Yara. There's a depth to these woods that only those who've lived in it can fully understand. Even I struggle to keep up.

We snake through the Forest like a herd migrating to find greener pastures. Yet we don't search for the bounty of fertile land; we flee from an invisible foe. One that could lurk around every crest or at the top of every cliff. And it's the knowledge that the Gaz scour these woods looking for us that doesn't allow me to enjoy this beauty. Because make no mistake, it is *breathtaking.*

The little Ko that accompanied Riley through the recent days sits draped along her shoulders. She's named him Jabo. Jabo's tail is wrapped around her neck and weaves through her armpit as he bounces along with her every step. He seems to be the only thing that can distract her from the gaping hole left in her heart. Jabo will grab two strands of her hair at times like he's a miniature conductor holding the reins of a human stagecoach. It brings a smile to our faces, our adorable aversion to the terrible emptiness that floats among us without Remmy.

Riley stares down at a crude map that she's pulled from her pack, the oversized straps slipping off her shoulder every few steps.

"Hey, let me carry that for a little," I say to her. My voice breaks a silence so long it startles her when she hears it. She glances up from the map with reluctant pride, but I can see the raw skin on the top of her shoulders.

"No, I've got it," She says, returning her attention back to the map. "We should be approaching a small pond soon; we can stop there and get some water." I don't let her dismiss my help. I touch her arm.

"Hey..." She glances up at me again. "Your shoulders are almost bleeding, let me carry it for a while." She heaves the pack up, readjusting the straps, wincing when the worn material rubs her chafed skin. Her eyes, prideful and resistant, tell me to drop it.

I hate it.

I want to help, yet every time I offer, I feel her push farther into herself. Apparently, Remmy used to carry their pack. He was responsible for it, watched over all of their belongings. I sense she feels like I'm trying to replace him; I'm not. I just want her to know she's not alone anymore. Riley pushes ahead of Yara and steps through a thick bushed area surrounded by a tight formation of thin trees, out of sight. Yara quickly hurries ahead.

A step through the brush opens the world to a small pocket of paradise.

The wall of trees soon meets jutting stone that raises tens of meters in the air, vines, and moss crawling up its face, encircling a pool of crystalline orange water. Vibrant and still, the water dazzles in our eyes. I've never seen anything like it. Pat, Bryl, and Spri all push through the trees and stop to take in the bizarre beauty of the glowing pool. A lethargic waterfall drools over the edge of the rocks and spills into the pool, its waters the normal shade before entering the waters below.

Riley drops her pack, a relief washing over her face, Jabo leaping to the ground as well. She pulls her shirt off and uses it to wipe the sweat and grime from her face. She begins to unlace her boots.

"You're not getting in there, are you?" I say in disbelief. The pool is beautiful, but it's orange. Bright glowing orange. For the first time since Remmy's passing, I see a warm smile stretch across her face.

"Get in. Trust me." She rips off her boots and wrestles out of her dirt-covered shorts. She hurries to the foot of the water, glancing back as she ties up her hair. My cheeks flush as she catches me unintentionally staring. Patawa glows, watching me fawn over her. Hugging me, an excited expression across her.

"Stop," I say to her.

"I didn't say anything." She grins uncontrollably. I roll my eyes with a smirk and peel out of her hug.

Riley dives from the rock and glides into the water.

When I saw her last, we were both kids, in mind and body. The woman in front of me now is a far cry from the rough boyish teenager of my memories. She's fiercely lean. Her skin is gorgeously bronzed by life under the sun, and even though I can see the pain under them, her eyes sparkle with a wild, untamed nature. We grew up in a world where no one looked like us, our perception of physical appearance was founded without any comparison to ourselves. And yet, even without anyone to compare it to, I know this is what beauty looks like.

She has a different appeal than Gwinn does, though. She's covered in blemishes and freckles and scars and scratches, where Gwinn's skin is flawless like a glass sculpture. She's thin, not possessing the seductive curves like Gwinn. Riley's hair is wavy and wild. Gwinn's is meticulously manicured. The two women couldn't look farther apart, yet I find myself drawn to both. Riley possesses something Gwinn doesn't, though. Something intangible that radiates from her, pulling me in. An energy to her spirit that beckons life to come to her. Gwinn has a cold depth within her that swallows the vigor of life of anyone nearby.

"Get in!" Riley yells.

I glance reluctantly to my crew, but Bryl is already stripping down beyond his socks, always eager to take his shirt off. The rest of us follow suit, tossing shirts and shoes about. We run, diving headfirst into the pool as Yara and Spri remain along the moss line.

My body submerges as I knife into the water. I arc up and pop my head out, laughing at Spri's worried expression.

"This seems highly questionable." Spri kneels down, bringing his massive eyes inches from the glowing liquid.

"I'm ordering you to get in," I say with a smile. He doesn't like that. He blinks harshly, a heavy film sliding across his eyes.

"Understood. But I'm enacting a formal notice that my recommendation was to avoid the glowing jungle liquid." He can't find anything to write with, so he digs his finger into the mud and streaks his name across the back of Riley's map.

"Ok, notice acknowledged, now get in."

He tiptoes into the rocking shore of the pond. Still dressed in his rig suit's under layer.

Four of us float effortlessly in the orange water while Bryl struggles to keep his insanely dense frame above the surface. A curious look twists onto his face as thousands of tiny orange beads roll from our bodies back into the pool.

"What the hell is this?" He asks, scooping up a handful, treading with his bottom arms. I inspect the beads as well when I realize I'm not treading. I'm just... floating.

I feel a light buzz around me as if the water gently crawls

over my skin. Riley catches my realization.

"Watch."

She cups her hands, bundling a heap of the orange beads, and presses them firmly against the raw skin on her shoulders. The rest of us inch in closer. After a moment, she removes the beads, and the skin on her shoulder is calloused over. The blood and blisters, replaced with rough clear skin. She smiles as she shows us.

"The Gaz call it, *Gan' da Noko*, the lifeblood," She says. "Remmy and I have found small pools like these all over the Forest. He'd always find them right when we needed them the most." She chuckles as she wipes her watering eyes.

Patawa scoops a handful and brings them close to her face, the gears of her medical brain churning.

"I have no idea what they could be. Maybe some sort of microbe?" She floats onto her back and lifts her leg from under the water. The wound on her thigh has closed over, replaced with a fresh scar. Spri pokes at it.

"Ow!" She flinches. "It still hurts, just the skin healed." Spri stares back, unremorseful.

"For the good of science."

She sarcastically swipes at the back of his neck to jokingly say thank you.

The orange beads pool in my cupped hand, a shovel filled with glowing mystery. I press it to my shoulder. My gunshot wound howls at me. After ignoring the pain, I'm welcomed with the same result. I shoot a smirk to Riley.

"Good as new!" She grins and splashes me.

We build camp there for the night.

The low hum of bugs fills the air. Riley builds a fire and encircles us in myrite, the combustible powder glowing a soft blue. She caught some plump floor-grazing animal earlier in the day, and now it roasts over the flames. Looks like it's related to a Fyza or a Jutoga; it's about three times the size of Jabo.

The fire crackles and thin smoke climbs its way into the night sky. Tonight's the first night I've felt at ease since leaving the well. Riley seems to be enjoying the night too. She smiles and laughs to herself at Spri's wandering stories. Yara stares longingly at the moon, the occasional twitch of his head his only movement. He hasn't spoken since we've left. Riley, who sits beside me, sees me looking at him. Her head is down, gazing into the fire as she tosses twigs and pebbles into the blaze.

"I know he didn't mean to," She says to me, her voice soft. The laughter and words of the others become indistinct chatter as I hear her voice. "But it's still hard to look at him." She rubs her thumb across a small twig and tosses it into the fire. "I'm trying though, I want you to know that."

I take a sip of water from our canteen.

"I know, Ri."

"I really miss him." She bites her lip.

"Yea I'm sure. I miss him too." I hope it's not insulting, but it's true. I was always close with Remmy. Fargo and Victor had such a tight bond, I tended to gravitate toward Remmy for a brotherly connection. As kids, Tanya and I were the only ones who grew up alone. Vic, Fargo, and Miku all had each other in Groga while Gwinn, Riley, and Remmy all had one another in Okotall. Only Tanya and I had no else around. How I would've given anything for a brother or sister to share my life with.

"Tell me more about what's happening outside the trees?" She asks. "You and Gwinn, huh? You two have some little cottage on the shore by now?"

I snort and watch her lightly blush.

"You saw how she was before you left, right? Well, she didn't get better; she got worse." I keep my gaze into the fire, thoughts of the years dedicated to her rattling through my mind. "It was hard when you left... I wasn't in a great place, and neither was she, and I don't know... she was just there..." My words trail off. Is that really how it happened? I'm not sure I've ever admitted that to myself, let along anyone else.

"You don't have to justify anything to me, Leo," She says, tucking her knees into her chest. "I don't have that right."

Maybe she doesn't, but I still have an aching desire to explain it. I don't really know why?

"Well there's nothing really to justify anymore," I say.

"...really?" She asks, sensing my tone.

"Nope. Not for a few months," I say. The words ring against my heart as I say them out loud for the first time. "I'm trying to figure things out, but she's made it clear she's not interested in that."

"What happened?" She asks. I glance at her. "... if you don't mind me asking?" She adds.

"We're just really different people, who want really different things from our lives, I guess."

"Well you've always been different; why was it an issue

now?"

I run my fingers through my hair as her questions begin to dig up the most painful memories I have.

"Things happened, and she chose a path that I just couldn't be a part of." We sit in silence for a moment. The warmth of the fire rubbing against my palms. Tears begin to welt in my eyes.

"... Leo... you can't tell me I'm not alone anymore and then keep me at arm's length with your problems." She finds my eyes, and that wild spirit of hers calls to me. "You're not alone anymore either."

My eyes fix on hers. They beg me to open the hatch to the depths of my pain. But I don't think I can. Every time I think of that day, a small piece of me dies.

She looks at me like she can read my thoughts. As if I don't have to speak a word and she'll understand. But she couldn't possibly. She grabs my hand and pulls it toward her.

"Please Leo, tell me."

A tear streams down my face as I replay it all in my head. I take a deep breath and begin to tell her everything.

Yara remains placid, staring up at the moon, the responsibility of Remmy's death unhinging the few sane parts he had left. He mumbles to himself. Wild, conspiratorial words. The ramblings of a madman combined with the elusive memories of his rational self. Like a spirit trying to whisper through the veil to his own husk.

I wish I knew with certainty what details of his incoherent mess are valid and which aren't, because the significance of his accusations is monumental. The only truth I'm certain of is the one I've seen with my own eyes. The Vault. The rest... I pray to God is not true.

Yara claims to know the way once we've reached Berban Falls but needs Riley to get us there first. He was insistent that we get there immediately. I understand why I'm so desperate to go, but the others? I don't know if they follow out of loyalty or a lack of other options. I guess I don't mind either way. Selfishly, I need them with me. Guilt has stifled my judgment over the past week. I've led my crew into the face of pure evil in the Rift, all the while lying to them about the Vault. Then, obsessed with my own impulsive curiosities, toppled the dominos that led to Remmy's death. And now, the six of us spend our days wading through the tall grass of the Forest, like the foot soldiers of primitive wars, hunted like animals.

This all rifles through my mind as I explain everything to Riley.

I tell her how everything that's happened over the past few days started months before the night I discovered the Vault.

A day designed with the intention of *escaping* the turmoil of my life sprung into motion an irreversible course of death, sorrow, and betrayal. Yet I wish I could look back, and say with conviction, that day wasn't the beginning of it all. That there was some other cause to all the heartache that followed. But that'd be a lie. I'd be just another attempt of mine to shield Gwinn from the culpability of her actions. A reprieve from her selfishness, I'm just now realizing, she does not deserve. I tell her a part of me may always love Gwinn. But what she did months prior will never be forgiven. The day she snatched a piece of my soul that I didn't even know existed is the day this all began. I take responsibility for the pain I've caused since that moment, but that moment broke a part of me that can never be replaced. And had she not done it, the lives of everyone involved would be far different.

I tell her how for so long, I was convinced I could change Gwinn, help her see the miracle of our being. But since the day Emoss died, she believed herself to be nothing but a plague. Ruining everything in her path, incapable of good. The longer time went on, the more people blamed her for his death, so in return, her self-loathing grew and grew. She didn't take a turn for the worst until she became obsessed with Human Anthropology, though.

In the same way I obsess over it, she became consumed with the roots of our people. I tell her it's what brought us together in the first place. But everything she read and learned, she viewed with unwavering cynicism.

She used the ruin of Earth to claim humans are a self-destructive menace. I chose to see the response and pointed to the Redemption, a work that clearly shows humans can come together toward common good.

She would cite war after war, through era after era, to prove humans aren't sophisticated enough to preserve life. I pointed to the individual acts of bravery from within those wars. Those willingly sacrificing their own lives for their fellow man. The selflessness that takes.

She referenced the cyclical natures of slavery and genocide and poverty and famine and all the horrible things that happened throughout our history. I would counter with art and music and charity and tradition and all the incredible aspects of our history.

She demonized the Earth's religions, claiming them all barbaric. I thought they were beautiful.

And the worst of it all, she would try to use my father's journal against me, arguing it showed that when faced with inevitable extinction, humanity still tried to destroy itself. All I needed as a rebuttal was our very existence.

I tell her the more Gwinn read, the more radical and entrenched her beliefs became. There was nothing I could say to alter her disposition. In her mind, humans were a failed breed. Natural selection deemed us unworthy of the second chance we were given.

But I tell her it wasn't until that fateful night, the night where this all started, years after Emoss had died, years since we first started dating, that I understood her cynical disposition was more than that. She truly believed humans no longer deserved life. And I tell her as long as I live, I will never forget the buzz of the city outside, the stale smell of rig vapor in the air that night, the utter despair I felt.

And then, I tell her what happened.

"...She looked directly into my eyes, as cold as I've ever seen her, and told me she was carrying my child... but she wasn't keeping it."

32

GWINN DEMARCO

Oblige

Russa slams the door of my apartment behind him as I pour a shot of antique Earth bourbon to calm my nerves. Leo found it in a small salvage pile out in Su Hoz somewhere, an anniversary present. It was supposed to be for a special occasion, not exactly what I had in mind. I gulp the brown liquor down, burning my throat as the numbing sensation soothes my anxiety. What the fuck just happened? Russa storms to me and pours himself a shot as well. His eyes steam with rage.

"I... You... I don't even know where to start with you." He slams the glass onto the tray as he finishes and marches off to nowhere. I bring another to my lips and toss back the shot.

"You're in way over your head here, kid, way over!" He paces to the window and stares out into the city. Rigs whiz by, and the neon signs that tattoo the metal towers glow softly through the vapor trails. "I can't help you..." He says.

"Who said I needed your help?"

He doesn't turn to face me.

"So, you've got this all figured out, huh?" He mumbles something else to himself that I can't hear. "Do you understand the position you've put me in? Not only do I know, but I know how, I know who, I know where, I know when..." He turns to stare at me. "What am I supposed to do when I'm confronted about this? Because you know I will, right? You understand this isn't just going to disappear because Trakstull elected you? The people will still have doubts, and you saw Meelo... He's not gonna rest until he finds out the truth."

"He won't. I made sure of it."

"Made sure of it? Gwinn, you made a deal with the devil; he's in control of this, not you."

His words linger in my mind. Doubts raining on my conviction like an artillery bombardment. But inside this bunker, inside my head, I'm safe. I push those thoughts out immediately. *Doubts are weakness, and I have no time for that.*

"Look, we have a deal, I get what I want, he gets what he wants. End of story." I pour myself another drink because I want this moment to be a fog, deep in the corner of my mind.

"That's another thing we have to talk about, your *plan*. I don't know where you got your information from, but have you stopped to consider the possibility that your entire set of beliefs about the Rotting and it's cure are way off base?"

I walk out to my balcony, staring into the dying embers of the city night. The Savron street workers begin their daily routine, the one I usually watch during the yawning hours of morning. The last of the night's partiers cling to Slidewalk railings as they're transported back to their homes. Nocturnal commuters flow easily through the uncongested airways of the night sky, the world just continuing on.

The muzzle flash of Victor's pistol plays over in my mind, along with the burst of dark blood erupting from that man's skull. A soul was taken today, in cold blood, but the world continues to churn. The deaths I ordered no different than the one I witnessed tonight. But again, the world continued on. I think most people would feel a sense of dread in these moments, an overwhelming sense of guilt at the realization of lives taken at your will, but not me. Watching the gears of the city turn as if nothing happened shows me life is a selfish pursuit. Death is only mourned because of the emptiness it leaves behind, not the death itself. If a death leaves no void in your life, you don't mourn it. Therefore, life isn't a precious pillar of existence designed to be treated with such fragile hands. We are mere specks. Here a moment, gone the next.

For if life was as paramount as people claim, all death would be mourned equally. The act of dying would be what was grieved, not the absence from another's life. And I refuse to feel guilt for the selfish sadness of others. No one will mourn when I pass, so why should I mourn for others?

"...Gwinn!" Russa barks from inside. I'd been so lost in my thoughts, I forgot he was inside. I turn back to look at him.

He's an entirely different person around me than the rest of the world. I sense this protective veil he covers me with, but the look isn't natural for him. He's self-interested, just like me. Spent millennia protecting his reputation and power within the High Council. Regardless of what he thinks, he has no moral high ground to scold me from.

"My information is rock solid," I say. He'd be less condescending if he knew I got all my information from bugs I planted in *his* office.

"You haven't the slightest idea of what's really going on," He says. "Even if you thought the Bytrol was in that Vault, you're not positive... you're willing to risk your life on chance?"

"But it *is* there, isn't it?" I say, my arms folded over one another. He stares at me as if beginning to contemplate the chances I've been spying on him.

"Gwinn, I don't know what you *think* you know, but I promise you, there's a lot to this world that's not what it seems," He says, eyes firm, almost challenging me to back off. "This world may look clean and pretty now, but I've lived this life for hundreds and hundreds of years, and we've had to do things many of us aren't proud of to get here. Things that to this day still haunt me, things I will never forgive myself for." He hangs his head for a moment. "But you need to understand, if you're going to lead this world, you will have to bear the weight of its secrets and do things asked of you, you couldn't possibly imagine." He steps closer in, his voice now checked. His eyes no longer tremble with anger but sink with an onus far more terrifying than any rage. "The moment you join our ranks, your life is no longer yours. It becomes property of the people, and right now, you must protect those very people from yourself... You made me do this." He steps back, face sullen with regret, and presses a button on his comm. "Bring him in."

The door to my unit swings opens as Trakstull and Lyrell enter, dragging a bound man behind them. I glance nervously to Russa. The two Ancients approach, and from beyond the darkness of the hallway, they emerge. Russa grabs a chair and positions it just in front of me. The other Ancients wrestle a massive man into the chair, their cords slithering and wrapping around his limbs and neck, making easy work of the considerably larger man. They settle him into the chair, cutting his binds and retying them to the arms and legs of the wood. Their cords leave behind constriction marks all over his body, so it looks like he's been whipped hundreds of times.

Trakstull's face is blank, the expression of a man so powerful no action can phase him. Lyrell pulls the cover from the man's head and tosses it to the side. The mountainous Olt, Meelo, sits bound and gagged in the chair in front of me, hair disheveled, eyes wild with panic. His gaze meets mine first, and his brow tightens in rage when he thinks he understands what's going on.

"What the hell is this, Russa?!" I snap. He doesn't answer. Trakstull steps in front, the cords of his arms now twisted into solid ropes and tucked behind his back.

"What a mess you created, foolish girl," He says, the words purring out from the thinnest of openings of his beak. Velvety and terrifying. "This man sought to expose you. Expose the actions we all understand you did. And yes, child, we know." He stares at me with wretched force before gazing off into the distance once again and pacing back and forth in front of Meelo. "But I knew of your plan before it happened, and I still allowed it." I recoil, and he sees my surprise. "Nothing happens in my kingdom without my eyes watching over it, little bird." I can't combat his tone because he makes me feel the size of an insect. The power behind his words, the knowledge that he see's things I didn't think possible.

"This man was hell-bent on bringing you to justice. Not stopping until the truth of your transgressions were unveiled for the masses to consume." He drags his cord ends along Meelo's face as he makes another pass. "Meelo is a noble man. Honorable. But a noble man cannot lead. Because there is no nobility in choosing who lives and who dies. Nobility is saved for men who *follow* orders. Inglorious burden awaits men who *give* them. And therein lies the issue," He says, dropping to eye level with Meelo. "He believed seeking out justice was the noble action, and he was probably correct, but nobility has no place in leadership. And he never considered the impact his *noble* actions would have on the world. I anointed you High Councilor shortly after Wylk's death; do I look culpable if the truth comes out? If the people lose faith in their Regal, they lose faith in the High Council." He turns his back to me and looks eye to eye with Meelo, just inches apart.

"Meelo, can people lose trust in their Regal?" Meelo glowers in anger, unresponsive. Trakstull grabs his jaw and slowly shakes his head side to side. "No?" Trakstull looks to Lyrell. "Lyrell, what do you think would happen if the people lost faith in their Regal?"

"The world would know darkness, my Regal." He answers as he picks at one of his frayed cords with a knife.

"And what about you, Russa? Surely you can imagine a society without stability and faith?" He asks.

Russa glances at me. He doesn't seem interested in partaking in the show like the others. He glances once more, almost ashamed.

"Yeah..."

"So, the Ancients understand, wonderful!" He snatches Meelo's face up, a cord slithering up the Oltish brute's nose. Meelo staggers as it snakes deeper into his head. "We built this world from the rubble of ruin and didn't claw our way to power just to have some muscle-bound white knight come to weaken the foundation of our society because he's incapable of seeing the trees from the Forest."

Lyrell leans down.

"I believe it's, *see the Forest for the trees*, my Regal," He says as he retreats back to his spot behind Meelo. Trakstull glances up at him.

"Ah, yes, my apologies. It seems I've misused one of Earth's idioms. I'll try another one. Meelo, you've made your bed, now you must lie in it." He stands up and pulls a pistol from under his coat. He turns, pushing the butt of the gun in my face. "Councilor." I stare at the weapon, unsure of what he wants. "Gwinn... take the gun." I quickly glance at Russa. He stares helplessly.

My fingers wrap around its handle. The chilled metal sending sparks through my mind. I hear the pounding of a heartbeat too loud to possibly be mine, but I'm the only person in the room with one. It throbs in my ears.

"I sentence this man to death for charges of attempted treason against the High Council of Valenia. As Regal of the High Council, I mandate the High Councilor of Okotall, Gwinnett DeMarco, perform the execution." I gawk in disbelief. Meelo fumes with rage and panic, his body violently trying to free himself from his binds.

"Trakstull, I'm not going to murder this man in my living

room, are you crazy?" I ask. I glance again to Russa, imploring him to help, but he keeps his distance.

"You must share the burden we all do. For the betterment of the people," He says. "Unless you'd like to switch positions with him?"

I stare helplessly at the Ancients who wait for my decision. Three of the most powerful men in existence exerting the entirety of their force upon me. And then I meet Meelo's eyes. The anger from that day on the lift, gone. Replaced with the pleading desperation of a man realizing his life rests at the tip of my finger. But they're right. He has to be taken care of.

I raise the gun and press it to his forehead.

There's a sobering weight to killing someone yourself. When I spoke with Deterro, the words flowed easily from my lips. I never saw it happen, never saw the aftermath, just said the words, and four men disappeared. This is different. Cold sweat streaks the inside of my palm. My tongue so dry, I may choke on it. All my cynical thoughts about life from before washed away by the mind clouding effects of adrenaline. My heart clamors. I can't look away from this man, and the longer I do, the more I see beyond his flesh and see the soul within him.

"Gwinn. The time is now."

My breath is wild. I can't stop blinking. My legs tremor, begging to collapse. I press the barrel harder against his forehead. *Doubts are weakness, Gwinn. Just fucking do it.* Meelo squirms in desperation. I close my eyes, unable to watch the life leave his body. My hand tenses, but my finger resists. *He would do the same to you. Life means nothing. Do it!* Every muscle of my body contracts as I prepare myself for the recoil. I take a deep breath as I turn my head away.

Doubts are weakness.

I pull the trigger.

There's nothing but deafening silence for a moment. I turn my head back and see tears streaming from Meelo's face, unharmed. Tension explodes from my lungs as I drop the gun and crash to the floor. It was empty.

My chest bucks as I sob. Why am I so glad to have not killed him? I can't explain it, but relief pours over me that this giant brute's brain matter isn't decorating my bedroom walls.

Lyrell removes the gag from Meelo's mouth, and he immediately begins to curse.

"You Surg bastard, mother fuckers!" Tears roll down his

cheeks, face bright red with panic. "Fuck you! Fuck you!" I stare at Russa from the floor. Eyes burning with overwhelmed tears. He walks over.

"Get up," He says, yanking me from the ground and tossing me onto a nearby cushion. "Do something stupid again, and it'll be you in that chair, but I can't promise the end will be the same." He looks at me like he never has before. The way I've always wanted him to, but now wish he wouldn't. The way he does to everyone else. "Understand?"

I nod my head and swallow hard as the tension in my bones continues to gnaw at me. Meelo's broken ramblings persist. Trakstull hushes him with a cord to his lips.

"That's enough. Do we have to put the muzzle back on?" He asks. Meelo shakes his head, breath still heavy, eyes wild. "Good." Trakstull smiles. "Now, do we both have an understanding?" He glances at Meelo and me.

"Yeah... I got it," I say. Meelo nods as he looks at me, terrified. A bizarre expression coming from such a massive man. Trakstull nods to Lyrell, who cuts Meelo's binds from the chair, and Meelo rubs his wrists.

"Get out of here," Trakstull says to Meelo. He darts up and hurries out of the room as quick as he can, nearly stumbling on the way out. "As for you, what is your plan for the little *snake king*?" He asks.

All in one moment, embarrassment slaps me across the face at my groveling.

Doubts are weakness... cut this shit out.

I rediscover my spine and suck away the emotion, powering to my feet.

"Get the cure from the Vault and trade it to Deterro for his silence," I say, doing my best recover from the pathetic display just moments ago.

"I thought you understood? The Bytrol cannot be made available to the public. It most certainly cannot be given to some crime lord. Nor can the knowledge of your agreement to remove Candidate Wylk from the equation remain outside our trusted circle. So, he must be dealt with," Trakstull says as if it's that simple to just *deal* with the most dangerous gang in the world.

"I can't just waltz onto the Viper compound and shoot him?" I say. "Why don't you send a legion in, wipe them all out?"

"Child, don't be foolish. They are a band of criminals, not the Gaz." He scoffs. "The High Council cannot take full military action against its own citizens. Think before you speak."

"But they *are* criminals. Don't you have the authority to detain whoever you want? No one would question a compound raid of the Vipers." Trakstull looks annoyed.

"I have the authority to do whatever I please, girl. That does not mean I should." He inspects my bottle of bourbon resting on the bar. He sniffs the rim and balks at the harsh scent. "I will not sacrifice the lives of my men to cover for your mistakes. This is your problem to solve, Gwinn, not mine." He takes a swig from the bottle, grimacing as the liquor pours down his throat.

"I understand that, but if you claim my deal with Deterro is unacceptable, how do you foresee me fixing this? You are the Regal for good reason, surely you can think of some way to help me learn from my mistake?" I say, playing to his ego. He's not fooled but enjoys the stroke anyway. He grins.

"Well, Russa explained to me that your human counterparts have a similar vested interest in the death of Deterro, do they not?" Trakstull says.

Miku. Through all the commotion, I forgot he has her too. I shudder at the thought of what the past few days have been like for her; there are most certainly worse fates than death.

Clearly, whatever plan Fargo and Victor had to get her back failed miserably the moment Victor pulled that trigger. That scene rifles through my mind over and over. Why the hell did Victor do that? I haven't had a moment to process the insanity of it, until just now. I know I've grown apart from my friends on Groga over the years, but Victor was always the most reserved and rational. I have no idea what could've set him off to commit such a heinous crime?

"Yea, they do, but I don't see how that helps. Not to mention, Victor is in custody right now," I say.

"You used illicit means to claim your seat, now you must use them to keep it," He says. I shake my head, still confused at what he's implying.

"Trakstull..." I say, Lyrell glares at me. I correct myself. "Regal... I don't understand."

He signals to Lyrell, who disappears out the door for a moment and returns with a small case. He sets the case on the table, opening the lid. Inside are encrypted datacards, lined in a row along the top with accompanying power cells lined along the bottom. Trakstull removes one of the power cells and holds it up between his fingers, staring magically at the compact energized cube, the gears of a plan already in motion, stirring in his head.

"You needn't a legion to dispatch of your enemy, Gwinn. Just two or three untethered Warlords."

33

FARGO SHEPHERD

The Enemy of My Enemy

My soul melts to a puttie as the toxic green vapor is sucked in through my nose. The world downshifts to a crawl, Venom beginning to hijack my nervous system. The drug doing precisely as I intended, transporting my mind away from this nightmare.

I inspect my fingers inches from my face. They feel swollen. Like they could shoot lightning from their tips. I sink deeper into my gel chair and worry if I close my eyes, they may never open again.

Cyto continues to bark at Zina, who is shackled to a bench along the far wall. He's been at it all night, ever since she came to. But it's no use. She won't hand it over. I don't blame her either. She's damned if she does and damned if she doesn't. The worst part is she doesn't even know Silva is dead yet. Whatever clumped mass that's replaced my heart attempts to feel guilt, but the Venom doesn't allow it.

I stare up at the ceiling, through the pentagon window and out at the jutting mountain peaks of the Valley. I wish I could teleport to its summit. Be away from this all. The disaster of my creation. I roll through the memories of my life and wonder which one set me on this path. Which defining moment of my life led me to becoming... whatever the fuck it is I am now. All my life I've prided myself on being so at peace with who I am, so connected with the intricacies that brought me joy, so defiant against accepting a pedestrian existence. But now, as I wallow in my self-pity, as alone as I've ever felt, I realize I'm completely full of shit. I didn't create my persona to feed the desires of my own headstrong independence. I created it because I was desperate for attention. A cry from a pathetic child, jealous of the admiration of his siblings. A boy who was so terrified no one would love him, he pretended no one did.

But people did love him. They loved him through his flaws and his selfishness. They loved him all the same. And now those very people will be destroyed by that selfishness. It's a thought I can't stand to bear.

I reach for another vile of Venom, but Cyto smacks at my hand.

"Enough slick!" He says. Cyto snatches all the drugs and haze from the table and dumps it into a crate along the counter. "Get off your ass and do something." His tiny pebble eyes glare in frustration with me. I moan and roll to my side. "Fargo! Get up." He tries to pull me from the chair, but his frail arms can't budge me. He kicks at my legs that dangle off the edge, but I barely feel them. "Alright slick, have it your way."

Cyto hobbles up a flight of stairs and digs feverishly through a metal storage bin. I lean back, hand outstretched as far as it will go, and try to pull the Venom crate off the ledge. The drugs cause me to hallucinate, and my arm stretches on forever. I try to pull it back, but it goes limp, and I yank on it like slack from a rope. My heart rate climbs as my arm doesn't come back to me. I pull and pull and pull, but it doesn't get any closer. My hand continues to stretch farther and farther away until I can barely see it. I think I scream out for it, but I'm not sure if I actually make any noise. And then I feel a heavy thump rock against my chest.

I snap violently back to reality, all the emotion blocked by the Venom surging to the forefront of my mind. My legs nearly fail me as I jolt to my feet. Lodged two inches into my chest is a cardiac spike pulse. My eyelids locked tight against the tops of their sockets, and my pupils gaped wide. Adrenaline roars through my body and flushes away every drop of toxic Venom that numbed my soul.

Cyto stands shakily next to me, the force of slamming the spike into my body more exertion than he's used to. I gargle a throaty cry as emotions flood my senses. Cyto says something to me, but my ears ring like a bomb detonated in the kitchen. I stare at him wildly.

He smacks me across the face.

"Hey!"

The jolt settles me, and my body begins to recalibrate.

"You with me, slick?" He says. My breathing calms, and finally, the world begins to reveal itself once again.

"What the hell, you old toad?!" I brace myself and yank the spike from my chest, blood droplets bead from the three needle-thin prick marks.

"You weren't cooperating. I need your mind here! We gotta' figure this out, slick," He says, voice firm and raspy. I shake my head and toss the spike off to the side. Cyto's face is riddled with worry. I can see how much he cares. He's not going to let me just give up and die. I think of all the other people who've loved me and tried their best to help me, no matter how many times I failed them and understand it has to stop. Cyto braces, preparing for me to scold him, but not ashamed of his actions. But I put my arm on his shoulder instead.

"Thank you," I say. I look into his eyes and see the hope he sees for me that I've pretended not to care about for so many years.

"Let's fix this," He says.

We walk back over to Zina, my chest still sore, who sits brewing in her restraints. Her amber and gold eyes glow with gorgeous rage. I killed so many of her family, but she doesn't steam with vengeful heat. It's a more graceful anger. I wonder if she knows how many of her people are dead by my hands?

"Zina," I say.

"Fargo," She says, eyes sparking with life. Even now, I find myself being pulled into her spell as quickly as I did the first night. Her pheromones sneaking up my nose, overloading my mind. I should want to slit her throat for causing all this, but instead, I gaze in wonderment at her, as one would a caged Tyko.

"You took something from me. I need it back," I say. I glance down at her leg. A heavy gash pusses over where I sliced her with the stun blade. It's definitely infected.

"Still a man of no mystery, Fargo. I expected more theater from you this time. Straight forward doesn't match your

317

reputation." She grins villainously. A sadness sinks within me. This isn't the game of sparring thieves and dueling intellects she thinks this is. This is real. People will die. People have died. And she has yet to fully comprehend the gravity of the situation. Her smile recedes as she senses the harshness of my expression.

"Silva is dead." I don't have time for subtly. Her face twitches, eyes blinking wildly. She scours my face, searching for a tell.

"Lair," She says, voice shaking. She stares into the grimness of my eyes, and I can tell she sees the truth.

"I'm not."

Tears begin to form in her amber eyes. She tilts her head away so I can't see them.

"How?" She asks, anger spilling from beyond the watery film that coats her eyes.

"After you passed out in the compound, Silva and I struck a deal. He needed the killing to stop, and I had someone gravely wounded," I say.

"The killing?" She asks. Shit. She didn't know. I stare sorrowfully at her, the images of their red eyes melting before me stained in my nightmares. Whatever I was before... that night has made me something far more wicked. She clenches her jaw. "How many?"

I pause.

"How many Fargo!" She cries, voice cracking, as panic quickens her breath. The slit of her nose flaring.

"... a lot," I say, the guilt choking at my throat. They weren't callous, murderous criminals like the Vipers. Just a group of people doing the best they could to survive a world that had forsaken them. Her lips purse together as silent tears stream down her face. She stole from me, caused me to raid their compound, caused Miku to get kidnapped, caused it all, and yet I still feel like the bad guy.

"He saved a lot of your people with that deal," I say, pity forcing me to grant Silva a martyr's death he doesn't deserve. She glances up to me, the attempt appreciated.

"Silva is many things, selfless isn't one of them," She says. "What was the deal?"

"He would get to eliminate Victor in the Arena and win his first match, and in exchange, he would return the Bytrol you stole from me."

She winces, the knowledge of so many of her loved ones dead, sucking the fire from her fierce Brushu eyes.

"Everything was going as planned until something happened in the Arena, and Silva was killed," I say, trying to avoid the particulars. She hangs her head, chest deflating with a heavy sigh.

"Can you unshackle me?... Please?" She asks. I glance at Cyto, who shakes his head. But as I look into her eyes, I see someone exhausted. Not filled with the heat of violence, ready to attack me at her first sign of freedom. But she's fooled me before. We've both hurt one another, I see someone who just wants it to stop.

"Slick!" Cyto opposes as I reach my hand up to her shackles, but I wave him off. I unlatch the restraints, and she immediately wipes the tears from her eyes. A proud soul.

"Thank you," She says, voice soft. She buries her face in her hands and shakes her head.

"What is it?" I ask. She glances up at me in frustration.

"Silva didn't even know where I hid the score," She says in disbelief. "He couldn't have led you to it even if he wanted to."

That little weasel...

"Maybe he planned on telling you about the deal and having you agree to it afterward?" I say. She appreciates me giving him the benefit of the doubt once again, but she knows him better than that.

"No, he saw his opportunity and went for it. He used you," She says. "Tried to at least." She shakes her head again in frustration, this time with her predictably selfish brother. I can't help but see the parallel between her and Victor in this moment. This is how he sees me. It pains me to finally understand the disappointment.

"What happens if I don't give back the Bytrol?" She asks, not necessarily negotiating, merely asking. Maybe trying to comprehend how much more pain can come from all this.

"Well, if I don't get it back to Deterro in two days, he kills me, and kills Miku, probably kills Victor, don't see why he wouldn't kill old Cyto over there, certainly hunts you down and kills you too, then finishes off the rest of your family. And to make matters worse, even though giving the Bytrol back to Deterro is the only way for all those things not to happen, that's not an option anymore." I pinch my brow, exhausted. And thank God I am, because if I had more energy, the sheer impossibility of my situation would have me balled up in a corner crying.

The weight of our reality is equally prevalent on Zina's face.

"Wait, why is giving it back not an option anymore?"

I take a seat next to her, head buried in my hands.

"Because we have the worst luck of all time and Bytrol is apparently, like, the *greatest* creation in the history of Valenia and can save humanity from extinction, cure the Rotting, and expose the High Council for being murderous lunatics." I chuckle as an overwhelmed tear streams down my cheek. "Who knows, it can probably end world hunger too. Why not?"

The full gravity of what she has entangled herself in must be cementing itself in her mind. She doesn't speak. She just sits there. Bottom hands rubbing at the shackle marks of her top hands.

"The Princess of Groga? What's she got to do with this?" She asks, staring blankly ahead, her eyes a million miles away.

"He kidnapped her as ransom," I say. Her eyes widen in fear. It's incredible the effect Miku has on people who she's never even met. Her allure stretches the entire planet.

"I'm sorry to hear that. It's hard to lose those close to you," She says. In this moment, we share the weight of loss. Of the unbearable consequences of our own actions. I feel as if I see the real her for the first time. Not as the sexual conquest I viewed her as at the party. Not as the bane of my existence at the compound. And not as a simple tap of critical information from the moments prior. But as someone desperately trying to do right by her people. Carving out a place in this world. Trying anything possible to pull her family from the quicksand of poverty. A woman who's operated behind a façade for years that's finally beginning to crumble. She's tired. Just like me.

"So that's the situation... And I have no clue what to do."

There's a loud rapping at the door.

It shatters our moment.

I whip my head to Cyto.

"Who could that be?" I ask. Cyto quickly hobbles to the gun rack and primes a pulsecannon. Its firing chamber whines. Ready to disintegrate anyone who barges through that door. I hurry over to the security monitor. Gwinn and Russa bang continuously at the door. I signal it open, and the two spill in quickly.

"What the fuck are you doing here?" I ask. "Actually, how did you even find this place?"

"Trakstull," Gwinn says in passing as she tosses a case onto the table and begins to open it.

"Who's that?" Russa asks, nodding to Zina. I glance at her.

"Don't worry about it," I say. They can't know she has the

Bytrol. That'll be a disaster. "What is all this?" I ask. Russa and Gwinn begin to pile all the contents of the case onto the table.

"Fargo, get over here." Gwinn barks. Her eyes are spears, deadly, and sharp. She's terrifying. I hurry over.

"Are these power cells?" I ask, a small cube shining in between my fingers.

"We have a plan," She says. I glance nervously to Russa, Cyto sharing in my apprehension.

"These power cells are industrial grade; they only supply maybe two or three things. Why do you have them?" I say. My brain reels, cycling through what uses they could have. "Airboats, construction bots, and..." My words trail off when I realize what they want to do.

"Warlord suits." Cyto finishes. My brain doesn't even know how to comprehend that information.

"Your plan is what, exactly? Use Warlord suits to raid Deterro's compound?" I ask. "You understand they don't function outside of the Arena's encrypted signals, right? Plus, you haven't the slightest idea how to operate one of those."

She holds up a datacard, yellow encrypted coding speeding in a line across the bottom.

"These will make them work outside the Arena." She hands me one.

"Holy shit, where did you get your hands on these?" I ask. "You'd end up at the bottom of a Surg feeding pit if anyone caught you with these." I stare up and realize I'm looking at two of the most powerful people in the world, holding some of the most illegal contraband that's ever been created. Who exactly would do anything about it?

Gwinn ignores my question.

"And we know exactly who can operate them." She adds. I'm so consumed with the rarity of the datacard, I don't fully comprehend what she implies. But then it hits me.

"Victor? But he's in holding?" I say.

They don't reply. I glance back down to the absurdly illegal datacard and realize there's nothing the tentacles of power can't reach. If they have access to these, surely getting Victor out is manageable.

My stomach aches.

There's a flaw in their plan... and they don't realize it. They have no idea of the state Victor is in. The last I saw of him, the madness on his face was beyond human.

"We are in the middle of extracting Victor now. Gwinn's

made assurances that we've distanced ourselves from it," Russa says. It shocks me how at ease he is with all of this. Gwinn, I understand, she is as ruthless as anyone I've ever met. Someone with a vested interest. But Russa is an Ancient. Someone who has led for centuries. Why does he subscribe to such drastic measures?

"Guys, Victor is..." I pause, not sure how to describe it. "He's not in the right state of mind to be asked of this," I say.

"Victor is a warrior. A killer. We're gonna use him for what he's meant for," Gwinn says. I hate the way she talks about him. He's not a killer. He's sick. Victor is the best man I know. I wish I could be half the man he is. "Your bodyguard, Geeva, she knows how to operate a suit too, right?"

I picture Geeva's pale skin sheening under the harsh lights of the MedCenter. I don't want her involved any more than she already has been.

"Fargo!" Gwinn snaps impatiently at me.

"She's hurt," I say. "She has to rest."

"Fuck that. We're all dead if Deterro isn't killed. She's in."

I know she's right, but I can't stand putting Geeva's life in danger yet again.

Cyto limps over and puts his hand on my shoulder.

"She'll be fine, slick," He says to my surprise. "She'll never forgive herself if something happens to you, and she did nothing to stop it. I know my daughter." He stares up at me with mourning eyes, the father in him wanting to protect his daughter but another side of him telling him he may lose her if he loses me. Does he know about us?

"So, we have Victor, Geeva, you, and one more power cell," Gwinn says.

"ME?" I ask, nearly puking as she says it.

"Yea you! This is your fault; your ass will be there."

"My fault? He'd never know about it if you didn't steal it from Su Hoz?"

"Fargo, you're going."

"I don't know how to—"

"Enough!"

My world begins to spin.

The thought of climbing into a machine of death more terrifying than anything I can imagine. My knowledge of Warlord suits, a fraction above passable. All residual experience from Victor.

"Do you know anyone else who would be willing to help and knows suits?" She asks. Willing to help? Has she lost her mind?

"Well, where the hell will you be during all this, *storm queen*?" Cyto snorts. Gwinn glares at him for using the insult. The skeptical corners of the world branding her many unflattering titles since her inauguration. *If they only knew the truth.*

"Russa and I are heading down to the Vault to recover the..." She glances suspiciously to Cyto and Zina. "... package, before Deterro sends his own men there to get it first. It's the only leverage I have over him."

Convenient, we charge forward into the mouth of a beast, and she goes underground to cover her own ass. But as much as it pains me, the plan might be our best option. The Bytrol can't fall back into Deterro's hands. Not that the High Council is much better. But one thing at a time.

Gwinn's steel eyes gnaw at me.

The only way to ensure all of our safety, for now, is if Deterro is dead. After that, I'll figure out what to do.

"So, do you know of anyone else?" Gwinn asks. "You may be able to handle it with just three, but our assault plan is built for four," She says.

Assault plan... I don't know how I went from slimy drug parties to murdering entire Rojo bloodlines, to carrying out assault plans. Everything around me is crumbling.

I shake my head.

"I've got no one," I say. She glances at Cyto.

"No luck here, your majesty," Cyto says.

"Well then you'll have to make do with three," She says.

"I know someone..." Zina chimes in from behind me. I had almost forgotten she was there. All eyes turn toward her. She stands and slowly approaches as if we were beasts she didn't dare startle.

"My father," She says. I glance at Cyto, he said she no longer had parents.

"I thought your parents were killed by Deterro?" I ask. She glances at me, surprised at my intel.

"My mother was. My father had to fake his own death to end Deterro's pursuit of our family," She says. "He couldn't risk Deterro finding out who he truly was."

"Who he *truly* was? Who is your father?" I ask. She pauses before answering.

"My father's name is Rozza... but you may know him as Pyra the Immortal."

The room is silent.

"Your farther is Pyra the Immortal? Greatest Warlord of all time, Pyra the Immortal?" I ask as my eyes widen.

"Yes, he is."

"Would he help us?" Gwinn asks, not aware of the history between our families. I stare earnestly at Zina. Victor ruined Pyra's career, killed his son, her brother. Could he possibly put all that aside?

"He would do anything to kill the man that took my mother from him," Zina says. "Silva was a derelict child. If it wasn't for me, he would've been cast out of our family some time ago. I know father doesn't mourn his death." The coldness of it strikes me. "But my mother, Tyra, was the light in my father's world. When she was killed, a part of him died with her. I didn't see him for years after Victor defeated him in the Arena, just weeks later. I don't know why he's come back around, especially to train Silva, but I know there is nothing the man will value higher than this vengeance."

"Then you have four," Gwinn says to me. Four? We barely have one. The fact that she's blindly accepting Geeva, Victor, and Pyra as confirmed is beyond logic. But she doesn't skip a beat. She projects blueprints and diagrams onto the table and goes over the plan with Cyto, who we'll need for comms.

"The Viper's compound is a fortress at the northmost point of the Valley where the cliffsides of the Elkowa mountains wedge to a stop and form a narrow pass. The *Gate,* as it's called, controls all ground transportation from Su Hoz into the Valley and indirectly all air traffic as no one would dare fly overhead..."

Gwinn continues on with the logistics as I check with Zina.

"Are you sure about this?" I ask.

"I'm tired of the violence too. Our families have caused each other enough pain, let's end this," Zina says, her eyes swollen and red.

I hand her the keys to a rig I have parked in an adjacent structure and a custom datacard with a randomizing sequencer. She glances up, confused.

"Listen, I want you to go get Pyra and the Bytrol, where ever you hid it, and bring them back here as quickly as you can. If things go south and the plan fails, I need you to deliver that Bytrol to Deterro." She recoils. "Him in control of something so vital to the world is the last thing I want, but hopefully this way, you can at least save Miku and your family. If the plan works and we kill Deterro, take the Bytrol to this address." I scribble Leo's address on the back of one of

Geeva's noodle boxes. "I don't know what to do with the Bytrol, it's way beyond me. All I know is those two back there shouldn't have it." I subtly nod to the two murderous tyrants in the living room. "And if anyone would know how to use it for good, it'd be Leo." She balks at the swarm of information I just poured onto her. But I keep going.

"Once you do that, take this datacard to Dwual Fir Central Depository and ask to see repository 0714. Got that? 0714. Cyto will activate the sequencer, which will unlock it, and you can have all the cash inside to get your family out of the Valley."

She stares at me, unsure of how to react to the gesture. I ease her suspicion.

"My entire life I've claimed to be one of the people, the commoner fighting to scratch his way to the top. But I've realized I've done nothing but perpetuate their standing in life. Climbing my way to the top, from the skin of their backs." This attempt at beneficence is awkward for me; I don't know how I come off. "Our families owe each other quite a debt. Rozza helping us is your payment. This will be mine."

She admires the datacard, a tear in her eye. She gazes up at me softly, for a moment, peering under my rouge exterior, seeing *me.* Just as I saw her.

"Thank you," She says.

Her gracious smile piques the little optimism left in my heart. Maybe I can change? Zina takes the keys and leaves the building as I ignore every morsel of my brain that signals for me to stop her. But if I want to change, I have to trust her. I just hope it's worth it.

34

RILEY HOLT

The Secrets Within

Leo's words haunt me through the night. How could Gwinn do that? A baby. A *human* baby could've been born to this world. The first organic child born since our extinction. I don't care how dour my outlook became; life of our kind is too rare to deny it access to the world. I don't understand...

I begin to imagine what a child of my own would look like. I've only seen a handful of images from our youth, the earliest are pictures and videos of our days as toddlers, so I haven't the slightest idea how we look as infants. I picture a small girl of about six running happily through a flowing field of Golden Grain. Her bright blonde hair matching the shade of the silky fiber. She pulls at a long stalk until it yanks from the soil, and she falls to her butt. A snaggle-toothed smile rounds through her plump cheeks as she giggles. Her uncle Remmy scoops her into his arms, and she squeals with glee. The vision begins to slowly dissolve as I desperately try to remain in that paradise. My eyes open, met with the merging rays of dawn and the fleeting darkness of night, and the illusion is gone.

Thoughts of the girl linger in my mind, though. She would be loved. Set out into the world with the knowledge that she will always have a home, something stripped from me at too young an age.

I would protect her from the harshness of life. Give her the companionship Remmy provided me in my darkest of hours.

The love Leo gave me before our worlds fell apart. She would not know loneliness. I wouldn't allow it. She would never experience the suffocating torment of a life lived devoid of acceptance. I would give her the greatest gift Remmy ever gave me, devotion.

Leo sits on the edge of a rock in his bottoms, toes just barely splashing against the water, staring longingly into the glowing orange pool, its reflections gently bouncing off his face. He seems so deep inside himself, he hasn't noticed I'm awake. His face reveals a somber grief I've never seen on him before. The unwavering optimist I grew to know, defeated by the unconquerable hollowness of loss. I empathize.

"I've caught him like this a few times myself," Patawa whispers to me as she leans over, the both of us inspecting Leo. "I don't know what's wrong, I've never seen him so despondent before."

I glance at Patawa as she peers at him, painfully trying to solve his woes. She doesn't know? I turn my attention back to him, inquisitively. Why did he tell me and not her?

"The day I met him, I could tell he was special," She says. "He has this infectious positivity about life that's remarkably admirable." Her bubbly personality is even more prevalent the more endearing she becomes of him. "He has been so great to us for so many years. I just wish there was something I could do to ease whatever pain he's in."

She leans her head on my shoulder, weaving her arm under mine.

"Sometimes, pain can't be eased," I say, Patawa flinches as she thinks she's insulted me. "What I mean is, there are things that happen in your life that are so painful, they change who you are."

Thoughts of Remmy rumble through my mind.

"You cannot ease them, or erase them, or forget about them. They alter who you are, how you see the world, how you *interact* with the world. Our job is to make sure we change for the better, not the worse," I say as I look up, Patawa intently listening. "The pain he feels, the pain *I* feel, is a part of us now. We cannot run from it. We have to face it. The problem is, it hurts." Her eyes slink back to Leo, no less sympathetic than before.

"I get it, I just wish I understood why. Not that understanding makes it any easier to watch," She says.

"No. No, it does not," I say as Leo turns and sees us staring at him, an adorable smile breaking on his face. "I'll give him

327

this though, at least he pretends."

"You two spying on me?" He jokes from the rock as he climbs to his feet.

"Just admiring the view," I say with a grin. He playfully runs his fingers through his hair, trying to act seductive. "And... you ruined it!" Patawa snorts a chuckle, as I smirk at him. Despite everything I just said, sometimes pretending can be therapeutic.

"And *you* ruined my sleep." Bryl groans as he rolls away from us onto his side.

"Get over it, ya big brute!" Leo says as he pulls the thin blanket out from under Bryl. "It's time to get moving anyway."

"The sun's not even out yet, boss." Bryl grunts and yanks the blanket back from Leo. Spri and Yara both begin to stir as well.

"Everyone up!" Leo orders. "Up. Up," He says as he pulls on his crew members one by one until they reluctantly concede that their day has begun.

I inspect him closer than ever, searching for the cracks in his cheery performance, trying to find the anguish buried under the gleeful eyes. For a moment, I think I can see it. The manufactured hopefulness beginning to become more apparent, like one of those paintings in Okotall's Museum of Fine Arts. The ones that contain hidden images blended within the bigger piece. Emoss would take us there as children, and we would stare for hours upon hours at the paintings, always trying to be the first to find the concealed mysteries. You had to look so intently at the figures to discover their secrets, you would look beyond the painting itself. And the moment you found them, it became all you could see. This gorgeous canvas of intense color and detail, reduced to a single defining point. I look away from Leo to spare him from a similar fate.

I'd rather never see the real sadness woven into his soul then shatter his hopeful, splendid veneer, no matter how enticing the comfort of shared struggle can be. We are all broken in some way; I chose one way of handling it, he chose another. I'm beginning to understand why his way is better.

Bitterness is easy. I know that all too well.

Remmy shared the same sanguine disposition Leo has. He was never seduced by the tragic state of our hapless life. He was strong, firm. I look again to Leo and see the same confident presence in his eyes that Remmy had. An expression that calmly whispers, everything will be alright. A twinge of helplessness runs through me as I see their similarities, yet understand Leo's true pain. Was Remmy acting too? Did he hurt to his core the way I know Leo does now? Did he live his entire life sharing the load of my burden, while he carried his alone? The thought tremors an unfathomable sadness through my heart, and I may very well collapse.

I'm so angry with myself that I never saw it, self-absorbed in my own sea of pity. He needed me to be more. More than an angry girl who hated the world for hating her. Leo glances at me with a warm smile, kind, genuine eyes, and I realize he needs me even if he never admits it. There is good still in this world, and he is it. I will not let him down the way I did my brother.

The midday sun bakes us inside the sweltering, dense jungle. My legs itch, irritated from the tangled weeds of the unexplored patch of the Forest we trek through, sweat running down my back and pooling near the ridge of my waistband. Our caravan trudges along, the promised sanctuary of the cool waters of Berban Falls powering our exhausted legs. Leo carries my pack. I feel naked without it, but I'd be lying if I said I wasn't relieved when he offered.

Sweat coats his shirtless body, more muscular than I initially gave him credit for. He's not the granite carved man Bryl, but he's not feeble either. Spri, on the other hand, looks more skeleton than Reyllion. We may have to anchor him down, else a breeze could sweep him away. Yara is the one who amazes me. He leads the way, setting a pace only I can maintain. He slinks through cluttered brush without ever looking down, eyes scouring the terrain for the Gaz. The Ancients are a miraculous breed, their longevity, their intellect, their efficiency. Why are there so few left? What happened hundreds of years ago to dwindle their numbers so immensely? Do they all eventually suffer the same levels of mental deterioration Yara experiences? The answers all vanished with the dark times well before humanity encountered this planet.

My wandering mind snaps to attention as we approach a worn path, a traveling merchant visible ahead. I raise my hands in the air, signaling everyone to crouch as we disguise ourselves among the tall plants. We approach silently, crouch walking through the brush like predators stalking their prey. Voices become audible as we get closer. I can see two sets of legs under the cart. One thin, dressed inappropriately for the weather, and the other, thick, powerful legs. Warrior legs. Gaz legs.

Leo crawls to my side.

"What is it?" He asks.

"A Su Hozi Merchant Envoy," I reply.

"In Berban?"

"E'Zuu struck a deal with A'gorr years back, allowing access for a select few Su Hozi traders to establish routes through Berban, so remote villages could trade for goods and supplies." He glances at me, surprised.

"The Gaz accepted that?" He asks.

"Well, not all of them," I say with an apprehensive look. "A'gorr's word is law, but he's given most villages the autonomy to decide to what degree they have sworn off the technology beyond the trees. Some make good use of the envoy's, some... well... don't." As I finish, another Gaz warrior approaches, war staff sheathed against his back. He speaks calmly, from a more native dialect, but I can make out some of what he says.

"What's he saying?" Leo asks. Yara answers before I can attempt to interpret. His voice startles me; I haven't heard it since we've left. I didn't realize Yara spoke the Forest Tongue.

"They ask about the Children," He says. "They ask if he has seen you during his travels," Yara says as he looks at me. The warriors seem placid, yet the threat of violence drips from them like sap from a branch. Constant and thick.

The three move to the back of the envoy's cart, revealing themselves for the first time. The Su Hozi is a Reyllion. A squatty man with chubby features squeezed inside a dated Grogan outfit waddles to the opening of his trunk.

He's dwarfed by the two Gaz warriors, both a darker shade of greyish green then the Gaz of Pom'do'kon. Closer to A'gorr. The Su Hozi man opens the trunk and reveals his merchandise as one of the Gaz steps into the transport. It buckles under his weight, the Hotógo hauling it, snarls in agitation. The Reyllion man follows him inside, as the other Gaz remains behind.

I don't like the look of any of this. Nor am I crazy about the look on Leo's face. He doesn't know these woods like I do...

It's less than a minute before the crate rumbles, and the Reyllion man is launched like a ragdoll from the opening, spilling onto the Forest floor. The Gaz from inside yells something I can't make out and sheds his staff from his back, pinning the man to the ground. The Gaz jumps off the trunk bed and smashes his staff into the shoulder of the envoy. The plump man squeals in pain.

Leo flinches as if to sprint from our concealment to aid the man, but I snatch him before he can.

"What are you doing?" I ask, dragging him back to the cover of the weeds.

"They're hurting him, we have to stop them!" He says, a naïve righteousness operating his mind.

"Leo, they're looking for me and Remmy..." I remind him. "They don't even know you're here, let alone the others. If they catch us, they may spare you and me... but not them." I glance back to Leo's crew and know I speak the truth. The only thing that saved us from execution that day in Pom'do'kon was the fact that we are human. If I was Heplin or Olt, I would've died right there in the grass next to my campfire.

"Well, we can't just sit here!" He says.

"We have to..."

The Gaz warrior continues to torment the envoy. Bryl crawls his way to us, along with the others.

"Boss, what's the move?" He asks. "Give me the order, and I'll drop these big green shits." Remmy's rifle is wedged into his shoulder, one eye squinted shut, the other peering down the sights. It pains me to see someone else wield it. Leo glances at me uneasily.

"No, hold."

"What the hell, boss? We just watchin' this happen?"

Leo shoots another look at me.

"Let me smoke 'em boss, they're gonna kill the poor bastard."

"Put it down, Bryl," I demand.

"Bryl, hold!"

"Leo, do something." Patawa pleads.

His eyes meet mine, dangerous sparks of courage erupting from within them. He's getting antsy, I can feel it.

"Leo... don't..." I say, my hand clasped against his forearm. The Gaz sweeps his staff across the merchant's face, and blood spills from his mouth. Leo sits still for a moment, eyes locked on mine, begging for my permission, but I won't give it to him. For once, I'm thinking clearly.

Leo is still. Squatting in the weeds, the cogs of his mind

churning as he inspects the situation. I squeeze his arm.

"...Leo..." I say. He glances at me, almost apologizing, and quickly spits out an order.

"Take him!" Leo says.

The thunder of the rifle roars the instant he says it, and the Gaz standing off to side bucks to the ground. I jump at the blast as Leo breaks away from my grasp and charges the other Gaz.

"Leo, no!" I cry out. Yara panics as he sees Leo sprinting head-on into danger.

"Child!" He stumbles ahead to protect him. Bryl begins to load another bolt, but I snap at him.

"Stop!" I grab the barrel of the gun and yank it away from him. "You may have just killed us." I hurry from the brush to join Leo and Yara, rifle flush against my shoulder now. I load the bolt in myself as Bryl sprints past me. As I chamber the round, Leo crashes into the Gaz attacking the Su Hozi man, his shoulder plowing against the warrior's ribs. The two tumble to the ground, a swarm of limbs and flesh. Yara races to Leo's side and helps him off the ground as Bryl and Patawa help the merchant to his feet. Spri remains in the weeds, cowering behind the hollow shell of a downed tree.

The six of us back away from the massive warriors as they regain their stance, anger smeared across their piercing blue eyes. The uninjured Gaz helps the other stand, as blood pours from a gaping hole in his shoulder. They twirl their staves into their fighting stances, rapping them against their horns. I pull Leo, Patawa, and the merchant behind me. Bryl flanks to my left, carrying the hatchet from my pack. And Yara aims the pistol we should've taken from him, on my right.

I would have Yara interpret for me, but I don't trust him. I yell out in the best Forest Tongue I can.

"We are leaving the trees. Let us pass and no blood," I say in choppy, crude sentences. The Gaz snort at me.

"There will be blood if we wish it, Cho'wa." The Gaz's word for outsider. I cock my rifle again, trying to intimidate.

"We are not your enemy, but we will be if we must."

"All Cho'wa are enemy. Even ones from the sky." He twists his wrists, and his staff unfolds into a circular shield, striking blue eyes peering over its edge. He slowly inches closer, shrinking the distance between us, as we back away. We cannot fight him; it's suicide.

"Don't come any closer!" I yell hollow threats with my rifle fixed on his head. He doesn't slow. The six of us press

together. Panic charging my heart like static. We run out of room to retreat. Think, Riley. Think.

Yara steps in front of me, placing his pistol on the ground and dropping to his knees. He speaks in fluid, clean Forest Tongue, the stutter and commotion of his normal idiolect, subsiding for the moment.

"If blood is what you desire, take it from me. These Children have brought Gaz no harm; I cannot say the same for myself. My race has spilled the blood of all hearts that beat, Gaz no different. These Children only seek the woods because my kin gave them nowhere else to go." Yara recites with beautiful composure, his voice dancing and gentle. His body is calm, his eyes steadfast. Beak perched with poise. Spectating the brief lucid grandeur of this lost man pulls at the resentment that burns in my core. His gaze meets mine, tranquil. His face searches for words that don't exist, his present consciousness unable to mend the wounds he's caused. His face pleads for forgiveness but understands there are no words capable of asking for it. The conflict grows inside me as I watch.

"Honorable warrior, what is your name?" Yara asks. The Gaz inspects us momentarily over the rim of his shield, then answers.

"I am Urok," He says. *"I grow impatient of your words Cho'wa, are you offering your blood as penance for their crimes?"*

"I will, but I offer you life instead of blood?" Yara says, confusing Urok. *"Let me save your partner and spare us."*

Urok carefully checks behind him to see the other Gaz strewn across the ground, blood pooling softly under him. Urok snaps his head back to face us, brow pressed, jaw clenched, fighting emotions.

"There is honor in giving your body back to the Forest." Urok says through clenched teeth. He begins to glance back to his partner again, but resists, fighting the rising tide that visibly builds on his face. Yara stands, slowly, cords only gently waving, and utters a phrase I can't quite make out.

"D'ya wo cha'ka, co tara sa noko co gan'da."

The Gaz cautiously lowers his shield as Yara pulls a vial of the glowing orange liquid Patawa bottled at the Life Blood pool. The Gaz twists his wrists, and the shield coils back into a staff, as he sheaths it, taking the glass from Yara. He whispers to himself, staring in wonderment at the glowing vial.

"...tara sa noko co gan' da." Urok glances back to his

partner, then to us, his warrior code struggling with the desire to help his fallen comrade.

"Take it. Use it," Yara says. *"And we will leave now."* He looks nervously to Leo, who seems appalled to give it away. Urok glares in disgust at Leo's crew, but caves.

"Very well. Leave now before I change my mind." Urok says, hurriedly turning to tend to his partner.

We quickly gather our gear and begin to flee when the Su Hozi envoy stops us.

"Wait!" He cries out. "We cannot leave my cart." I turn back and grab him by the arm.

"Fuck your cart, we have to go now!"

"No, you don't understand, it can't stay here."

He tries to scurry back to the trunk.

"We will get you another Hotógo, pay for the supplies you've lost, who cares, come on!" I pull open my pack and reveal the Tyko horns concealed within. "See, these are worth far more than anything you could have in there."

His eyes light up at the horns, but he shakes his head and gathers himself.

"No, they are not," He says as he slips from my grip and runs back to the cart. Leo hurries to my side.

"What the hell is he doing?" He asks.

"I don't know."

Urok balks as the Reyllion man approaches the cart, grabbing for his staff, but the envoy climbs atop the Hotógo mount and urges the beast our way. The creature snarls and snorts as the man yanks him to a stop just meters in front of us. He bangs on the metal face of the trunk.

"Out!" He waits a moment, eye skittish, then pounds against the wall again. "Out, out!" The crate begins to stir, and we take a step back. The caravan bounces and jostles until I hear the sound of feet landing on the dirt behind it. The Reyllion man snaps at the Hotógo and takes off in the opposite direction.

"It's clear I can no longer help her. I'm sorry."

As the cart speeds away, it kicks up dust and debris, creating a cloud that hides the image of a frail figure standing within it. Leo steps closer, his eyes wide. The dust settles, and my mind surely plays tricks on me.

She stares back at me with the same level of bewilderment.

I carefully place my pack on the ground and take a step closer. Is it really her?

"... Tanya?"

35

VICTOR BELLS

Witness the Flesh

L ife seems distant as if the world plays through a small screen across a dark room. I have to squint to see it. All around me is darkness. The cold empty depths of my mind. I know harsh fluorescent lights flood my holding cell, but they appear faint as the stars on cloudy nights. Nights where the storms of the Su Hozi plains rage with menace until they run out of steam and settle over the Grogan islands, masking the sky in grey mist. I miss those nights. Lying next to Miku on the perch of our home, staring into the murky air, feeling the cold vapor rub against our cheeks. I've thought of nothing but her all night.

The magnetic cuffs that clamp my arms to my thighs dig into my wrist. I don't bother trying to adjust them; Hades doesn't care. He bangs my head against the impenetrable glass window, bottled rage unable to release. I've relinquished my body to the monster. Life bearing no meaning any longer. I spend the maddening hours of my incarceration trying to sear her perfection into my memory. Fighting the intrusive thoughts of her inevitable torture. I refuse to let her face melt away from my mind; it is all I have left.

All the memories I have of Fargo, though, I give to Hades.

Across from my cell paces another insane man. His eyes never leave Hades'. He's a disfigured, obscure, grotesque looking psychopath. Face surgically altered in an attempt to look human. The signature touch of the cultish society that clings to the underbelly of the world, obsessing over the human race... the Proselytes.

The Proselyte *reborn*, as they call themselves after their transcendence from Valenian form to their pure Earthly being, grovels at my presence. A laughable ideology. Who would choose this curse?

His surgically tightened face is disgusting and hardly resembles anything close to human. The Proselytes look far more mutant than anything related to my species. I can tell he speaks to me because his bizarre lips move, but the soundproof cells mute his words as if they never existed.

I try to ignore him, but Hades growls at him like a feral dog. All pointless rage and fury.

The *reborn* gazes at me with deranged mania, the same way one would a fiery golden God. A guard strolls by and casually presses a button along the outside of his cell, sending sparks of electricity erupting from spouts in the walls, jolting the man until he falls to the ground, shivering. The guard smirks to himself and taps the same button on my cell.

Hades roars at the guard as I brace for another round of aggression suppression. My entire body clenches as my eyes nearly roll into the back of my head, and I crash to the floor. I spasm uncontrollably. The current stops and my body lays immobile, writhing in pain.

I come swarming to the forefront of my consciousness for a moment after the jolt, Hades temporarily repressed. I don't know why, but the first thing I always want to do when it happens is to close my eyes. Feel the warmth of my eyelids. Revel in the control of my body, perhaps. But my brief access to the control center of my mind fades quickly, and I'm shoved back into my cold, dark corner by the unstoppable demon.

I can feel Hades try to climb to his feet, but my muscles still don't cooperate. The guard crouches and tilts his head so he can meet the eyes of the Proselyte.

He says something to the man, but I can't hear it. The reborn stares past him to Hades. Glued to our presence. The guard bangs the glass, then remembers he didn't activate the comm. He reaches up and clicks on the hall's speaker system.

"Hey, freaks! Stay on your benches, or you get shocked again," He says, looking back and forth between us. The Proselyte nods, but Hades spits at the window and cackles.

Fuck.

The guard smiles wickedly.

"Have it your way, *warlord*!"

This time he presses and holds... Power surges through my body. It doesn't stop. I begin to choke on my tongue. My vision caving in on itself. Blood begins to drool from my nose. Capillaries in my brain erupting. What a pathetic way to die? Shackled like a beast, my organs cooking from the inside. But at least I'm in control. Hades flushed away by the tortuous volts. What good am I to the world without Miku anyway? I accept my fate and let the world around me plunge into darkness.

I wake to the blaring scream of sirens, red lights pulsing through utter darkness. Shattered glass is scattered along the floor. My head throbs. Am I dead?

Soldiers in jet black body armor glide menacingly through the halls, green lasers attached to their rifles, dancing in the dark.

No, I'm not.

I flinch as gunfire erupts.

The guard from earlier lays dead in a pool of his own blood. Reinforcements barricaded behind portable shields fire wild, terrified rounds at the storming force. The deafening madness of battle blossoms in my ear.

My training kickstarts my mind as a bullet screams past my head.

I roll to my side, inching against the wall, body in agony. My vision clears, and I realize I'm here. Hades zapped away once again.

Could this be how I control him?

Bullets careen off the guard's portable shield, sparks igniting from the metal. I scramble to hide from the crossfire. Threads of death, knitting an impassible sheet across the corridor. The guards scream orders at one another. Eyes bulging in panic. One lobs a riot control explosive over his shield. Concussive thumps ring out. They use the moment to inch closer. But the high pitch whine of a railcannon churns.

"Rail!" One shouts. The guards dive into adjacent cells just before a heavy magnetic round rips a hole in the shield and tears into the wall next to me. Rubble explodes into the air. Jagged shards of stone tearing into my leg. They peek around the corner cells and return fire.

Bodies begin to accumulate.

I crawl to the downed guard who electrocuted me, errant rounds screaming inches above. I gather his rifle. Every ounce of blood in his head, now drained onto the floor in a pitch-black pool. If only they would've left him for me. I roll into the cell where the Proselyte was and press my back against the wall. Rounds continue to shred the stone blocks. Where is the zealot whose cell this was?

I gather my breath and peer around the corner to assess the situation.

Half a dozen of the armored men remain standing, surgically moving through the corridor. Only four of the nearly twenty guards remain, cowering against the cell walls, surely running low on ammo. I watch one attempt to signal for help on his comm, but can't.

"Comm's are down!" He yells to his partner across the hall. Bullets slam into the edge of the wall, and he dives back deeper into the cell. The mayhem plays out in slow, haunting frames of pulsing red light. Pulse. Dark. Pulse. Dark. Every frame, the attacking forces push closer and closer to the ill-prepared guards. The certainty of their death, written morbidly across their face.

One by one, they collapse.

A bullet dives into a guard's skull.

One into the stocky neck of another.

Morbid shrieks fill the air as those who don't go quickly wallow in agony.

The last guard is a Savron man with wings clipped so short, you can barely see them. His eyes flutter. In and out of consciousness. Until a hole is bored into his head, and the fighting suddenly stops.

An eerie tension floats throughout the hall, the siren screaming its rhythmic cry. The sound of cautious footsteps creep along the corridor floor, green lasers scanning for threats. I carefully peek again to get a better look at who the men are.

Red light flashes and illuminates the terrifying figures. Jet black armor, sharp, pointed helmets covering their faces, massive men that make their rifles look like toys. They have to be Deterro's men. Coming to tie off the loose ends of our botched deal.

I follow a green laser, anticipating its origin, and wait for a patch of darkness. The light recedes, and I whirl my rifle around the corner, squeezing unmercifully on the trigger. The bullets spill from the barrel, storming blindly into the blackness, and a body crumbles to the ground.

The other soldiers dive behind cover, barking out orders.

No one moves.

My heart thunders against my chest. I have no idea how Hades hasn't clawed his way back to life. Something metal clangs against the ground and rolls its way to me. I use the butt of my rifle to smack it away just before it erupts into blinding bright light. A soldier calls out down the hall to no one.

"Who is in charge here?!" He yells. All the guards are dead, nobody answers. "Whoever is in charge, surrender now, and you will be spared." Again, no response. "Hand us Victor Bells, and you will leave here alive."

"Fuck you!" I yell back. "You want me, come, take me!" Anger rises in my throat, and for once, I wish Hades would come here and dismantle these pieces of shit. I check my ammo, as a long pause lingers in the air.

"Victor? Jah?" A soldier calls out. "Can you make it to us?"

I glance around the corner, confused. *Make it to us?*

"Victor, we've been sent to rescue you. Are there any guards alive?" He asks.

The rough spackling of the wall digs into my back as I peer down the hall, suspicious.

"Throw your gun down the hall and come out with your hands up," I order.

"Victor, we are *disciples*. DO. NOT. SHOOT!" He says. I blanch at the way he says it. A rifle is tossed down the hall, followed by a helmet. A young Proselyte man uneasily steps out from behind his cover, hands raised above his head. The cult's divine star symbol branded on his neck. He's not yet reborn, but he wears colored eye lenses and dyed his short, groomed hair brown, to mask his Oltish ethnicity. As if anything could make him look less beastly.

"Victor. Chosen soul. Please come out." He asks, his voice shaking. I launch out of the cell with my rifle trained on him. He steps back, hands shoved higher in the air, but eyes full of wonder. "Put the gun down, Jah. Please."

What the hell did he just call me?

The other soldiers step out from their cover, removing their helmets, and all toss their rifles over their shoulders. I lower my aim, and the men slowly approach. Their leader reaches out tentatively, as if he'll be burned by my skin, and touches my arm. His face bursts with life. He looks to the sky, eyes flooded with joyous tears.

"Witness the flesh." He whispers to himself. The others stare on in disturbing admiration, some reborn, some not.

His eyes close, and he lingers on my arm. I pull back awkwardly.

"Gwinnett DeMarco, starfallen, has sent us! We are honored to serve the chosen." The men all touch their brand, then their heart.

Gwinn?

"I don't understand?" I ask. "Why?"

"You'll understand when we get to the Valley," He says, ushering me by the arm. The Valley? *Fargo...* I yank my arm from his grasp.

"No!" I yell. "More destruction in my name? It won't happen. I am many things; a fugitive will not be one of them." Nothing of value waits for me outside these walls, anyway. Miku is gone. My world destroyed. For once in his life, Fargo can solve his own problems. "Failure must have consequences... and those consequences are here. I am exactly where I should be."

The Proselyte cranes his neck, confused.

"You can do no crime Jah, you are the chosen," He says.

"What the hell are you talking about?" I shake my head and begin to walk back to my destroyed cell, unsure of what will come next.

"You must come with us, Jah, tonight we save another starfallen."

I halt.

"What are you saying?"

The prisoner who was held across from my cell approaches from behind us.

"There is a plan to save the Princess, and it has already begun."

36

LEO

ABERNATHY

Hunted

Tanya's hair is clumped together in greasy, thick strands, a foul stench wafting off her. She fidgets anxiously, scratching nervously at her pasty skin. Dark needle marks line her left forearm and must continue up her torso because similar impressions are left on her neck. She self-consciously tucks the arm behind her when she catches me glancing at them. Her eyes avoid ours, either by choice or she's simply overcome by the jungle. I disregard the smell and give her a hug. She stands awkwardly, not returning the gesture. Her eyes dart uncomfortably through our group, swallowing painfully.

"Do you want some water?" I ask.

The others stare in disbelief at her.

She nods quietly. Riley removes the canteen from her pack and slowly approaches. Tanya's eyes finally rest on her. The two women stare at each other as if they were holograms. Not positive that they would actually feel the other if they reached out their hand. Riley extends the canteen, and Tanya takes a desperate pull from it, eyes remaining glued to each other. We stand awkwardly in silence.

Tanya finishes her swig and hands the canteen back to Riley. She begins to speak but stops herself.

"Tanya, what is going on?" I ask. She ignores me and speaks to Riley.

"Where have *you* been?" She says, her voice raspy and filled with contempt I don't understand.

Riley seems confused by the suddenness of the question as well.

"Me?"

"Yea, who else would I be talking to?"

Riley is taken aback.

"Excuse me?"

"What's it been? Five years?" Tanya asks, an odd harshness to her voice. "This where the Holt's been hidin' out this whole time?" She glances at me, rolling her eyes. "Oh... not you too, Captain Valenia? Say it ain't so? Was someone mean to you too? You poor things!" Sarcasm drips off her words, and her eyes narrow. "Where is your other half, Riley?"

"Tanya... do you need more water?" Her face is pale, sweat colors a dark ring around the collar of her shirt. She looks like she's about to pass out.

"Don't patronize me!" She snaps. Her legs stagger, eyes glossing over, and I rush to catch her.

"Whoa, easy."

"I don't need..." She shoves me off of her and passes out face-first into the weeds.

We've walked for hours in the unrelenting heat. Bryl has begun to fall behind with Tanya draped over his shoulders. I'd offer to help, but I don't think I could carry her very far. We couldn't use the sled idea that Riley proposed because we traverse through Forest too dense, having to remain concealed from Gaz search parties. He'll have to lug her a bit farther.

We can't yet see it, but the constant crash of Berban Falls whispers to us in the distance. A hushed rumble teasing our exhausted bodies with the promise of relief. We're close.

Riley leads, hacking at plants with the ax, carving us a narrow path ahead. Yara trails just behind, his gun primed and ready. Bugs nip at our necks and legs, heavy humidity weighing on us. We need to find this water soon.

Bryl groans behind me as Tanya comes to, squirming and demanding he put her down.

"Hey, hold up," I call to Yara and Riley ahead of me. I toss Bryl the canteen after he places her on the ground, and he sucks down the last of my water, catching his breath on a knee. Tanya sits leaning against a large plant stock, rubbing her head.

"What happened?" She asks from under her hands.

"You passed out," I say. "Got abandoned by that merchant, said some nasty stuff to us, then immediately fainted."

"Not ringing any bells?" Riley adds, arms crossed. Tanya glances up, embarrassed.

"Sorry..." She says. "Blame it on the heat." Riley kneels down beside her and offers her some water. The two exchange a delicate look. Tanya gratefully accepts the gesture and tilts the canteen back. Riley glances at Tanya's forearm, a sympathetic look on her face. She doesn't hide it this time. "Yea, not much has changed, as you can see."

I place the pack on the ground and pull a pouch of the dried Luta meat from within.

"Everyone take some." I ration out the meat to the seven of us, taking the moment to regain some energy. Tanya chews wildly on the meat like she hasn't eaten in days.

"Tanya..." She looks up at me. "What are you doing here?" She stops eating mid-chew, her face falling bleak.

"You don't know?" She asks.

"Know what?" I ask. "My crew and I have been here for days. And Riley has... well, you know." Riley's face is flush with remorse. Tanya scans our caravan of people, searching for someone.

"Is Remmy not with you?"

I instinctively take Riley's hand. She doesn't fight it.

Her lips scrunch as she tries to hold off tears.

"Remmy is dead..." She says. Reflective, bittersweet eyes peer at me, clearly thankful for my help during this time, but no doubt still troubled with my role in his death. Tanya's face pales.

"That's terrible," She says. Riley glances at Yara, then changes the subject as she wipes the wetness from her eyes.

"So, what the hell is going? What are you doing here?" She asks. Tanya's voice becomes frail, the words barely escape her lips.

"Miku has been kidnapped..."

"What?!"

"I snuck out of the lab and was heading to help the others get her back, but I would've never made it all the way across Su Hoz. The High Council would've caught me. So, I had to come through Berban, it was my only option."

"Are you serious? Do they know by who?" I ask.

"The Vipers..." She says. My heart drops.

Yara rushes to us when he hears the news, but before he can say anything, a throaty growl trembles from within the deep brush.

"What was that?!"

We freeze in fear. Fallen branches and plant stocks crack and snap. Another growl echoes from the other side. Beasts hunt.

We all silently scramble to our feet, crouched. Riley hands the ax to Bryl as she arms herself with her rifle. Yara stands ready with his gun, and I grab a large tree limb to use as a club. Movements haunt us in all directions. Something circles. Riley's Ko, Jabo, scurries up to a treetop in fear.

A flash darts through our open path and vanishes back into the brush, all I could make out was a golden yellow tail lined with spikes.

"What was that?" I whisper. Riley saw it too; her face tells me all I need to know. Trouble.

"Jymira..." Riley calls to me in a hushed voice, eyes locked on the lurking noises.

"Leo, in the left pocket of my pack, there should be a green canister with a screw cap. I need it now!"

I hurry to open the pocket.

"It's empty."

"The canister?"

"The pocket."

"Oh shit, are you serious?" She quickly darts a glance into the empty pocket. "No..."

"What was it?" I ask.

"Trogaro pheromone spray. Trogaro's favorite meal... Jymira's. It's how Remmy and I kept these monsters away for so long."

"What do we do without it?"

Her expression worries me, fear etched in the creases of her brow.

Golden eyes flash through the cracks of the weeds, stalking us. How many are there? Four? Five? More? Small, compact machines of violence. Hardly bigger than Jabo, the agile varmint hunt in packs, armed with razor-sharp claws on their three legs, teeth, and a tail studded with needle-like pricks. They're shattered glass covered in fur. Death by a thousand blows.

The Forest rustles all around us, the pack of Jymira

closing in methodically.

Suddenly, a spiked tail launches from the brush and swipes at Tanya, just missing. I slam my club blindly into the weeds, hitting nothing but plants. The predators toy with us. Stabbing and hissing. My pulse crashes against my arteries. I don't blink.

They've stopped moving.

Silence fills the air.

We stand in a narrow pass carved by ax, prey snared in the hunter's trap. It's so quiet. I can hear the subtle tremor of Berban Falls again. My spit struggles down the constricted tunnel of my throat. Breath sharp. Our path is no more than three bodies wide. Riley stands guard to my right, the farthest in front, Tanya just behind her. I stand with my back to Patawa facing the brush, tightly wedged between Yara, who guards Spri. Bryl trails in back, watching down the path to my left. It seems an eternity since anyone has moved, but I know it's only been minutes.

Then finally... chaos.

A bolt of golden fur launches from the brush. My reflexes are all that save me. I bash the Jymira across the face and send it flying back into the thicket. Another vaults from a tree branch high above to my left. Yara spins and shoots it in midair. It shrieks and scurries back into the weeds. Two more scream from the weeds farther back down the trail, overtaking Bryl. Their claws dig into his shoulder. He roars in pain as he fights them off. Ax swinging with reckless abandon. Two more attack from my right, at the front, where Riley has yet to carve. She tries to shoot, but they're too quick. The butt of her rifle clubs at one but the other is on her. Tail piercing into her calf over and over. Blood drenching her leg. Oozing into her shoe.

"Riley!" I scream.

Tanya sprints and tackles it off of her. She tries to pin it to the ground, but its barbed tail jabs into her shoulder. She buckles but doesn't yelp. No stranger to needles. I run to help, punting the screeching beast away. It spills back into the brush. Spri screams in agony behind me. I snap around, and three Jymira tear at him, Patawa trying her best to get them off. He helplessly cowers, their claws and teeth shredding into his skin. I dive to help, scooping all three beasts off him, squeezing them to my chest as we roll over Spri and nearly on top of Bryl. I'm so close to him I can feel the swoosh of his ax speed over my head as he fends off another swarm. Their tails puncture my chest and arms as we roll. Like diving onto a bed of nails. My momentum stops, waist tangled in the brush, and one of the Jymira skids off me. Patawa grunts and smashes it with a huge rock. Yellow, viscous fluid erupting from the body. The other Jymira hiss in anger as one their own dies. They shriek in unison. Rage intensifying. I throw the other two off me in a panic, razor-sharp limbs skewering my chest as they go. I don't see where they land. Claws and teeth and tails gash at us all.

My family is screaming.

I'm shell shocked. Blood pouring from the dozens of holes pierced into my chest as I stand. I look down. My shirt drenched a dark red. Mind numb. An evil golden swarm rips through every member of our party, but me. Someone cries my name, but I don't know who. My legs buckle. Vision spots. Hearing muddled. Then, like a flying golden demon, a Jymira soars through the air from the other side of the brush in slow motion, his trajectory aimed right for my face. My arms fail me and do nothing. I watch the beast speed toward me, unable to move. But just before the creature's claws spear into me, a violent concussion reverberates through my skull, and I watch the predator's head explode into a yellow mist as its corpse hits me in the chest with a thud and falls to the ground dead. Yara's pistol smokes from where he lies on the ground. Two Jymira continue to endlessly rip at him. My ear sears with pain. Scalding, stomach-wrenching agony. I reach up and feel a wet stump where it used to be. The pain slams me back to reality.

To my left, Bryl is still battling two. He's losing. One is clamped down on his bottom right arm. I snatch it off him, a chunk of Bryl meat coming with it. Its tail swings up, sticking me in the cheek. Pain racks through my body. Blood spilling into my mouth. I stumble, delirious in pain but gather myself enough to snap its neck. Bryl hacks off the other's tail. It shrieks and screeches until the ax meets its head and the beast is silenced. Bryl collapses, exhausted, face coated in a horrifying blend of red and yellow blood.

"Bryl!" I yell. I reach a hand out and yank him up. "Let's go!" We stagger back to the others, helping Spri first, who isn't moving. The two Jymira I stripped from him earlier, returning to finish what they started. Riley fights hers off at the end of the path and fires a round at Yara. The Jymira chewing at Yara's cords is slugged in the torso and is thrown down the path toward us, dead. I stomp on one attacking Spri, crippling it. Riley swings her rifle at the other, crushing its head against a tiny tree stump in the middle of the path. I pick my club back up and heave it at the beast attacking Patawa. Tree bark and violent fur become one. Knocking the predator to the ground. Pat scrambles away behind Bryl, holding her arm, and Riley fires at it. Missed. I drag Spri to safety down trail. Then I hear Tanya cry out in pain just next to Yara, as a Jymira claws at her back. Riley swings her rifle and knocks it off her. Tears flood Tanya's eyes. Riley steps on its tail, pinning it down.

"Bryl! AXE!" She shouts over her left shoulder. She screams as the beast bites into her thigh. Bryl tosses the ax to her, and she hacks the Jymira in half. I flinch at a fired shot and see Yara throwing his last enemy off of him.

We all turn to face the last Jymira that was attacking Patawa. Its back pinned against the brush on the left side of the pathway, our backs to the right. Outnumbered and without its pack, the beast slowly retreats. Riley aims and shoots at it, but just as she does, it darts away into the brush and flees.

I crumble to the ground.

My world is a dizzy dream, blood oozing from my mouth as I tilt my head. My chest rings in agony. Ear missing. Our group groans like wounded soldiers lying scattered along a war-torn frontline. Blood is everywhere. I nudge Spri.

"Spri..." I say, spitting blood every few seconds, utterly exhausted. "Spri..." I nudge him again. "Come on, buddy. I need ya. Come on!" I shove him harder this time, yelling. "SPRI! Wake up!" I roll to Patawa. "Pat..." She trudges to us, covered with gashes and holes over her arms and left side. "Pat..." My voice is weak, flooded with delirious panic, overwhelmed. "He's... Pat..." My eyes flutter.

"Leo, I got it..." She manages. She tends to Spri as a horrible thought jolts me back awake. Riley!

I hurry up the trail to her with all the energy I have left.

"Tell me you're ok?!" I beg, my hand cupping her cheek. Blood smears across her face from my thumb. Her eyes overflow with tears, traumatized. Mine are too. I rest my forehead on hers and close my eyes, the life left in me clinging to this moment.

Her hands rest gently around my neck. I meet one and hold mine against hers. Neither of us can let go. Infused into each other's soul. Hanging onto life by a shred, it's the closest I've ever felt to someone. I look into her eyes and know she feels it too.

"Are you hurt, child?" I hear Yara ask Tanya. His shirt mangled, many of his cords shredded to pieces, lying scattered along the ground. But he kneels by her, ignoring his own wounds to tend to hers.

Bryl crawls to Pat.

He helps her rip a chunk of her shirt to use as a tourniquet, and she desperately wraps it tight around Spri's left arm. She leans all her weight onto a rag she's pressed to his neck. Blood pools heavily under him. I hurry back.

"He's ok right?" I say, praying more than asking. Pat glances warily to me. She double-takes at my shirt, soaked completely through now. "Bryl, hold this as tight as you can." She passes the rag to him. "Leo, take your shirt off now!" I pull the blood-drenched shirt over my head, nausea growing in stomach. She covers her mouth, balking at the damage. "Leo..."

"Bad?" I say, the world around me spinning.

My chest is peppered with dozens of pin-sized holes, blood bubbling and oozing its way down my trunk. A small notch is punched clean through my cheek, and the bottom of my ear dangles from one frayed tendon. Misery chews at me.

Jabo squawks continuously from a tree limb. He throws something from the branch and hits Riley.

"What do you want?!" She barks.

Jabo hops up and down madly, squawking and pointing to our east. He throws another stick at her.

"What?!"

Jabo points empathetically over and over, shrieking.

Riley groans and climbs to her feet, holding herself up with a tree branch.

"What the hell are you pointing at?"

She trudges down the path, hacking her way through meters of jungle.

"Ri... where are you going?" I ask, my world melting.

She disappears down trail for a moment to investigate.

Patawa tries her best to tend to all my wounds, but she's running low on resources. Her eyes nervously catalog my injuries. Yara gently helps Tanya to her feet. Both spattered with lacerations. Bryl hangs over Spri, face in ruin, pleading our brother to make it through. I crawl to his side, Patawa demanding I stop. We put our arms around each other, Bryl's face a shade I've never seen. Patawa joins us, tears welting in her eyes. The three of us sit embraced together as we watch the life drain from a member of our family. Bryl's tough exterior cracks, laying his head on Spri's chest, ribcage bucking with sobs. Patawa wipes her eyes and checks. And in one fading moment, our zany, curious, beautifully wild minded friend is gone.

Sorrow sinks my heart.

Another loved one, dead because of me.

My mourning lasts only but a moment before it's cut off by Riley's shouts.

"RUN!" She screams from within the brush. She reappears in the trail, dragging her leg behind her as she runs frantically. "GAZ! RUN!"

We scramble our tattered bodies to their feet. Moving slowly like in waist-high mud. I corral the pack, swinging it over my shoulder. My body begs me to put it down. Riley doesn't stop as she hacks us a clear path ahead. Tanya and Yara follow.

"What about Spri!" Bryl yells. I turn back to look at my deceased friend. Blood soaked through every fiber of the thin man's body.

"Grab him." Bryl tries but can't; his injuries too severe. He stares up at me, desperate.

"Boss, we can't leave him!" I glance back to the others, and they hurry through the weeds.

"Shit... Here switch." I hurry to toss the pack off my shoulders, and Bryl slings it over his back, wincing in pain. I take a deep breath, my legs shaking, jaw clenched. This is going to hurt. I bend and pick Spri up, draping him over my shoulders. I scream in agony. Pain searing my mind. Blood pushes through the makeshift bandages Patawa applied on my chest. "Let's move!" I yell through clenched teeth.

Bryl and Patawa help each other weave through the new trail Riley has carved. I follow behind as quickly as I can, torture in every step. It's hard to keep up, blood loss fogging my consciousness. I stumble over a vine, Spri's body thrown from my shoulders as I spill to the ground.

"Leo!" Patawa cries. She hurries back to me, helping me to my feet. I bit through my lip as I hit the ground. I try to pick Spri back up, but I no longer have the strength, buckling under his weight. I try again but don't even get him to my shoulders. Exhaustion sucks at my lungs. Riley has backtracked to us, yelling.

"Hurry!" She yells. I stare apologetically to Bryl. I can't carry him. His expression melts my heart. "Leo!" She yells again.

"Boss... please..."

I try once more but to no avail. Tears spill from my eyes as I look at him.

"I can't..."

I begin to move again, but before I do, Yara slides in from behind Riley and scoops him up over his shoulders. I stare at him with infinite gratitude.

"Thank you..."

"Children. RUN!" Yara takes off again, his wounds somehow not affecting his speed.

We push ahead, legs beginning to fail us. We breach through the brush and onto a wide path. I turn to see an army of Gaz warriors charging with menace. The fear sparks adrenaline into my body, masking the pain.

We sprint as fast as we can. The charging forces gaining on us. A thrown war staff slams into the ground next to me, just barely missing. Just beyond the break of the trees, a pool glows in the sun, crashing water spilling from massive jagged rock. Berban Falls.

"The Falls, hurry!" Riley points. We run, harder and harder. My heart straining. The Gaz so close I can hear the stampeding behind me.

"*Cho'wa!*" One yells. I glance back, eyes bouncing as I run. A'gorr leads their charge, a slew of Precursors outpacing the other Gaz warriors. Another staff slams into the ground in front of me, and I nearly fall trying to avoid it. The water is close.

"Where do we go!" Tanya yells.

"Under the falls," Riley yells back.

"Under?"

"Just follow me." She hits the water first, diving in like an arrow. Then Tanya, Yara, Bryl, and Pat. I still lag behind. My feet dig into the soft soil, and I launch myself from the ledge and into the water.

Red clouds of blood patch across the water. I swim frantically, chest screaming in pain. The water burning my ear and mouth. Huge splashes thump behind me as Gaz barrel into the pool. I turn back to watch them struggle to keep their massive bodies afloat. We begin to pull away, the Gaz unable to swim. A'gorr stands atop the cliff, watching the streaks of red-coated trespassers escape once again. Gaz bodies begin to sink to the bottom, their allies desperately trying to save them. I turn back around and push myself forward to join the others. Where are we going?

The roar of the falls is deafening as we approach. It's power unrivaled. The cloud of mist from the crashing water blocks out the surrounding world. We convene in the hidden fog, the rest of my group treading water, waiting for me. Riley yells at the top of her lungs, but she's still hard to hear.

"FOLLOW ME AND TAKE THE BIGGEST BREATH YOU CAN!"

We all suck in as much air as we can and dive under with her. The volume of the Falls mutes under the water to a low rumble. Riley dives deep, avoiding the swirling underbelly of the falls. We follow behind, Bryl struggling to keep up. Yara somehow drags Spri's lifeless body with him as he plunges. We go under the raging riptide and push our way to the surface on the other side. I gasp for air as I burst to the surface. Lungs wheezing.

Coughs racking against my chest.

"Oh my God..."

Behind the Falls is a tremendous hollow cavern, the water diving off a massive arcing sheet of rock impossibly high above our heads, that extends hundreds of meters out. The water breaks over every inch of the arc, concealing a small island behind the curved wall of water. Some form of war-era stone outpost sits atop it. It's hard to see, the sunlight dulled in here. The surrounding cavern's dense rock curves its way around the island connecting to the falls on either side, insulating us in a pocket of stone and crashing river.

Yara is already ashore, disappearing inside the outpost for a moment as I plod through the water, my limbs hardly working. There's a bright spark, then blue light ignites along a basin against the outpost wall, wrapping around the hexagon-patterned building, until it reaches the opposite side of the door. What is this place? I finally reach shallow water and try to stand, but all I can muster is climbing to a knee. I collapse. The adrenaline washes away, a flood of pain gushes in behind it.

Pruned hands drag me ashore. Curtains of darkness pulsing in my vision. Riley and I lay entangled along the sand. Exhaustion beyond control. She moans something, but I can't hear it. The roaring of the Falls pounds against my ears, and it's the last sound I can make out before everything around me vanishes, and I go limp.

37

RILEY HOLT

The Second Truth

The fire crackles gently, plumes of smoke filtering up the primitive chimney. Its light dances off the stone walls of the outpost, twinkling in dour eyes. Our battered group lays defeated in a circle around the blaze, entranced by its memorizing pull. There is something majestic about fire. Hypnotic. As if staring into its flickering tongues transports you to a realm beyond ours. One where life isn't so gratuitously removed from existence. And there is no pain, no heartache, no grief. Just a sound wholeness. Like the warmth of the flames can seal shut the fractured foundation of your soul. And the deeper into the fire you give yourself, the clearer that world becomes.

But *my* world is far from that place. And no fire will be able to take me away from it tonight.

Leo lies unconscious on a cot to my left, his body is nearly mummified by the amount of gauze and bandages Patawa applied. The fire illuminates one side of his face, a bloodied patch covers his cheek. He looks peaceful as he lays there, but I know a storm of pain surges under his serenity. Not physical pain, though, I'm sure there is plenty. But emotional pain. I know it because it's the same storm inside me. The swirling, drowning flood of sorrow. Of loss. And of guilt. I stare at the outline of Spri's body under the cloth we've draped over him and understand the devastation of family lost.

It's a hollowness.

A void with only one shape that fills it, and that shape no longer exists. But when I felt Leo's hands against my cheeks and his breath against mine, I understood that though some voids may never be filled, it does not mean you will never be whole again. Because at that moment, I felt it. Felt the spark of life I thought extinguished forever the moment Remmy died. Felt the engines of my soul begin to churn once again, beckoning me to that feeling. Urging me to embrace its energy. For I know the sensation of love, but I have never felt *that*. I've known love for a brother. And love for a father. And for a time, love for a sister, yet that ember has begun to cough its last breaths. But this was a different burn. One with intensity and vigor. I felt it radiating off him, words not spoken, but still understood. Processed in a different section of my heart. One unexplored and foreign. One not reserved for family, not for Remmy, or Emoss, or even in some odd manner Gwinn. But someone else. For a bond I thought I may never experience again. A bond I thought I destroyed the moment I left for the Forest. Love in the form I barely recognize anymore.

But could I possibly still love a man I haven't seen in five years? Could he? Could the feelings of two naïve teenagers be something more than delusional fairytales? Something with weight? Something that could stand the test of time? Something that could survive an absence of such magnitude?

The night under the stars, he told me he still loves Gwinn. But I know what I felt between us. His eyes. His smile. The way his fingers lingered between mine. Love is spoken through the body, not the lips.

Memories of my life roll through my mind as I watch him sleep. He will never replace the hole in my heart Remmy left behind, but I realize now, that's not where he belongs anyway. He belongs in this new, mysterious chasm of my heart I've never quite understood. Not until now, at least.

It's quiet in the outpost. No one speaks. The gravity of the past days weighing on us like the massive snowdrifts of the Valley, caving in the weak tenement roofs and burying everyone underneath. Wet, blood-stained clothes hang draped over a bench in front of the fire, drying. We tried to rinse out as much blood as possible, but some of the garments will be stained forever. Now, we wear a random assortment of time-worn military garbs we found scattered throughout trunks along the bunks of the barracks, their rough material scratching at my skin, but at least they're dry. Tanya was lucky enough to find an oversized animal pelt in one; she has it wrapped tightly around her shivering body across the fire from me. Her face has trauma cursed across it. I don't know the last time she's blinked. But at least she's had a chance to wash the sweat and mud and filth from her hair in the outpost's cleansing room.

Patawa's head is nuzzled into the chest of Bryl, our dear friend, lying cold on the floor next to them. Sadness settled deep within their eyes. Yara is the only one who doesn't sit by the fire. He stands behind me against the far wall, staring at the Falls through the open window port.

It's a lonely experience, even though we all surround each other. Each of us sinks from a separate devastating loss we all assume no one else could appreciate. Though we all can. I see it written on all of their faces. The same depression I thought no one else could possibly ever fathom, present in each of their eyes. If Remmy were here, he would find a way to bring us together. Create the pillars of support needed to slog our way through this swamp of sadness. Leo could do it too. But all they have right now is me. And even though I'm trying to be better, I'm not them.

"Spri was a gem," I say. Everyone's eyes draw to me, the sound of words welcomed. "I know he never meant to, but he always made me laugh."

Bryl smiles in agreement but can't maintain my gaze. He looks back into the fire.

"Spri was *one of a kind*, that's for sure." He glances down at Patawa with warm eyes. I miss that look. Remmy would give me the same look, many a night, as we were curled up under the canopy of the Forest. "Did you know he was convinced he could speak Surg?" He asks with a chuckle.

Patawa rests her head on Bryl's shoulder, wiping at her eyes, smiling in remembrance.

"I'm going to miss the little maniac," She says. "Funny part is... I honestly don't know if he liked us. He once described Leo as an *unobjectionable companion*."

A genuine smile creases from my lips for the first time in days. Bryl and Pat snicker with one another. "Leo didn't know how to react. It was amazing!"

The laughter of the moment fades, and we're left back in the ugly silence.

I don't know how to diffuse the awkwardness.

"Tanya..." I search for something to say, but she cuts me

354

off before I can find it. Her eyes are harsh, the lighthearted moment from before doing nothing to thin her pain.

"Not really in a small talk mood there, *Ri*." She groans sarcastically and wraps the animal pelt tighter to her chest.

"What is your problem?!" I don't understand why she constantly has an attitude with me.

She glares at me. "Excuse me?"

"You've been at my throat since the moment we found you. What is your deal?"

"My deal? Riley, you abandoned me." She snaps. "You abandoned us! We were a family... all of us. Together. Until you and Remmy ruined it."

Her face streaks with red splotches, Patawa and Bryl sitting idly by, not knowing how to react. The words punch me in the gut as she continues plowing into me.

"We weren't the Eight after you left. Gwinn imploded without you two. Then, we were down to five. You broke Leo's heart." I wince, and glance to Patawa whose somber eyes confirm it's true. "He became obsessed with his studies and started clinging to the unraveling Gwinn. Then, we were down to four. You can guess what the fuck happened to Fargo without enough of us around to babysit him. He started hanging out in the Valley and got mixed up with the Vipers. Three left. Victor didn't have his support cast around him, and his anger issues exploded. Two remaining. And Miku did her best to visit, but she still had a life to live. Which leaves just me. By myself. For years. Alone. Trapped. Scared. Miserable. Hopeless... and I haven't even told you the worst part. It was all a fucking lie. My entire life, a lie."

Tears begin to overwhelm her eyes. What does she mean a lie?

"Do you know how hard it was to have *nobody*..." Her anger fades, dissolving into a distant, forlorn gaze. "Riley, I had *nobody... no one.*" Her lips tremble. "You broke everything..." Tears stream down her cheek until they dampen her fur pelt. She looks up at me, her eyes, desperate and exhausted. "Do you even care?"

The question shatters my heart. She's right. All of it. I didn't understand until seeing them again, but I left a wake in my path the night I decided to flee Archler House. And those rocky tides have crashed down on every member of our group. But how do you apologize for the mistakes of a child? Is it possible to mend the pain of half a decade? I don't know... but I have to try.

"Tanya... of course I do."

The ceiling is grey and drab and splintered with cracks. I can't sleep. The betrayal on Tanya's face is impossible to wipe away. It's seared into my mind like a brand against the hide of a Nuvu. The metal supports of my bunk dig into my bank, creaking with the slightest movement. They remind me of the orphanage. Those horrible beds, in that horrible place.

I climb from my cot and jump down to the floor, the stone, ice-cold on the pads of my feet. I tiptoe through the barracks. Past ill-formed bunk beds and simple latch and hook trunks. Past a closet filled with war-era guns. And through the doors and back into the common grounds where the firepit's ashes sizzle for the last time. Yara is exactly where I expected him to be, still standing by the window port. He hasn't moved in hours.

"I don't believe I've ever seen you sleep," I say. He doesn't turn as he answers me.

"A sleep far longer than one turn of the moon awaits me soon. I choose not to run towards it." His words are silky and clear. When he has his wits about him, the man can seem quite dignified. But no matter how elegant his cadence is, I know what awaits me in due time. I will always see the unstable man who took my brother from me, that will never change.

"Tanya is correct, you know." He peers out one eye down to me. "You should have never come to this place."

I join him at the window, the Falls glowing against the moonlight.

"I'm beginning to understand that," I say.

Despite it all though, I did learn to love the Forest. I was not built for the bright lights of the Dwual Fir or the tidy walls of Celestial City. I was born to live free. Among the plants and the stars and the trees. Yet if never coming here means Remmy is never killed and our group doesn't break apart and the string of despair we've encountered never happens, then of course I would change it. But if not... I can't say I wouldn't do it again.

"But not for the reasons she gave," He says. I glance at him, puzzled. "Your purpose is elsewhere. That is why you should not have come here." Yara pulls some form of trinket or vial from his pocket. Orange luminescent fluid glows inside the clear spokes of the vial's ladder-shaped design. Yara weaves his cords through these spokes as he admires the Ancient symbols etched along the diamond formation at its bottom. He presses the vial into my hand and gazes into my eyes like he's entrusting me with the key to the universe. "You need to give this to Leo. He will rise soon, and when he does, and I've determined he's safe, I must go help the other Child in need."

A soft warmth pulsates from the vial. Breathing life back into my palms.

"What is this?"

"The Children's purpose."

"And what exactly is that?"

He pulls his eyes back away from me and into the Falls.

"I do not know. I only know it is the end of the path that Emoss set you Children upon many years ago. Your destiny. An answer."

"An answer to what?"

"I cannot know. Only the Children may." Even in his rational states, his cryptic nature is exhausting.

"Yara, none of that makes sense."

He purrs.

"Child, you will learn one day not to fear ignorance. I am glad my Master sheltered me from the secrets of which I need not know. For now, I do not have to lie to you, nor am I in danger. I can perform the oath I made to him without the burden of knowledge that does not belong to me—"

"Hold on..." I say, squeezing the bridge of my nose between my fingers. What the hell is he talking about? I can't tell if I'm wasting my time with the ramblings of an insane man or just don't have enough information to comprehend what he's trying to say. "Yara, I want to understand what you're saying, but you're not making any sense. You say we are supposed to know what to do with this, but I have no clue what this is?"

"Leo will."

I shake my head.

"How am I supposed to believe any of this, Yara? You hand me something, tell me it's important, yet you have no idea what it is. And earlier, you told me Emoss didn't get sick. Well, I was there for that. I saw him with my own eyes. He melted away just like everyone else who contracts the Rotting. I was there! By his Med Bed as he was pronounced dead. So that was clearly wrong... why is this any different?"

My heart races as I begin to grow frustrated with him.

Those memories will never fade. How could he possibly try to convince me otherwise?

Something about his demeanor shifts. A discomfort settling within him.

"Your eyes did not deceive you, Child, but you still do not understand..." He fiddles with the collar on his surcoat, eyes darting, the edges of his cords beginning to squirm in angst.

"Master learned the truth, yet he was not supposed to. This truth was so dangerous, he knew one day it would cost him his life. It is why he set you all upon this path and asked me to protect you. And when the keepers of the truth discovered he planned on telling the Children, my Master was silenced. Emoss did not contract the Rotting... he was given it."

My heart grinds against my chest.

"What are you saying..."

"The High Council built the Rotting and unleashed it on their own people. That is the truth they killed him to protect."

My mind spasms. It's unfathomable.

"That can't be true..." I say.

Tanya's voice startles me from behind.

"It is."

I turn and watch her creep from the bunk room with the animal fur still wrapped around her. She meets my eyes with an apologetic gaze.

"Qwillow told me before I escaped. She's the one who gave me that vial." She points to the device in my hand. "The fluid inside is called Bytrol, and what it's capable of... is terrifying."

The orange fluid gleams with mystery. I meet it with reservation.

"They create strands of the Rotting from the Bytrol. And they build the Bytrol from me... that's why I was never allowed to leave the lab. I wasn't the cure; I was the supply."

Our group closes in as secrets beyond comprehension are revealed. Whatever I say won't be enough to express my sympathy for her, so I just let her keep talking.

"I planned on using it to bargain for Miku's freedom, but Yara insisted Leo needed it more. Said he'd come with me to ensure we got her back in exchange."

A hand caresses my shoulder, and I turn to see Leo's tender smile. *He's awake!* My arms are wrapping him in a hug before I can blink. We pull apart, and he runs his thumb along my cheek, our eyes fused to one another. He pulls my head into his chest as I hand him the vial, and he turns his attention to Tanya.

"No wonder I wasn't allowed in Su Hoz... they knew if I could study you, I'd figure it out," Leo says. "I'm so sorry, Tanya." She simply nods, the damage already done. What else can be said?

Leo is mesmerized by the vial. I can feel his heart drumming through his bandages as he marvels at it.

"There's a small observatory in the Vault with a slot shaped just like this. It has to be what Emoss wanted us to find... but do you know what it does?" He asks Yara. Yara shakes his head.

"All that I know is that Emoss had something he needed to show the Children. Something he claimed would change their lives forever. But he feared the High Council would kill him to protect the truth of the Rotting before he could do so." We share an apprehensive look, each word casting an ominous cloud over the room.

"What you hold is the key to a secret he kept from *them!* The key to what he needed the Children to find in the Vault. And whatever it is, it extends beyond the scope of the Rotting and exposing the High Council for their crimes. I do not know what it is. That is yours to discover. But I know the High Council is incredulous to this secret. They still believe the Vault to be connected to the Rotting. And that Emoss was going to somehow use it to expose them. None of that is true. That was a convenient cover he used to hide the true purpose of the Vault. The purpose meant for you all."

Yara strides past us to an outdated weapons rack and pulls two of the war-era railcannons off the wall. He checks the chamber of his and hands the other to Tanya.

"Another Child is in danger. My first oath is to protect the Children, *then* to get them to the Vault. You are awake and no longer need my protection. You know the way from here, so, go, fulfill your destiny, discover what Emoss died to preserve for you. I must go help the other Child in need."

Leo, Pat, Bryl and I don't move. So much to digest in such a short time.

Tanya hustles through the outpost, gathering supplies, readying to leave. She hugs everyone goodbye and eventually reaches me.

"I'm sorry for earlier..." She says, having a hard time looking at me. She pulls me into a soft hug. My mind still rattles with all the information Yara dumped onto us, but it's nice to feel her forgiveness. I needed it more than I realized.

"Go get Miku back," I say. We share a strained smile, and

she turns to leave.

But as her and Yara head out the door, what keeps crawling through my mind is the fact that the High Council killed my father.

"Wait," I say. The pieces of a horrific puzzle beginning to fit together. "Trakstull killed Emoss?"

Yara stops at the door and stares back grimly.

"The Regal *orders* deaths, those closest to him carry them out."

Those closest to him?...

My heart sinks. Eyes spreading wide.

"... it can't be."

Yara's eyes narrow as he can tell where my mind is heading.

"...Yes, Child... It was Russa."

38

FARGO SHEPHERD

Split Souled

Pyra is a demiGod.
He must be.
I refuse to believe someone of this magnitude can consist of mortal binds. He is simply ominous. A monumental being, a statue not built of stone and metal, but massive bone and muscle wrapped in weathered skin. He towers over me, the ridge of his jaw impossibly wide. His hands looking as if they could crush my skull whenever he pleased. Violent tattoos stream down his bare arms, depicting gruesome battles for control of the afterlife. I begin to believe he very well may *actually* be immortal. How did Victor ever manage to dismantle this... deity?

I shudder.

I don't know which is more terrifying, the man himself or the fact that even this titan could not stop Hades...

He runs his massive fingers along the cold metal of the Berserker suit mounted in front of him, eyes as if he stares at an old friend he hasn't seen in some time. On the third level of my headquarters, three other Warlord suits sit stationed in mounts next to him. A Phoenix, a Scorcher, and a

Banshee. Pyra admires them, pacing slowly until he reaches the Banshee suit. Something about him sours. He gathers the helm in his hand and unclicks it from the torso. He peers coldly into the dark visor, no sentiment to his gaze. I can see his hands tense as he squeezes the metal with vice-like force. Is it... bending? I swallow harshly. No, just my mind playing tricks on me. An angry father being reminded of the legacy of his offspring. He catches me looking at him and immediately tightens his jaw. I snap my head away, terrified.

A hand on my shoulder startles me.

I turn and am greeted by Geeva's candy green eyes. A sight desperately needed.

"On edge?" She says.

"You're not?" I say, unable to keep myself from glancing continuously at Pyra. "This is so fucked."

"Yea, it is. And whose fault is that?" She asks with a cocked brow. Mine obviously...

"Are you positive you're good to go?" I ask. She rolls her eyes.

"I'm not the one we have to worry about Fargo, you know that." But I do worry about her. "If you think I'm leaving you alone with Thing One and Thing Two, you're crazy. We need to get this over with as quickly as possible, I don't trust either of 'em." She cautiously inspects Pyra. "I don't trust men with nothing to lose." She begins toward the suits, but I grab her by the arm.

"Hey..." My words fumble along my lips. "I wanted to say... to tell you... I'm sorry." The apology spills out awkwardly.

"Sorry? For all this?" She gestures all around us.

"For everything..." I say. She smiles faintly.

"Fargo." She clasps my hand with hers, running her other along the back of my neck. "Do you think I've stuck around for so long because I just *love* the Valley?" I stare expressionless at her. "If you don't think I knew a day like this would eventually come, you are not as smart as I gave you credit for. We've taunted fate so many times, I'm surprised it's taken this long to catch up to us." She leans in and kisses me gently on the lips, whispering just inches from my face. "There is nothing you've done that I'm not at fault for too. I'm with you to the end... no matter what."

Geeva pulls away and joins Pyra near the Warlord suits, leaving my heart cringing. I don't deserve devotion that strong. I turn to begin down the stairs, and Cyto stands planted on the last step, staring at me. His face isn't one of surprise or anger, though. He simply stands there. Gaze fixed on me, eyes speaking for him. They say *you better protect my daughter.* Geeva may have chosen to share the burden of responsibility with me, but Cyto certainly does not.

The low rumble of a rig's engine note plays above us. I stare up through the ceiling window into the pitch-black sky and see blue blinking lights alternating on either side of a bulky silhouette. The pounding of boots on the roof echo as people spill from the hovering craft. *He's here.*

The rig's engine drowns away as it leaves, and all that's left is a small symphony of footsteps as they approach the roof hatch. How many are there? There are far more than I anticipated...

Gwinn and Russa join Zina, Pyra, Cyto, and me on the third story. Gwinn walks ahead to greet her cavalry. The roof hatch opens, and the first person through is something from a nightmare. More ghoulish men spill down the stairs behind him, and I have to get closer to ensure my eyes see clearly. Proselytes... As if there weren't enough psychos in the building.

Russa purrs as he sees the fanatical men descend the narrow staircase. He hurries to Gwinn, protesting into her ear, but she dismisses him. Then finally, as the last Proselyte soldier empties from the hatch, Victor appears.

His eyes meet mine immediately, dominating every part of me. My chest tightens when I see his restraints. The last Proselyte soldier guides him down the stairs carefully, a metal chain attached to a harness around his chest. A muzzle is clamped across his mouth. Oh no...

The only reborn not in full military armor leads the way.

"Abraham, I presume?" Gwinn asks. Her lips curl in disgust as he approaches. "Good to put a... face, to a name."

He touches a brand along his neck, then his heart as he reaches Gwinn. The others follow suit. She scoffs at the gesture.

"What the hell is this about?" She says, pointing to Victor, or should I say Hades. The reborn glances back as his squadron finally makes it down to our level.

"The starfallen had become an endangerment to himself. We've... temporarily restrained him for his protection." Victor's brow is pointed, and I know his mouth snarls behind the muzzle.

"Well, get him out of that. Now!" She orders. I interject quickly.

"Wait, not yet... Gwinn, a word." She glances at me, annoyed.

"What is it?"

"Remember when I told you Victor wasn't in the right, *state of mind*, to pull this off." I gesture to him with my head. "This is what I was referring to."

She cocks her back to inspect him.

"What? Is he suicidal or something?" Gwinn asks. "Join the fucking club. We don't have time for this."

I scratch my neck.

"Not exactly..." I search for the best way to put it. "Victor is... sick. He can't control his anger." She stares at me as if I'm wasting her time. I'm not.

"I don't give a shit about his temper; we're wasting time, Fargo." She shakes her head at me, then yells over her shoulder. "Unhook him."

"Don't!" I yell. The Proselytes freeze, unsure of what to do. She snaps her head back to me, aggravated.

"Fargo, do you want to die? We have to move now before it's daylight."

"You don't understand..." I glance apologetically to Victor as I have no choice but to reveal his secrets. "Victor is not Victor right now. His Warlord name, Hades... that's not just a name. It's an entirely different person."

"What the hell are you talking about, Fargo?"

I hang my head, not wanting to speak the words aloud, but I must. Russa watches on in horror as if he knows what's about to come from my mouth.

"Victor is—"

"*Split Souled.*" Pyra finishes. I stare in amazement at him. He strides, stopping just in front of Victor, peering into his eyes over the Proselyte soldiers uneasily shielding him, in such a way that I am convinced an explanation that has eluded him for years has finally been revealed. Gwinn is skeptical.

"Split Souled isn't real. Everyone knows that. That's nothing but a fabricated High Council myth to make the world fear humans. You cannot be two people at once." Gwinn turns to Russa, positive he will concur. "Tell them, Russa."

He looks at Victor with devastating pity. As if he watches a noose wrap around a man's neck at the gallows and knows the horrible fate that awaits him.

"...Russa," She says again. He turns to her, face ghostly.

"It's real," He says. Gwinn's demeanor shifts

uncomfortably. "We learned of its possibility from Redemption medical logs. Although, the translation didn't make much sense at the time." Russa steps in closer, now curiously inspecting Victor. "The translations described humans as having the ability to hold multiple forms. I understand now, they just meant in the mind." A cord end lifts Victor's chin, turning his head side to side. Hades bucks violently, Russa doesn't flinch. "Also seems it's a debilitating sickness, not a useful trait." He pushes Victor's head away and returns to Gwinn's side. "It's a shame too, for a moment I almost thought you rodents were interesting."

If my world wasn't filled with such insanity right now, I'd be insulted, but I have no time for pride. I ignore Russa and instead continue to plead with Gwinn.

"Do not let him out of those restraints..," I say. Hades' eyes pierce through me, and I wonder if Victor curses me or thanks me under the demon's veil.

"Well, we need him... what do we do?" Geeva asks. Gwinn and I turn to Russa, hopeful for answers. He shakes his head.

"I don't know."

Our legion stands at an impasse, arguing what to do as precious time melts away. I scour my mind for answers but can think of none. Cyto nudges me out of the way as he hobbles past. *What is in his hand?* He sneaks his way behind the reborn guarding Victor and hoists himself onto a crate so he's eye level with them. *What is he doing?* Abraham catches him out the corner of his eye and whips around, but he's too late. Cyto slams a stunner into Victor's neck, and a surge of electricity courses through him until he crashes to the ground.

"Jah!" A soldier yells.

The Proselyte squadron snaps their rifles onto Cyto, and I quickly dart in between them.

"Stand down!" I yell. "Stand down!"

"He attacked the chosen!" Abraham cries.

Cyto shoves me to the side, ignoring the rifle barrels bearing down on him, and wedges his way past the Proselytes.

"I didn't attack shit. Time is ticking. You guys weren't acting. Shove him in one of the suits and deal with him when you get there. Our window is closing."

The soldiers look to each other restlessly.

"We listen to Chosen only. Not some lowly Valenian being." A soldier says, glaring at Cyto. He turns to me. "What say you, Jah?"

"Stand down. NOW." I bark. The Proselytes obey, their twisted faces snarling at Cyto. A huge sigh of relief washing over me. Crazy hag.

"Cyto is right, though. We have to move. Let's suit up," I say. Nobody moves, the tension of the moment still lingering in the air, and my leadership skills subpar at best. "...Now!"

People begin to swarm all over.

Zina helps Pyra into the Berserker suit, the colossal man transforming from a mountain of flesh and bone to a nightmarish tower of metal. Gwinn and Russa argue amongst themselves as they leave. Geeva eagerly climbs into the Phoenix without the help of anyone, her eyes light up as she clicks her helmet in place. The Proselyte squad scurries in all directions. Raiding my munitions closet, stuffing Victor into the Banshee suit, and stealing my clothes. Every single one of them steals at least one article of clothing from me. Creepy fucks.

I search for Cyto to help me get in my suit and see Abraham lording over him, aggressively whispering. I only make out the end of what he says.

"...Jah ever again, and I will skin you alive and grind your bones into dust. Do you understand me?" Abraham glowers at Cyto.

He dramatically nods to me as I approach, touching his brand then his heart.

"Jah," He says to me. "Are you ready?" I glance at Cyto to ensure he's ok. He is, but he seems surprisingly shaken. I take a deep breath and answer.

"I am."

My heart races as the suit's mechanical hinges hiss shut along its spine, sealing me in. Abraham tries to attach my helmet, but Cyto rips it from him and climbs up the mount's back to insert it himself. The two share a spiteful glare. The helmet latches into place, and the world around me subdues.

My breath now seems the loudest noise in existence.

The visor in front of me fogging with every nervous exhale. *Through the nose Fargo.* I try, but my anxiety requires more oxygen than I can bring in through my nostrils. I attempt to bring my hands to my face, but they don't budge. My legs don't move either. I squirm, and panic as claustrophobia begins to set in, and every flail makes the suit feel as if it closes in tighter and tighter.

"I can't move! I can't move!" My breath is out of control,

and I may hyperventilate. "Get me out!" I yell. "Get me out!!"

Cyto's face appears in front of my visor.

"Calm down, slick! We haven't inserted the encrypted datacard or power core yet." He disappears for a moment, and I think I may faint. But just before I do, gauges and numbers flicker to life in my visor, and the building hum of power surges into the suit. The mount disengages, and I buckle as my legs weren't ready to hold myself up yet. I hurry to buck about wildly, shaking the panic from my body and my heart rate falls back down to a livable rate. My breath steadies, and my nerves calm, and I finally gather my faculties as I fully comprehend just what is going on.

I am wearing a Scorcher suit. And it's absolutely terrifying...

39

VICTOR BELLS

The Gate

G et your guns out of my face! It's me..." An army of Proselyte soldiers glance cautiously to Fargo for approval. He looks ridiculous in his Scorcher suit. He motions his metal arm, and the soldiers disarm.

The rig silently chews through the night air, our legion, tensely keeping their distance from me.

"Glad you're back..." Fargo says, his voice drifting off. I hate the way they stare at me. Not just the Proselytes, all of them. I've went from a God to a wretch in only two words.

"Power," I say impatiently. A reborn soldier fumbles to install the power core. He glances up nervously, his face sickly altered. "Left hatch... slide it open." The reborn follows my instructions poorly. "Left!" I shake my head. "Push the core in until it clicks, rotate it toward Fargo, then push it completely in, and slide the hatch back." A moment later, my visor sputters to life. The air filtration system kicks on and flushes the horrendous stench of body odor that's sat ripe in my suit for hours. A bead of sweat that ran from my forehead stings my eye. My puppet masters dressed me incorrectly. *This is why I wear a skull cap, Fargo!* The coward can't even look at me. He's pathetic.

Our pilot calls back to us. Whose flying?

"Strap in, we're throttling down, going tactical. Rig won't be as steady, but she'll be silent." Amber hair spills around the corner of the cockpit, and as she turns back to speak to us, I recognize her fiery golden eyes. That can't be her... I've seen this woman before. This is the woman from the party, the one I saw in the rig with Silva, his sister, the one who started this all! Pyra is here as well? My blood boils.

It wasn't a dream, atop Fargo's headquarters. A nightmare where all the people who have caused me such dire pain stand in unison, watching me be led down the staircase in restraints like some animal. I was sure of it... I could find no plausible explanation for why Pyra would be there, or this Brushu woman or at this point, even Fargo. I assumed it was another of my hellish reveries. Hades playing a cruel trick on my mind. But I was wrong, and the realization makes me angrier than the dream ever could.

"What are they doing here?!" I slam Fargo into the wall of the Rig. He stares back sheepishly. "...Fargo!"

"They're here to help..." He manages. I glare nastily at Pyra and step into his face.

"Help? Why would a poisonous creature like this want to help?" Pyra narrows his eyes. "I was curious why you finally reappeared after being gone for so long... and to train Silva none the less. But then that Serpent Arrow hit my shoulder, and I knew. Knew you needed someone despicable enough and who hated me enough to exact your revenge. Because you are not man enough to do it yourself." Pyra's jaw clenches, and he presses his visor to mine. I don't relent. "And how did that work out?"

"Mind your tongue, boy. Before I yank it from your throat!" Pyra says. "That is my kin you speak of." It takes a moment to connect the dots, but I laugh as I do.

"You're Silva's father?" I laugh hysterically. "Her father?" I point to... Zina, that's her name. "Wow, you must be *so* proud." Pyra slams me into the wall, but I don't fight it. I just laugh. "What a legacy you've left, *Rozza.*" I grin arrogantly at him as I can see his composure begin to falter. "To think I ever idolized you... I guess that's why they say never meet your heroes." My words come out with such venom. Am I speaking? Or Hades? Or some horrible new combination of the two. The distinction has become less and less clear.

The ship rumbles.

"Victor, enough!" Fargo says. He wedges his way in between us, and I can smell his anxiety through my suit.

"Growing a spine finally?" I ask.

"Shut the fuck up!" I do actually see his confidence grow. "Shit has happened, ok... This is far bigger than me and you

369

now. We're all here for one thing, to kill Deterro. Kill him, we get Miku back, the bounties on our head are gone, the evidence against Gwinn disappears, Pyra and Zina get their revenge, and we may just save the entire human race in the process, alright. So, get on board and get on now because we all have something at stake here, and we can't do this without you."

He shoves past me to compose himself.

"...evidence against Gwinn? Save the human race? What the hell are you talking about?" I ask. Fargo glances apprehensively at Abraham as if he's said something he regrets. He quickly skirts the question.

"The details aren't important. You need motivation? Miku should be all the motivation you need."

"Bay doors are opening!" Zina shouts from the cockpit.

I stare firmly at Fargo as the rear ramp unfurls and exposes the dark Valley night. Abraham leads his battalion of Proselytes down the ramp first, followed by Geeva in the Phoenix suit, Pyra in the Berserker, and then finally, Fargo peels away from our locked gaze in the Scorcher.

I remain in the holding bay, the repercussions of this mission beginning to materialize in my mind. Fargo's right... She's gone if we fail. I push aside my hatred for them all and focus on Miku. She is my salvation from this torment. I cannot lose her.

My eyes meet Zina's for a moment. I expected a spiteful, sour expression, but instead, I'm met with something far softer. She's weary. Is she not angry I killed her brother? What kind of sister would that make her?

"I'm sorry," She says. Guilt. *That's* what I see. "I never meant for any of this to happen. I hope you understand that." I can see the remorse on her face, but what good will that be if I don't get Miku back. I turn to walk away from her when whatever tiny sliver of my conscious that remains intact reminds me of my actions. Miku could very well be in my arms already if it weren't for Hades. Her brother, however vile, would still be in her life as well. I stop. It's all I can manage, but I turn back to face her and give her a solemn nod. Our eyes linger on one another for a moment, and then I step out onto the frozen ground of the Valley, and the mission has begun.

Our team moves stealthily along the ragged building facades of a tight pathway as Zina's rig soars away. The buildings are barely shells of structures, crippled heaps of bent metal. Litter lines the street, their wretched stench choking the air. I deactivate my air filtration; even my body odor is better than this. The street is narrow, our footsteps echoing off the metal rafters just a stone's throw across the street. Shadowy figures silhouette darkness filled corridors, watching in fear as we spill down the alley.

An old Heplin woman with a small hybrid girl at her hip appears at an open window port to investigate the muted landing. Our eyes meet as I pass by in a crouched pace, my Banshee's bow drawn, and she gives me an indistinguishable look. It's cautious and reserved as she pulls the small girl behind her, but she knows only evil awaits me in the direction we head, and somehow, I think she understands our intentions.

"Hi Hade..." The old woman quickly covers the little girl's mouth and takes her away as she sends me one last stern look that says, *do you what you must then be gone from here.*

I flick my visor shade down and push ahead. What has become of this place?

Our team has split into two groups, flowing swiftly down either side of the cold empty street as we rapidly approach the Gate. Fargo and Geeva lead Abraham and two Proselyte soldiers in black body armor along the left while I lead Pyra and three Proselytes on the right.

We hurry to the pitch blackness of an intersection of alleyways just before the entrance of the Gate as Fargo signals to hold. How absurd to think he leads the way...? We tuck behind the metal siding of a tower, and he speaks to Cyto back at base, through our connected comms.

"In position Cyto. Mark 'em up." Cyto's rover drone silently purrs past us, no bigger than my hand. Along the perimeter wall, four guards stand invisible in the darkness, hidden to all but Cyto's thermal lens. Four green dots highlight their chests as he designates the targets.

"Go ahead, slick," Cyto says. Fargo turns his thumb up and circles his index finger, signaling us to climb. Fargo and his team cross the street to us, and together we breach through the open doorway of an abandoned tower and ascend the ten stories to the roof.

Atop the roof, we get a full image of the fortress we're trying to penetrate. I catch a glimpse of a Proselyte soldier's face as he comprehends the magnitude of our undertaking. I can read his mind; *this is suicide.* Probably so. Yet my death is not what I fear; it is *her* death that terrifies me. And even though the Gate is crawling with armed Vipers, we have one advantage. No one in that compound is ready for an assault because no one in their right mind would ever dare do such a thing. Tonight, they're wrong!

Fortress is not a strong enough word to describe the Gate. It's a *citadel*. The compound is encased in two impenetrably thick walls, one facing Su Hoz and one facing the Valley, and the east and west are both blockaded by the jagged cliffsides surrounding it. One small access tunnel burrowed in the center of the walls is the only way through. For travelers, that is. We have our own plans.

The Gate is the only lit structure for nearly half a mile, spotlights oscillating from half-constructed guard towers sweep across the ground below. The entire compound is lit well for Valley standards, a random assortment of light fixtures illuminates the interior. String lights drape across pathways between buildings, the occasional standing lamp dots the main corridor, soft light colors the musty windows of a rickety four-story tower to the right of the Gate's tunnel. Three squatty warehouses line the compound's far left side, a chemical distortion spilling from stacks on either side, just barely visible in the low light. Their Venom lab's no doubt. A guard sits casually under the faint glow of a single bulb in front of each entrance.

A larger, poorly lit warehouse rests just in front of those three, on the Valley side of the compound, where I follow the lights of a rig into its dark opening then disappear as a garage door is pulled closed behind it.

Dozens and dozens of small buildings made of rusted and chewed metal are packed tightly within the walls, some dimly lit, some completely dark. This may be a stronghold, but it is still the Valley.

Only one building stands out from the rest, and it is undoubtedly where we will find Deterro.

Directly in the center of the Gate, a five-story complex shines brightly. The passenger tunnel is built clean through the middle of the complex, wings of the building spilling onto either side. It's sleek and clean, modern construction. Crystal clear windows glow brightly with white light and are immaculately carved into the building's glossed stone. Guards patrol along the roof, long-distance rifles in their hands. A frenzy of activity whizzes by through the windows. I motion to

Fargo.

"There." I whisper. He nods and contacts Cyto.

"Need two more marked. Roof, center building."

The rover drone climbs higher to not draw attention, and two more green dots mark the guards' chests on the roof.

"Ready on go," Cyto says. Two of the proselyte soldiers lay down, mounting their silent rifles on bipods and activate their synch signal. A small green ring blinks on the body of their rifles as the soldiers center the guards in their scopes. We sit motionless for a moment, a tension hanging over us as we wait for the first bodies to fall. This is it. Once this trigger is pulled, there's no going back.

The adrenaline of war stampedes through my body.

I close my eyes, trying to keep the burning itch of Hades at bay. But that lava rises. Scorching the fringes of my sanity. I want to do this without him, but I don't know if he'll let me.

One of the Proselytes gives Fargo a thumbs up.

Fargo stares out at the guards waiting for the drone and rifle to synch. The two green dots on the roof and the blinking rings on the rifles snap to red.

"Fire!"

Two muted thumps ring out instantly, and the guards on the roof spill to the ground. The sharpshooters quickly readjust their aim to the guards patrolling the ground and each prime an additional shot. Two green rings now blink on each of their rifles. The green dots on the ground snap to red.

"Fire!"

Four deadly rounds silently find their targets.

"Move!"

It has begun.

The sharpshooters scurry to their feet, and the ten of us back our way to the far edge of the rooftop. This has to work.

Fargo glances to me, so much needing to be said but not nearly enough time to say it. My anger with him still burns through my veins. Endangering Miku, something I'm not sure I'll ever be able to forgive him for. He looks to me with one last desperate look.

"...I love you, brother." And with that, he takes off sprinting.

He plants his foot on the edge of the tower and launches himself into the air. The rest of us follow, diving off the tower's lip, soaring through the darkness like bats shrieking from a cave. The ground below speeds by in a dark blur, and I activate my glider. A massive synthetic tarp whips out of the mechanical pack on my back and outstretches wide, catching the wind underneath it. My body bucks at the resistance, but it holds. Gliders breach from the other's backs as well, and together we silently coast across the gap in between our rooftop and the perimeter wall.

The Proselytes soar higher above, not weighed down by the metal of the Warlord suits as the wall rapidly approaches. It's going to be close. I continue to fall lower and lower, the interior of the compound becoming visible now. I have to make it! I arch my back as hard as I can to flatten out, but the wall is on me. I slam into the corner! My body rolls along the top, and my glider tears in half as I begin to slide off the edge. I desperately claw at the metal, but there's no leverage. I continue to slip down. Fargo sprints atop the wall and slides to a stop grabbing my arm. He begins to inch over the edge as well, my heavier suit dragging him down.

"*Help!*" He calls over the comms, and Geeva runs to his side. She grabs him and tries to haul us up. The material of our suits was built to deter grip, not cater to it. I can feel myself beginning to slip. Fargo grunts as he pulls with all his force, but then I feel it.

The weightlessness.

Fargo and Geeva speed away from me as I plummet to the ground. Only one thought whispers through my mind as I desperately reach out for them... *Miku.*

My head rocks against the back of my helmet as I hit the ground, and I'm stranded on the outside of the compound.

40

FARGO SHEPHERD

Into the Fire

"*Fargo!*" Geeva protests over the comms, but it's too late. Her eyes glare into the top of my helmet as the metal of my boots chew into the soil when I land harshly next to Victor. Our plan is in shambles mere moments into its life. "*What are you doing?!*" She says. I nervously glance up the wall to meet her furious gaze.

"*Improvising...*"

The offer of my hand is met with contempt by Victor. He stares at it in disgust like I'm some subhuman animal.

"*Get up...*" I say.

He knocks my hand away and climbs to his feet, ripping off the shattered visor shade from his helmet. Have his eyes always been so cold? Victor is a stoic man, but he is not without emotion. Yet, these eyes he pierces through me have nothing but spite in them. Forgiveness surely cannot exist within those dark hollows. Chills run down my spine as I realize he's losing the battle that wages inside him. These eyes have only belonged to Hades. I worry they now belong to Victor too.

I glance nervously at him, then issue orders to the others

atop the wall.

"Victor and I will enter through the tunnel now and search for Miku. Geeva, you will have point on the inside. Run contingency C and combine our two original approach paths into one. Everyone will follow her lead."

Abraham's voice interjects over the comms.

"Jah, I must stay with..."

"No! Follow Geeva! We can't afford any more of us outside the perimeter."

"But, Jah..."

"Enough!" I bark. Abraham glances at his other Proselytes, concerned. *"Do not, by any means, go loud until it is absolutely necessary, or we have signaled that Miku is safe. Understood?"*

Pyra pushes impatiently past Geeva.

"I only care for Deterro, if I have a shot, loud or not, I will not hesitate. Your friend's safety means nothing to me..."

Victor and Pyra lock into a menacing sneer.

"Get her killed... and I will happily finish what I started all those years ago!" Victor says. My stomach twists into a knot at the terrifying smile that has scratched its way across his face. In any other situation, I'd try to squash this before we start, but we're wasting time.

"Let's move."

Victor and I hug the perimeter wall on our right as we approach the tunnel, stepping over two of the downed guards from earlier. I peer around the corner to inspect it as we arrive. What the hell are we going to do? The tunnel is well lit. On either side are glass encasings, surely entrances to either wing of the complex above. Head-high metal fences snake their way through the middle, forming jagged inspection lines. Ten exhausted guards scattered throughout the complex fight to stay awake. I don't share the same apprehension I did the night of the Rojo compound raid. These men are monsters; this is the fate that awaits them.

There's a small landing along the left wall that runs all the way to the glass where mountains of confiscated belongings create the only cover we can use.

"There!" I point to the heaping mass. *"On my count, we push to those stacks. Stay low, move quick."*

Victor says nothing. I wish he would.

"Ready... Go!" I dart from behind the corner, trying as hard as I can to condense the massive metal suit I'm wearing. I have no idea how loud my steps are. At this point, I can only hope no one can hear them. The metal fences buzz by as I

slide to a stop behind the farthest stack. *"Alright, let's... Victor?"* I turn and see Victor walking across the tunnel grounds. *"Victor mov—"* In the blink of an eye, he snaps three arrows from his bow, each hitting their targets seconds after the other. Three guards are down, and I didn't even seem them.

"Victor, get over here now!" He cocks his head towards me, and for a moment, I think he may just shoot *me.* My fingers cautiously curl around my deployable shield. Sweat beads down my neck. I can't do this without him; he has to keep it together.

Come on, Vic... Come on...

Movement down the tunnel breaks his stare, and he slowly squats down under the fence line.

Air spills from my lungs as my fingers relax. We need to hurry.

I don't dare acknowledge that tense moment when he gets to the stack. He's a ticking time bomb, and who knows what could set him off. *"How about you lead? I got your six,"* I say, avoiding eye contact.

We weave silently through the mounds of stolen goods. Junk piled up over our heads. It's eerie. The chaotic masses whisper like echoes of abandoned lives. The shed souls of men whose bodies continued on, but spirits remain trapped here. Paid like a toll to enter the world to the south. Can Su Hoz be that bad? Surely the Valley isn't the sanctuary they were imagining while passing through these gates. What an awful life they must have been leaving if so.

Geeva's voice crackles in over the comm.

"Half of east compound cleared so far. Haven't met much resistance. Avoiding east tower, pushing to complex now."

"Understood."

We reach the final mound and can see into the clearing between the glass encasings, where the fences stop on either side to allow guards access to the lines. Four of them stand casually talking amongst themselves. No one usually migrates this late at night, so they're not paying any attention.

I scan for the other three but have lost sight of them. We need to separate them somehow. There's a small suitcase about halfway up this mountain of junk. If I pull it out, I bet this tower will collapse and create a diversion.

"Victor, here's the plan, backtrack to the front and go to the far-right line..." I explain the rest of the plan, and Victor thankfully obeys.

I can't see him, but I feel it's been enough time for him to get into position. I wrap my hand around the handle of the suitcase and take a deep breath. This better work!

I yank it out from under the load, and sure enough, everything crumbles to the ground with it. The avalanche nearly buries me, but I'm able to put my back to the wall and avoid the crashing debris as I watch Victor devour the four distracted men in two vicious strokes of his Greatsword. Bile ejects from my mouth as the guard's bodies slump to the ground in halved heaps of blood and organs. I've never seen anything so grotesque.

Climbing my way out over the junk, I can tell something is wrong. Victor stands over the mutilated corpses, staring at them. I click my comm on.

"Victor..." I creep my way toward him, shield deployed already, scorch cannon primed on him. *"Victor!"* He doesn't move. I snap my eyes frantically around the tunnel, searching for the last guards. *"Vic, brother, I need you to answer me..."* My heart is racing. Slamming against my ears like the mallets of construction bots on the steel rafters of a tower. Pounding away. My feet don't want to work. Every step I take towards him feels like my last. *"Victor..."* I've gotten as close as my body will let me, but it refuses to move another inch. Victor remains posed over the bodies, so much blood pouring from the carcasses that it's reached my boots.

"V—"

Victor twirls and snaps an arrow. The Serpent tip drives halfway through my shield and shatters a tiny hole in my visor. Glass slicing into my face. My scorch cannon roars to life with a blazing stream of fire as I panic and retreat down a fence line. Rifle shots ring out at Hades as the remaining guards have been alerted. One panics as he passes by my line. Spinning and spraying a cluster of bullets my way. I brace behind my shield, then melt the poor man like a dragon of Earth lore. His skin sizzles and cracks as I sprint through him to cross the clearing.

"What the hell is going on?!" Geeva calls out.

"It's Hades!"

I bash a guard with my shield and cave in his skull as bullets dig into my chest plate. *"Go loud now!! Forget Deterro—"* A skin-peeling scream echoes against the tunnel as Hades rips the last guard in half with his hands. Blood sprays his armor like morbid graffiti. *"Find Miku! Go!"* I race from the fence line and tackle Hades. Our suits tangling together. My scorch cannon begins to charge, but before I can unleash it, he hurls me through the encasing. Glass shards exploding in all directions. Bullets spill into my suit as I struggle to get my shield up. The noise is horrifying. Like thousands of furious demons crashing into the metal. The impact of my shotgun knocks Hades off his feet, and I scramble to mine, darting out the door and into the complex.

I'm met immediately with an army of Vipers in a cramped room. I can't count how many. Muzzle flashes explode like a lightning storm over the Lotopi. Rounds refuse to stop chewing into my suit. One plate along my thigh finally caves, and a bullet stabs into my leg. Pain sears through me. An inferno erupts from my scorch cannon as I fire back, replacing the deafening clamor of gunfire with the nauseating cries of agony. Screams no man should ever hear. Charred men beg for death. Gauges in my visor seize red, isolating breaches in my suit. Before I can move again, a proximity alarm warns of an enemy behind me. I whirl my shield around just in time to block a ferocious strike from Hades' Greatsword. My body is thrown across the room, landing among the bubbling Vipers. The smoke begins to thicken, and I scramble to activate my air filtration as the dark vapor begins to slither into my suit.

"Breaching main door!" Geeva yells. *"Cyto scan for Miku. We need her location now!"*

"Scanning," Cyto says.

Hades stalks toward me. His suit drenched in blood, metal charred by my flame. The eyes of the devil pierce me. Cutting through the smoke and the fire, they crave violence. I scurry to my feet and up the staircase before he can fulfill any of his twisted desires, smoke coughing out behind me as I crash through the door.

The main level is anarchy. Vipers scramble throughout a massive cafeteria, some attempting to get into defensive positions, some desperately seeking out their weapons. Waves of thugs, cascading from the floors above, race to reinforce the room. I sprint and slide behind the food trough, where terrified Savron cooks huddle together in the kitchen. My trigger finger spasms, but I stop.

"Get the fuck out of here!" I yell at them. The Savrons hurry away, not knowing just how close they were to being incinerated. My body trembles.

The cafeteria looks more like a fortified beachhead now. Tables have been flipped, portable barricades planted in the ground, heavy chain guns, and railcannons mounted all over.

379

But as I carefully peer over the edge of the metal trough, I can see into their eyes. They may be monsters, but they're still men. Terrified, frozen men. Faces that stare at the main door don't blink. Men that have committed atrocities under the notion they were untouchable, now cower from the reckoning that awaits them. Only the vilest of creatures do not fear death. And those are the true monsters.

Hades smashes through the basement door and roars with the insanity of a hundred madmen. *That* is what pure evil looks like. His Banshee rifle and one he picked off a scalded Viper sing out destructive, horrid notes. Bullets rip through the cafeteria as the flanked Vipers dive to find new cover. But across the battlefield, a Viper's railcannon hisses behind a deployable shield. It's payload charging, coils zeroed in on my rampaging brother. He doesn't see it. *Victor!*

I sprint from behind the trough, Vipers now returning fire at both of us. The railcannon coil is almost red, and I urge my legs to move faster. Hades sees me charging and turns to fire on me. More of the nightmarish sounds wail against my shield, and I tackle Victor as the railcannon's pulse sucks in, then unleashes. Stone explodes against the wall behind us as we crash to the ground. Tumbling over one another, we grind to stop behind a huge support pillar. Our eyes meet, and for a split second, I think I can see Victor under his demonic veil. Then, his mechanized fist rocks my helmet, and I snap back to reality.

I kick his rifle from his hand and flee, tears welting in my eyes as I run. My brother can't be gone!

A detonation rumbles, and a gaping hole explodes at the main entrance. Geeva and the others pour into the cafeteria, guns blazing.

"About fucking time!" I yell. Geeva launches into the air, flying overhead and carpet bombs the Vipers below. Explosions trail her like choreographed fireworks. Wiping men from the world as if they never existed. She lands on the second-floor loft and continues to pick off enemies with her precision rifle. I use the commotion to push in, being no use at this range.

Pyra charges in as well, hammers drawn and swinging wildly. It's odd to see those mallets in the hands of anyone but Victor. They're his pride and joy.

"Abraham, keep your soldiers at a distance, maintain the perimeter. Don't let anyone else in!" I yell.

"Yes, Jah!" Abraham and his Proselytes spread out covering the main entrance and the staircases, holding off more reinforcements.

My scorch cannon bellows, searing everything in its path. Bullets continue to pelt my suit, gauges shrieking. Pyra chews through a group of grunts, men flying through the air from his unstoppable hammers. One charges from his right with a stun lance, but his head disintegrates from the legendary man's bolt pistol.

Pyra is flawless.

He moves like the wind. Tearing through enemies even though they swarm him like a pack Jymira. His brain moves so much quicker than mine. A railcannon churns again, and Pyra detonates a scatter core over their head, sending shards of jagged metal death down upon them. He's calculated. Precise. Every move he makes, perfectly efficient. In a different setting, it'd be breathtaking. But here, it's just another piece to the horrifying scene.

I, on the other hand, am run by fear and stress. My limps flail and spray flames with frantic hope.

I somehow touch a setting on my suit that mutes the roaring battlefield. Only fractions of sound from the raging fight seep in through punctured holes in my suit.

The sounds of my panicking breath are all that fills my helmet. Somehow, they're more terrifying than war.

I scramble to fix it, an overwhelmed sob choking against my throat as I catch a glimpse of a charging Viper. I fall to my ass in panic. His head evaporates before he can carve a spear into my chest. Geeva already switching targets.

This is not the world I was meant for.

I was built for a posher life. One without destruction and misery. A life full of pretentious parties and arrogant excess. How did I end up here? I lay paralyzed for a moment. A battle I have no business being in surges around me. Nothing but trained ruthless killers in every direction I look. I buckle as I find the sound setting, and the deafening wave of battle returns to my ears. Another overwhelmed sob bubbles from my chest, but I push through.

The world is on fire.

Flames rage, and plumes of smoke engulf the corridor.

Men cry out in despair. Awful, heinous cries. Limbs scatter along the ground like fallen leaves of the cold season. Rubble and debris make the stone along the floor and walls appear gnawed and chewed. It's an unbearable scene.

Three of Abraham's Proselytes lay dead along the west stairwell. Our warlord suits, mangled heaps. My visor has splintered so many times I can barely see out of it. Maddening sirens ring in my ears, and I would give anything to figure out how to turn them off. The stench of vomit has cemented itself in my nose. Putrid and rank. This is hell.

"Fargo, we have to keep moving!" Geeva says. She signals for us to regroup with her atop the second-floor loft, but I struggle to move. The others have no issue, apparently unfazed by such barbaric carnage. Yet I don't see Pyra or Victor...

The maimed skull of a Viper stares at me from the floor, dislodged from his body. A murky, cloudy eye is frozen in time. Fixated. I can't tell which parts of his face are covered in blood and which are just his merlot skin, but I can see the fear etched in his expression as the life left his body. I said I feel no sympathy for these men, but that is a lie. I can't help but look at him and wonder if I would've suffered the same fate had I been born Valenian instead of Human. Would the Valley's hardships have pushed me to the Vipers like it did so many of these lifeless souls? If it did, could I have been as horrible as these men were? My mind convinces itself I wouldn't because it has to. But as I scour the appalling aftermath of my actions, take inventory of the carnage I'm responsible for throughout my life, a secluded chamber of my soul understands I am no better than they are. I never have been. I'm no better than Deterro, who exploits everyone in the Valley. Thriving on the despair of others. I'm no better than the Rojo who steal and cheat. Prioritizing their needs above anyone else. And I'm no better than Gwinn and the other horrible creatures that make up the High Council. Exterminating my alien race before it had a chance at life. Poisoning their own people. Murdering those in their way. No. I am capable of unforgivable things, just as they are. The only difference is, this entire time, I've thought I'm the good guy.

41

GWINN

DEMARCO

Bluff or Burn

I don't need Russa here, but I'm glad he came. Our small platoon hustles off the transport rig's loading ramp and onto the ash-coated streets of Paradise. Protective suits shielding us from the poisonous air.

I suppose I didn't give him a choice but to join; he stumbled into the self-incriminating web I carefully wove for him. Securing the Bytrol, now just as vital to him as it is to me.

Four of my grunts shield us on either side, weapons scanning the darkness. Oblivious to the fact that knowledge of the Bytrol's existence is far too powerful for any of them to possess it beyond this mission. They march toward their grave. Unquestioned obedience. They receive an order, they follow it. Misplaced loyalty to, what I can only assume, is some higher sense of duty to province. I pray it's not to me. That would be tragic. Because as I walk these men to their graves, not an ounce of guilt drips through my veins. As Russa says, *'there are two things absolutely necessary to protect power: stomach and sacrifice.'*

The old Trakstull Chateau is a crumbling pile of rocks. It sits perched upon the hill we climb, dilapidated, and sad. The entire annihilated town of Paradise is no different. Massive chemical clouds hang in the sky, spewing soot and ash, blanketing the cratered streets in poisonous fluff. The High Council ordinances really did a number on this place. How anyone ever believed the destruction here was caused by a power center explosion is laughably pathetic. The sheep will believe whatever we spoon feed them.

Mutilated skeletons line the streets. Souls that were doomed well before the detonations wiped this place from existence. I step over them without a second thought.

I never understood Leo's fascination with this place. It was our romanticized interpretation of the failed society of Earth. If he thought it was anything other than that, he's wrong.

The eroded statue of Trakstull lays mangled along the ground of the Chateau's entrance. It's never resembled him more than it does now. Seemingly half a man, withered and decayed by time. But still, even as he lays crumbled along the ground, covered in soot, it is him who looks out over the world and decides the fate of the masses.

The roots of power dig deep.

The leader of our squadron halts us at the entryway arch. The beam of his rifle peering into the labyrinth of pitch-black corridors.

"You two, guard the High Councilors while we clear the building." He orders, and two grunts dart to position. "You three, perimeter sweep. You two, with me. Move." The guards spill to action, the leader and his men disappearing into the Chateau as the others follow their orders.

I take a seat on Trakstull's stone face as we wait for clearance to enter and pull a leather journal from a storage pouch in my suit. It reads Archie B. Abernathy across the cover.

It sat hidden in the same place Leo always kept it if he didn't have it with him. Concealed in a small rusted Redemption crate in his room.

I wasn't sure if we'd need it, but there isn't a better source of information about the Redemption on the planet. Seemed like a justifiable detour.

How many times did Leo read this damn journal? I bet he knows it word for word. It's no doubt where his delusional sense of pride in humanity comes from.

I run my thumb along his name on the first page, a twinge

of worry pricking at my side at the fact that he's never checked in with Russa.

Where the hell are you?

The pages are hard to turn with my gloves on, but I manage. This thing is filled with years and years of nonsense. It honestly does explain why Leo's mind has been warped so drastically. Unfortunately, Leo could never grasp the fact that his father lived his entire adult life inside a metal ship. What could he possibly know of life? The man never had decisions to make. His entire life had one goal. To find a new planet. No one else has the luxury of simplicity like that. The majority of lives are spent searching for meaning in an existence that does not require one. What exactly was mine supposed to be? To carry on the human race? Well, that's not possible... and for him to expect me to participate in his delusion, let alone have the audacity to grow angry with me because I wouldn't, is something I don't know if I'll ever forgive him for. Because for all of Leo's obsessions with the Redemption, he conveniently ignores one crucial detail of the mission: the number of crew members.

A crew of 330 wasn't a random decision. It was deemed the absolute bare minimum amount of genetic diversity to repopulate humanity.

330.

We have eight. And two are fucking related.

So, he can argue all he wants that if he solves the womb formula that the issue disappears, the fact of the matter is, he didn't. And between the eight of us, there's enough genetic diversity to create two generations without inbreeding. That's it. My grandkids would be the very last of humanity.

How cowardly would it be to push that fate onto my children when I could carry that burden for them?

This is what Leo couldn't understand.

There was absolutely no way I was going to bring one more human life into this world just to let him die alone. What exactly would his purpose be then? No, I know that isolation, and I wish it on no one. I will live out the rest of this miserable existence, and that will be the last of us. Humans had their chance, we failed. Now it's time for one of us to have some courage and let mankind fade away.

"High Councilor." A guard calls out. "Let's go." Ash coughs from the book as I slam it closed and am escorted into the building.

We're guided through a maze of rubble-filled hallways until

we reach the destroyed wing of the Consulate. Trakstull's old throne still stands in its center. Hovering over a massive pit, connected to the edges by small arching walkways. Like the mouth of a gargantuan beast is stretched open wide, ready to devour the stone perch.

Three levels of destroyed balconies wrap the throne room. Ash pouring in from where the roof should be.

I scale down the debris and rubble until I'm peering into never-ending darkness. Even my light is swallowed in the bowels of the pit. It's an uneasy feeling being so close to such an unknown depth.

"Obedience lived at the bottom," Russa says. He stares into the pit like he misses the days of ruthless authority. When the world feared the merciless word of law.

"Did you know about the Vault underneath?" I ask.

"Of course," He says. "During the Gaz war, we needed a way to sneak into Berban undetected. The tunnel at the bottom leads to an outpost we stationed inside Berban Falls."

"Inside?"

Russa glances at me.

"Live long enough, and the planet can't hide its secrets from you."

My men begin to set up a harness lift at the lip of the hole, but Russa stops them, annoyed.

"Do you think the Regal repelled down into the tunnel from a fucking rope?..." He shakes his head. "This way."

Russa leads us to a hidden door off a side wing of the throne room. There, we pile into an antiquated lift, descending two levels under the floor to an old strategy room to strip from our suits so we don't drag chemical fallout into the Vault.

The lift groans as we descend once again, plunging deeper and deeper into the ground. Bodies packed tight against one another.

Inside another damn lift. I can't escape these things.

Our flashlights shine over metal rafters as we drop lower and lower until we croak to a stop. The gears hissing. The door rattles open and what's on the other side is nothing short of miraculous.

There was a time when I was young and naïve enough to believe in human decency. To believe we could be capable of something other than self-destruction and pain. But the more I became exposed to the alarming legacy we've left behind, the less confident I grew. Humans are not sophisticated enough to handle existence, that became unarguably clear to me. But I will admit, seeing such a grand piece of the Redemption in this state does stir a sense of pride. The fact we were capable of making such an awe-inspiring machine does make me wonder what we would've been capable of as a species. But it also took the imminent threat of extinction to create, so maybe the Redemption is evidence *in* my favor, not against it.

Charred metal and millions of screws, wires, and sensors. It's an impressive feat, I'll give them that. Russa stands next to it with a distant gaze.

"I still remember that day," He says. "I don't think I'll ever forget it." His cords stretch out over the ship's hull. "Everyone was so scared... There was no mistaking it for anything else. We knew." He tilts his head to absorb the towering metal vessel. I can see the memories playing in his eyes. "Things were a lot different back then. This technology was so beyond what we had; we were convinced it was the end. And it very well may have been if anyone was inside. But it was just you." He smiles at me for the first time in years. "We didn't know that obviously, but..." A softness takes over his face, an odd look piecing together along his beak. What has gotten into him lately? "... when you're in charge, sometimes you have to make decisions where no matter what you choose, someone gets hurt. And even if you oppose, you still must obey. That's the burden of power."

He stares at me with solemn eyes. Guilt of some sort weighing on him.

"Destroying the other eggs, the day you were born, was one of those decisions," He says. "My life has been filled with those moments."

His sentimental aura makes me uncomfortable.

We stand in silence for a moment.

"Never took you for the apologetic type, old man." A smug voice startles us from the other side of the ship. Someone's here! My men spring their weapons to ready. Boots click along the hard tile and echo in the vast cavern. My heart sinks when I see his devilish eyes as he turns the corner. His black tunic drags on the floor behind him. Tattooed skull tilted for us to see. He wags his finger at me and sucks his tongue against the roof of his mouth. "Tsst, tsst, tsst... Gwinny, I thought we had an arrangement, no?"

My jaw clenches as Deterro saunters toward me. My men step between us, rifles primed. He stops and smirks. A sharp curling whistle shrieks from his lips, and Vipers appear from behind concealments in all directions. He's supposed to be at the Gate. Fargo putting a bullet in his head. Instead, we're surrounded.

"Now... if you all would be so kind as to drop your weapons, that would be lovely." His eyes don't leave mine. How is he here?! "...Gwinn? I'm waiting."

My men nervously glance at me for orders. What the hell am I supposed to tell them? Out of the corner of my eye, I can see Russa's cord ends slowly curl around the heel of the pistol clamped to his belt. He's not exactly a rational thinker. I have to act quick.

"You don't know how to get into the ship, do you?" I ask. Deterro grins. "You would've gotten what you needed already and been gone." His posture changes ever so slightly.

"Or... I have what I need, and I've been waiting here to deal with a breach of contract. Are you familiar with how Vipers handle broken deals?" Deterro inches closer, nodding to a grunt holding a silver canister. I know what's in it. I've seen the aftermath of that acid. The Rotting seems like a quaint death compared to it. "It's not pleasant."

My throat tightens as the Vipers around the room seem to enjoy the charade.

"Gwinn..." Russa whispers to me. "Do not put those guns down." I glance at him, an eagerness about him. He wants to fight. But that's suicide. Not that I'm desperately clinging to this world, but foolish pride seems like an embarrassing way to go.

"Hand me the torch," I say. One of my men hands me the torch we brought in hopes of melting a hole in the hub. I guess we'll see who's better at bluffing. "This journal in my hand contains the only information available on how to access this ship. And I've memorized everything I need to know from it." Blue flame bursts from the nozzle as I spark the torch. Its tongues dancing inches below the leather book. "If this goes up in flames... you'll never get in without me. And you'll never get the Cure." I have to mask my terror in thick false confidence. Deterro is a professional psychopath; he can see right through me. "Think of the power you'd have if you controlled it."

He smirks at my conviction. The sides of his mouth peeling apart to show his second row of teeth.

"Burn it, Gwinny..."

I stare into his eyes, desperately searching for a tell. The Vipers seem to close in. Russa has pulled his pistol from its holster, and it dangles behind his leg. My men fidget anxiously.

But a calmness settles in my stomach.

These men always think they're in control. But what they never fully comprehend is that, at the end of the day, I just don't give a fuck.

"Have it your way." Flames birth along the ridge of the book.

"NO!" Deterro yells out! Vipers spring from their cover. Weapons primed. My grunts squeeze together in front of me. Everyone shouting. The powder keg ready to erupt.

A massive rumbling shakes the Vault. Gears and cogs, hiss and clank along the far wall. The entire room trembles, drowning out the shouts. The Viper grunts snap their attention to its source for a split second. This is our moment.

"Go!"

We scatter up a set of stairs behind us. Vipers panic and clamp down on their triggers as we sprint away. Deterro shouts for them to stop, but not all can hear him. One of my men crashes to the ground, a stray bullet plunging through his throat. Voices roar over rifle discharge. Superheated ammunition shattering the glass panels along the staircase. We fire back blindly. Climbing the stairs until we reach the top and dive behind the thick stone observatory walls.

Huge gears rotate along the far wall, their teeth grooving perfectly into one another. It begins to move. It's not a wall at all but a massive circular door. The door pulls apart from its center, and massive plates tuck away into opposite sides. The entrance finishes opening with one final pound that echoes against the hollow Vault, and the bullets cease. Then there is nothing but heart-clenching silence.

A thin stream of smoke dances its way to the ceiling as the flame begins to inch its way up the book, Deterro struggling to put it out.

A herd of boots cautiously thump along the ground as the Vipers try to get a line of sight on the Vault door.

And a haunting gurgle escapes my downed man's throat as he drowns in his own blood, the life seeping from his eyes.

I try to ignore it all.

Because four shadowy figures approach from within the darkness of the tunnel. Guns outlined along their dark silhouettes. It can't be... I stand up slowly as the first one walks into the light.

My heart trembles when I see her. Can that truly be her? I wasn't sure I'd ever see her again.

"...Riley?..." The name falls from my lips.

Two more walk into the light, their faces telling me exactly who follows behind them. And then... My stomach twists. All of the conflicting emotions I've convinced myself I haven't felt storms back to me with just one look from his gentle eyes.

"...Leo......."

42

VICTOR BELLS

The End of Evil

Rage. It's intoxicating. I've never been ashamed of my love for it. Even at my darkest moments, when Hades worked my limbs like a demented puppet made of flesh and bone, I knew that rage was who I was. The lifeblood of my soul. And I sought it out. The unmatched power of fury was too electrifying to ignore. And as I watch him tear through this building, shredding men to pieces, unable to do anything about it, it is not the rage that I plead to stop. It's the hate. Poisonous, wrathful hatred. It's where I lose myself to the monster. Because I don't know if rage is possible without hate, and though I accept my need for the anger, I reject the notion that I am a man filled with scorn... Hades impales a Viper pinned under his boot, the helpless man screaming in agony as the demon roars with a frenzied bloodlust. But I do hate these men... And I want Hades to tear them piece by piece until we find that stupid motherfucker who thought he could threaten my family and live to tell about it. I've let go of the reins and told Hades to do his worst. God help them.

Hades walks up the fourth flight of stairs, ignoring bullets pouring into his suit from the landing above. The rounds finally punch through the metal plating, and one digs into my shoulder. We both ignore the pain, body numb from deranged furor. Razor-sharp arrows dispatch of the enemies with deadly precision. His appetite grows.

"Found her! Top-level, north side..." Cyto's voice trails off over the comms.

"Cyto... What's wrong?" Fargo asks, erratic breath choking his words.

"There's... no more guards..."

Their voices sound like faint murmurs trailing off at the end of a long hallway. Distant and vague.

"Anywhere..." Cyto finishes.

"What do you mean? That can't be all of them?" Geeva asks, slamming to down on the top level.

"I don't know what to tell you."

Hades strides to the last squirming Viper on the floor. The man suffering as the Serpent arrow has shredded his insides. He compresses the man's head to the blood-stained floor with his boot. I can feel the bones of his skull begin to splinter.

"WHERE IS HE!" Hades' voice is horrifying. His throaty growl originating from somewhere in the heinous crevices of my soul. Splinters of myself that I lost too long ago to remember. The words squeeze out from behind a clenched jaw, knifing through the cracks in his teeth and terrifying the helpless man. The grunt writhes in pain, pinned under a metal heel.

"Who?!" The man cries. Hades pushes down harder and sends him into a panic. "Who?! Who?!"

"DETERRO," Hades says. The man desperately tries to push the boot off his face.

"A Vault!" I can feel his skull giving. His squeals intensifying. "I don't know! Somewhere near the Trakstull Chateau. I'm just a recruit. They don't tell me details... Please!"

Fargo's voice kicks in over the comms.

"Did he just say Deterro is at the Vault?"

Hades glances down to the pinned soldier, the man's wild eyes begging for mercy... Not today. Hades slams his boot into the ground and crushes the man's skull to pieces. To Hell We Go...

The metal door dents as Hades kicks it open. His mind trembles. It craves violence, yet there is no one left to hurt. He scours the top floor, empty room after empty room. He has to be here. Images of his face sprint through my mind. How desperately I want to watch the life fade from those cloudy yellow eyes.

Another door, another empty room.

"I've got her!" Geeva calls over the comm. *"She's alive!"*

Her...

Miku.

I'd become so lost in my sea of rage, hellbent on destruction, that I lost sight of the very reason for my existence. The very reason I haven't fought against the raging storm inside me.

"Zina, we need extraction immediately!" Fargo says. *"Cyto, can you contact Gwinn?"*

"Already tried, slick... must be in the Vault already." Cyto answers.

"Shit."

"Fargo, we have a problem..." Geeva's voice continues on but isn't directed at Fargo any longer. *"Put your gun down... What are you doing? Put it down!"* Hades sprints down the hall, eager to hunt more souls. He smashes through a door and spills into a large barren room, a standoff happening just feet in front of him.

Hades' eyes narrow. Saliva wetting his lips. His neck crackles as he twists it side to side. He's ready once again for pain. But as I squint at the tiny screen displaying the world around me from inside my mental prison, I realize these are not enemies he's ready to attack.

Geeva's precision rifle juts from her shoulder, like a deadly thorn. Her Phoenix suit, horribly mangled. At the receiving end of her aim stands Pyra, the moonlight through the window bouncing off his metal Berserker shield. What is she doing?

Hades stalks them, swinging out widely to get a better angle.

"Fargo, Abraham, I need you guys here now!" Geeva urges, her eyes skirting between Pyra and I. Pyra doesn't bother turning around, his head is cocked down, looking at something below him.

My blood hardens in my veins, stomach plummeting. The barrel of Pyra's bolt pistol rests flush against Miku's temple, who is bound and gagged to a chair, some contraption wired to her chest. Pyra turns his head and meets my eyes. *My* eyes, not Hades'. He looks beyond the monster and into me, years of anguish embedded in his gaze.

"Put the gun down, Pyra!" Geeva orders. His eyes don't leave mine. Hades spins his bow through his arms and primes an arrow, its Serpent headed tip itching to drive through Pyra's skull.

"Victor, you too! Put it down," She says. Geeva's face trembles.

Hades eyes her, annoyed. He adjusts so quick it makes me flinch inside. An arrow snaps from his bow and punches Geeva in the chest, knocking her off her feet. He spins, and another arrow is primed at Pyra in the blink of an eye. Geeva shrieks. Gasping for life over the comm.

"...Fargo... Help." She wheezes, searching for air.

"Geeva!" Fargo yells.

Pyra's voice shakes ever so slightly. Something is wrong.

"You've taken everything from me." His eyes speak to me, but it is Hades who destroyed his world. A differentiation he knows yet doesn't seem to care. *"Your brother butchered my people, you murdered my son... destroyed my career... and then, you promise me revenge against the man who took my love away from me... and you've stripped me of that as well."*

I don't understand? We know where he is. We can leave right now and head to the Vault. Panic begins to consume me. A tidal wave of fear. I'm sorry. Dear God am I sorry. Please don't... But Hades just grows angrier. Fuel on the fire of his demonic furnace.

Miku's eyes flood with tears, sitting perfectly still. They shred through my soul. Hades' anger and my sorrow ripping at either end of my sanity, like fangs chewing through soft meat. The room swirls, horrible screeching noises plaguing my mind as two people fight over one consciousness. Blood begins to ooze from my ear. This battle inside, killing me.

Pyra turns his body to face me, gun still pressed into Miku's head, and I go cold. I understand now. Sticking from his abdomen is a massive jagged piece of shrapnel. Blood courses from the wound and streams down both of his metal suit legs.

"Life can only be repaid with life." He coughs, and blood splatters against the inside of his visor. *"But I am not a monster like you, I won't collect her life... Just yours."*

Pyra twitches and my visor shatters! Pain rattles along my face. The bolt gashed the side of my cheek and plowed straight through the back of my helmet. Hades spills to the floor, bow crashing to his side. Pyra's on us before we can move. A hammer slams into our back. We crash into the wall. Bullets rage from his rifle, piercing into our metal hide. Hades keeps our exposed face away as he counters. The two Warlords crash into one another. Swords and hammers collide with vicious intent. Blood smears across the ground. Pyra swings with a brutal uppercut. It connects. Launching us into the air. Hades and I tumble to the ground in pain, but we land just next to the bow. Three arrows snap out, lightning quick. One burrows into Pyra's thigh, and he belches out in pain.

My head snaps to the left as I hear Fargo whisper over the comms.

"Hey, hey... it's me. I gotcha." He whispers to Miku. He must have snuck his way in. He crouches next to her, carefully peeling off her restraints. I watch him remove the gag from her mouth, and she spills out in violent sobs.

"DON'T!" She yells as he goes to remove the contraption from her chest. *"It's a bomb!"*

Pyra capitalizes on the distraction.

Rifle rounds break through a destroyed plate along my back and plunge into my torso. Agony singes my nerve endings, and I no longer feel anything. I float through a blank sea. Numb to the pain, numb to the heartache, numb to the fear. I don't even feel my body move as Hades' Greatsword carves through Pyra's suit and chunks into his massive trunk. Pyra staggers.

Existence becomes foggy. Distant. Similar to the first time I ever encountered Hades. Like I'm watching a nightmare unfold but am trapped inside a glass case and can do nothing to end it. I hear words over the comms but don't understand them. Distorted and warbled. The roof explodes, and blocks of stone debris erupt into the room.

Is this real?

People pile out of a rig that hovers overhead. Bullets clatter against me from all directions. Hades snaps arrows wildly. There's yelling. I know there is, but where from?

Pyra kneels half-dead, blood gushing from his mouth now. Who are these people? Is that an Ancient? A woman with amber and gold hair stands between Hades and the dying warlord. The veins of her neck bulge as she screams at me. What is she saying? I recognize her... but I can't figure out who she is. The shooting has stopped, the world stills, and I realize I don't know who any of these people are.

A man kneels in front of me, tattered and beaten. Two people in mangled Warlord suits, one with an arrow sticking out of her chest, stare at me. They look so incredibly familiar. Three grotesque men wearing black armor have rifles pointed at me. And a short... human... wearing oversized military garbs stands next to an Ancient man with chaotic eyes. I don't know any of them.

Then I see her.

Hades stands still. Our body paralyzed in some form of trance. Her skin is flawless, eyes gentle, and soft. Her lips move, and she speaks to me, but I can't hear it. Yet I know she calls to me. Beckons me back. And I know that *she* is where I belong. With her. I can feel it. Feel her in the fibers of my heart.

Miku......

Slowly, life begins to creep its way back, and warmth crawls its way to the surface. I recognize the man next to her, too. It is a brother filled with love and regret. I can see him. A man defeated. Life spiraling beyond his control, and the shattered remains of his mistakes displayed around him. He looks to me for help. Desperate. Overwhelmed. Like he has no idea of what he's become.

Fargo......

The sensation and the pain and the emotion begin to surge back. Flooding my mind. My body aches and trembles and the stress of passion tingles through my nerves. I can see them all. And I feel the hate rinsing away.

But then, I cringe.

Because I can feel *him* now too. Hades. And he now knows just how powerful my love for *her* is. It will eventually defeat him. The rage bubbles and boils, and he knows now what he must do to rid himself of me once and for all.

Fargo sours. He can see it happening.

He fumbles for Pyra's bolt pistol, priming it.

"Hades..." Fargo warns. *"Victor, if you're in there, I need you out here right now, man!"* His voice pleads. Sobs cracking his breath. *"RIGHT FUCKING NOW, VICTOR!"* He screams.

A heinous smile scratches across Hades' face.

I fight with every ounce I have, but Hades knows how to defeat me; he's not letting go.

Miku simply smiles at me, wiping a tear from her cheek. Tears of mine flood from Hades' eyes as well. I have to tell her.

Inside, I scream as I push my way to the surface. Hades grows restless, fending me off. It makes the room nervous, watching us squirm.

I push harder and harder until I can finally see the light. Hades roars as his anger with me grows.

"Victor, please..." Fargo whimpers, but there's nothing that can be done. His face is bright red, tears pouring from his

eyes as mucus staggers his breath. *"Please..."*

I wish I could tell him thank you. For always being the brother I needed, not the one I deserved. Of how proud I am of him, regardless of all the stupid shit he's done in his life. And it pains me to know that I will leave this world with him thinking I hate him. Because nothing could be farther from the truth. For a moment, sure, I blamed him. Blamed him for all of this, but the truth is, Hades and I were destined for this moment. Destined to endanger everyone around us. Destined for one final moment where the waters of the broken damn would eventually wash me away, and Fargo would be responsible for cleansing the world of the evil left behind. A burden I unfairly thrust onto him. And as I stare into his hysterical eyes, his desperate pleas falling on deaf ears, all that I want to tell him is, thank you.

To tell them all thank you.

So, if Hades plans on taking my body, I plan on keeping my soul. I will not spend my last moments full of hate and anger. For once, it'll be love.

I storm ahead, pushing past waves of anger and poisonous wrath. Past the hate and the blame and the wickedness to the tiny crease of light where *she* lives.

And just like Fargo, I would do anything for her. And even though we will never be together, it warms my heart to know that she will finally hear me say it. Because there has been no one in this world that has helped me grow more than her. No one who has loved me unconditionally like her. And no one who has helped me combat this evil being inside of me, like her. Miku is my heart and my soul, and I live to love her.

I burst through the crease of light and am present for just a moment. I stare into her eyes and smile as the words tiptoe from my lips.

"I love you."

Hades claws his way back instantly and lunges for her.

Fargo has to look away and wails as he fires.

The bullet wedges through my skull, and the world finally falls beautifully and totally silent. Hades, you can't have her, she's mine...

To hell we go.

43

FARGO SHEPHERD

Before We Go

I drop the pistol to the floor.

If I wasn't such a coward, I would kill myself. Maybe Gwinn and her twisted views of humanity are right. Maybe we *aren't* worthy of life. Look what I've done with mine. With Miku's, and Victor's, Gwinn and Tanya's, I've nearly destroyed them all... And for what? Greed? Was that really it, though? Or was it merely stupidity? I honestly don't know which would be worse? Abraham is hunched over Victor's body, mortified. Zina over her father. Geeva lies unconscious against the far wall, and Miku sits frozen in the chair, overcome with heartbreak, Tanya draped around her neck. I can't believe she actually escaped. How do I even begin to process everything happening around me? My chest clinches even harder when I hear Cyto's voice over the comm.

"Geeva..." He says. *"Geeva?! Fargo, where is she? Is she ok?"* Cyto's drone probes side to side. The lens on its undercarriage gyrating to find her. A silent tear puddles in the corner of my eye as I block his view of her. *"Slick... you promised me..."* I take a breath and lie.

"She's ok. Just a busted comm." My heart cringes as I turn

and see her folded into herself, groaning in pain, the massive arrow beaming from her chest. Cyto breathes a sigh of relief and pushes back the emotion in his voice.

"Well, alright. You had me worried for a moment there, slick..." I wish I had some reassuring response, but I can't lie to him again. So, I say nothing.

"Guys..." Tanya backs away from Miku cautiously. Two small metal arms extend from her vest holding thick plates that face each other like opposite sides of a vice grip. Hovering between the plates is a compact blue sphere, pulsing and glowing with dark navy and royal. Distorted air fills the space between the plates and the orb as some form of energy field keeps the orb in its stasis.

Miku tries to flash us a crooked smile of assurance, but that lasts all of one second before she glances back down in horror to the glowing orb on her chest.

"Cyto, are you seeing this?" I ask. His drone hovers just in front of Miku's vest.

"Oh shit... I see it, alright," Cyto says.

"What is it?" Tanya asks. We lock eyes for a moment. Everything happened so fast it hadn't struck me yet that I should be dumbfounded she's here. Is that an Ancient too? Who the hell is that? Tanya stares at me in disgust, knowing I'm to blame. But there's no time to beg for her forgiveness. I doubt I'd get it anyway.

"A particle diffuser." Cyto answers.

"What the hell does it do? And how do I get it off her?" Tanya asks. Miku nervously smiles again at us. Trying to keep *us* calm. I can't even begin to return the gesture. Every second claws at my nerves.

"It's basically a ball of concentrated energy particles. The plates emit a frequency that keeps the energy from expanding. If the frequency changes, or stops, the energy expands until it explodes..."

Tanya can't contain the tears that are bubbling in her eyes. She stares at the vest just like I do, helpless. Miku takes her hand, trying to comfort her.

"Hey... it's going to be ok," Miku says through stifled breaths. She glances at me as Tanya hangs her head and sobs. I place my hand on Tanya's shoulder, and she instantly smacks it away.

"Don't fucking touch me." She growls. Her anger cleaves through my heart. I want to fix it, but time is running out.

I click off my comm.

"Abraham," I yell. He's rocking back and forth over Victor's body. "Abraham!" He finally turns to face me.

"Yes, Jah?" He says, trying to compose himself.

"I need you to get everyone out of here. Drop Geeva, Victor, and Pyra at my safehouse and then get your men and... what is your name?" I ask the Ancient.

"Yara... I was supposed to protect..." He trails off, staring at Victor with complete devastation like Abraham does. He doesn't finish his sentence, so I return to barking orders.

"Get your men and, Yara, to the Vault because Gwinn and Russa don't think anyone will be there. They'll be in trouble."

Yara's beak snaps toward me.

"Russa has found the truth?!" He asks. I stare at him, confused.

"What?" I ask.

"Guys... the bomb!" Tanya pleads.

"Russa. You said he is at the Vault?"

"... and Gwinn." Yara's face goes stone cold. He shouts over to Abraham.

"You must go now! The truth is exposed." He hurries to my side, still yelling out to Abraham. "If you care for the Children as I do, you will protect them at all costs. I will stay and protect these."

Abraham also scurries to my side, opposing the orders.

"Jah, the Proselytes will not leave Chosen behind. We've already lost one starfallen, I refuse to lose more."

All eyes fixate on me. As if I have any idea what to do. Stress detonates in every corner of my mind.

"Abraham, go! We will be fine, go help them." I yell as sweat beads down my forehead.

"The other Children will be there too. You must hurry." Yara adds. I glance at Tanya, hoping she can translate.

"Riley and Leo... They're heading to the Vault."

I don't know how to react when I hear their names. What is happening?

"Riley?" There are too many moving pieces for me to try to figure them all out now. "So, Riley and... *Leo*... are heading to the Vault right now? Not Remmy?"

"Yes."

"Where's Remmy?"

Tanya gives Yara a solemn look, the Ancient's face falling ghostly pale once again. Miku covers her mouth.

"Shit..."

I look back to Abraham, and the compounding deaths

400

seem to be enough to convince him to leave. He nods, understanding.

"Be safe, Jah. We will protect the Chosen." He glances back at his remaining soldiers. "Witness the flesh." They touch their brands. "Let's move."

I click my comm back on, and Cyto has been yelling in my ear the entire time.

"Slick, what the hell is going on? Where did you go?"

"I'm here, I'm here. Listen, I need you to get the others up to the rig." The Proselytes begin to hustle all around, Zina glaring at me as she drags her dead father toward the ship. If she betrays us all right now, I wouldn't blame her. Hopefully, my earlier gesture is enough to keep her loyalty.

I glance up to Miku and give her a tentative smile.

"We're gonna get this off you, alright?!" I say. She smiles as if she doesn't believe me and is making peace with her fate.

"Tanya, go with them," She says, her voice calmer than mine.

"Not happening." Tanya stares firmly at her. "I'm not going anywhere."

"Yes, you are!" Miku insists. "I've overheard the Vipers talking, the cure is in that Vault. *Your* cure!" Tanya's head drops.

"Listen, there's too much to explain, I'm not leaving. That's final," She says. Miku doesn't understand. She tries to resist, but Yara stops her.

"Child, please be still," He says, probing at the pulsing orb on her chest.

Across the room, Cyto's drone has finished hauling the others up the hole in the roof to the transport rig, and it flies back over to us.

The last body he hauled was Geeva's.

"Cyto..."

"I know... she'll be fine," He says, clearing his throat. The lens of the drone stares at me for a moment then returns to Miku.

The rig punches into the night sky and leaves us alone atop the Viper compound. We all exchange one last reserved look, and Cyto begins to walk me through the plan.

"Alright slick, there should be a metal box about the size of your thumb at the bottom of the vest. Do you see it?" Cyto says.

"Yea, I see it."

"Great, you need to pry that open."

We frantically search for something to wedge under the

small paneling.

"Here." Tanya tosses me one of Victor's Serpent arrows. The image of his face just before he lunged at Miku flashes across my eyes. That'll forever be burned into my memory. I stare at the arrow and whisper a final apology to him.

"...I'm so sorry, brother." The arrow's metal shaft is splintered and broken, just like he was.

"Fargo!" Tanya yells. I snap to attention and hustle back to Miku.

"Now wedge that arrowhead under the panel, but be careful not to touch anything inside it."

Miku and I share an uncomfortable look.

I try to hold the arrow precise, but my suit's fingers are too thick to be accurate.

"I gotta strip the suit," I say.

"I wouldn't do that if I were you, slick. If that thing goes off, that's the only thing that's gonna protect you." I glance to the others, glad that they can't hear my comm.

"Tanya, I need your help," I say as I unlatch my helmet. Tanya and Miku both recoil at the stench that plumes from within my suit. "I need you to slide open my hatch, and press the release valve." The suit hisses and peels open as she does. My body aches as I step out. Blood runs down my leg. My entire body, scattered with wounds. The others stare at me in disbelief. "I'm fine. Let's get this open."

Now able to control the arrowhead, I pry open the panel cover. Cyto's voice spits out over the drone speakers now.

"Great job. Let me see what's here."

The drone hovers in closer and inspects a datacard encased within, streams of code cascading down its screen. The drone's analyzer scours the data as the four of us wait anxiously. The warbling frequency grows louder.

"Come on, Cyto, what do we got?" I say, nervously.

"I'm working, I'm working."

Miku takes my hand.

"Hey. It's ok," She says. My lip begins to tremble.

"Miku, I'm so sorry. I never meant—" She stops me.

"Fargo... It's O.K." She gives me a soft smile. "I'm just glad you're alive." A tear slips down her cheek. "I don't know what I'd do if I lost both you and Victor." How is she not furious with me?

"Miku, this is all my fault. None of this would've happened if I—"

"It's not your fault," She says. Tanya huffs in disagreement.

"Our lives have never been our own. Look at what they did to Tanya, to Riley and Remmy and Gwinn, to all of us. A moment like this was inevitable." Tanya has heard enough.

"How can you say that?!" She barks. "*He's* the criminal, *he's* the one who partnered with these monsters, *he's* the reason they came after you." She turns and points at me, "*You* are responsible for this!" She's right, but Miku shakes her head.

"If it wasn't Deterro, it would've been someone else, for some other reason," She says. Yara paces nervously behind us. "Tanya, they've had the Cure this entire time, don't you understand? They've stolen your life too, and you don't even see it."

Even though Miku doesn't fully understand the truth about Tanya and the Rotting, her point still applies. They did steal her life. Lied to her. Lied to all of us. We were never in control.

Tanya folds to a knee as Miku continues.

"The Princess of Groga? I act that way because I know we only live as long as they want us to. It's unfortunate but true. You think Trakstull cared about me? I don't see him here." Miku locks eyes with Tanya. "We are outsiders to them and always will be. Think about it. They kept you locked away in a lab. Kept Victor around for entertainment. Used Leo for information. Pushed Riley and Remmy to the Forest. Hell, they've even turned Gwinn into one of them!" Miku is calm like she's speaking of things already understood. "I knew they had to love me. That's how I could survive. Fargo's been the only one allowed to be himself. How can I be mad at him for exploring his life?" She gives me a smile I don't deserve. She can say it was all an act, but nobody is as genuine as her.

Cyto's voice worries me when it kicks on over the comm.

"*Slick... we have a problem.*" Tanya weaves her fingers into Miku's, waiting.

"What's wrong?"

"*There's nothing we can do,*" He says. The room falls unbearably silent. Just the air-jets of the drone whistling as it hovers in place.

"There has to be something," I say.

"*The datacard has a fail-safe command if tampered with. It'll detonate the moment we try to hack it.*"

Panic closes my arteries. Black dots poking holes in my vision. This can't be how it ends.

"What if we just pull the orb out manually?" I ask.

"You'd have maybe... ten seconds before it exploded. But you couldn't grab it anyway. That thing would melt right through your hand."

Tanya whimpers. Wrapping herself around Miku's leg. I scour the room, looking for anything that could help. The frequency begins to screech louder.

"Guys!" Tanya yells, panic ripe on her voice.

"Move." Yara shoves me aside. He strips off his surcoat. His cords unwinding into hundreds of strands. His head twitches. Beak snapping. Purring uncontrollably. "Yara will save the Children. Yara can hold it."

He twines some of his cords around the hook of the drone. Bucking and twitching violently. More strands weave together into a single dense vine.

"Yara will grab the danger." He squawks at me. "Machine, lift Yara to the stars when he does," Yara says to Cyto's drone. He turns and gazes upon all three of us. "Yara must fulfill his oath. Protect the children. Prepare to run."

He glances at the hole in the roof, then back down to the orb and, without a second warning, snatches the orb.

"OH SHIT!"

We scramble to our feet. I pull Miku from the chair. The drone yanking Yara toward the roof hole. He screams in agony as the orb sears through layers of cords. Our feet pound the floor as we sprint away. Yara climbs higher. Bright light swelling around him. I turn and don't look back. Urging us forward. Bursting through the door, out into the terrace. A stone overhang adorns the wall across the bridge. We need to get there. Blood gushes from my leg with every stride. Tanya and Miku running beside me, hand in hand. Moonlight passes overhead as we cross the bridge. The stars shine through the glass of the roof. They bounce as I sprint. Yara speeds farther into the frigid night. Screaming light swallowing him whole. He drifts silently through the sky until the light blinks away for an instant... then detonates. Blinding light engulfs the world. Glass erupts. A blue fireball plows through the terrace just as we dive behind the stone wall. A shockwave tremors through the building. Rattling the walls. The fireball sucks back up in the sky and disappears, leaving behind a scorched and silent world.

I'm sprawled onto my back. Eyes awash with tears. Arms wrap me in a hug the moment I sit up.

"Miku..." I cry. Stroking her cheek, her beautiful smile

shining back at me. I pull Tanya into our hug as well. "Tanya, I'm so sorry." She doesn't smack me away or fight with me. She just surrenders. Collapsing into our arms. Sobbing. I stroke their hair. Kisses them both on the head. Tanya gazes up through the roof.

"Thank you, Yara." She whispers. His name reminds me that our family is still in trouble. As much as I want to sit here and never let these two go, the others still need us. I spring from the ground. "What are you doing?" Tanya calls out. I hurry across the bridge back to my Scorcher suit. The metal is charred, but the suit is built for destruction. I signal Cyto through the private comm.

"*SLICK?!*" He yells.

"Hey, ya old toad."

"*Is everyone alright?*" He huffs, sounding like he's on the verge of a breakdown.

"We're all good," I say. He croaks.

"*Oh, thank God.*"

"Listen, the day's not over. We need a rig. And we need it right now." Tanya and Miku finally make it back to the room with a puzzled look on their faces. I click the comm off, pick up Victor's bow and turn to face the girls. "We need to get to the Vault."

44

LEO

ABERNATHY

Redemption

The Vipers make their way around the ship while Riley, Patawa, Bryl, and I sprint to the observation deck. That's where I see her.

Gwinn's diamond eyes pierce through me. Filled with the same cold harshness and exquisite beauty, that's always been an impossible blend of intimidating and intoxicating. She looks like an angel dipped in frost, flawless and powerful. But for the first time in as long as I can remember, I don't yearn for her love. Grovel or embarrass myself, throwing my heart at the mercy of her frigid soul. I sympathize with her. Because she doesn't know a lie has poisoned her mind. Turned her into someone unrecognizable. And although my love that I so desperately wanted her to reciprocate for so long has begun to find a new home, that doesn't mean she deserves a life afflicted with such an awful burden. She deserves the truth, but I worry the truth may be too devastating to handle.

A thin vine of smoke twists its way up from the embers of something burnt on the ground, a man in a black tunic tending to the charred remains. Deterro... Vipers branch out in an arc, closing off every escape route we have. My eyes meet Gwinn's, waiting for her to say something... She doesn't. What could she say? She turns away and murmurs something to Russa.

Of all the nights I spent picturing this very exchange, I was too naïve to predict silence. Too foolishly optimistic. But now that I'm out from under her spell, I realize I shouldn't have expected anything else.

"Well, what a treat!" Deterro says as he hands the burnt book to one of his lackeys. "Leo Abernathy and Riley Holt? To what do we owe the pleasure? Is this a *daring* rescue attempt?" He smiles wickedly and picks at the corners of his teeth. "I must admit, after getting to know her, I don't think she's worth saving." He winks at Gwinn.

Deterro knows her?

"Gwinn, how does the leader of the Vipers know you?" I whisper to her. The first words I've said to her in months... But before she can answer, it hits me. "...Gwinn... you didn't..." She clenches her jaw and looks away, yelling down to Deterro as my heart sinks for her.

"Enough of this shit, Deterro. We need to come to an agreement," She says.

"Gwinny, we had an agreement. *You* broke it. I am owed the cure to the Rotting. The time for negotiation is over. Let me in the ship, or I slaughter each and every one of you and figure it out for myself."

Riley squeezes my arm so hard her nails nearly dig into my skin. Blood flushes her face with anger.

"Leo..." Riley whispers to me as she glowers at Russa. I take her hand.

"I know, I know..." I glance at her, trying to calm her down, but a fire storms through her.

I catch Gwinn looking at our hands, then she meets my eyes. I look past her and call down to Deterro.

"I don't care what *she's* promised you, this ship is mine!" I say, wedging my old war-era rifle through the railing. "You've made a mistake coming here."

Deterro smirks and opens his arms, displaying his horde of Vipers.

"Look around you, Leo, it is you who has made a mistake."

Bryl leans over and whispers in my ear, surveying the Vault.

"Boss... there's too many of 'em."

I dart my eyes to him, then subtly gesture toward the Vault door. He squints for a moment, then his eyes widen in horror.

"Oh shit..."

Cleaving through the utter darkness of the tunnel are five glinting sparks of cyan blue light. Approaching steadily until their glare illuminates the outlines of bulky vessels. The myrite torches flash shadows of oars rowing in a haunting rhythm. Pushing ahead with every stroke until they're nearly at the beachhead and the torches extinguish. And all that's left behind are the dreadful silhouettes of massive warriors. Their unmistakable short-horned leader, striding in front. The Gaz are here...

"Leo, are you insane? We can't fight them," Gwinn says.

"You've given us no choice."

I squeeze the trigger.

Pandemonium erupts inside the Vault.

My bullet plunges into Deterro's shoulder and knocks him to the ground. His loyal guards absorb the next shots. They collapse to the ground in agony, and Deterro is drug away to safety.

Metal and magnetic rounds explode in all directions.

Glass of the observation deck shatters in front of us, their tiny slivers of pain diving into our skin. My crew pushes farther down the deck, behind a hip-high metal wall, their bodies trembling with the vibration of gunfire. Gwinn and her people flank to the other side.

I dart my weapon over the top of cover and take aim at a grunt. But before I can shoot, his body is crumbled at the end of a war staff. A'gorr roars, and Gaz flood the Vault.

"WHERE IS THE GIRL?!" He howls.

Warriors rap their staves against their horns, stampeding through the Vipers.

Rounds deflect off their circular shield until they've gotten close and then staves crush skulls with ease.

The echoes of war are deafening. Ringing harshly in my ears. A round from Gwinn's weapon plunges through a Gaz warrior's neck, and he crashes to the ground. His ally howls, and I watch him charge toward her.

"Cover me!" I yell.

I sprint from behind cover. Bullets snap into the wall behind me. My body shrieks in agony as none of my wounds from the Forest have healed. The warrior rushes up the stairs behind his shield, Gwinn's men dumping rounds into the metal. He reaches the top, snaps his staff back, and crushes two men's skulls with thunderous strikes. Gwinn and her soldiers vault over the railing and spill onto the floor below. Russa and the warrior remain, glaring at one another, and I can hear them yell as I sprint to help.

"YOU!" The warrior yells at Russa. He rips the armor from his left arm and throws it to the ground, the scar of an exit wound, twisted on his shoulder. "KAN'DOR HAS NOT FORGOTTEN! HAVE YOU, ANCIENT?!"

My legs shake as I run, chest singing with pain. This Gaz is different. He's covered in armor unlike the others, my dated weapon incapable of harming him from behind... I have one play.

"All you mongrels look the same to me, but I do remember shooting one. There's nowhere to run this time!"

Russa twirls his pistol and darts out a round just as I toss a pulse grenade at the feet of Kan'dor. The grenade detonates, launching both men from the deck. A thud slams into my chest. Russa's round missing the Gaz and flattening me to my back. I stare up at the ceiling, lungs seizing.

"LEO!" Riley screams and hurries to me. "Patawa, help!" She cries. Pat hustles to me, staying low. Bryl roars as he provides cover fire.

"Why did you help him!" She yells at me. A mix of rage and desperation paint her face. Patawa fumbles through a bag of supplies she bought.

"Where is it? Where is it?!"

"Hurry, Pat!" Riley says.

My vision begins to fade. The deafening clamor of battle muting away.

"Got it." Her blurry arms rise above her head and slam into my chest. Life erupts inside me! Lungs swelling with air. My heart squeezes with every beat. Blood bursting through my veins.

A cardiac spike pulse juts from my chest. A shriek spills from my lips as I shoot upright.

Riley wraps her arms around my neck and kisses me.

"Thank God!" She says. Our eyes linger. Her nose still against mine. She kisses me again. I press her tight to my lips, her cheek cradled in my palm. The world becoming so clear. "I love you," She says. I go to tell her I do too, but before I can respond, fury ignites in her eyes. "Where is he!"

Russa has regrouped with Gwinn and her remaining men, and they are sneaking their way along the backside of the ship, making their way to the Vault door as the battle continues to rage around them. Riley takes off sprinting after them.

"Riley, don't!" I yell. Patawa finishes patching my wound, and Bryl helps me to my feet. I chase after her. Sprinting down the stairs, firing my gun wildly as the others follow. A Gaz strikes at my head. I roll out of the way, and the staff grazes against my sleeve. A bullet digs into the warrior's skull before I can counter. He crashes to the ground.

"Jah!"

I turn and see soldiers in all black armor spill into the Vault. Weapons spraying. Vipers and Gaz collapsing to the ground. One slides to my side and offers out a hand. He's a Proselyte. Face mutilated and altered. But I vaguely recognize it.

"You once saved me, Jah! The night in Paradise. I would have died at the end of that rope. But you cut me down," He says as he pulls me to my feet. "I am Abraham, and it is an honor to repay you." He touches his brand, then his heart.

Bryl rumbles to our position holding a Gaz shield. Bullets crackle against it.

"Boss, what's the move," He says, double-taking when he recognizes Abraham. "Holy shit, what the hell are you doing here?"

I look up, knowing I just stare at rock, but picturing my father. This has to be him giving me a sign. Telling me this will all work out.

"I am yours to command Jah. Tell me what to do."

I glance at Riley, who still sprints away. Vipers and Gaz and Proselytes and High Council grunts clash together. Bedlam consumes the Vault.

"Bryl gets us across to the others. Abraham... just keep them off us."

We share a nod, and Abraham hustles to join his squadron.

I have to get to Riley.

She still powers ahead. Betrayal operating her thoughts. Bryl and I take off after her, but she finally skids to a stop, jutting her rifle into her shoulder. She takes a steadying breath, and I call out to her, but it's too late. The gun claps, bucking against her armpit, and Russa falls to the ground.

"Russa!" Gwinn yells. She turns and sees smoke sizzling from Riley's barrel. "Riley, what the fuck are you doing?!"

Gwinn's men drag a groaning Russa behind bulky lab equipment. They mount their rifles atop it and chunk out protective fire.

Gwinn spins and jams her weapon into Riley's face as we arrive.

"Riley?!" She shouts, her jaw clenched tight. I slide in between them and knock the weapon from Riley's face. Gwinn stares back, dumbfounded. "Leo, have you lost your fucking mind? What are you doing?"

My chemically induced rampage begins to fade and, with it, follows a numbing wave of coldness. I drop to a knee.

"Gwinn... You didn't kill Emoss." I blurt out. We don't have time for subtly. My world begins to slow around me. Russa's fleeting eyes leer at me. He shakes his head, telling me to stop. He'll get no sympathy from me. "You didn't kill your father, Gwinn... Russa did."

I fall to my ass, head leaning against the back of the lab equipment, hand clutched to my chest. Riley hurries to my side.

Gwinn's face goes cold, tension building in her neck.

"Bullshit!" She says. "What the hell are you talking about?" She glances at Russa, who closes his eyes. Head spilling back to the ground.

Bullets crackle against the lab desk. We crouch down lower.

Riley meets Gwinn eye to eye.

"Emoss was planning on going public about the Rotting. The High Council found out about it, so Trakstull ordered to have him killed..." A tear forms in Riley's eye as she glares at Russa. "Gwinn... He injected Emoss with the Rotting that day at Widow's Wing, and they blamed it on you... On us... He killed Dad."

Gwinn bites her lip, shaking her head.

"No... he wouldn't. He loved Emoss. He'd never do that," She says, trying to convince herself. She peers down at Russa. "Look at me!" She orders. Russa opens his eyes and shakes his head.

"Lies. All of it," He says, fading in and out.

"Why would they think that?!" She asks. I can see the wheels turning in her mind.

"I don't know," He says, wincing in pain. "But Emoss was like a brother to me. I loved him."

Gwinn darts back to us, now more unsure than ever. She shoves her pistol back in Riley's face.

"I'll ask one more time. Why do you think that?"

Riley doesn't back down.

"An Ancient named Yara told us," She says. Russa purrs at

the mention of the name. Gwinn's face shifts uncomfortably when he does. "Dad ordered Yara to protect us and bring us here. Gwinn, I'm telling you the truth."

Gwinn pulls at her hair. Overwhelmed tears slipping into the corner of her lips.

"Yara is a lunatic." Russa croaks.

"Shut up, let me think." She's nearly hyperventilating at this point. Chest heaving up and down until she screams. Slamming her fist against the desk. The pistol is now in Russa's face.

"Tell me your quote." She growls at him. He doesn't respond. "Tell me... what you always say to me." She stands now. Smacking away my attempt at pulling her back down behind cover. "TELL ME!" She screams.

His beak drops.

All the cords of his body still. Hostility baked into his voice now.

"See, this is why you didn't pass the electability tests." He purrs. "You thought you were tough and cold and calculated... but you're not. You're just scared. You're always scared." He leans forward and presses his head to the gun. Eyes narrow. Venom spitting from his words.

"You were too scared to be a good daughter. You were too scared to be a Councilor. And you were certainly too scared to be a mother."

The color drains from Gwinn's face. Gun trembling in her hand. She asks him one more time, her voice quivering. The words barely creeping from her lips.

"Tell me... the quote."

Russa grins.

"Very well. There are two things... absolutely necessary to protect power: stomach... and sacrifice."

She pulls the trigger.

The pistol drops to the floor, and Gwinn buckles, scattered sobs overwhelming her.

"I'm sorry." She cries. "I'm so, so sorry."

I pull her into a hug, and she begins crying harder when she meets my eyes. She tries to apologize again, but I stop her.

"Shh. It's ok."

Gwinn wipes at her eyes, glances at Riley, then looks around.

"Where's Remmy?" She asks. Riley bites her lip and shakes

412

her head. "Oh, Ri..."

She's interrupted by Abraham sliding over the desk.

"Jah! Move!" He shouts. We flinch, no idea what is happening. We scramble to our feet.

Across the Vault, I'm met with the red, whining coils of a railcannon. Deterro, attached to its trigger.

"Shit!" I fumble for my rifle. The world still fading in and out. His body is blurring in my vision. I can't line up the shot. Fire cracks from my barrel, but I miss. Riley and the others scatter from cover. Deterro bellows in rage. Stepping closer. The railcannon mere moments from firing. Then, suddenly, his face goes limp. An arrow bores clean through his skull, and he folds to the ground. The railcannon unleashes into the ceiling, exploding and massive stone chunks avalanche to the ground, burying everyone across the Vault from us.

The battlefield settles.

Dust coughing up from the landslide.

All those wishing to hurt us, crumbled under a mountain of stone.

Fargo struts in from the Vault entrance, pacing toward Deterro's body, a bow splashed across his back. He puts his foot against the side of the Viper's skull and yanks the arrow out.

"Fuck you," He says and spits on Deterro's body. He glances at me with an arrogant smirk. "Nice shot, huh?"

I stagger to him, blood still drooling from my chest, and slam him into a hug.

"Have you ever shot one of those before?" I ask.

"You want the answer to that?"

I shake my head with a delirious grin.

Miku and Tanya have arrived as well, and together, they step over littered bodies and destroyed lab equipment to meet us.

Tanya clings to Miku's arm like she may never let go of her again. For someone who's life has been filled with such torment, it warms my heart to see her smile.

Riley and Gwinn, on the other hand, hunch over the man who took their father from them. A dark pool forming underneath him. There's a stiffness between the two. Old wounds still yet to heal. But they push those aside for the moment and lock hands. Two sisters understanding they cannot go at this life alone. No matter their differences. Regardless of their past.

Riley smiles at me over her shoulder, but then her brow

scrunches as she notices something behind me.

I turn around, confused until something catches the corner of my eye.

Buried under rubble, just a burnt corner exposed, is a thick book.

"What is that..." I dig through the stone blocks. Pain searing across my chest until I pull it free. It's half-burnt and covered in debris, but it's still in one piece. A smile pinches my cheeks.

It's my father's journal.

"I brought it," Gwinn says. "Took it from your room. Figured it'd be my way into the ship," She says it with a hint of shame. I try to absolve her of that.

"It can." I smile at her and run my fingers along the beaten leather, pulling the orange glowing vial from my pocket. My excitement pushes away the pain in my chest for the moment. I order Abraham to insert the vial in the observatory slot and hustle to the airlock. Everyone gathers around. Abraham inserts the vial, pulls the lever, and orange fluid begins to streak through the tubes that connect the ship and the observation room. I thumb through the pages until I find the entry that contains the airlock code.

0966-8874-2250

The doors hiss open.

"Oh my God."

Riley wraps me in a hug. Mesmerized as I am. The metal creaks under my weight as we step inside. The others follow.

Faint running lights sputter to life.

Glass smudges as I streak my thumb across the shell of an artificial womb.

This is a habitation unit.

This is the secret Emoss hid for us.

Salvation. The redemption of humanity.

Hundreds and hundreds of metal eggs sit perched in rows throughout the hub. Tubes filled with the orange glowing Bytrol spool along the ceiling and connect to their bases.

Tears spill from my eyes to the metal grates of the floor as I watch the liquid flow through the hub.

The womb formula... this is it.

I skim through a journal entry where my father wrote

about the habitation unit's terminals. One is docked a few feet ahead, somewhat resembling the awful sketch my father made of it.

The terminal sputters to life, asking for a facial scan. I glance at Riley, shrug, and lean my face down to the podium, and the terminal scans my features.

A digitized female voice comes on over the hub speakers, and a low, energized buzz begins to build intensity.

"Facial Recognition success. Clearance approved: Captain Archie B. Abernathy."

I run my hands along my face. Across my cheek and my mouth and down my jawline. I must look just like him... My reflection shines in the curved, glossy edge of a cryopod. I stare at it. Feeling my father staring back at me. Standing in this very spot hundreds of years ago, hoping he can save humanity, just as I do.

Green lights illuminate the bases of the pods when I activate their row from the terminal. Row after row flicks green until the entire hub is activated.

Riley and the others gather closer around. Staring down at the terminal with me.

One button that reads *proceed* blinks across the screen.

I give my family a final look, pull the charred skin of my father's journal to my chest, and push the button.

"Cryopod defrost, activated. Womb accelerant, injecting. Embryo growth sequences, initializing. Estimated time until births: six months, three days..."

I close my eyes as tears push through the folded lashes, our group merging into one embrace and whisper to my father.

"From the last human to the first."

15 years later...

EPILOGUE

LEO

ABERNATHY

Journal

Wet soil oozes in between my fingers and crumbles back down into the soaked Valenian crust. I bring the soil to my nose, and my chest swells with the scent of nature.

My eyes fold, the therapeutic scent cleansing my soul. I'd hold it there for longer, but my fingers begin to go numb, and I drop it, blowing on my hands to bring them back to life.

I miss the warmth of the Capital.

In Su Hoz, the whistle of the wind is my only companion. Tall grass gently sways back and forth as it blows, and I carve the blade of my shovel into the ground once more.

I wince as the handle rubs a blister on my palm. It's been another long day.

I spike the shovel into the ground and lean against it. Water from my canteen soothes my aching tongue as I stare down the irrigation line I've dug. The sweat and grime plastered to my face streak my shirt as I wipe it away.

Warmth is all I miss, though.

At the origin of my irrigation ditch, a thin column of smoke rises into the air and disappears into the cloudless night. A village surrounds it.

Cheers of celebration seem to echo out the top of the village and rain down on me in the field. I grin, listening to the chants of 2000 birthdays happening at once.

The cheers almost muffle the sounds of something rustling in the grass nearby. But I hear it. It scurries for a moment, then stops. Darts in another direction then freezes again. I yank the shovel from the ground and peer out into the sea of waist-high grass.

Stalks bend as something moves to my left. I spin the shovel in my hand, creeping into the grass. I follow it cautiously until it comes to a halt once again.

The rustling stops. For a moment, I stand there, still as can be. The faint uproars of the village still drifting out to me. Whatever is in this grass rests an arm's length away. The edge of my shovel slowly parts the thicket. It's dark but is that...?

A young boy pops out of the grass to startle me.

"BOO!"

I flinch. Clutching my chest with a relieved smile.

"God, Army, you scared me," I say. I toss the shovel into the ditch and pick him up out of the grass, cradling him under my arm. His chocolate hair is covered with dirt and debris. "Why are you sneaking around in the grass, mister? You're filthy." A snaggletooth smile spreads across his face. He giggles.

"Mom told me to tell you to stop working and come play," He says.

"Oh, she did, huh?" I say. "Did she tell you to scare me too?"

Army giggles once again as I tickle him.

"No," He says, his little feet kicking and flailing. "Dad, stop. Please." He laughs, face turning red as he squirms all over.

"Ok, you've had enough." I stop tickling him and toss him onto my shoulders. "Let's head in."

The celebration gets louder as we get closer to the village. Rows of long wooden tables in the village center are filled with people eating and drinking and laughing. A bonfire rages just next to it. The grass ends and slowly transitions into a crude stone road.

"Do you know how old the other kids are today?" I ask. He counts on his fingers until he runs out.

"Firteen?" He guesses.

"Fifteen." I correct. "So, since mommy had you eight years ago, how much older are the other kids than you?"

His brow scrunches as he thinks. His fingers folding one at a time.

"This many." He holds up seven fingers.

"That's right! Good job," I say and give him a high five. "You definitely got your Dad's brain and not your Mom's," I smirk, but he doesn't get it. "Speaking of, where is your Mother?" I ask. Army points to a table at the edge of the celebration.

There she is.

Chest filled with laughter; eyes filled with love. Her table sings. Arms wrapped around one another, belting out the words of this glorious holiday. The stanzas linger in the air as they seep out into the silent isolation. I love when she sings. I love why she smiles. I love how she loves.

I let Army down, and he scurries to the table, climbing into her lap.

The song finishes just as I arrive.

"I've been summoned?" I say with a grin as I bend down to kiss Riley. She tilts her head back and returns my kiss, rubbing her thumb along my cheek.

"My little messenger delivered once again," She says, squeezing Army to her chest.

"Dad said I have his brain and not yours," Army says. Riley looks at me. "Well, let's hope that's not true." She grins that firecracker grin that made me fall in love with her all those years ago. "Come sit. You can work tomorrow, its Redemption Day. Celebrate with everyone!"

I study the herd of people celebrating tonight, rubbing my hand along Riley's back.

"It's just hard, ya know?" I say. She weaves her fingers into mine and leans her head on me.

"I know," She says.

Throughout the crowd, the faces all burn bright with the joy of life. 2000 humans, pimpled and energetic, turn fifteen tonight. Our mission in the vault saving our kind. Yet, even with humanity saved and our species given its second chance, this day still reminds me of those we lost to achieve it.

Geeva sits next to Riley, but the seat next to her is empty.

"Where is he?" I ask. Geeva nods, and I glance to a small dirt patch that breaks the circle of dwellings that make up our village. "I figured. How's he doing?"

"About as good as you are, I guess?" She says. Cyto hobbles up with a plate piled high with roasted meat and roots. He plops down hard. Army giggles.

"Did you save some for the rest of us?" Geeva asks. A crooked eye sneers back at her as he strips leg meat from the bone with his teeth.

"Had to make sure I got enough before the Savron twits got to it." Geeva shoots him a disapproving glare. "Don't even think about it, kid." He swats at Army's hand before those little fingers can pluck away any food from the plate. Army giggles again.

"Those Savron *twits* are the only reason we could raise all these kids... try showing them a little respect," I say. He sloshes down another hunk of meat and huffs.

"Yea, *real* noble. Be homeless and die of starvation in the city, or move here to Serenity to take care of humans. Not much of a choice." He croaks. "Vagrants... the whole lot of 'em."

He can think what he wants, but the truth is, we needed them. And sure, they were second class citizens in the mainland, but they weren't complete outcasts like we are. Cut off from everything. No aid from the Capital or any other province. Those that came here came knowing they'd never be allowed back. And without them, this beautiful celebration wouldn't be possible. So, I'll be forever grateful for their aid. Cyto, on the other hand, hasn't been useful as a mechanic in years and spends most of his days stuffing his face and griping about the miserable weather.

Geeva gives me a look that says he's a lost cause, and I drop it. I kiss Army on the head and leave them to deal with the curmudgeon. "I'll go check on Fargo."

Tonight's celebration is filled with laughter and noise and music and games.

These teenagers, unstoppable balls of energy.

Two blur by me as a streak of cyan blue, sparks from their myrite torches crackling in the air.

"Careful!" I say. It's no use. They storm through the village with reckless abandon. Fearless. As children should be.

Tanya and Miku play acting games in front of the bonfire. Kids yelling out, trying to guess what the pair is demonstrating. They squeal with laughter when Tanya gets frustrated at their wrong answers.

Tucked away in a subdued corner of the courtyard, a small group sits cross-legged in front of Gwinn as she shows them salvaged relics of Earth we negotiated away from the High Council. She'll surely be warning them of the mistakes we've made in our past and preaching about how important it is that we break the cycle of self-destruction that has punctuated every prior human civilization.

Her eyes flick to mine. She points in my direction, and the kids turn around and wave. We share a smile.

We are not what we once were, but we're still good for one another.

I've helped her rediscover her pride in humanity, and she's helped me understand criticism is necessary for the growth of our species.

I leave her to her flock of rebellious spirits and tend to the emperor of rebellious spirits.

Fargo sits in a dirt patch with his back against a tombstone, eyes red and wet. Eight stones, half-buried in the ground, form an arc and have the names: Victor, Remmy, Yara, Emoss, Spri, Klawka, Qwillow, and Archie carved on them. Fargo leans against Victor's.

I hand him a mug and use Remmy's stone to ease myself to the ground, making sure not to spill mine and sit back against it, staring up into the pristine Su Hozi sky.

We sit there for quite some time. Watching the flicker of distant stars, wondering if someone is doing the exact same thing at this very moment, light-years away.

"Do you ever think about Earth?" I ask without looking. I can hear him wipe his nose and readjust against the tombstone.

"Sometimes," He says. "Now, more than before."

"I think about it all the time," I say, wondering if any of the stars we look at right now are Earth? "You want to give the speech this year?" I ask, finally glancing over to him. He seems surprised by the question.

"You're asking me?" He chuckles.

"Who else do I have?" I ask. Fargo shakes his head with a smile.

"I don't remember signing up for second-in-command duties."

"Yea, well, life's a bitch ain't it?" I say.

"That it is." He offers out his mug, and I tap it with mine as he takes a drink. He rubs the rough handle of the mug, something clearly weighing on him. "I miss Vic." He glances back up to the sky, a tear streaming down his cheek. "Big fucking ugly bastard."

I laugh.

"He was huge, wasn't he?" Fargo laughs as well. My eyes drift to the left. Bryl hacks at tree stumps with four axes to make more firewood. "Who do you think would win in a fight,

Vic or Bryl?"

Fargo snorts, the image of those two brutes going at it, clearly rumbling around in his mind.

"Vic," He says. "But it'd be a good fight."

Another moment of silence sits between us.

"I miss Remmy," I say. I'd have never guessed it, but it's easy to open up to Fargo. "I just still feel guilty. Ya know?" Fargo nods. "The night Remmy died just plays over and over in my head," I say, digging at the dirt with my heel. "Wondering if I could've done something different. If I could've stopped it."

Fargo snorts, wiping at his nose with his sleeve.

"Ah, yes, *those* nights," He says. "To wondering..." He clanks my mug again.

I search the masses until I find Riley and smile. She dances with our beautiful son. Remmy would adore that child.

Fargo puts his hand on my shoulder.

"Grief doesn't make sense. That much I've figured out," He says, taking a long drink. "The rest... well, I got no fucking clue."

A grin crawls onto my face. Fargo notices, trying not to grin himself.

"What?" He asks.

"Oh nothing, you're just quite the poet."

He chuckles out a laugh only someone whose been sobbing for hours and has exhausted every ounce of tears they have can understand.

"I'm full of shit is what I am."

I reach over and put my arm around him.

"Well, full of shit or not, I don't think I'd have made it this long without ya."

Fargo winks and hoists me up as he stands.

"Who else did you have? Right?" He says with a smile.

We admire the shrine of our lost loved ones and those who sacrificed themselves for the human race, as those still with us join at our side. Patawa holds Army's hand as she leads him to Remmy's grave. She tells him of when his uncle saved her life. Riley rests her head on my shoulder, wiping a tear from her eye as she watches. Bryl wraps his arm around me on the other side. Geeva slides underneath Fargo's arm, Cyto begrudgingly shuffling up next to him.

"Nice mix you made this time," Fargo says, holding up his mug. "For an old hag that is..."

Cyto's face tilts up ever so slightly.

"You wouldn't know a good mix if it bit you in the ass, slick," Cyto says. Geeva grins and opens up her arms as Tanya squeezes in.

Miku kneels by Victor's tombstone, planting a kiss against it then returning back to us.

Gwinn is the last to arrive and, after a moment with Emoss, joins us.

Army wobbles back to me and yanks at my pant leg.

"Dad, will you read us what you wrote today?" He asks. My heart swells when I'm near this child. Like all the hardships of the past melt away and what's left behind is nothing but pure, unfiltered love. Every sacrifice, every heartache, every loss... worth it when I look into his eyes.

"Sure, buddy."

I hoist him into my arms as I pull a small leather journal from my jacket pocket, glance back at the new civilization of mankind... then read.

ACKNOWLEDGMENTS

If you've made it to this point in the book, I must first take this opportunity to thank you, the reader, from the bottom of my heart. The thought of anyone committing time out of their busy lives to read my story is incredibly humbling. I hope you enjoyed reading it as much as I enjoyed writing it.

This story has been in the making for close to four years and it's honestly still hard to believe that it's actually here... in my hands. And yours. And countless others. That fact still floors me.

The first person who deserves not only my praise but all that the world can possibly offer, is my wife Danielle. If it seems like all my female characters are gorgeous badasses who don't take shit from anyone and are smarter than every person in the room, you can thank her for that. Danielle, you have been so supportive through this entire journey and there is absolutely no way I finish this book without your love, motivation, trust, and most importantly, patience! Writing love seemed so incredibly easy with you as a subject, so thank you for being by my side for the last 14 years.

Next, I have to give a monumental shoutout to my editor, Sarah Kolb-Williams. She is as good as it gets! I dumped a 400-page circus on her lap and said "HELP!" And help she did! Sarah was my writing Sherpa, guiding me along this new journey I was taking. She sent me a 70-page report on my book that I cherished as much as Leo cherished his father's journal. This book would be a shell of itself without her guidance, recommendations, suggestions, and criticisms. So, thank you Sarah and I hope to work with you again in the future!!

I also want to show some love to Amanda and Tyler at Faceout Studios for designing an INCREDIBLE cover and book exterior! Getting those first mockups blew me away! You all knocked it out the park and captured exactly what I was looking for to visually represent the book! Thanks for being superstars!!

When writing a book, it's also crucial to have people you trust to show your early drafts to because they're usually terrible! The Eight of Earth was no different. So, having friends that understand what you're trying to do, but can still shoot you straight and will actually take the time to read your drafts, talk to you about it, and legitimately care is invaluable. I had two such friends I met in 2017 and they were the very first eyes on my writing. Eric and Cole. Two teammates I had when playing for the Cleveland Indians' AAA team, the Columbus Clippers, that would read my early drafts and talk to me everyday before, during and after games about the story. They gave me confidence in my work, helped me navigate this plot, and always mirrored my excitement. Thank you both for never growing annoyed with my constant questions and obsession with this story!

To my family that taught me what it meant to care for one another, thank you. To my mother and father who instilled in me the work ethic needed to complete this story, thank you. To my brother who showed me how special a sibling relationship can be, thank you. To my Filthy Musc boys and all my close friends I met in baseball who showed me you don't have to be blood related to be family, thank you.

There are countless other people responsible for shaping my experiences in life that helped infuse this story with personality and to all of you, thank you for being a part of this wild ride I've been on.

What a fun, exhausting, frustrating, rewarding, draining, challenging, and nerve-racking experience this has been. I can't wait to start this adventure all over again with a new story, in a new world, and with new characters and I hope you'll join me on the next one!

If you enjoyed the book, please consider leaving a review on Amazon. Reviews are so incredibly helpful for self-published authors and a main ingredient in the exposure a book gets! I appreciate the consideration and thank you once again for reading!

ABOUT THE AUTHOR

Richie Shaffer is a former Major League Baseball player that spent the countless hotel room nights, cross-country trips and never-ending rain delays trying to entertain his teammates with outlandish stories. They eventually grew annoyed and told him to just write a book already, so he did just that. The Eight of Earth is his debut novel and he currently lives in Charlotte with his wife. When not writing, he spends his days livestreaming videogames on Twitch and considers pizza an essential food group.

For more information on upcoming books and free short stories, visit his website:

Shafferstories.com

Also, come say hello to Richie on Twitch as he plays video games, talks about his book, gives insight into his past career in Professional Baseball and has endless fun with his community at:

Twitch.tv/dickydanger

And finally, stay up to date with everything going on in his life by following him on social media:

Twitter: @rshafff8
Instagram: @richieshafferofficial

Contact email: richieshaffer@shafferstories.com

Made in the USA
Columbia, SC
10 December 2020